THE RETROSPECTIVE

A *New York Times Book Review* Editors' Choice
Winner, 2012 Prix Médicis Étranger
Winner, 2012 Prix du Meilleur Livre Étranger

"Genius . . . Yehoshua evokes the complexities of growing old — for men and women, and for a country that is no longer fledgling — and the entrapments of regrets and broken memories that make it hard to part 'from what might have been but was not.'" — *Jewish Daily Forward*

"An ambitious, engrossing, playfully testamentary novel." — *Moment*

"Longtime readers of Yehoshua will surely recognize in this dialectic the shape of the master's career, which began with severe allegorical tales and moved toward the finely observed psychological realism of *A Late Divorce* and *The Liberated Bride*. Yet despite this move away from allegory, what strengthens the claim for A. B. Yehoshua's being the greatest Hebrew novelist is the rustle of higher meanings that attends his every incarnation." — *Jewish Review of Books*

"A pure pleasure . . . Yehoshua's best book in years." — *Maariv* (Israel)

"Yehoshua is concerned with the inadequacies in our quotidian sense of history, our inability to comprehend its violent grandeur. Though the history he has in mind may be Jewish and Israeli, the final words of Ralph Ellison's *Invisible Man* may apply: 'Who knows but that, on the lower frequencies, I speak for you?'"
— Robert Pinsky, *New York Times Book Review*

"[Yehoshua] achieves an autumnal tone as he ruminates on memory's slippery hold on life and on art." — *The New Yorker*

"*The Retrospective* is intelligent, sensitive fiction ... In his inimitable style, Yehoshua crafts a powerful and engaging allegory of modern Israeli Jewish identity. " — *Haaretz*

"Yehoshua delivers a stunning explanation of the ethics of art ... A fluid and absorbing novel of ideas; highly recommended."
— *Library Journal*, starred review

"A truly international book, a serious set of reflections about coming to terms with the past—with a surprising ending ... His recent novels have a wonderful restraint, an increasingly elegiac feel."
— *Jewish Chronicle*

"Yehoshua's intelligent and refined novel ... about an aging Israeli director reviewing both his films and his life ... recalls once again Faulkner's famous dictum that 'the past isn't dead. It isn't even past.'"
— *Kirkus*, starred review

"Resolutely realistic." — *Los Angeles Review of Books*

"With beautiful wordsmanship, Yehoshua entangles dignity and humiliation, repugnance and rapture, showing us how difficult they become to distinguish." — *Booklist*

"A compelling meditation on art, memory, love, guilt ... A hugely pleasurable read, it shows that in his seventies, A. B. Yehoshua is still producing some of his best work." — *Independent*

"Fascinating ... Beautiful." — *Ha'ir* (Israel)

"Thoughtful ... Yehoshua has mentioned Faulkner as an influence, and it shows ... [His] insights into realism and surrealism, religiousness and secularism, and the creative process deserve greater exploration." — *Publishers Weekly*

"Richly plotted." — *Jewish Week*

THE RETROSPECTIVE

Books by A. B. Yehoshua

The Lover

A Late Divorce

Five Seasons

Mr. Mani

Open Heart

A Journey to the End of the Millennium

The Liberated Bride

A Woman in Jerusalem

Friendly Fire

The Retrospective

THE RETROSPECTIVE

A. B. YEHOSHUA

Translated from the Hebrew by Stuart Schoffman

Mariner Books · Houghton Mifflin Harcourt · BOSTON · NEW YORK

First Mariner Books edition 2014
Copyright © 2011 by Abraham B. Yehoshua
English translation copyright © 2013 by Stuart Schoffman

For information about permission to reproduce selections from this book,
write to Permissions, Houghton Mifflin Harcourt Publishing Company,
215 Park Avenue South, New York, New York 10003.

www.hmhco.com

First published as *Hesed Sefaradi* by Hakibbutz Hameuchad, Tel Aviv, 2011.

Library of Congress Cataloging-in-Publication Data is available.
ISBN 978-0-547-49696-2   ISBN 978-0-544-15798-9 (pbk.)

Book design by Melissa Lotfy

Printed in the United States of America
DOC 10 9 8 7 6 5 4 3 2 1

In Hebrew, the title of this book is *Hesed Sefaradi*. *Hesed* (with a guttural *h*) eludes precise translation and connotes compassion, kindness, love, and charity; a fair equivalent is the Latin *caritas*. *Sefaradi* means "Spanish" but also "Sephardic," referring specifically to Jews whose ancestors were expelled from Spain in 1492 and more broadly to "Oriental" Jews from Arabic-speaking countries in North Africa and the Middle East. The double meaning helps the reader get the picture.

THE RETROSPECTIVE

one

SANTIAGO DE COMPOSTELA

1

ONLY AT MIDNIGHT, when they arrive at the massive, stark stone-paved plaza, bare of any statuary or fountain, its only ornament a boundary of heavy iron chains, does the director sense that his companion's anxiety is finally beginning to wane. By the time two silver-haired bellmen hurry down the front steps of the former royal hospice for pilgrims, now the Parador hotel, the actress, who made the trip at his request, is beaming with gratitude. But after the luggage is collected, their host, undeterred by the lateness of the hour and obvious fatigue of his guests, insists on hauling them to the heart of the square so they may marvel in the stillness of the night at the famous cathedral, between whose yellowed towers saints and angels stand erect, as if in their honor. In strange but fluent English he recites the names of its builders and luminaries, taking personal pride in the size of the square that draws throngs of believers, determined to prove to his guests that the holiness of the place they have come to is in no way inferior to the holiness of the land from which they came.

Indeed, given the grandeur of the cathedral and the elegance of the adjacent hotel, the director, Yair Moses, is pleased he did not refuse the embassy's request and has journeyed despite his age to this remote region to attend a retrospective of his films, not just as a passive guest of honor but as an active participant. Again, as in recent years, he mourns the absence of his cinematographer, who would surely have shouldered his camera by now and in the wintry glow attempted to capture the entire cathedral, or at least the pale moonlight cast upon the iron chains, or even the shadow of the broad stone steps leading into the Old Town. And if the director complained, as he used to do, about the waste of valuable film stock, the cameraman would have smiled and said nothing, since it was proven time and again that shots with no clear purpose, unconnected to plot or character, could be intercut in the editing room to enhance the imagery, and also to add, even in a purely realistic film, the mystical and symbolic touches sought by his former screenwriter.

Toledano, the cinematographer, were he still alive, would not stand still for the host's pedantic explanations – which will have to be cut short – but would hang back and satisfy his camera, surreptitiously or otherwise, with the profile of her face, or the contour of her body, or even its silhouette. His love for Ruth had led to his death.

Perhaps it's because of her that the director has been thinking often of Toledano, all these years after his death. For the actress, object of the cameraman's unrequited love, has become Moses' occasional companion, or, more precisely, a "character" given him for safekeeping. Here she is beside him, wearing a ratty fur coat, bent over and a bit clumsy but still attractive despite signs of age, and her friendly attentiveness, which looks real even when it isn't, now stimulates the flow of words that need cutting off.

"Yes, sir" – the guest grabs the arm of the host, whose name has already escaped his memory – "your cathedral is indeed worthy of admiration. And I hope that tomorrow morning it will still be here, so in our three days as your guests there shall be plenty of time to come back and marvel." And the director of the Archive of Cinematic Arts, a short man conceivably of Celtic stock, moon-faced and bald, smiles and humbly but firmly repeats his name, Juan de Viola, and warns against the illusion of "plenty of time." The program of the retrospective, which the guests have yet to receive, is full; each day, at least two films will be screened, and of course there will be discussions and meals. Not only at the film archive but also at the institute itself, there is great interest in the art of cinema in the Jewish State.

2

AT SOME RETROSPECTIVES, two separate rooms are reserved for the director and the actress, because their Internet biographies are vague regarding the true nature of their relationship. Nonetheless, there are hosts who, based on knowledge or rumor or simply a wish to save money, provide only one room at the hotel. When two rooms are offered, the director and the actress take both and use them as they please, but if only one is available, they accept the verdict.

In this historic hotel, where every nook bespeaks an aesthetic effort to convert its pious past into elegant comfort, the guests have been given a large room on the top floor, an attic with wooden beams that support the ceiling with perfect symmetry. The furniture is old but polished to a high gloss, and the velvet curtains are festooned with silken tassels whose color matches the soft carpet. The armoires are enhanced by artful carvings, and inside them, wide shelves lie in wait alongside a wealth of padded clothes hangers. There are no twin beds, but the double bed is generous in size, made up in fresh linens with rustic embroidery. The bathroom is spacious too, its tiles scrubbed clean and fixtures chic and clever, apart from a huge old bathtub with feet, preserved perhaps as a medical exhibit, for its style and girth suggest that in the distant past it held two ailing pilgrims, not one. The discerning eyes of Ruth — who grew up in an immigrant town in the south of Israel and is always eager to stay in places that don't remind her of her deprived childhood — confirm the beauty of the room, and without delay she gets undressed and curls up under the big quilt, ready to succumb to undisturbed slumber.

Moses — a man of middling height who in recent years has developed a potbelly, unprecedented in his family, that he counterbalances with a small, intellectual goatee – is pleased with the room and the ample dimensions of the double bed though concerned by the overbooked schedule of the retrospective. Despite the lateness of the hour, he does not rush to join the sleeping woman but takes off his shoes and moves about silently, allowing her to sink into deeper sleep. Lately he has been treating her with special tenderness – he has yet to inform her that there will be no role for her in his next film. Though it is well past midnight, he cannot rely on fatigue and takes a pill designed to alleviate anxiety. He would like to lower the heating but fails to find the thermostat, so he opens a window to let in the winter air, only to discover that the ancient cathedral had not been content with its vast stone-paved plaza and had sprouted to its rear another square of significant size at whose center, on a tall pedestal, stands a stone angel brandishing a sword at the visitor.

Moses joyfully gulps the chilly air before shutting the window and closing the dark velvet curtains so the light of dawn will not wake them, and carefully, without touching the sleeping body, he slides under the big duvet. Ruth's family doctor has urged her, more than once, to repeat a blood test whose results were worrisome, but, despite Moses' nagging, she keeps postponing the test. Yet when the date was set for this retrospective, Moses thought it preferable for the bloodletting to occur after their return from Spain. If it turns out there is a real problem, there'll be time enough to deal with it later on; for the moment, it's best to take advantage of the trip to quiet the anxiety, his more than hers.

He turns off the room's remaining light, for only in pitch-darkness can sleep overpower his imagination. But on the wall by the bed, close to the ceiling, one stubborn point of light stays on, apparently intended to illuminate the picture hanging below it in a gilt frame or to draw attention to it, and as he deliberates the need to get up and struggle with so faint a light, he feels the sweet pull of exhaustion and curls into fetal position, stealing a glance in the darkness at two mythological characters – a bald man, his upper body naked, sitting or kneeling at the feet of a bare-breasted nymph. Then he takes off his glasses, removes his hearing aids, and falls asleep.

It was Ruth who first diagnosed his hearing loss; she noticed that in public appearances he was raising his voice and giving answers not always pertinent to the questions. Although such responses might be appreciated by courteous people who'd been touched by his films in the past, the younger generation, whose questions are more precise and demanding, are less inclined to accept irrelevant answers. Sometimes a member of the audience will rise kindly to the occasion, restating the question and perhaps supplying an answer, but such assistance, even if well intended, does not enhance the dignity of any lecturer.

Moses was thus persuaded to acquire hearing aids, which, though minuscule, cannot entirely escape the notice of keen-eyed observers, thus calling attention to his age. When he sticks the pinkish gadgets in both ears, they emit a brief tune — as if to say, *At your service* — and immediately amplify the hubbub of the surrounding world. Now and then, they chirp and hum as they please, perhaps because a stranger's hearing aid has sent them a friendly signal or because some clandestine military radar is checking their identity. When one of the batteries runs down, it announces its demise with an insistent, continuous ring that can't be ignored, and thus in social situations or in the middle of a lecture, he has to remove the device and replace its battery.

All in all, the hearing aids have been good to Moses. When he is directing, the dialogue between him and the actors and crew is clearer now, and at public events he appears focused and relaxed. In an odd way, these tiny devices have taught him that deafness is not merely a physiological issue but a psychological one too. When he forgets to stick them in his ears, he can occasionally still pick up subtle overtones in the speech of others. His prostate, which has become enlarged in recent years, has taught him a similar lesson. He and it are able to ignore each other for many hours, even after the consumption of liquids, but sometimes, for no apparent reason – the stimulus of a new idea or an emotional reaction, or a slow descent in a narrow elevator – the prostate can threaten its master without warning. In which case, if the toilet is far away or its location is unknown, there may be no choice but to dart behind a parked car or find a hidden spot among the trash bins and gas canisters of a nearby apartment building. Once, in desperation, he slipped into a private garden, where the owner lay in wait and rebuked him. "What if I were just a stray dog," protested Moses with a smile, "would you insult a dog?" "But you're not a dog," retorted the man with a sneer, "and you couldn't be if you tried." Moses zipped up his trousers and retreated in silence, though he could have told him that at the beginning of his directing career, he and his screenwriter Trigano had made a thirty-minute surrealistic film about a jealous husband who fears his wife is cheating and so, to follow her, he masquerades as a dog. To their great surprise, the film turned out to be more than a comical sketch. The ingenious script and nuanced camera work, along with the right music, enabled the dog who played the jealous husband to exhibit credible human gestures. He still drifts through Moses' thoughts – a big yellowy mutt, hairy and melancholy, looking more like a hyena than a dog, with drooping ears suggesting spaniel ancestry. The dog was so faithful to the director's commands that it seemed his canine soul had absorbed the obsessions of the jealous husband. After the filming, the dog stayed on with the director – a strange companion, loyal, tormented, as if Moses had actually succeeded in imbuing him with human spirit, until in the end he recklessly crossed a road and was run over by a car.

3

THOUGH THE DARKNESS is total, the clock does not disappoint. It's 7:30 A.M., not 5:00. Sleep overcame consciousness and vanquished anxiety, and if during the night a strange dream had flickered, it didn't bother the dreamer. Yair slips out of bed and tries not to disturb his surroundings as he makes his way to the bathroom. His companion, asleep but not oblivious, instinctively occupies part of the vacated territory.

From the bathroom window, he can see people walking by the walls of the cathedral. Today is the first day of the retrospective, and it would be nice to rest a bit more before the commotion begins. Random rays of sunlight that have filtered onto the big bed cast a golden glow on the actress's bare feet, protruding from the quilt. Moses covers them, then carefully inspects the reproduction hanging on the wall. The stolen glance at night was superficial and misleading. Perhaps the picture represents some obscure mythological tale, not of an old man's lust for a young woman but rather of a hungry and desperate person. The old, muscular man is plainly a prisoner: his hands are tied behind him, and his naked, dirty feet have just been released from the stocks that rest nearby. His jailers have starved him so badly that he is drawn to the merciful breasts of a young nursing woman, who delicately guides his bald, sunburned head to the whiteness of her bosom.

Moses looks for the name of the artist and finds only two words in ornate script: *Caritas Romana*, meaning "Roman Charity," and as if struck by a flash of distant lightning, he wonders whether Trigano knew of this strange and brazen painting hanging randomly in a hotel room in the Spanish province of Galicia. Is it conceivable that in the dawning light, by sheer coincidence, here in Santiago de Compostela, he has uncovered a secret source that long ago sparked the imagination of his former screenwriter? He was a talented young man, a near genius, but also fanatically inflexible, and because of one dropped scene, he had broken off relations with not only Moses but also his own lover, the actress, thus imposing her on the director — if not as an obligation, at least as a source of worry. Could this mythological picture have inspired Trigano to devise the crazy, provocative ending of their last film together?

The location chosen for the scene was a rundown back street not far from the fishermen's pier in Jaffa. The drizzly weather that day complemented the somber tone of the film. The cinematographer and the soundman, the makeup artist and the lighting man, were ready to roll, and despite the out-of-the-way location, a sizable crowd had gathered to watch. In the early 1970s, shooting a feature film on location was rare in Israel, and passersby were enchanted as if by magic. Moses has not forgotten that morning after all these years, for on that day the creative covenant between him and his screenwriter fell apart. On the street corner, on a stool, sat an elderly beggar dressed in rags – a well-known thespian from the National Theater. It was particularly important for Moses that in the final scene, it was not some anonymous extra playing the part, but a familiar and respected actor who would surprise the audience in the role of a miserable beggar and be engraved in their memory. The actor, however, demanded that his character be given a touch of intellectual flair, perhaps a top hat and not a mere cap to receive donations, or a pipe whose smoke would slither from his lips. As the final directions were given, Moses could sense the old actor's anticipation of sensual contact with a young woman's breasts, not least because the scene would doubtless be shot several times, with the most shocking yet plausible version to be achieved in the editing room. Despite its boldness, the scene wasn't difficult to stage. A young woman departs a private maternity clinic after leaving her newborn for adoption and wanders the streets anguished and forlorn, and when she sees the old beggar, she opens her coat, takes out a breast, and nurses him.

It's because of the nasty fight that broke out that morning that small details stick in the memory. The long old coat Ruth wore. Her face made up to look sickly and tormented. A rusty iron door on an abandoned house, meant to be the entrance to the clinic. But most memorable is the distress of the young actress. Toledano reshot her exit from the clinic door, hoping to strengthen the credibility of her action, but Moses sensed that something was amiss. Her gestures became more hesitant and hollow, as if her whole being was in rebellion against the scene written for her by her lover, the screenwriter. At first Moses assumed she was embarrassed by the presence of curious onlookers and suggested they film the breastfeeding behind a partition. But it became clear that it wasn't the gaze of strangers that unsettled her, since she had stripped for the camera before, and even craved it, Moses thought. Nor was she repulsed by the touch of the old actor's lips on her breast. Her spirit rebelled against the absurdity of a young woman who, right after giving up her child for adoption, feels impelled to breastfeed an old stranger. Knowing Trigano, she decided to dodge the scene decisively, without getting tangled up in words. As she approached the street corner, tracked by the camera, she suddenly dashed into the cab of the production truck, locked the doors, and rolled up the windows.

Moses instantly empathized with her action. Notwithstanding the disruption and the time and effort spent in preparing the location, he told Toledano, who had so looked forward to this scene, to turn off the camera, shut down the lighting, dismantle the track. And since in those days Moses was both the director and producer, he hurried to inform the beggar from the National Theater that the scene had been canceled and paid him right there in cash, the full amount. He still remembers the hot flush of insult on the face of the rejected actor, who had once played classic roles in the theater but in recent years couldn't find a job and thus needed something, however marginal, that would revive his reputation, or at least his self-worth. First the actor wanted to know if the actress was repulsed by him, and after Moses assured him that he wasn't the issue, it was the credibility of the scene, the actor let fly a curse, flung the burning pipe into the top hat, and demanded a taxi. A year or two later, reading the actor's obituary, Moses wondered if the shock he had dealt him that drizzly morning had perhaps hastened his death.

At first Trigano refused to accept the violation of his script and tried to convince his lover to reverse her decision. But since she knew it was in his power to subdue her rebellion, she decided to ignore him. She covered her face with her hands and refused even to lower the window. Trigano slammed his fist on the glass as if to break it. And Moses, trying to forestall further violence, took quick responsibility for canceling the final scene. Let's find a different ending, he suggested, something more heartfelt and plausible, a scene that conveys simple compassion, not intellectual provocation. And though he knew he was wounding the pride of his partner and former student, he got carried away and complained about the boring nonsense he'd had to direct lately, the sick and twisted situations he was increasingly expected to bring to life. He deliberately chose extreme language – *boredom*, not *difficulty*; *nonsense*, not *oddity* – that would undermine the self-confidence of his young collaborator. Trigano, who had been Moses' loyal and beloved student, had convinced him that together they could create visionary art, something utterly new, and persuaded him to switch from teacher to filmmaker. And now, suddenly, the teacher had denied not only the artistic value of his student's work but its moral quality.

Trigano bore the offense with a quiet hatred that undermined any chance of continued collaboration. True, creative differences had flared up between them before, arguments over characters and relationships, the content and style of dialogue, camera angles that had been spelled out in the screenplay. But a good partnership had endured, resulting in six films, admittedly unprofitable but unique and original and praised by those whose opinions mattered. But when the actress rebelled in the last scene of the seventh film – a scene that for the writer was the very point of the film – and the director not only made no effort to get her back in front of the camera but supported her action, Trigano quickly tore their collaboration to shreds. For it had been agreed that the screenplay could be discussed and debated during the writing process, but once the shooting started, the director was to honor the script.

And even though many years have gone by with no contact at all between the two, Moses still feels the stump of amputation, and he believes the screenwriter feels it too, even if he is too proud to admit it.

After all, once they parted ways, Moses continued to make feature films, first from screenplays written by others and later, as success favored him, from scripts he wrote himself based on original ideas or adapted from books. Whereas the screenwriter's output was confined to short, esoteric films, and then, when his new collaborators proved incompetent and saddled the productions with financial problems, he stopped making films altogether and went into teaching.

Sometimes Moses feels a vague desire to get back in touch, but he never does. Reconciliation after a serious breakup is harder than smoothing feathers after an argument. When they ran into each other at public events, at festivals or symposia, they barely exchanged more than a few empty words. Moses had at first believed that Trigano left him because of the affront to his professional dignity, but when he saw that the writer had left his friend and lover too, Moses understood that Trigano's pride was injured not only by a director's excessive indulgence of an actress repulsed by a twisted script but also by the extreme kindness of another man to a distressed woman whom Trigano regarded as his own. For had Moses not truly melted at the sight of a frightened female refusing her breast to an old street beggar, he would never have dropped a scene he was previously willing to direct — one never seen on the screen before. Toledano, the cinematographer, in love with Ruth, had adjusted the lighting and the camera so the moment at the end, when the beggar's head touches her breast, would project the nuanced eroticism, the sense of longing and nostalgia characteristic of Ruth's performance in those days.

Now, contemplating the picture of Roman Charity, Moses dismisses the possibility that Trigano had known about this painting, or another one like it, when he came up with his scene. Shaul Trigano had been a pupil in his class, and he was the type who relied more on imagination than knowledge, which in his case was spotty. Besides, Trigano had not described an old prisoner, hands bound behind him, who can't touch the woman dispensing kindness, but rather an old beggar on a street corner who grabs like a baby for the breast that feeds him.

4

WITH THE FIRST glimmer of consciousness, Ruth expands her conquest of the big bed, assuming a diagonal position that sends a clear message: *Don't come back to bed, my friend.* Other companions might have sought an alternative interpretation of the angle — such as *Come, I wait upon your pillow* — but Moses' stricter reading had been proven right in the past. He doesn't go near her except if she asks, and she doesn't ask unless he gives her a sign that he is willing and able to respond. In essence she is not a partner but a companion; more precisely, a character who reappears in his films because he feels obligated to take care of her. They've never lived under the same roof, and she has a social world of her own, where she stays in touch with friends and lovers. She has a modest income from her work as a drama teacher for children, so she is not dependent on movie roles given her by Moses or any other director. But lately, despite her long experience and lingering beauty, she is not exactly in demand. And as she is unfit for the theater, since she can't remember long stretches of dialogue, Moses has been trying to find her smaller parts in his films, and he recommends her for others. It would be a shame if her career ended in commercials for insurance companies or organic foods. Her intellectual resources are not deep. She came from a religious background, and in her father's house, not one unholy book sat on the shelf, and all the record albums were Jewish folk songs. Her mother died in childbirth, and her father, a tall, silent man who was a respected rabbi in their village of Debdou, in eastern Morocco, left his community to make aliyah to Israel, where to support himself and his only daughter he became a farm worker. Therefore, when Trigano began to take an interest in her and plan her future, her father wholeheartedly turned her over to the energetic young man, who persuaded his girlfriend to drop out of high school, believing that whatever he learned and knew would be hers too.

Moses doesn't want to turn on the light but opens the curtains a bit to take another look at the picture, to decide whether to call it to Ruth's attention, possibly awaking painful memories, or let her discover it for herself. But the winter sun is in no hurry to visit the westernmost province of the Iberian peninsula, and in the faint gathering light, Ruth's diagonal position has exposed her legs, which are rubbing each other to keep warm. He takes the quilt and carefully covers them. All these years later he still remembers the praise once accorded them by an old painter who came three times in one day to see the first film she starred in.

That was in the 1960s, in a small movie theater in north Tel Aviv that specialized in unconventional art films, mostly foreign, some of them without subtitles. But ambitiously avant-garde Israeli films unable to make their way into the bigger theaters were also welcome to try their luck, which is how Moses and his collaborators came to show their film there.

In most of his early films, Ruth had significant roles, since as the scriptwriter's girlfriend she was available to work for free. The director and cinematographer were curious to feel out the audience, so they would sneak into the first screenings, with no expectation of favorable response. These were modest films, made under primitive conditions. Yet at their core lay an intense and arresting surrealism that attracted sophisticated viewers.

The very first showing of the aforementioned film was at three in the afternoon. A few viewers walked out in the middle, but a man with a hat planted firmly on his head watched attentively till the end. He came back for the first evening show, the hat again conspicuous as the lights went down. At somebody's request, he removed it, revealing a big and shiny pate. Moses and Toledano were determined to find out what drew this man to watch the film twice in a single day, but he slipped out of the hall in darkness before the film was over. To their astonishment, he turned up at the third showing, at nine that night, and sat down in the back row. This time the director and cinematographer blocked his path before the lights went up and asked what compelled him to watch so unpolished a film three times in a single day.

He was evasive at first but then quickly complied, introducing himself as a painter. He thoroughly analyzed scene after scene, listing its strengths and weaknesses, and though his reservations were substantial, he also offered encouragement. The filmmakers were intrigued: If the film had so many flaws, why see it three times in one day? The painter hemmed and hawed, but finally admitted that it was because of the young actress, who had so moved him that he came back to engrave her image in his mind, for who knew when he would again see her on the screen? Strange words of praise, as he had not spared criticism of her acting, yet he came back, drawn by her charms. The cinematographer asked for a fuller explanation, if only to know how to capture that magic in the future. Whereupon, with precise professionalism, the painter proceeded to describe the nature of the sensuality that had spoken to him, sketched her facial structure in the air with his hand, detailed the shifts of expression in her eyes, marveled at the lightness of her gait, her ease as she sat down, and, above all, the perfect form of her "heavenly legs." Those were the very words he spoke in the darkness as the last lights went out in the lobby of the movie theater. Moses was disgusted by the libidinal enthusiasm of the old, foul-smelling man. But the cinematographer hung on every word, as if in the future he would be able to translate the artist's professional lust into perfect lighting and camera angles.

Was that the moment that sparked Toledano's secret love for the actress who was bound body and soul to the scriptwriter? For even after Toledano married, he would often remind Moses, half seriously, of the keen observations of the "man with the hat," to guide him in the staging of scenes that preserved the magic. Years later, when Trigano abandoned Ruth, the cinematographer remained faithful, and if there were no jobs for her in films by Moses or others, he would find work for her in commercials, where he was free to film the fading magic from every conceivable angle. One day, when he attempted to film her from a cliff as she lay nearly naked on the beach below, he carelessly lost his footing and crashed to an untimely death.

5

THE BLACK VELVET curtain grows lighter, and hunger too makes its demands. Ruth is an inveterate night owl, late to bed and late to rise. But since this retrospective will require long hours of attendance, it would be good to hurry up and use the morning to explore the city of pilgrimage. Moses is careful not to touch the sleeping woman, but he draws the curtain back and opens the window too, so that light and air will wake her. And when he emerges from the bathroom, fragrant with cologne supplied by the hotel, he finds her curled under the covers with smiling eyes, and since she knows how addicted he is to sumptuous hotel breakfasts, which in recent years have become the most satisfying benefit of his travels, she urges him to go to the dining room and not wait for her. Lately, Yair Moses often imagines his meals in advance, and in his pursuit of a precise naturalistic style, he prolongs the eating scenes in his films, insisting that real food be served, colorful and appealing, not sterile replicas, and he instructs the cameramen to shoot close-ups of full plates and wineglasses, not just long shots of the dining table. Within scenes he sometimes has actors cut short the dialogue and improvise personal reactions to the food. You are not dogs, unable to express opinions of what they eat, he likes to tease the actors, but intelligent beings who need to understand not only what comes out of your mouths but also what goes in.

He himself, though, prefers to eat in silence. As the years have gone by, he has become increasingly convinced of the value of being alone and keeping to a daily schedule. He is content to embark on flights of imagination and planning, especially at a sumptuous breakfast, a feast for the eyes and palate, such as he has discovered in the dining room on the ground floor of the historic hotel. A small sign by the entrance informs guests that this same dining hall was in operation during the Renaissance, serving the weary pilgrims who lodged at the royal hospice and those who cared for them. The wait-resses' traditional attire arouses interest along with appetite. He looks around for a table suitable for a lavish but introverted meal, and then a woman, thin as a bird and not young, approaches him tentatively and informs him that she has been sent by the film archive and insti-tute to be his guide for the day.

If he asks her to wait for him in the lobby, his meal will be hasty and unsatisfying. But neither does he want her to watch as he gorges himself alone, so he urges her to join him. "Before my companion arrives," he tells her, "come advise me on the fine points of Galician cuisine, so I won't miss the best or be tempted by the worst." She is embarrassed by the invitation, but since the flimsiness of her phy-sique enables Moses to steer her with a light touch to the multi-tiered buffet and shove a big plate into her hand, she cooperates, naming the local dishes, listing their pros and cons. And as Moses, acting on her recommendations, piles his plate with tiny pigeon eggs and pick-led fish in bluish brine and golden pastries shaped like shells, she too talks herself into an ample plateful of the same. The name of the birdlike adviser is Pilar Carballo, who identifies herself as a teacher of animation at the film institute. Despite her tiny frame, or because of it, she turns out to be an energetic eater, or maybe she arrived at the hotel especially hungry. In shared pleasure, they eat their fill, and to ensure orderly consumption, he asks many brief general questions about the institute and its personnel, the city and its residents, so his guest may reply at length and in detail while he continues to eat. Pilar is happy to oblige and also spells out the plan for the day.

The schedule, as promised, is jam-packed: First, a visit to the ca-thedral, which considering its importance is worth additional visits. From there, a courtesy call on the mayor, who has promised to at-tend one of the films at the Israeli's retrospective. From the mayor's office, back to the cathedral to see its museum, and then, time permitting, a taste of the Old Town. At noon, a lunch-and-study session with teachers from the institute and employees of the archive. At three, the screening of the first film, followed by discussion; at six, the second film and discussion; at nine, the third film, plus discussion. Around midnight, top off the day with a meal at a superb restaurant.

"No, that's enough." Moses touches the little bird's hand. "Did you all forget how old I am?"

"How could we forget?" she counters with a cheerful smile. "We studied your biography." As proof she produces from her handbag a folded sheet of paper with an old photo of Moses, along with his resumé in Spanish.

"No," protests Moses, "midnight is much too late for a gourmet meal. Let's work it in between the second and third screenings."

"Impossible. In a restaurant like this, the break between the two films would barely be enough for a first course."

"So there'll be only a first course, and maybe a quick dessert. What can I do, Pilar? It's how I was brought up. Nights are for sleeping, not eating."

She shrugs, as if to say the nights in Spain are long enough for both eating and sleeping. Suddenly she shifts her gaze, eyes flashing, and rises to invite Ruth, wandering among the tables, to join them. "Here's your companion," she says, in keeping with his resumé. "How charming to meet such a lovable character in person and not just on the screen."

The two hug and kiss as if they were childhood friends. Moses has observed in recent years that Ruth is quick to throw her arms around anyone still excited to meet her, maybe to seize the connection before she is forever forgotten. Moses puts his napkin on his plate and hangs his scarf on the chair to indicate imminent return, and hurries back to the room, which Ruth has tidied up. He inspects *Roman Charity*, still hoping to discover the name of the artist, but to no avail.

Before returning to the dining room, he inquires at the reception desk about the reproduction of the painting hanging by his bed. Who was the artist, when was it originally painted, and in what museum may it be found? The desk clerk writes down his room number and the location of the picture and asks him to describe it, and Moses obliges.

"If the picture is disturbing to you, sir, we can replace it by this afternoon —"

"No, on the contrary, I like it, it's very nice, but also quite intriguing."

It will be difficult to find a quick answer, but the desk clerk promises to forward the question to the director of the cathedral's museum.

On his way back to the table, Moses asks the waitress for another cup of coffee. At the table, the two women are deep in conversation. "All right, then," says Moses, "let's get going and see the cathedral."

"But wait," insists Ruth, "which films were picked for our retrospective?" Linking herself, as usual, to Moses.

"What's the difference," Moses says in Hebrew, "we know our own films."

"But if we have to explain, or defend them . . ."

"Defend?" Moses pats her arm affectionately. "You mean discuss them. But even if we need to defend them, so what? We won't know how to defend what we created?"

Pilar pulls out a piece of paper with the titles in Spanish of the three films to be screened that day, improvising their translation into English, and the visitors do not recognize a single one. "You're sure these are ours?" asks Moses with a laugh. "Or did you bring someone else's films by mistake?"

It turns out that here in Spain, foreign films are freely assigned titles that appeal to the local audience. It takes a bit of wit and ingenuity to excavate the old titles hiding behind the new. There has been no mistake. These are indeed Moses' films, from the dawn of his career, forgotten films made in full collaboration with Trigano.

"Why did you pick such ancient films of mine?"

"For you they are ancient," says Pilar, "but not for us. We have silent films here in which the mother of de Viola, the director of our archive, performed as an actress."

"She's still alive?"

"Barely. But if she feels well enough, she will personally present you with the award you've been promised."

6

"IF THESE ARE today's films," says Moses to Ruth as they walk into the giant square, whose majestic emptiness in daylight is no less glorious than its nakedness at night, "we won't be able to go shopping during the screenings. We'll have to sit in the dark and try and remember the details, or we won't be able to answer the audience's questions intelligently."

The day is cold and bright. The plaza is lined by imposing palaces, which Pilar identifies by name — Palacio de Rajoy, where the mayor will soon receive them for an official visit, and the former Colegio de San Jerónimo, today the Institute of Galician Studies, whose rector, says Pilar, hopes to honor them with his presence at one of the screenings. And of course the massive cathedral itself, built atop a Romanesque church, its towers looming above a grand quadruple flight of stairs, the battered, greenish steps leading to the entrance. An aficionado of European cathedrals, Moses enjoys the novel experience of a long climb from ground level to the towering church. At the northern face of the cathedral stands a statue of Santiago, Saint James, one of the twelve apostles of Jesus and the patron saint of Spain; his sacred remains migrated to this place and since the Middle Ages have attracted pilgrims from all over the world who seek blessings and healing.

Therefore, in contrast to many European cathedrals, where often one finds only an African or Korean priest celebrating the Mass for a handful of foreign workers and a few local women, here the cathedral is crammed with tourists, who upon entering are transformed into pilgrims; they kneel and make the sign of the cross, sing sweet hymns at masses performed in small chapels. Near the stairs leading to the crypt housing the relics of the saint, believers wait patiently in line, hoping to draw strength from the dry bones.

Because the birdlike emissary of the archive is not sure if Jews draw strength from a competing religion, she leads them instead alongside the pews, pausing occasionally at statues and explaining their significance.

One cannot help but notice the brisk activity in the confessional booths. Along the interior walls, on both sides, the booths are arrayed one after the next, many more than generally found in cathedrals. Remarkably, even at this early hour, the confessionals are manned by priests in robes, some hidden behind a curtain, others on view awaiting prospective clients, immersed in books that through the lattices of the booths appear to be novels rather than holy scriptures.

Moses is impressed by the vitality of the religious rite of confession, which he had naively assumed was on the decline. "Decline? Not in Spain," Pilar replies, "and surely not in this cathedral." She blushes, her eyes glinting with mischief. Perhaps the visitors from Israel wish to confess?

"I don't rule it out," Yair Moses says with a smile, "but I would first need to put my sins in order."

"In order? How so?"

"Separate personal from professional sins, for which I would need a priest who is also an expert in film. But is it possible for a priest to take confession from someone who is neither a Christian nor a believer in God?"

"It is possible for him to take confession from such a person, but he cannot grant absolution," answers Pilar confidently, "and don't be surprised if you find a priest here who also understands film."

"Then I'm ready to confess," Ruth chimes in, attracted by the idea of confession at a safe distance of a few thousand kilometers from home, though it is unclear whether her fractured English could express her sins adequately.

The animation teacher smiles faintly, steering the pair toward the large altar at the front. Here, too, one last confessional, isolated and closed, apparently in use. Pilar asks the two to wait until the curtain is opened, and after a huge red-faced man emerges, wiping away tears, she approaches cautiously and pulls from the darkness a short priest in a big robe. His face brightens at the sight of the Israelis, and he cordially inquires whether their hotel room was comfortable and their breakfast satisfactory.

Ruth recognizes him and speaks his name, but Moses is still grappling with the fact that Juan de Viola, their host and the director of the film archive, is also an ordained priest.

"Films and the Church?"

"Why not? If painting and sculpture, music and poetry, choral performance and theater have been nurtured for centuries under the wing of the Catholic Church, why not include their younger sister, the seventh art? What's wrong with that?"

"Nothing wrong at all," says Moses, "but it is odd that I was not warned in advance that my retrospective was organized by a religious institution."

"Warned?" says the priest, flaring his robe with mild irritation. "And if you had been warned, you would not have honored us with your presence?"

"I would have come."

"And why not? Especially," says de Viola, "since the municipality and the government are partners with the institute and archive, which also receive contributions from private individuals. My mother, for one, who in her youth acted in silent films by Luis Buñuel, is a generous contributor. This is why the bishop has freed me from certain obligations, to enable me to join the administration of the institute and make sure that my family's assets are squandered only on worthy causes." He winks.

A friendly and unusual fellow, thinks Moses. *On the third day, before we leave, perhaps I'll make a small confession in his booth.*

"And your mother," says the director, leaning closer to the priest, enthralled by the notion of an ancient actress from the silent era, "your mother also lives here in Santiago?"

No, his mother lives in Madrid. She is ninety-four, sharp of mind, though her body is infirm. She knows about the Moses retrospective and is one of its financial backers, and if she feels up to it, she will attend the prize ceremony on the third day. She is even familiar with a few of Moses' films and believes in his future.

"My future?" Moses blushes. "At my age?"

"'When the future is short,'" the son quotes his mother, "'it becomes more concentrated and interesting.'"

They cross the big square on their way to the mayor. About thirty sanitation workers are staging a demonstration, banging pans and blowing whistles, lustily shouting rhythmic protests and waving red flags. Two bored policemen stroll calmly beside them, making sure the demonstrators do not overstep some invisible line apparently agreed upon. Yet every so often, the agreement gives way to rage, and one of the protesters bursts forth with his whistle. As the policemen casually approach him, he retreats with equal ease.

On the magnificent steps of the municipal palace, Moses realizes he left his hearing aids at the hotel. A simple courtesy call should not be a problem, provided he sits close enough to the mayor and tilts his head at a certain angle, but what if the chambermaid thinks they are used earplugs and tosses them into the wastebasket? For a moment he considers asking his hosts to wait a minute on the stairs while he runs to the hotel, but the actress, always sensitive to his anxieties, calms him. "I have brought them, though you seem fine without them."

"Yes, my guardian angel," says Moses shakily, "sometimes I can manage without them, but it's better to have them with me."

She removes the hearing aids from her bag and sneaks them into his hand, so as not to reveal his disability to strangers. But he no longer considers people who know his biography, and honor him with a three-day retrospective, to be strangers, and he sticks the devices in his ears in front of Pilar and the priest, noting with a touch of irony: "This way I can better hear the possibilities for my short but concentrated future."

Good thing he has improved his hearing, for the mayor, Antonio Santos, a thickset man and as short as the priest, turns out to be amiable and curious, and to the joyful sounds of the sanitation protest, he shifts the routine courtesy call into a serious interview.

"I've read your bio," he says in Spanish, waving the printout from the Internet with the blurry photo, "but I ask that you expand on it a bit."

A surprising and flattering request, and though simultaneous translation by Pilar requires that he pause every few sentences, Moses expands a good deal, and looking over the great square of pilgrimage on this dazzling morning, he unspools his life story, the full director's cut, outtakes and all.

He was born into an upstanding, educated Jerusalem family before the outbreak of the Second World War. After the establishment of the State of Israel, his father and mother both went to work for the state comptroller's office, in which capacity they spent most of their time scrutinizing the faults and failings of the new government. At work, the mother outranked the father, who reported to her, and so at home, as compensation, she served and coddled him. Yair Moses was an only child, and he learned from his parents that every politician had a little back pocket filled with secrets worth investigating. His parents insisted that after his military service he pursue higher education that would enable him to follow in their footsteps and be useful to society. At first he studied economics and accounting, but then, breaking free of his parents, he switched to philosophy and history, and ultimately got a teaching job at an elite Jerusalem high school, the same one he had attended as a youth. He had no trouble controlling his students. If a teacher maintains a cool distance and occasionally erupts in spontaneous rage, students are careful not to defy him. In those days he still lived at home to save on rent, and his parents would pester him to go out at night to get free of his dependence on them. But as an only child, accustomed to solitude, he didn't tend to seek the company of others and often found himself wandering about Jerusalem or going to see a film alone, never thinking he might someday want to make motion pictures and certainly not believing he had the capacity to do so.

Then, after three or four years, there appeared in his eleventh-grade class an unusual student whose creative originality and aura of self-confidence deflated the standoffish pose of the teacher. This talented young man was from a small town in the south of Israel, formerly a transit camp for Jewish immigrants from North Africa. While still in elementary school, the boy had lost his father, and was sent to a vocational school in the hope he would find employment as an auto mechanic or factory worker and support his mother. But the power of his imagination and ideas prompted his teachers to put him on an academic track, and a modest scholarship was arranged so he could attend a first-rate school. It was under the influence of this student who happened to land in his class that the teacher of history and philosophy became a film director.

"A student?"

"Who later became my screenwriter."

"This fellow . . ." murmurs the mayor, perusing the bio sheet, looking for the name.

"I don't think you'll find him there," Moses quickly comments, "he was the writer in only my very first films."

"The marvelous ones . . ." whispers the priest to himself.

"And perhaps may again be in the future," graciously suggests the mayor.

"Perhaps . . ." softly repeats the actress, closely following the detailed story she knows so well and will soon be part of.

"In the future?" Moses chuckles. "But the future is so short and concentrated . . ."

"If a student turns a teacher of history and philosophy into a film director," says de Viola, "it proves that students can revolutionize the lives of their teachers, not just the other way around."

Of course, the director continues, but if the connection had existed only in the classroom, it's doubtful even so special a student would have had such an influence. The student's stipend was small and he had to work. He found a job as an usher and janitor at a local movie theater beloved by Jerusalemites for the caliber of its films and its location in a pleasant, formerly Arab neighborhood outside the shabby city center. In those days — because Ben-Gurion, the legendary prime minister, prohibited television broadcasting in the young country lest hard-working citizens waste precious sleeping time — people went often to the movies. Moses would usually go to a second show, and he'd bump into the usher on entering and leaving. It wasn't right to give only a passing nod in the evening to a student so active and intelligent in the morning, and Moses was agreeable when the young man wished to hear the teacher's impressions of the film just seen and, even more, to offer the teacher his own opinions.

Given the advantage of being an usher, who sees a film many times, the boy achieved a deep understanding not only of what went on in films, but also of what went wrong, of missed opportunities. He knew how to link what he learned in the morning with what he saw and heard in the evening, and so Moses, to encourage him, would engage him in late-night conversation about the movie just ended.

The protest songs outside grow louder, but the mayor stays on track. Patiently, almost like a therapist, he asks his guest to continue. In recent years, ever since his wife left him, Moses has avoided personal disclosures, but he is won over by the interest in his professional development on the part of a mayor of so famous a city. The hearing aids pick up every word, and Pilar's translations of questions and answers seem accurate in rhythm and tone. And while she translates, he feasts his eyes on the mayor's office, on whose walls, amid portraits of the city's mayors and other dignitaries, hang pictures of hunting scenes, replete with straining dogs and bleeding stags, and young women in states of undress, adding a splash of sensuality to the severe vista of the cathedral outside. Now and again, he exchanges a tender glance with Ruth, who follows the conversation, eagerly anticipating the moment when she will appear in the story.

And there is no doubt that she will.

The late-night discussions with the student involved close analysis of the films — of characters and plot, ideas and emotions, questions about what touched the viewer's heart and what left him cold and sometimes angry and disappointed, what provoked laughter and what brought a person to tears, what was believable, what seemed arbitrary, what would surely be remembered, and what was eminently forgettable.

This is all about Trigano, de Viola explains to the mayor, who nods as if he actually recognizes the name, and for a moment Moses is alarmed that the name of the screenwriter he broke off relations with so many years ago has come up here, in this strange and distant place, but he quickly reminds himself that Trigano's name appears in the credits of his early films. Relieved, he continues to speak well of him.

"Yes, that's his name, and although he was younger than me by almost ten years, I found nothing wrong in the intellectual connection between us in those nighttime conversations, particularly because the boy never tried to exploit this connection to gain privileges in the morning. In class, he continued to meet his obligations, was as well behaved and focused as ever, answered questions concisely and to the point, with none of the excitement he displayed at night. Slowly I sensed that the young man was not content to analyze and understand films made by others but was dreaming of making films of his own. And so I was therefore not surprised when at the end of his last year, he asked me to help him make a short eight-millimeter film about the school, to be shown at the graduation ceremony."

At first it appeared that Moses' role in this short film would be limited to oversight of the budget provided by the school. But he soon found himself offering advice, getting involved on the artistic side. In the end, the work was widely praised, so much so that this amateurish film, lasting all of ten minutes, was Trigano's admission ticket to the film unit of the Israeli army. During the years of his military service, he would come in uniform to visit his teacher, to tell him of his activities and consult about the future. Also in the film unit were a cinematographer and a lighting man who were both, like Trigano, North African immigrants from Israeli development towns, and Trigano tried to interest them in working with him after they were discharged. But his friends were ready to collaborate only if somebody serious supervised his fantasies — in short, they demanded a senior partner who would see to the proper management of the production. Trigano invited his teacher to join his young group. It'll bore you to repeat yourself year after year, Trigano said. You can have a real connection to young people only by working with them, not from a teacher's podium. But Moses imposed a condition: If he was a partner, he would not be just a bookkeeper and production manager, he would also participate in the creative process. Trigano would dream up the plot, make up scenes, and write the dialogue, and Moses as director would bring Trigano's vision to life. Why not? The screenwriter overflowed with ideas, and his friends took care of camera work and lighting, but they needed a leader, a man whose authority people were glad to respect.

Pilar translates, and the mayor and the priest regard the old man fondly — but Moses is suddenly sick of talking about himself.

"And so, ladies and gentlemen, to be brief, I took leaves of absence from teaching and joined these young people, whose enthusiasm swept me onto the path that has become the center of my life. During my first leave we were able to complete our earliest project, a short and unusual film that to my surprise was well received, and so we began right away to plan another. And after my confidence as director grew — and as I read the memoirs of famous directors who started making movies without special training — I gradually reduced my teaching hours, then finally quit, with no regrets. And though he had become my close collaborator, my former student made sure to maintain polite boundaries and treat me as if I were still his teacher, perhaps a surrogate of sorts for the father he didn't have growing up. He decided that he and his friends wouldn't call me by my first name, only by my family name, and I also addressed them by their family names, as in the classroom, and it was more or less agreed that everyone in the group would call the others by their last names, including the lady who sits here before you, who in those days was the writer's very close friend."

"You also called him Moses?" de Viola asks Ruth, who sits next to him with her legs crossed, her colorful woolen scarf brushing the hem of his robe, her eyes twinkling as she tries not to miss a word.

"Yes." She laughs. "Even now, Moses is like a teacher to me."

"But how did you come to belong to the group back then?" asks Pilar. "According to your biography, you were still a child."

"Whoever wrote my bio was generous about my date of birth," says Ruth, "but by now, believe me, I'm tired of hiding my real age. Besides, my connection with Trigano began when I was still a child. I grew up with only a father — my mother died in childbirth, and my father got help from the neighbors, including Trigano's family. I am in fact younger than Trigano, and when I was in elementary school, he would create roles for me in little skits that he wrote, and it sometimes seemed that he was inventing these stories just for me. And so when he put together the group, I was naturally a part of it. I wanted so much to be an actress that I dropped out of high school. Now I'm over fifty, and I still don't have a diploma." Suddenly, she falls silent.

"What was that first short film about?" the head of the archive asks Moses. "We know nothing of it."

The director begins to answer, but Ruth beats him to it.

"It was a film about a jealous dog."

"A dog?"

"A dog."

"Just a dog?"

"No," Moses quickly explains, "it's about a jealous man who disguised himself as a dog to secretly follow his cheating wife."

"But in the film, there is also a real dog?"

"Yes, of course, the dog who played the husband."

"A metaphorical dog, as in Buñuel's *Chien Andalou*?"

"A real dog, not metaphorical."

"The film still exists?"

"No. Film preservation was so bad then, all that's left is a sticky pile of celluloid."

"You should know, Mr. Moses, that we at the archive are able to resurrect even films that have been given up for dead."

"This film you could never resurrect."

The windows of the office are rattled by trumpet blasts and the pounding of drums. The sanitation workers have brought in musical reinforcements, finally snapping the mayor from his tranquillity. With a wave of his hand he summons his aides. Moses seizes the moment and rises to his feet, poised to take his leave. He is unaccustomed to talking at length about himself, especially to foreigners whose intentions have yet to be made clear. The others also get up. "Maybe you should advise him to raise their pay," he jokes to Pilar as the mayor gives orders to his staff. "After all, in such a holy city, sanitation workers are little angels."

But Pilar furrows her tiny brow, disinclined to translate for her mayor the advice of so foreign a guest.

7

THEY EXIT THE municipal palace, and Moses hurries toward the sanitation workers to congratulate them on their spirited performance. And in light of the day's crowded schedule, he suggests that Pilar postpone till tomorrow the visit to the cathedral museum, and that before the meeting with the institute teachers, they take a walk in the Old Town. It is a great pleasure to wander aimlessly in narrow streets that suddenly become little plazas with statues, to peek into hidden gardens. The pure, refreshing air reddens Ruth's cheeks, and her eyes shine. Outside of Israel she does not expect to be recognized; she can walk around relaxed, without wondering if someone will come up and ask if it's really her.

The souvenir shops here are so numerous and well stocked that it seems sinful not to take home some knickknack, proof for their twilight years that the trip to Santiago was not just a dream. Moses chooses two traditional walking sticks of blackish bamboo, each with an iron tip to stick in the ground for support, and topped by a big reddish shell, the shell of Saint James, in honor of the angel who steered the shell-shaped ship bearing the body of the saint to the shores of the village of Padrón.

"What do I do with a stick like this?" She laughs.

"You can lean on it when I'm no longer at your side."

When they return to the hotel they find de Viola in civilian clothes, waiting beside his small car. They quickly deposit the walking sticks with the desk clerk, who has not forgotten the request to clarify the source of the painting *Caritas Romana* hanging by the bed but also reiterates his offer to replace it with another, more modest picture. "Certainly not," insists the visiting Israeli, "this picture is important to me personally."

The director of the archive was gratified by the conversation in the mayor's office. It's good that foreign artists honor the city fathers, since unlike the locals, the guests cannot be suspected of ulterior motives. Spread under the sharp blue sky, the vast pilgrim plaza is empty now. The sanitation workers have gone for their siesta, and a bored lone policeman waits for them to come back.

The drive to the film institute takes a while. It is located outside the city limits but exploits its famous name to attract students and visitors. The car heads west, toward the Atlantic coast.

During the reign of Franco, a native of the region of Galicia, the building that now houses the institute functioned as an army barracks. Located in an open area that offers a plethora of parking spots, it provides ample space — three screening rooms of varying size, dining halls, studios and classrooms, and dormitories for students. Even so, exchanging the stately old palaces and glorious cathedral for the nondescript quarters of his retrospective depresses the Israeli director a bit.

In the staff dining room, a large table has been set, around which a small group of senior faculty await him, men and women of various ages. As he feels their warm welcome, his mood improves, and after everyone present introduces himself by name and specialty, a simple but generous meal is served, with vestigial flavors, or so it seems, of army food.

De Viola doesn't want to waste time with small talk. Having seated those who know English well next to those who do not, he taps a knife on his wineglass without waiting for dessert and poses a question of aesthetics so urgently that Moses almost suspects it was the sole purpose he was invited to a retrospective at this provincial archive.

"We welcome you with pleasure and interest and thank you for taking the trouble to travel so far to your retrospective," begins de Viola, "a retrospective where we shall screen primarily films from the early period of your creative work. We will discuss them one by one after each screening, but a general question has arisen regarding the sharp stylistic shift that took place in your films. It seems to us, Mr. Moses, that in the past two decades you have turned your back on the surrealistic and symbolic style of your early films and have become addicted to extreme realism that is almost naturalistic. The question is simple: Why? Do you no longer believe in a world of transcendence, in what is hidden, invisible, and fantastical, so much so that you are mired in the mundane and the obvious? For example, in the film *Potatoes*, which you made five years ago, your main characters eat lunch for sixteen minutes."

"Eighteen minutes," Moses corrects him, impressed that a stranger in a distant land is such an expert on a recent film of his, "if you count the two minutes I made the audience watch the table being cleared and the dishes washed."

"True," proclaims the priest triumphantly, "I even remember the hesitation of the Arab waiter as he wondered whether to empty the plate into the garbage can or salvage the leftovers in a container for the poor of his village. Yet this long meal scene is within a film that is not especially long. One hundred and twenty minutes?"

"One twenty-three," notes the director for the record, again with a smile.

Whereupon a young teacher, pale and handsome, raises his hand to push de Viola's question further.

"There is a feeling, sir, that in your latest films, the material aspect has assumed supreme importance, and not necessarily out of a new aesthetic. As if you are sanctifying the materialism of the world or succumbing to it, whether in lengthy cinematographic takes of locations and landscapes or in the physical appearances of people. You slow down movement and employ extreme close-ups to dwell on the most banal things. Sometimes the camera spends an entire minute following the gesticulation of a speaker without showing his face. Sometimes, in a long dialogue scene, we see just one of the speakers; the other we only hear. Does not such naturalistic realism smother any possibility of mystery, of rising to a higher vision? Have you permanently broken away from the strange, the absurd and grotesque, the elements that were so important and well developed in your early films?"

Moses has heard such sentiments in his home country as well as abroad, though here the questions seem tinged by a certain antagonism. And as the English speakers finish translating for their friends, there is a murmur of general agreement, after which the room falls silent in anticipation of an answer. The director exchanges a quick glance with his companion. Trusty Ruth, her eyes sparkling, knows the answers to come. And Moses feels that despite the many years that have gone by since Trigano first introduced her to him as his friend and lover, her beauty has not faded, and it holds a clear advantage over the looks of the two chic young teachers sitting alongside her.

For a moment Moses considers rising to his feet, to add force to his response, but the female hand placed gently on his knee keeps him in his seat.

"Yes, ladies and gentlemen" — he smiles serenely — "I am familiar with this contention and taste its hint of bitterness. Yet in recent years I have witnessed a new phenomenon among filmgoers, especially those considered intelligent and perceptive. I have a name for this phenomenon: the Instant White-Out. People are closeted in cozy darkness; they turn off their mobile phones and willingly give themselves, for ninety minutes or two hours, to a new film that got a four-star rating in the newspaper. They follow the pictures and the plot, understand what is spoken either in the original tongue or via dubbing or subtitles, enjoy lush locations and clever scenes, and even if they find the story superficial or preposterous, it is not enough to pry them from their seats and make them leave the theater in the middle of the show.

"But something strange happens. After a short while, a week or two, sometimes even less, the film is whitened out, erased, as if it never happened. They can't remember its name, or who the actors were, or the plot. The movie fades into the darkness of the movie house, and what remains is at most a ticket stub left accidentally in one's pocket. A man and a woman sit down a few days after seeing a film together and try to squeeze out a memory of a scene, the face of an actor, the twist of a plot, but they come up with nothing. The movie is erased from memory. What happened? What changed? Is it because the TV shows dancing before us on dozens of channels reduce feature films to dust in the wind?

"Amazingly enough, live theater, no matter how weak or shallow the play, always manages to leave some impression. Of course, people don't remember every turn of the story, and whole scenes are forgotten, but there's something about the tangible reality of the stage or the living presence of actors that sticks in the memory for years, and like a locomotive it can pull a whole train out of the darkness. Therefore, in honor of the art of cinema, I have decided to combat forgetfulness by means of the staying power of materialism.

"I'll give you an example. Three years ago, I saw a Korean or Vietnamese film about a village girl who gets pregnant and is determined to have an abortion but there's no one she can trust not to expose her shame to the community. Eventually she convinces a young boy to help her, and by primitive, life-threatening means they succeed in aborting the fetus. But while the girl is writhing in pain, the director doesn't back off; he forces the young man to look at the dead fetus, at four or five months of development, that lies on a towel in the bathroom. At first the camera lingers on the frightened face of the boy looking at the fetus, and then the director moves the lens toward the fetus itself, and suddenly the screen is filled with a creature, smeared with blood, that appears to be not an artificial prop but the real thing, an actual fetus. The camera stays on it for twenty seconds, which seems endless. Many viewers squirmed in their seats and averted their eyes, but I decided to meet the director's challenge, and I saw, in that bloody mass, the image of a primal man, something in the chain of evolution, that looked dimly back at me and filled me with deep sorrow but also with strange excitement.

"The following day, I went to see the movie again, this time freed from the suspense of the plot. And when the bloody fetus on the bathroom floor again spoke to me of humanity brutally nipped in the bud, it was clear that despite the film's simplistic story and amateurish acting, I would remember it to the end of my days. And I told myself that if I wanted a movie of mine not to be quickly erased from memory, I needed to strengthen it with something along the lines of this fetus."

"Fetus?" says Pilar, as she leans to whisper translation to two teachers.

"Fetus as a symbol, a metaphor," Ruth explains to her, knowing well both the story and its conclusion.

"Therefore," continues Moses, "in recent years I have been using two cameras, and even three, to explore the realm of reality in search of the fetus that can never be forgotten. First I collect available morsels of reality, rare or commonplace, and then my scriptwriters and I choose the ones that can be strung together into a story."

A tense silence falls among the film teachers, who try to fathom the depth of thought and technique while also eyeing the chocolate cake that has been placed in the middle of the table. Darkness deepens in the narrow windows, and for a moment Moses imagines he hears an echo of his words in the roar of a nearby ocean.

But when the housekeeper brings the coffee, the tension lifts. The visitor looks around with a reassuring smile, as if he'd been jesting all along, and those present respond in kind. Idle conversation has begun, a packet of slim Spanish cigarillos is passed around. Moses takes one, sucks the smoke with pleasure.

Prior to the screening, de Viola takes his guests on a quick tour of his little empire, the film archive that occupies the chilly basement of the barracks. First they visit the film lab, dominated by an old-fashioned editing table, still apparently in use, with film on its reels. Then they go to the modern editing rooms and see the big AVID computer and a row of screens. From there, they head for the up-to-date sound studio, where the dubbing is done, and then the director of the archive leads them down a narrow, chilly passageway, and on its shelves, instead of shells and bullets, are reels of old celluloid film. Before they ascend from the cellar, the host takes them for a peek at a small museum of the history of the barracks. Amid pictures on the wall of officers who killed one another in the Spanish Civil War dangle a few rusty pistols from the same era.

"Can they still shoot?" asks Ruth.

"Can they?" The priest laughs. "Maybe, but at whom? The dead are dead. And the living want to keep on living."

two

CIRCULAR THERAPY

1

THEY ARE GREETED with applause as they enter. The screening room is small, but the guest prefers a small and crowded hall to a big one half empty. Every seat is taken, and several young people are sitting on the stairs. Can it be, wonders Moses, that everyone here is a student or a teacher? But then he notices a few heavyset senior citizens in the room. It turns out that the provincial administration extended support to the retrospective on condition that the film archive set aside seats for old people from the area.

De Viola begins with words of appreciation, and an announcement. The first two films will be shown in the small hall, but the third, *The Train and the Village*, will be screened in the evening in the big auditorium. As is customary, before the lights go down, the director is called upon to say a few words of introduction. Moses keeps it short, to lessen the burden of translation, not failing to mention his surprise at the decision to open the retrospective with such an early, rudimentary film, one made more than forty years ago and whose concept, let alone details, the director can barely remember. Therefore, he tells them, in everyone's interest, it is best not to offer explanations that will turn out to be inaccurate. He also issues a warning: "Even if the film, in your opinion and also mine, turns out to be amateurish and full of holes, I will try to defend it to the best of my ability, but on condition that you will treat me with mercy."

Laughter ripples through the room. The priest raises his hands in a display of piety and says, "Don't worry, even though artists are not allowed to ask for mercy for the fruit of their imagination, compassion and forgiveness are plentiful around here." He motions to dim the lights.

The opening credits appear in Spanish, replacing the original Hebrew. The editing facility in the cellar is clearly capable of high-caliber work. The screen is flooded with glaring, undiffused Israeli sunlight as the names of the filmmakers — actors, editors, set designers — drift among old buildings of Jerusalem. The name of the scriptwriter, Shaul Trigano, tarries long on the screen, fading only as the camera focuses on a noisy old Chausson, a clunky French-made bus popular in Israel in the 1960s; it was eventually retired from service, and the chassis were used as storerooms at building sites.

From the toxic black smoke belched by the bus emerges the name of the director, Yair Moses, also in Spanish transliteration; it is towed behind the Chausson as it pulls into the old central station. Moses is wondering if it was he who decided to stretch the screen time of his credit or if the Spanish film editor took it upon himself to immortalize the director's name until the first passengers exit the bus.

And now he senses that the woman who sits beside him in the dark does not recognize herself in the village girl wearing the flowered mini-dress and straw hat and clasping a cardboard suitcase to her chest as she makes her way out of the bus station. He whispers, "See what a cute dress we picked out for you," and she seems puzzled. But then a jolt of memory prevails, and she watches her character approaching passersby, asking directions in a voice not her own in a foreign tongue, and she turns to Moses, half smiling, half panicked.

Who would have thought that such an ancient film would be dubbed in Spanish, the Hebrew soundtrack a dim echo in the background? "What can we do about this?" he whispers to the archive director sitting to his right. "I can't explain a film if I can't understand a word that's spoken." "Of course you can," the priest says to calm him, "it's still your film, and even if you can't recall the dialogue, you'll be able to recognize the thrust of the film. And besides, my friend" — he touches the guest on the knee — "although the film you made at the beginning of your career may seem naive or primitive to you now, it nevertheless contains religious truth. It was not by accident that we chose it to open your retrospective."

The words *religious truth* put Moses oddly at ease. Yes, why not? Perhaps it's when you skip the dialogue that forgotten details of directing and cinematography come to light. He settles comfortably into his chair and grins at Ruth, who, having recognized her youthful self, leans eagerly forward, as if to embrace it. It is now clear that owing to its flimsy plot, the film will unfold at a snail's pace and give its heroine plenty of time to reach her destination. But walking is not easy. She keeps shifting her suitcase from hand to hand; suitcases in those days did not have wheels, and Moses insisted that suitcases carried by his characters not be empty, to heighten the authenticity of the act. Toledano's loving camera clings to the village girl who makes her way through the divided Jerusalem of the sixties — a provincial city but content within its clear boundaries, so that even an ugly concrete wall stuck in the middle of a street to mark a border between two countries doesn't perturb the young woman walking by, accompanied by soft music. She pauses to read the Hebrew street signs, asking directions in Spanish. Moses takes note of inventive camera angles and interesting bits of montage that offer images of Jerusalem before the Six-Day War, including streets and buildings that no longer exist and vacant sites built up in later years, like the field where the president's house went up; it is virgin land in this old film, strewn with rocks and thistles.

The young woman descends the steps of a stone house and rings the doorbell, and Moses is shocked to discover himself opening the door — a thin young man with wild hair, naked to the waist, a pipe in his mouth. The priest casts him an impish glance. *Yes, it's me,* nods the director, who hopes, but is far from sure, that this was the only time he cast himself in a film, since the shift from one side of the camera to the other undermines his control and authority. But in this beginner's film his acting part was small and brief, and the Spanish voice they've given him sounds more like yelling. He thinks of asking de Viola to tell him what he is saying, but the priest is glued to the screen, and Moses doesn't want to break the spell.

Yes, even without the dubbed dialogue, it's clear that the careless young man knows the visitor on his doorstep and doesn't deny his promise to put her up at his house. Except someone got there before her, a woman emerging now from the bedroom in a flimsy bathrobe, a tenant, a lover, and the hostile look she shoots at the newcomer stops the girl cold. Humiliation and confusion flush her face, enhancing its beauty. Which is perhaps why the young man shows signs of doubt and regret, opens the door wide for the village girl to enter, and carries her suitcase into the hallway, and it seems this will be a story about two girls in a rented apartment, competing for the kindness of a mixed-up young man. But the lodger in the skimpy robe is unwilling to share her rights. She sends the young man to get the visitor a glass of water, and when he is gone a conversation ensues between the two women, of which Moses cannot recollect a word, but whatever is said, it is strong enough to convince the guest to give up her claim, enabling the screenwriter to derail the plot from a banal story into a strange and different one, a story that will struggle to be meaningful and credible.

Moses' performance is not over. As penance for breaking his promise to the girl, he carries her heavy suitcase in the harsh white Jerusalem light that Toledano favored in their early days, failing to understand how many subtle and important details he was bleaching out.

To rest his arms, the young man places the suitcase on his head, taking a few hesitant steps that suggest, at least in the mind of the director, that he regrets that the extra room in his flat was not saved for this attractive young woman but rented instead to a bony, depressive tenant. Moses is shaken at the sight of his childhood street on the Spanish screen, and of his parents' house, with some of its furnishings removed to give the camera room to maneuver.

"Wasn't that your mother?" whispers Ruth as the camera slowly closes in on the woman of the house, indeed his mother, an impromptu actress in her own living room, which thanks to camera angles has never looked larger.

In the 1960s, his mother took early retirement from public service so that her husband could be promoted into her job, and the free time tempted her to take part in her son's directing adventure, first by reading the script and suggesting minor changes, then by persuading Moses' father to offer their house as a filming location. In those years, the filmmakers preferred to cast amateurs, not merely to save money but also because professionals who'd been trained as stage actors were prone to theatrical excess. Perhaps out of gratitude to his mother for turning her house into a set for a dubious movie project, Moses gave her a part in the film. His mother rose to the adventure over the objections of his nervous father, and the opportunity provided by her son to become a fictional character added joy and excitement to the last years of her life.

A long time has passed since her death, yet it pains Moses that Trigano's script aged his mother beyond her actual years. They not only whitened her hair but also added wrinkles to her face that he is sure had never been there before. Yet she retains the wise humanity of a lonely old woman who offers shelter to a confused young woman in exchange for housework and personal services. This, as the film progresses, will prompt the old woman to evolve from a recipient of care into a caregiver, an angel of mercy for a woman more impaired than she is. Through the convolutions of the plot, that woman, despite her disabilities, will herself come to the aid of a dying man, who will assume a mission of his own and with superhuman effort postpone his death. With the remnants of his strength he will drag himself at night to a shabby cafeteria in the empty bus station, not to sip the last drink of his life, but to lift the spirits of the village girl who had come to the capital filled with hope and who now waits for the first bus to get her out of there.

For this was Trigano's vision: everyone who receives therapeutic care can and must become a caregiver. And as this simplistic, seemingly unfounded idea circles in scenic waves of black and white, crafted long ago by a young director, the original title of the film flashes in Moses' memory, and he whispers it to his companion.

2

THE FILM'S DIRECTOR sits in the last row, with de Viola beside him in the aisle seat; this way it won't be hard for him to get to the stage at the end of the screening. Meanwhile, his heart beats faster at the sight of his mother, her voice faintly audible under the Spanish dubbing. She is giving instructions to the new lodger, who unpacks her suitcase in Moses' childhood room and emerges in a lightweight shirt and shorts from a bygone era — very short and baggy, with an elastic waistband. She had arrived in Jerusalem only an hour ago, at the invitation of a young man who raised her hopes, and now, weary and dejected, she wields a mop and pail in the home of a sick old lady.

The two converse incomprehensibly, and the director notes that even at the dawn of his career, he could create a natural flow of dialogue. The Spanish dubbing is so sophisticated that it almost seems not to be the work of actors in a sound studio but that the Israelis had been hypnotized to speak another language. No wonder the audience feels at home with the foreign characters, and little Jerusalem, in the black-and-white of the 1960s, is perceived in the province of Galicia as a familiar and likable city.

Moses recalls that this early film was awarded a prize by the city of Jerusalem, but the prize didn't help draw an audience, and after two weeks in the theater, it had to cede its place to a hard-hitting action movie. His father, who was distressed to see his wife as an actress, even more so to see her as an old lady with white hair, was unabashedly delighted that the film was no longer playing, but his mother was upset that not everyone she knew had seen her. She, who never shied from self-criticism, had become a fan of her fictional character, and repeatedly praised her son for the quality of his direction, perhaps to hint she was ready for another role.

Even had he wanted to find her another part in later films, it was not possible. Two years after the filming, his mother was diagnosed with the illness that forced her to struggle in reality and not just in the imagination of a writer or director. And now, in the small screening room of a former military barracks, as he watches her resurrection of sorts, so long after her death – a brief resurrection, since she is present in the film only through the first half – he cannot contain himself, and in a whisper he turns to the priest on his right: "There, that one . . . the old woman, she was my mother." The director of the archive already knows – someone has told him, or he figured it out from the names of the actors – and he smiles and nods with approval at the audacious choice, and redirects Moses' attention to a strange silhouette that appears on the right side of the screen – a flaw that escaped the film's editor. A character unconnected to the plot is there, behind a curtain, and the cameraman did not notice the invader of the frame. Only after the film's conversion to a sharper digital format is his father revealed, hiding behind the curtain to make sure that even as a film director, his son took pains to honor his mother.

"You really don't remember what you talked about?" Moses quietly challenges his companion, who is fascinated by what she is saying, even if she doesn't understand a word. Indeed, how quickly dialogue is erased from memory, and only random images remain, such as the young lodger leaning gracefully on a broom handle, her bare foot carelessly brushing its bristles. Moses wonders if it was inexperience that led him in his early days as director to depend excessively on the power of spoken language, unfazed by the likelihood that overlong dialogue with no action would tire viewers and sap their empathy. Nonetheless, all around him are foreigners sitting attentively, murmuring pleasure, without the slightest idea where the plot will take them.

"You really don't remember what you said to her?" Moses persists in asking the actress, whose eyes sadly glisten, longing for lost youth. She shrugs, for she has acted in so many films and spoken so much dialogue, she says, who can remember. And yet, there is something she does recall. "In a minute you'll see how I cook a meal for this old woman, also known as your mother. That's what I do remember from this pitiful movie."

Here, then, is the lodger in the kitchen, cutting vegetables, slicing bread, frying an egg, which looks like a goldfish, owing to an error in lighting. Can it be, thinks Moses with a chuckle, that he already had the yen to poke the camera into pots and pans, or was it the cinematographer's idea?

The film unfolds at a sluggish pace, promising no dramatic developments yet able to sustain tension in the small hall. Is it the absence of the promise that commands continued attention? The old woman, listless and frail, eats the meal with trembling hands. When she drops her fork, she is too feeble to retrieve it from the floor, and the girl has to pick it up and rinse it off. This does not seem to be temporary weakness, and yet, after the young lodger clears the table, washes the dishes, and gets permission from the landlady to go to her room — where for a sweet second of screen time she appears in the nude — a metamorphosis takes place in the living room. The landlady rises energetically from her armchair, changes her clothes, puts on makeup, takes a basket and a cane, and, in keeping with Trigano's vision, switches from suffering invalid to efficient caregiver. She makes her way through a crowded market, a slow-moving yet confident old woman, tracked with deep respect by the camera. She walks purposefully from stall to stall, bargaining with vendors and selecting bread, eggs, and vegetables, even a cut of red meat, and then she heads down a lonesome alley to an old house. She climbs narrow winding stairs to a peeling door with no name, a door that admits her again into that same house, his parents' house, a place only Moses can identify, for through the skills of the cinematographer and set designer it has now become a different house, with no courtyard or garden, a dingy and neglected house with broken furniture and torn rugs, the residence of a big-boned woman confined to a wheelchair, waiting for help.

"Matilda . . . I can't believe it!" Ruth laughs.

And the laughter extends, like a fishing line, into the well of time, and out comes a colorful, almost mythological character of indeterminate age and identity, a distant relative of Trigano's, also imported from that immigrant town in the desert, who turned out to be a natural comedienne. Moses' mother, a refined and cultured old woman, approaches her tentatively and carefully lays the basket of groceries in front of her rickety wheelchair, apparently on loan from a nearby old-age home, and in the dark hall the filmmaker hangs his head with embarrassment over what he has created, though after many years of experience in gauging audience reactions, he can see that his message, puerile but humane, retains its grip.

Not in a sudden recollection but simply by looking at the flow of images on the screen, he discovers that as a fledgling director, faithful to the script, he did not spare his mother the indignity of feeding the invalid and cleaning her, washing her underwear in the sink, and there is no way of knowing if these actions were in the script or added by the director's inspiration. And perhaps also because he doesn't understand a word of the dialogue that flows cheerfully between his mother and the woman in her care, his eyes mist over and he chokes up; it is hard to bear his mother's humiliation. And like his father, who did not survive long after the death of his wife, he feels great compassion for the ghost of his mother, who plays her role with such devotion, and he rises from his seat. I'll be right back, he reassures the director of the archive, and hurries for the exit.

The long corridor of the barracks is filled with the shadows of the short winter's day, but since Moses had made a mental note of the men's room door, he locates it easily in the faint light. He rinses his face and closets himself in a stall and, after emptying his bladder, sits on the lid of the toilet to weigh his options for this strange retrospective of old films that speak a foreign tongue. Was the promise of a small cash prize, to be awarded at the end of the retrospective, meant to mollify him? Though, really, why be upset? After all, he is not here to represent only his own work, but also the spirit of his nation's rebirth. And Santiago is a city with an important cathedral. The hotel is opulent, the breakfast generous, and so far his companion is not unhappy. And even if the early films were based on the ideas of a young, opinionated, and unrealistic scriptwriter and are far from a full expression of Moses' professional growth as demonstrated concretely over the years, he can defend them, provided he can still discern their intention.

He looks at his watch. His mother will soon complete her role, and her departure from the screen will alleviate the remorse of the merciless director. He returns to the hall; the audience is still caught up in the film. He slides carefully past de Viola, who gazes with amused wonder at the Matilda character, now begging the elderly caregiver not to leave her, but his mother covers the huge invalid with a blanket, and before exiting, to relieve the emptiness, she turns on the radio, and an old marching song resounds in the small hall of the former military barracks.

It's a good thing that the Spaniards did not try to dub the words of the song, thinks Moses, for if they had, it's doubtful Matilda could have mustered the strength to switch from invalid to caregiver. But empowered by the Hebrew marching song, still wedged in her wheelchair, she wheels herself with astounding expertise toward her own patient as the film shuns the rational choreography of people and objects. By means of clever cutting, the wheelchair moves as in a dream, along streets and stairs and courtyards to a country cottage, again his parents' house, but this time the tiny residence of a dying man.

"Who was that?" Moses nudges Ruth, still delighted by the sight of Matilda. Ruth shrugs, unable to identify the actor with an oxygen mask on his white bloodless face, a jungle of intravenous bags hanging round his bed, tubes and needles feeding various regions of his body, and a microphone hidden among the IV drips that transmits groans and complaints in Spanish. But who is it? Moses shuts his eyes in the hope of teasing out the truth from behind the dubbing, the makeup, and the accoutrements of illness that fill the screen. For a tiny moment he suspects that it is he himself who, having no alternative, performed an additional role in his film. But surely he hadn't brazenly misled the audience, turning the muscular young man who had earlier greeted the village girl into a mortally ill patient lying in bed in a white hospital gown. Surprisingly, despite the scary and depressing appearance of the dying man, a few giggles are audible from the audience. Perhaps this is because the big woman, expertly maneuvering her wheelchair, has transformed her passivity as a patient into the hyperactivity of an industrious caregiver. Or maybe the original text was not just dubbed in Spanish, but altered? In any event, it would seem that hidden comic elements, embedded in the script and direction, have improved with the passage of time, and a gloomy moral drama has turned on foreign soil into farcical entertainment.

"Yes, I recognize him," Ruth blurts out, "concentrate, look carefully, it's Toledano himself." "Not a chance," retorts Moses, dismissing the possibility that the cameraman had become the one on camera. But Ruth remains firm, and even as he throws his arm around her to quash her outlandish recollection, she stubbornly clings to that man who loved her and is now bedridden, deprived of his original voice in the role of a dying man. "Yes, it's him, it can only be him, take a good look, the actor you picked was afraid of the part, and Toledano volunteered, because Trigano would never agree to portray any character he created. Why do you insist," she pleads, "on not recognizing him?"

She's right. The dying man's eyes above the oxygen mask are the eyes of the deceased and unrequited lover, but then, who operated the camera? "Apparently you," says Ruth, "and there was his assistant, what was his name?" "Nadav," says Moses confidently, thrilled to retrieve the name of a person not seen in forty years. "Yes, Nadav," she happily confirms, her memory merging with that of the director, the two jointly reconstructing the reality behind a forgotten film.

Their longtime cinematographer portrays a man on his death-bed with such understated grace that Moses is nostalgic for his antiquated film, and even the Spanish dubbing sounds familiar. Now the screen is a bit blurry, perhaps from a faulty focus or a smudge on the camera lens that shook in the hands of the director serving as a surrogate cameraman. Though it occurs to Moses that the unprofessional shakiness actually improves the scene, adding a dreamlike dimension at the twilight hour, as an immense woman in a wheelchair tries to soothe the suffering of a dying man in the final moments of his life.

And the viewers, who so far have patiently accepted the absurdities on the screen, must know, perhaps by some divine intuition, that it's impossible that the dying man, the receiver of merciful care, will end this strange old film with his own death. A terminal patient with a conscience will not forfeit his role as a caregiver. The big woman leaves, and the audience applauds as the dying man sits bolt upright in bed, rips the oxygen mask from his face, and stares in agony at the slightly unsteady camera. The shaking, deriving from inexperience, fits the mood of the finale. The dead cameraman, beloved by all, comes back to life without surrendering his status as a dying man. In his white gown he wheels the intravenous poles and rushes out of his house, and even the critical and suspicious director cannot help but marvel at this terminal patient wandering like a ghost in the dead of night at the central bus station, clattering his IVs between dark silent buses, pushing them into a workingmen's café, where a picture on a wall reminds Moses that this is his parents' living room, now taking the role of a cafeteria thick with cigarette smoke and a bar stocked with colorful bottles, a dubious-looking bartender jovially mixing his concoctions. In the moonlight, from the garden of his childhood home, the camera tracks the silhouette of the innocent girl who gave up on the young man of the broken promise and then let down the woman she took care of and who now waits for the first morning bus to take her back to her village. The familiar cardboard suitcase is at her feet, and along with the flowered sundress, which is no less charming in moonlight, she wears a pretty scarf over her skinny shoulders. She is sad, and when she sees that the one who comes to care for her is himself dying, her despair grows, and she begins to weep.

"When you were young and gay, it was so easy to get you to cry for the camera," Moses can't help teasing his actress, "and now it's hard to get one tear out of you." "What can you do." She sighs. "With all the tears I've shed in real life, I don't have any left for your movies, but don't worry, in your next film, if I must, I'll cry again." He nods, saying nothing, not only because he doesn't want to upset her with the news that there will be no role for her in his next film, but also lest he annoy the audience, hypnotized by the moonlight and the shaky camera. The dying man with his tangle of IV tubes becomes a heroic figure – a character who proves to the whole world, in whispering Spanish, that even in his last hour, a person can breathe hope into the heart of another. The embarrassed smile that breaks out in close-up on the young woman's face arouses real tears in the eyes of the aging actress watching herself. And after the screen finally goes dark, and lights go on in the hall, Moses promises himself that when he returns to Israel, he will find a copy of the forgotten film and watch it in its original language to determine its true value once and for all.

In the eyes of the audience scrutinizing the director, there may be wonder or bewilderment, but no antagonism or derision. He therefore hopes the questions will not deal with trivial points of realism or believability or with camera techniques, but with the ideas. Since the Spanish that replaced the original language did not allow him full mastery of the film's details, he asks the director of the archive, who will moderate the discussion, to relay several questions together, figuring to avoid the ones not easily answered.

To his surprise, the questions imply affection for this simple film, and Moses is careful not to undermine it with answers betraying his own ambivalence about his early work. Film teachers and students do not approach movies as consumers demanding satisfaction and enjoyment in exchange for the ticket purchased at the box office; for them, a film is first and foremost material for study and explanation. And since he realized at lunch that in this city of pilgrimage, people tend to seek a symbol behind every detail, he resolves to be tolerant even of allegorical speculation. When one of the older teachers offers a strange interpretation for the visible shaking in the last scene, Moses does not expose his unskilled hand operating the camera but praises the man for his perspicacity, adding that in hindsight he cannot be sure that was the intent. Though the students do center their questions on technical matters and not spiritual issues, the fact that an outdated film made by a group of amateurs in a young small country on a minuscule budget can hold its own after such a long time instills optimism in them too, these young people. And after the priest reveals that Moses' mother played the first old woman, obvious questions arise, such as: Was it hard for you to direct your own mother? Did she follow your instructions? Why didn't you try to include your father?

Attention shifts to the actress, her fetching screen presence still lingering in the room. A young woman asks whether the smile that brightened her face at the end of the movie was genuine or produced at the director's request. In other words, if the scene had happened in real life and not before a camera, and a white ghost dragging intravenous bottles had darted out of the darkness to console her, would she have welcomed it, or run away in terror? Ruth answers firmly, though in poor English. Yes, she would have happily welcomed the dying man, whose care that night would keep her in Jerusalem, and she would not flee the city in the morning.

Then an old farmer speaks. His bald pate reddening with emotion, he asks if he is permitted to think that this dying man, who earned the trust of not only the girl on the screen but also himself as a spectator, will wrestle with death after the film is done and overcome it. Is such hope possible, and was it the intention of the filmmaker?

"No, it wasn't, but neither does it contradict it," answers Moses. "The ending of a work of art is an absolute ending, and whoever imagines what happens next speaks only for himself."

The disappointed farmer slowly sits down, but several of his friends ask for permission to speak. Fearing the local farmers will lower the level of conversation, the priest urges them to keep their questions short, and he answers them himself hastily, and then, to bring the discussion to a close, he poses his own question to the honoree: "Do you yourself believe in the idea of the film you created? In other words, is everyone who receives care also a caregiver?"

Moses is startled by the question but is quick to answer.

"My screenwriter believed it, and in those days I respected his ideas and agreed to direct films based on them. After we went our separate ways, this idea seemed unrealistic to me, since there are invalids who are chronic and stubborn, concerned only with themselves. But today, after watching this film of mine, which I had not seen for decades, I'm ready to give his vision another chance."

3

THE ARCHIVE DIRECTOR has two options for the intermission before the next screening. They can further tour the film labs and classrooms, or they can rest in his office, which was once the apartment of the army base commander. It has a modest sofa on which one man can stretch out comfortably. As a devout believer in afternoon naps, Moses chooses the second alternative. In recent years, even on filming days, he has managed to arrange the working day to include an hour or so for a nap. Not even when shooting on location does he pass it up; he crawls, blanket in hand, under the production truck to grab a quick snooze in the oily darkness below the chassis, first making sure the vehicle is locked and the keys are in his pocket.

How good to enter a quiet, spacious room, albeit slightly monkish in character, with logs burning in the hearth. The priest removes two woolen military blankets from the closet, shuts the blinds, disconnects the telephone, and locks the door from the outside.

Moses goes immediately for the couch, but Ruth asks sheepishly if this time she could have it and he make do with the armchair. He is surprised, but he agrees. After all the excitement over her past beauty, she is probably depressed and seeks the consolation of curling into the fetal position.

He covers her with the blanket and turns out the light, hoping to catch some sleep in the chair. The next film is about the army, and he has a vague recollection of long nature shots and of soldiers fast asleep. He closes his eyes, pondering his mother's devotion to the role he entrusted to her. He knows a good many artists who avoid watching their past work. He, too, unless he must, watches his old films rarely. But it now would appear that because of the falling-out with Trigano, he went too far in completely ignoring them. For even in such a beginner's film, he can see a few moments of beautiful directing, worth going back to for inspiration.

Ruth's breathing grows deeper. She once told him that sometimes, when sleep eludes her, she imagines that she is in front of the camera, and a cinematographer and director and soundman are watching over her sleep, protecting her – then she relaxes. Now Moses fills all those roles, and in her sleep, she reaches out her hand from under the blanket and touches the director who sits beside her. Age spots that have lately surfaced on her face and hands are visible even in the dim light. But it's not a liver spot that will deprive her of a part in the next film; it's that his obligation to her character has been exhausted. Her talents have found expression in every possible role, and in the last stage of a long and varied career like his, one must be wary of repeating oneself.

The base commander's armchair is stiff and upright, and the priest who inherited it has shunned, perhaps out of asceticism, even a small cushion, so Moses has no hope of dozing or resting. If he wants to be alert during the next screening, he will have to take off his shoes, curl up on the rug at the feet of his companion, and remove his hearing aids.

As her breathing floats over him, so do melancholy thoughts about her future. If he has lately included her, now and then, in his travels, he does so not with an eye to the future, but as his debt to the past: as limited consolation for a career in slow decline. He remembers that Nehama, meaning "consolation," was her original Hebrew name, given her by her father, the rabbi, who came to Israel from the Moroccan town of Debdou, and who ended up as a farm laborer, planting trees. Sometimes Trigano would tease his lover and call her Debdou. After they parted, she dropped the name Nehama and, on the advice of an actors' agent, took a simple name, easy to remember, typically Israeli but also well established in the wider world.

But Moses did not forget the original name of the shy, gentle girl whom the usher, his student, introduced as his girlfriend at the movie theater in Jerusalem. Sometimes, in rehearsals, or even during a shoot, as he tried to get a deeper, more credible performance from her, Moses would confront her with her original name, using it as a talismanic word to rescue her from artifice and mannerism and prompt her to broaden her acting with the flavor of the disadvantaged, confused girl who had never finished high school. At first she was angry that he had revealed to the whole crew the old name she'd left behind. But when he persisted, she was forced to listen, through her given name, to the true voice of her identity.

He has no magic word to help her evoke shades of character she has not played in the past and so can help her only at a remove, recommending her to other directors. And because the cinematographer had also expressed his love through concern for her daily well-being, he feels he should take responsibility for the practical aspects of her life, in financial matters and health issues such as the blood test, which must not be neglected when they return to Israel. He covers his face and shuts his eyes tight, then hears soft knocking on the locked door.

"Nehama" – he pats her arm – "wake up, de Viola is here."

Her forehead furrows, and her eyes open, shining after deep and satisfying sleep. She rises gracefully and stretches her limbs, folds her blanket and his too, puts on her high heels, and adjusts her blouse. She takes a comb and makeup from her bag and does her hair and face before the windowpane, then runs the comb through his white hair to make him look presentable too. The archive director unlocks the door and enters. "What is this," jokes Moses, "you were afraid we'd run out without saying goodbye? I mean, it's downright illegal to lock up an old man with an unstable prostate." De Viola laughs. He serves the institute not only as archive director but also as priest, he explains; teachers and students take the liberty to enter his room at will, as they would a confessional booth. To ensure his guests a proper rest, he thought it wise to lock the door and also put up a Do Not Disturb sign. Two more films await them today, and judging by the reactions to *Circular Therapy*, there is great interest among faculty and students.

En route to the small hall, they learn of a slight change in the original program. The screening of *Slumbering Soldiers*, whose title in Spanish is *The Installation*, has been postponed till tomorrow, and in its place the film known here as *Obsession* will be screened — it's probably *The Flying Pen*, what else could it be? The switch has been made, says the priest, "to show the Spanish people that your early work deals with psychology, not just ethics."

"The same crowd?"

"Mostly."

"And I thought they'd had enough, after that superficial film you insisted on starting my retrospective with."

But Juan de Viola firmly dismisses this self-criticism. "The film is not superficial, simply a first effort, and a first work of art, if motivated by a religious inspiration or at least a metaphysical one, will always possess a certain power."

"You insist on the religious issue," protests Moses, "but you should know that neither I nor Trigano would define our work that way."

The priest is unfazed.

"There are many people with a religious temperament who are ashamed to admit it. Don't forget when you made the film. In the sixties, a strong secular outlook prevailed in the world, and religious faith was completely out of style. People like you camouflaged their longing for the absolute in foggy allegorical parables. But the world has changed since then, although not always, to my sorrow, for the better."

"And you see a religious aspect to my amusing little *Obsession?*"

"Of course," says the priest without hesitation.

"And this one has also been dubbed?"

"All of them."

"What is this? Again you're forcing me to watch a film I already forgot and now can't understand?"

"When it comes to a creative artist, this is not necessarily a liability. Perhaps you can get some help from the younger memory of your companion."

"In this movie, if I remember correctly, her role was marginal."

"But in the film to be screened this evening," declares the priest, "she's the star."

4

AGAIN, APPLAUSE IN the little theater, more crowded now than at the previous screening. Young people sit on the stairs, and a few older women have arrived, apparently housewives who've finished their daily work.

"You don't have TV reception in your province," whispers Moses, "so the locals come to see weird films in black-and-white?"

"Mediocre television is readily available, but in recent years we have persuaded the local people to look for something more. The films we screen for them are usually old ones, but admission is free, and sometimes they get a chance to argue with the filmmakers, so some are willing to take the risk."

The director of the archive again introduces his guests, this time briefly, and the Israeli director insists on saying a few preliminary words. Again he cannot resist carping about their choosing such a crude early film from his many decades of work. Yes, he remembers the lighthearted spirit of the original film, but he wonders if it will hold up after all these years, especially when dubbed in Spanish.

Juan de Viola orders the lights turned off. When the credits appear on the screen, Moses notices that the lead actor is listed as codirector with him. Had Moses merely agreed to this, or was it done on his initiative? Despite the jovial feel of the production and the film's moderate popularity among the young people, Moses himself had his doubts, so it could be that attaching the actor's name as codirector was meant to relieve Moses of full responsibility. But what was it that bothered him about *Obsession?* The Spanish title now seems more fitting than the Hebrew one.

He was essentially forced to direct this picture. Trigano didn't involve him in the writing process; he just handed him a finished script, written in collaboration with the editor of the student newspaper at Hebrew University — a handsome, talented young man Trigano had met in an introductory psychology course required for students in the humanities program. This young man came up with an idea for a film about the crazy power of Freudian symbolism. Trigano would write the screenplay, and the friend would secure funding, but on condition that he play the lead.

After the two managed to get financial support from the association of clinical psychologists, as well as a personal contribution from the teacher of the course, a woman of independent means, Moses had a choice: let the new partners run with an idea that he found peculiar and childish, or swallow his misgivings and preside as director over a fairly credible rendering of a preposterous notion. Fearing that if he refused, Trigano might drop him in favor of a young and gifted partner, Moses chose the latter alternative.

With perfect timing, a sudden burst of rain drums upon the roof of the small auditorium as the camera starts to wander through Jerusalem on a wintry night, this time focusing on the alleyways of a poor neighborhood, largely ultra-Orthodox yet tolerant of the secular young people living there. In a rented apartment, whose location Moses can't quite recall, a raucous student party is under way, dominated by a tall young man with long hair who transfixes his listeners with tales of his travels in India. He takes from his pocket a large fountain pen that doubles as a flashlight, and from the innards of the pen he produces a tiny scroll of parchment with a colorful picture of a beautiful, naked Indian woman, wreathed by inscriptions, devout or perhaps lustful, in an unknown tongue. The pen is passed from hand to hand, and the students examine it with amused curiosity, opening and closing it, testing the little flashlight, examining the scroll to have a good look at the Indian woman and try to guess the meaning of the writing around her.

Moses cannot remember what was said or wasn't in this party scene, but he is disinclined to listen to Pilar's simultaneous translation. She sits at his side in place of de Viola, who has gone to prepare for evening Mass. Yes, now he understands the priest's offhand remark: not knowing the language sometimes brings about new insights.

With no dialogue to distract him, he can see clearly not only the fakery of the main character who tries to pump up his manliness with a pen from the East, but the hollowness of the actor himself.

Is this what bothered him while they were making the film, so much so that he tried to disown it, despite its relative success? Could he actually sense that the charismatic young man who won Trigano over was morally damaged?

It wasn't the man's opinions or his smooth way with words that put Moses off. He was convinced that a man who believed in nothing could not, for all his cleverness and charm, penetrate the character of another human being and make it come alive. Moses refused to include the man again – "It's him or me," he told Trigano.

On the screen, the hour is late and the party is over, and on his motor scooter, the hero is giving a student, played by Ruth, a ride to her parents' home in Jerusalem. At the door, he takes his leave with quick hugs and a cursory kiss, then continues on to his rented room in a house not far from the Old City, which in those pre-'67 days was off-limits, an object of longing. A bit tipsy, he undresses for bed, listening to an upbeat tune on a foreign radio station, and in his cozy pajamas, before going to sleep, he decides he wants to fondle the Indian pen one more time, take out the piece of parchment, perhaps decipher the message on the lips of the girl. But he discovers the pen has disappeared, and he searches for it frantically, but in vain. And instead of waiting till morning, he gives way to the panic that drives the plot and plunges him into the abyss.

Step by step, Trigano cleverly escalated the insane obsession. After the hero turns his room upside down, he gets dressed, grabs a flashlight, and returns to the cold empty streets he crisscrossed with the student. He walks slowly, inspecting the road and the sidewalks, ultimately arriving at the girl's house, where he pounds on the door, wakes her parents, and insists that their daughter has pickpocketed his pen.

The search grows more delirious, and since the film's hero, unlike the audience, doesn't understand what the lost pen symbolizes, his madness becomes a tragicomic journey, offering glimpses of Israeli student life as each of his friends reacts to his behavior, some with anger and scorn, a few with compassion and readiness to help. Somehow this shoestring-budget film, eighty-five minutes long, evolved into a picaresque quest for the lost symbol, and Moses notices that despite the loony script, he made sure as director to maintain respect for the tormented character wallowing in humiliation, so as not to distance the audience from a man bent on surrender to obsession. But Trigano's script failed to bring the film to the open and generous conclusion found in the greatest picaresque works. After the hero goes from student to student, trying vainly to discover who at that raucous party had secretly coveted his pen, he breaks into their apartments to search for his lost object. And since the inscrutable symbol has so deeply permeated the soul of the hero that the psychiatrist, who enters late in the film, cannot free him of the obsession, it's only natural that the rigid, one-dimensional screenplay was given a radical ending that Trigano was unwilling to modify. And so, in the last scene, as the sun goes down, the hero lays his handsome head on a railroad track and waits.

The cheers at the end of the movie are more ardent and longer than at the previous screening, perhaps because of the young people in the crowd, while some of the older ones hurry to the exit before the lights go up. Ruth opens her bloodshot eyes and yawns. Moses wonders if there is any point to going onstage without the archive director at his side. The petite animation teacher who is to moderate will not be forceful enough to control the audience in discussing a film that contains a seed of perversion. He suggests combining this discussion with the one that is to follow the evening screening, especially since the railroad tracks that end the present film will open the next one.

Pilar appears relieved. She too is happy to avoid discussing a movie whose meaning is so obvious, and she hurries to the stage and announces the postponement of the discussion until the next screening. A few in the audience look disappointed; this time, many have wanted not only to ask questions but to attack. And Moses, who feels mildly guilty about avoiding the conversation, asks to attend the evening Mass conducted by the priest. For at the end of the retrospective, if he indeed decides to confess his professional sins to a film-savvy priest, he ought to know something about the confessor's style of prayer.

It's good to visit the little chapel where officers of the army barracks once prayed. In its modest way, its beauty and harmony are the equal of its mighty sister in Santiago. Hanging on the walls are pictures of beasts of prey of a sort not generally found in churches.

It's crowded. The old people who just saw *Obsession* have come to purify themselves through evening prayer, and, who knows, maybe evening prayer in so charming a chapel is the actual purpose of their visit to the film institute. Juan de Viola wears a white robe and chants the liturgy in a pleasant voice, and from the yellowed marble altar, bedecked with wreaths of white roses, he nods his thanks to the Jews.

After the service, Moses expresses due admiration of the chapel and pleads with the priest to drop the idea of taking them to a fancy restaurant after the third movie. "Don't strain your budget," he says. "The fatigue and excitement of revisiting forgotten films will make it hard for us to focus on an expensive meal. We should eat early and satisfy our hunger with a quick hop to the cafeteria. We can postpone the banquet till tomorrow."

Given no choice, Ruth agrees. During the break she slept on the sofa, and she napped in her seat during the screening, and she's ready for fine restaurant food. But Moses knows that in a foreign city, with her poor English, she will have a hard time going without him.

The cafeteria is jammed. Have all these people come to see *The Train and the Village*? Moses enters the self-service line and picks up a cheese sandwich wrapped in plastic. Ruth makes do with black coffee. Soon her character will propel the plot of a provocative film, and she is getting ready to encounter her old self.

5

THE WOODEN FLOOR of the big hall creaks, and the room is nearly full. Some of the elderly faces are familiar from the afternoon screenings; the number of younger viewers has grown, and middle-aged couples have arrived in groups from neighboring villages.

This time Moses takes no issue with the choice of film. He remembers this one and is confident in the quality of the plot and its execution. *The Train and the Village*, whose original Hebrew title was *Distant Station*, is the fourth film he made with Trigano. The idea for the film cropped up during the final shooting days of *Obsession*, as they were looking for railroad tracks they could film. They found a stretch of the track to Jerusalem, which in those days ran along the old border with Jordan, downhill from a divided Arab village. It was a picturesque section of the route, where the tracks made steep switchbacks on a rocky mountainside. The train from Jerusalem to the coastal plain passed through only twice a day, at a drowsy crawl, which meant they could march their desperate hero again and again between the iron tracks until they carefully balanced his head on one of them, found the proper angle, and shot several takes. It was clear that showing the severed head was taboo, so Trigano suggested ending the film with a close-up of a bloody, mangled jacket on the tracks, the missing pen glistening nearby in the moonlight. Moses, however, firmly rejected any improvised alteration of the original script. We have to respect the written word, and any change requires consensus, he said. Besides which, the planned ending, in which the train has not yet passed and only its faint whistle blast is heard in the distance, does not belittle the hero.

Trigano's disappointment with Moses' adamant refusal to decapitate his friend was apparently the inspiration for a new film, set entirely in the train station of a remote mountain village, in which the tight linkage of love and death would be crystal clear. And with these very words, *eros* and *thanatos*, Moses guides the audience to the symbolic heart of the movie they are about to see. Galicians not familiar with the Israel of the 1950s and 1960s and its sleepy local trains will not realize that a sleek, luxury express train – in too big a hurry to stop at a desolate mountain station, a train that races by each evening with sublime indifference and blind trust in a long bridge suspended over a deep abyss – is a product of pure fantasy. But according to the movie's internal logic – reveals Moses, to de Viola's chagrin – it is no wonder that, for the forgotten villagers, such a train inspires longing, helpless anger, and the desire to deal the indifferent world a dose of disaster and pity, to which end they must shunt the train from the main track to a rickety siding, causing it to plunge into the ravine below. De Viola interrupts and censors the translation to prevent giving away the ending, but Moses is swept up in his revelations and is explaining to the audience that the village they are about to see is in effect two villages in one, on both sides of a border, and the portion inside the kingdom of Jordan had to be filmed with a telescopic lens — at which point the priest tugs at his sleeve. "Come, my friend," he whispers, virtually shoving him from the stage, "it would be a shame to ruin the viewing experience with unimportant detail." The technician turns out the lights, and Moses has to feel for the step with his foot.

This was the first of their films that called for many extras to portray the villagers and the passengers on the train. In the past they had been able to draw on friends, and as backup they had members of Trigano's family, eager to immortalize themselves but also genuinely excited by the scriptwriter's ingenuity. This time they had to look for paid extras, young and middle-aged and a few elderly, and mold them into a frustrated community stewing in the humiliation dealt them by the speeding evening train, a village whose forbidden, repressed fantasy would be unleashed by a young woman, sitting now beside him, overwhelmed by emotion.

In a morning fog pierced by first light, the camera follows an old, creaking freight train, wearily twisting up a mountain track. Now and again, the camera skips to the tiny mountain station, where awaiting the train is the veteran stationmaster, wearing a cap with a brim and holding two signal flags, one red and folded in a downward position, and the other green and unfurled, which he will soon wave at the locomotive. Moses remembers the man. A dour-looking actor from the Yiddish theater, he accurately played the loyal and reliable official who would in the end be turned by wily villagers into the person solely responsible for a calculated act of terrible destruction.

Although Moses praised the actor for his nuanced portrayal of his character, he could barely get a word from the man about the movie's plot. Let's wait till it's done, the actor would say, elegantly dodging the question, we'll see how it all comes together. Moses could sense that this Holocaust survivor was repelled by the Israelis' fanciful catastrophe, and by the time the editing was complete, Moses had lost contact with the actor, who did not show up at the premiere. It was impossible not to interpret his absence as dissociation from the film, and especially from what his character had been dragged into. Moses once saw him walking in the street, straight-backed and gloomy, dressed all in black, as if he were still playing the tragic character of stationmaster in a godforsaken mountain village. He considered approaching him and telling him the reviewers had praised his performance, but he feared provoking the wrath of a man who had been led astray by the young people of his village.

But now, in the dawning light of the film's first moments, not only he but all the dreamers and deluders of the village, all the innocents and the inveiglers, do not yet know how they will fit into the story concocted by the scriptwriter. And while the locomotive of the freight train sways with the screeching of brakes as it braves the curving tracks, the stationmaster rushes to lean his weight on the railway switches — two metal levers constructed by the set designer to give the illusion that only when they are manipulated can the freight train diverge from the main track and come to a safe stop at the station. Toledano insisted on shooting the face of the engine driver — a real one, who was flustered by the film crew awaiting him at the station. The camera also follows two sleepy workers, who now speak fluent Spanish, as they jump from a dark railroad car and begin uprooting weeds between the tracks.

"Were they real railroad workers or extras?" Moses whispers to Ruth, who predictably doesn't have an answer.

Moses puts an arm around her, gently strokes her hair.

The light brightens, and the village awakens to a routine day. Men leave their homes, children go to school, women do laundry in a small artificial spring built for the occasion to give the village a primitive feeling — everything flows so smoothly that even the dubbing seems natural to Moses.

"The Spanish you planted in my movies is starting to grow on me," he whispers in Juan de Viola's ear. "Who knows, I might be tempted to make my next film in Spain, maybe in Santiago."

The priest's face lights up. "For that possibility alone, the retrospective was worth the effort." And in a surprising gesture of affection, he brings the director's right hand to his lips for a gentle clerical kiss.

Meanwhile on the big screen, the freight train crawls ahead, sounding its whistle, and in the station house a new character awakens, the stationmaster's assistant, a dreamy youth who will later turn out to be unreliable and perfidious. He emerges disheveled from a tangle of sheets, stands in his underwear by the window, and surveys the village streets through big military binoculars, spying on the girl he loves with all his heart.

"How and why have I forgotten his name?" Moses whispers to the woman at his side.

"Because he was a rotten son of a bitch."

"Yes, but . . ."

"His name was Yakir."

"That's right, Yakir. What happened to him? Where'd he disappear to?"

"I thought he was killed in a war but unfortunately I got him mixed up with someone else. A few years ago I ran into him on the street, but I avoided him. After what he did to me in the film — "

"He was difficult . . ."

"For you he was difficult, for me he was horrible. This animal dragged me into the bushes in the last scene, and you let him do it. He was a despicable person who exploited the opportunity you gave him to humiliate me."

"I gave him?" Moses laughs. "Why me? I just followed the script."

"But without pity . . . you didn't spare me." Ruth seethes as if they were discussing a scene to be reshot in a few minutes.

Moses tries to make light of it.

"Why should I be easy on a girl who charms the villagers to plunge an express train into a gorge just to attract a little attention from the world?"

"What do you mean, attention?" she protests. "You're forgetting the empathy that we, the villagers, experienced, the compassion and concern, the devoted care we gave the injured passengers. That was my mission in the movie, all without speaking a word."

"Without a word, how so? Look, here you are."

Through the cinematic cunning of Toledano, who had the young man watch his loved one through binoculars – thus visually annexing the Jordanian half of the village – a girl appears on the screen, speaking with the village mayor in strange, jerky gestures.

Moses is enchanted by the shot. "Brilliant to reveal your character from far away, through movement alone."

"But that's how it is the whole time."

"The whole time?"

"I don't believe you forgot."

"Forgot what?"

"That you and Trigano made me not only deaf, but almost mute."

Her whispering is so agitated, viewers are turning to look at them, and the priest's soft hand rests again on the knee of the guest to hint that it's rude to annoy people watching his movie. Moses leans forward, shocked – how could he have forgotten that Trigano decided to advance the plot through the machinations of an alluring deaf-mute girl?

The camera moves away from the young man's distant visual embrace and zooms in slowly on the village mayor, a vigorous man of about fifty, a professional actor who demanded and got the highest pay, and deservedly so, for here he is onscreen, ten years after his death, the picture of trustworthy authority. He looks patiently at a beautiful young woman, a deaf-mute who utters only noises and inscrutable syllables – which the Spanish dubbing replicates amazingly well – punctuating them with agitated hand gestures laced with charm and guile that are meant to inject into the sun-swept village the first spark of a carefully planned disaster.

The village mayor, who has known the young woman since her childhood and who over the years has carefully observed her blend of beauty and disability, is presumably capable of interpreting her distress from her hand motions alone.

"What were you telling him? Do you remember?"

"That we had to divert the express train to our station."

The sounds she is able to produce are desperate, those of an animal in distress, and in retrospect, the director understands that it was here, in this film, that the amateur actress began to turn into a professional, her beauty ripening in the process. She is no longer a skinny, androgynous girl, pale and embarrassed, as in *Circular Therapy*, but a determined young woman whose beauty is combined with emotional strength and the erotic expertise she brings to her part.

Moses has not calmed down. "Who coached you in sign language? Me?"

"You? Come on. What do you know about sign language? And it's not even real sign language — more like a private language. I took the gestures from Simona, Shaul's older sister, who was mentally disabled and also a deaf-mute. She always tagged along with us when we were kids."

"He never mentioned such a sister."

"Maybe he was ashamed, even though he loved her and took care of her. In any case, he wanted to immortalize her in the film, through me. Moses, it's about time you realized things are hiding in your films that you didn't know and didn't understand."

Patience is running out all around, their whispering has become a public nuisance. The head of the archive gets up, grabs Moses by the hand like a schoolteacher, and leads him a few rows away, as if to say, *In a couple of days you'll be back in Israel, where you can make as much noise as you like, but why disrupt a retrospective held here in your honor?*

It's a good thing the director and actress have been separated, because now that Moses has been banished to the rear, the storm of memory subsides, and he skips what is spoken in the film, in words or unique sign language, and concentrates on the images of the village, the changing daylight, the little houses, the behavior of the residents: a woman who opens her shutters and takes chairs out to the porch; a horse-drawn wagon that climbs the road to the village, followed by five workers on foot; a noisy group of boys heading toward a fig tree; someone who suddenly stops walking and stands still in anticipation; a boy who runs to the bridge and places a piece of scrap iron on the railroad track. Now it's clear to Moses why after this film he decided to leave teaching for good and exercise his talent through the screenplays of a brilliant and loyal student.

With simple but effective editing, intimations of sunset filter into the frame, as Toledano, the artist of shifting light, captures every nuance. Now come the first flashes of the express train, winding its way through the hills, still some distance from the lonely village.

Since in those days it was impossible to imagine a sleek Israeli train that would fit the film's plot, they had to borrow one from a foreign setting that resembled the Israeli landscape. The cameraman and his assistant were therefore dispatched to Greece to collect footage of fast trains in the evening and at night, to be intercut in the film. Not that it was easy to find what they needed in Greece. For ten days and nights the two wandered among railroad tracks, staking them out to capture a passenger train from a good angle. They returned to Israel with a vast collection of shots of speeding trains, each different from the next, and of hills and gullies, and near the big train station in Piraeus, they also filmed railroad cars and locomotives wrecked in accidents and removed from service. The filmmakers spent long days in the editing room patching together from the bounty of Greek trains and wreckage one fast train, devoid of recognizable national markings — sort of a universal, symbolic train — destined for disaster at the edge of an Israeli-Jordanian village.

The door to the hall opens, and in the rectangle of light stands a thin, tall man who scans the dark room and after brief hesitation heads down to the front, blocking the screen as he slips into a first-row seat. Moses' heart is pounding. For a moment he imagines his former scriptwriter has joined the audience. He has the urge to get up and move forward to get a better look, but he controls himself, not wanting to create a further disturbance.

Who is the composer of the ballet music that accompanies the young woman on her path to the little train station? In those days Moses got help from a young librarian in the music division of the National Library, a woman who found musical selections that could enhance plot and atmosphere. Trigano, however, objected in principle to the use of existing music. If we can't commission our own, he said, better to have none at all. But when the film reached the editing room, it entered the exclusive domain of the director, and Moses was steadfast in his belief – partly because he was falling in love with the librarian – that music had the power to clarify the feelings and thoughts of the characters, especially in the case of a beautiful deaf girl called upon to convey to her accomplices and the audience a complicated criminal plan by means of hand gestures and facial expressions alone.

The music now accompanies the girl along the tracks, continuing as she meets the young man who is in love with her and who at sunset returns the rail switches to their prior position and waves the green flag at the fast evening train on the main track, signaling its safe disconnection from the side track. The director senses that his heroine has won the sympathy of the audience in the big hall. Now she has to convince the man that any flag-waving is useless, that even if he waves the red flag to warn of danger, the train could not possibly stop in time. The young man looks bewildered, and there's no way of knowing what he understands from her pantomime, but his passion hijacks his hands and flags, and he gives her the red one; and as the speeding locomotive draws near and he waves the green one as usual, the girl waves the red flag and keeps waving it as a warning at faces that fleetingly appear in the lighted windows of the train – the nameless faces of Greeks who will become Israeli in the editing room.

Who is the composer? he asks himself again, for the music is bound up with his growing love for Ofra, the young librarian who later became his wife; they eventually parted ways, but she is still the mother of his two children. That's why he considers *Distant Station* to be a personal film, as if he too were a character walking the village streets.

Is Ruth's heart bound to this movie too? Sitting a few rows ahead, she seems to have forgotten him. But even without seeing her face, he knows that, like the rest of the audience, she is aware of the female power of her hand movements and burning eyes, beyond the quality of her acting.

Yes, it was the scriptwriter Trigano who added the muteness, which was original and brilliant, even if inspired by an unfortunate sister. But Moses is pleased in retrospect that he directed it without hesitation and to the best of his ability. A beautiful young woman, deaf and mute from birth, somewhere between disabled and strange, wants the express train to stop at her home village, even if this leads to disaster. She will succeed in persuading others to follow, for a satanic idea expressed in sign language that may or may not be understandable is not the same as a satanic idea explicitly worded. In the end, it is a floating idea, and it's hard to pin down who thought of it and intended it and who just imagined it and imputed it to others, so it's easy to deposit it on the doorstep of the stationmaster, who at this moment, after the express train has gone by, looks suspiciously at the young woman approaching him. Are her hands and fingers really demanding that tomorrow, when the terrible tempest comes to pass, no one should come out to shift the switches?

And so the film unfolds on the screen in a hall where during the Spanish Civil War officers were instructed not to have mercy on their countrymen. Artificial wind, generated by the blower next to the camera, accompanies a little yellow railcar, and out steps the chief railway inspector, recruited to assist the stationmaster who was asked to stop a fast train that never stopped here before. How hard it had been to convince the management of Israel Railways to allow the actor to drive, for only a hundred meters, the single small car designed to check the condition of the tracks. The chief inspector here is not an ordinary man but in effect a pagan god, an evil higher power who doesn't need a maintenance worker to drive him. But the Israel Railways people stubbornly refused to allow someone unlicensed to operate a railcar belonging to the state. And especially because the actor recruited by Trigano, a distant relative of his, a wedding singer and comedian, a dwarfish man of sixty with a red, pockmarked face, seemed unreliable to Israel Railways before he ever uttered a word. There was no alternative but to wear out the maintenance worker assigned to the railcar. With an empty camera, they filmed him ferrying the actor over and over, and then persuaded him to take a rest for just one ride and let the actor drive the railcar himself. So the tiny god and wedding singer was able to zip around a curve on a drizzly day and hop from the railcar into the station house. Moses feels an urge to walk down a few rows to whisper in the priest's ear, *You see, Juan de Viola, though we were sworn secularists, we still tried to enlist divine intervention to prevent a needless disaster, but we didn't succeed. We came to realize that God too lends a hand to absurdity.*

But Moses stays in his seat and watches the chief inspector. The latter sits and seems indifferent to the obsequious conduct of the loyal stationmaster, who breaks into a stutter as he reveals the existence of a plot to sabotage the fast train. The little man listens, sips slowly from his teacup, sighs, yawns, and finally rests his heavy head on the table like a child and closes his eyes. The director can remember how he made sure the camera stood patiently still and drank deeply of the slumbering comedian, who was thrilled to play God, and kept asking, What should I say in his name? "Don't say a word," Trigano said, calming him. "In this film God is silent, he only sleeps. Close your eyes and doze off, snore a little and give a sigh, the camera will do the rest."

The authority figure, giving no answer one way or another, confers by his silence the permission to execute the plot. And now, in place of the dumbfounded stationmaster, who closeted himself at sundown inside the tiny station, villagers stand by the rails, torches in hand, poised for their encounter with an arrogant train that will veer from its regular track. Since fewer extras than anticipated were available to the production, they had to hustle them down as agitated onlookers, and then transform them from local residents into passengers, after the crash, rip their clothes, smear them with grime, pour red liquids on them, to ensure their credibility as they screamed in agony. In the artificial lighting intended to improve on the moonlight and stars, Moses can see that he too was forced to abandon his post beside the camera and join the extras as a passenger writhing in pain. The camera closes in on his face as he lies among bushes in torn clothing, his face horribly gashed, waiting for the deaf girl to lavish mercy on his suffering. "As a living actor, you have no future," joked the film editor when they looked at the scene on the editing table, "but as a dying one, you're a big success, especially when a girl is stroking your head."

Yes, the beauty of the deaf girl lights up the screen, and the stationmaster's assistant does not wait long to exact his due for the wicked plan that came off well. Though in years to come the violent scenes in his films grew more and more audacious, one might still wonder about the license given here to the actor to express his lust. He wrests the girl savagely from the wreckage of the train, takes her up a dirt path, and drags her into the bushes, and though she knows that is the price of her exhilarating vision, she fights the arms that seize her, screams with her hands and fingers, and finally lets loose the wail of a wounded animal. Moses wonders if this brutal scene was simply to be faithful to the script or whether some strange desire was also a factor.

The lights in the hall come on. Moses scans the first few rows to locate the person who looked like Trigano. But if such a person had been there at all, he escaped before the lights went up.

At first the applause is stuttering and embarrassed, but gradually it becomes louder and rhythmic. As it continues, de Viola rises and invites Ruth to join him. He looks toward the rear to invite the director as well, but Moses is in no hurry to get up and gestures to the actress to go first. As she is led to the stage, the audience redoubles its applause, with scattered cries of *Brava!*

Ruth is nervous, and de Viola, to allow her time to compose herself, gives a lengthy introduction in Spanish. But when he cedes her the floor, her English is replete with Hebrew words in critical places. Then a man gets up — a Jew, or a former Israeli of the sort found everywhere and always — and offers his assistance in translation from Hebrew to Spanish.

There is relief as the Hebrew is freed from the filter of broken English. But even now, Ruth's words are confused and almost childish, suggesting that not only as a character in a film but as a woman, she is defending her former lover's notion that destruction and disaster improve and refine mankind. When the priest, smiling gently, tries to modify her remarks, she persists, her hands waving exuberantly, her eyes ablaze, as if at any moment she will revert to sign language. Now Moses raises his hand, to the relief of the moderator, who invites the director to the stage to restore order to the chaos created by the actress. And despite the temptation to continue in Hebrew, Moses prefers to speak in English, which allows him to digress more easily from moral dilemmas to tricks of the movie trade.

The hour is late. The aged farmers in the audience slip from the hall one by one, but the young people won't let matters rest. They demand to know if the director subscribes to the views of the actress. Moses is wary of an imprecise answer, so he speaks compellingly of obligation and regret and atonement, and how these alone can yield true compassion, as opposed to the self-pity that masquerades as sympathy for others. And he promises the inquisitive young people further discussion. The retrospective, after all, continues tomorrow.

6

"YOU SEE," HE says to Juan on their way to the hotel, "it is a wise man who knows the limits of his strength and declines in advance a meal in a good restaurant." "Wise or otherwise," answers Juan, "tomorrow you will not be able to shirk your duty. A distinguished lady, far older than you, will be making a special trip from Madrid to honor the conclusion of your retrospective with her presence."

It is almost midnight, and again the empty square is spread out before them in splendid gloom. "You don't want another little look at our cathedral before bedtime?" jokes the priest. "Why not?" says Ruth, still energized by the film. "No, the night is so short," Moses firmly interjects. But before they part, he expresses genuine appreciation, first for the fine hotel accommodations and generous hospitality, and for the quality of the dubbing and the high level of questions from the audience. He is especially grateful to the host for his excellent and efficient handling of the retrospective, yet he must ask that the pace tomorrow be a bit slower, and without giving the priest a chance to promise anything, he turns to the reception desk and collects the room key and the two pilgrim walking sticks.

How good to return to the calm of the spacious, pleasant attic, which is made up for the second night's sleep. The sheets have been changed, and little chocolates in gold wrappers glitter on the big pillows.

But Ruth, suddenly cold and distant, dives fully dressed onto the bed, in fur jacket and boots, quickly unwraps a chocolate, and pops it whole into her mouth.

Moses removes his two hearing aids and tucks them in their box. Then he steals a look at the picture of the old prisoner steadfastly suckling at the pure white breast. He still refrains from saying anything about the picture to his companion, who is watching him with something akin to hatred.

He undoes his necktie and takes off his shirt.

"You could have asked whether I also wanted to decline the dinner."

"I assumed you wouldn't want to go without me."

"Then you could have stayed with me, even if you weren't hungry."

"Again you ignore the age difference between us. When you're my age, and I am no longer among the living, you'll understand better how one feels at the end of a long and tiring day."

She closes her eyes.

"In the morning, a big breakfast, but if you're still hungry now, you can have my chocolate."

She reaches for his pillow, takes the chocolate, and puts it in her mouth.

Now, as he stands naked to the waist at the foot of their bed, he feels that in the many years since *Distant Station*, not only has her spirit remained fundamentally unchanged, but her older body has preserved the contours of the young actress, walking up the hilly path.

"How did you feel about yourself in the film?"

"I really liked what I saw."

"As always."

"More than ever."

"When you spoke, for a moment I felt you really believed disasters are a good means of true communion among people."

"You planted the idea in me when we made the film."

"You can actually remember what I told you then?"

"More or less, but what I do remember clearly is you didn't pay me."

Moses is surprised, breaks into hearty laughter.

"Suddenly you remember?"

"This evening, in the dark, I remembered."

"In our early films none of us got paid. We worked in partnership, in a cooperative venture. We shared expenses and would share equally in the profits, if there were any."

"I don't remember you including me in your cooperative."

"But you belonged then to Trigano . . . to Shaul."

"*Belonged*? What an awful word."

"What I mean is, you were included in the screenwriter's budget. You lived together, you were like a little family; whatever he got from the film was automatically yours too."

"Nothing was automatic. It was unjust and unfair. Tonight I saw that the character who carried the whole film was me. Without my sign language, nobody in the village would have lifted a finger. So even if you thought that Shaul and I were a little family, you should have paid me separately."

"I should've?"

"Who else?"

"Okay, then, I'll pay you now. I'll compensate you for all the injustice. Especially now that I've seen how exquisitely you played a character in sign language —"

"Which you didn't even remember was in the film. Apparently you are worn out in spirit as well as in body."

"I told you."

She says nothing, regards him with hostility.

"When I saw you watching your hands and fingers waving on the screen this evening, I asked myself if you could still understand them."

"Mostly."

"And if I spoke to you now in sign language, could you understand?"

She is surprised, even suspicious, as Moses makes broad hand motions and points at the bed.

She immediately gets what he means, perhaps because she guessed his intent from the start, and sits up to make room for her own gestures, which signal an emphatic no. And as a sly spark flashes in her eyes, she gives a few animalistic grunts, as if to say, *It's not me you want, it's the character you saw in your films, but even if you can get yourself satisfaction from the character you created on the screen, from me, tonight, you won't get a thing.*

Is that what was actually said to him in sign language at midnight in a hotel that was once a hostel for pilgrims, or was it convenient for him to interpret the signs that way? But since, according to the established convention between them, they could be together only if both sent the same clear signals, he shuffles to the bathroom, locks the door, and starts to fill up the big tub. As he waits, he examines his image in the mirror. Time has turned his hair white but has not yet bared his skull. And he hopes that the wrinkles that proliferate around his eyes offer a touch of humanity and not just an intimation of mortality. He gets into the tub and enjoys the water that lightens his bulk. He washes his hair vigorously, as if that could darken it. And when he returns to the room, clean and fragrant, he finds that his companion has turned out the lights, and to outwit her hunger she has let sleep swallow her whole, coat, boots, and all.

For a moment he wonders if he should wake her, remove her clothes so she can sleep more soundly. But he decides not to touch her, lest she think he intends to violate a clear sign just given him. On second thought, he decides to remove her boots, so they will not soil the white quilt cover. She moves slightly, feels his hands loosening the laces, sighs, and appears to struggle, but does not wake. Finally he manages to pull off the boots, and he removes her woolen socks too. White feet in the darkness, small and tired. Suddenly the young woman materializes from the first film of the day, standing in his family home, fearful and demoralized in baggy white shorts, leaning on a broom, and her pale, delicate foot strokes his hair. Was it the left foot or the right that Toledano's camera caressed more than forty years ago? he wonders as he gathers both her feet to him, kisses each one gently, and rests them carefully on the bed.

three

THE SLUMBERING SOLDIERS

1

LATER THAT NIGHT, when he gets up to go to the toilet, he sees she is still wearing her coat. In the dim light of *Roman Charity* he sits down close to her, careful not to touch her, and explains in a fatherly tone that such uncivilized sleep will not leave her rested. And she, without opening her eyes, mumbles that even uncivilized sleep can be restful, but nevertheless lets him peel off the coat and then, in utter exhaustion, curls up beneath the quilt and goes back to sleep.

But when he wakes up in the morning, her singing in the shower is louder than the roar of the water, and her hungry voice propels him from under the covers, in words not unlike his own: "Let's get down there fast, before other people eat it all."

As he emerges from the bathroom, she is dressed and made up, looking at the reproduction that hangs on the wall. But there is still no sign that the scene that repulsed her so in her youth and caused her to rebel against her lover triggers any memory. Moses, however, resolves not to give up. *If not today, then tomorrow,* he says to himself. *I will not let her leave Santiago without reconnecting her to the repulsion that inflicted years of obligation and worry on me.*

"Something wrong?" She is troubled by his look, but he waves her off, echoing her warning: "Let's hurry down, before others leave us hungry."

A new escort has been assigned for the second day of the retrospective. He waits now at the entrance to the dining room, the young teacher, handsome and refined, who at yesterday's lunch complained about the absence of abstraction and symbolism in the later films of the Israeli. His name is Rodrigo Bejerano, and although his English is not as lush or fluent as Pilar's, his thoughts are more complex and interesting. Moses invites him to breakfast.

Bejerano teaches the history of Spanish cinema at the film institute, but his field crosses borders; he is also an expert on French and Italian films of the postwar period. And he admits to being surprised by the three Israeli films screened yesterday.

"Why?"

The Spaniard tries hard to find the right words. "The determinism of the absurdist plot," he says finally. "I couldn't believe that in the end, Mr. Moses, you would actually plunge the train into the abyss."

"It was not I," says the disingenuous director, "it was the village people."

"Still . . ."

"So what could we do? Be content with just a threat?"

"Yes, why not? There is great strength in restraint, in a threat that merely hovers, an irrational threat that one can imagine but that does not spill blood quickly and sow destruction easily . . . After all, in that period, not long after World War Two, you were not alone in this genre. Not only in Europe, but even in the Far East and Middle East, there blew an absurdist and surrealist wind. Take for example Egypt, your close neighbor. A few months ago we screened some old Egyptian films, underground films, surrealistic, but their grotesque and absurd elements were gentle, much less violent than yours."

"The Nile relaxes them," suggests Moses. "The Egyptians are always certain of their water sources; their surrealism as a result is less vulgar."

The Spaniard's eyes open wide, then he smiles, as if he's heard a joke, but when the Israeli's expression remains serious, he tries to digest the answer, and a moment later he asks Moses if he really thinks the absurdist genre reflects national character or geography.

"No doubt about it," says Moses, putting down his knife and fork to avert the temptation to talk with his mouth full. "Don't forget, we belong to an ancient people; for us, absurdity and surrealism are second nature, and so, when our art blends reality with a surrealistic spirit, or just bends it in an absurd direction, it needs a shot of violence, an overdose of imagination, because only then can art be distinguished from the absurd reality. You want only a free-floating threat? Our daily lives are filled with threats, which is why we cannot limit ourselves in a film to the threat to a speeding train — we have to actually throw it off the cliff."

The young teacher closes his eyes to ponder the answer, his handsome face burnished by the glow of the copper pots and pans hanging on the wall. And then — after Moses picks up knife and fork — Bejerano wears a mischievous look as he challenges the director with a new hypothesis.

"If so, is it also possible to interpret the naturalistic detail in your recent films as a sort of inverted surrealism, a surrealism of calm reality?"

Moses chuckles with satisfaction.

"Let's assume . . . maybe . . . why not? That interpretation is yours and remains your property. I never get involved in interpretation of my films and I am willing to allow any interpretation, provided it's not an attack in disguise."

Ruth is silent, dreamlike, not following the conversation. She is no longer eating what she piled on her plate in the first ravenous minute and has pushed it half full to the center of the table. Now she seizes her tea with both hands, presses the warm cup to her cheek, its pallor only thinly veiled by makeup.

In her absent-mindedness, can she still appreciate the delicate beauty of the young man sitting opposite her, or does this sort of thing no longer interest her? Over the years of their collaboration, Moses learned to gauge every shift in her mood. Even when she was not in front of the camera, or in his field of vision, he felt he knew what was on her mind. And now, in the dining room, despite the lusty singing in her morning shower, he can sense a depression setting in. Is the picture of *Roman Charity* slipping into her consciousness, an old memory giving rise to new melancholy?

"And today?" he asks Rodrigo. "Which films are being shown today?" The young man, unlike Pilar, does not need to pull a list from his pocket but quotes from memory the Spanish titles of the two films designated for today, quickly improvising their English titles.

Moses also asks about the film to be screened the next day, but Bejerano doesn't know; de Viola had given him only the list for today. In any case, the final decision is based on the experience of the day before – the reactions of students and teachers, the nature of the discussions, and the level of interest displayed by the wider audience. For the institute is not just an art-film house but a center of learning, and a retrospective here is not only part of the students' curriculum but also – please forgive the presumptuousness – an opportunity for the artists themselves to reconnect with their past and understand it better.

A waitress in a purple apron arrives and asks Moses to go to the reception desk after breakfast for a brief word. He assumes it has to do with the picture hanging by his bed, and since he would rather receive the information with Ruth not present, he doesn't wait till the end of the meal, but agrees to go at once, asking Ruth to guard his near-empty plate.

His assumption is correct. The quick response of the hotel staff to an unusual request by a guest apparently stems from its tradition of caring for weary pilgrims. The clerk on duty, after seeing the picture for himself, located in a nearby town his former art history teacher, and to the best of his ability described on the telephone its content and style. On the strength of his report, the teacher offered a strange story of the picture's background and even suggested the names of several possible German or Italian painters but said she could determine the identity of the artist only after actually seeing the painting. There are two options: invite the expert to the hotel, or send her the picture and hang another, less troubling one in its place. Moses immediately rejects the second possibility, and reminds the man that the picture does not bother him at all, quite the contrary; it connects with an important private memory . . .

"A private memory?" The hotel clerk is somewhat taken aback by the leap into the modern era.

"I mean the memory of a film I once made."

In the end it is decided to bring in the art teacher, who can probably arrive within three hours.

On returning to the dining hall, he finds that Ruth has vanished. "She said," the Spaniard explains, "that she forgot to take her medicine, and also that she would not be visiting the museum, but not to worry."

"Why should I worry?" says Moses. Noticing the long line that has formed, he decides against another visit to the buffet, reaches for his companion's plate, and slowly finishes off her leftovers.

"The three films you screened yesterday," he goes on, "were very early ones. I had no idea your retrospective would dig so deeply into my youth. And if you surprised me, the director, you surprised her, the actress, all the more. To meet her young self, and in a foreign language, would naturally excite her and also exhaust her. It's best she should rest this morning and be ready for the screenings this afternoon."

Bejerano nods but adds that perhaps he is also to blame for her leaving; he may have worn her out with all his talk. Not often does a man get to sit face to face with an actress he has seen the night before in the full flower of her youth, and realize that despite the years, she has lost none of her magic.

Moses grabs the young man's hand with affection. "Your words are very generous, and even more if you actually believe them. If you get a chance to tell her how you feel, it will help her self-confidence, which naturally enough has faded in recent times. But don't torture yourself thinking she went back to the room because you talked too much. She loves conversation, and she enjoys listening to people talk, but her headaches are real, especially when she forgets to take her medicine. By the way, what did you talk about?"

"I talked. She listened. She asked what I thought of yesterday's films, and I told her frankly that despite understandable weaknesses, typical of such early films, I was pleased to find them free of a certain annoying flaw found in many films today. I mean the doubling of the plot in the last third of the movie."

"Doubling of the plot?" Moses is intrigued. "I can guess what you mean, but please, tell me."

"A film begins," says the young Spaniard, trying to formulate a thought precisely in his halting English, "I mean a realistic film, serious, psychological, with a believable plot." A film about human relationships, about people with a real problem that demands attention and a decision that is painful and not simple. The suspense is genuine, subtle but clearly defined. However, past the halfway point, the film drops off, not because the original problem has been resolved, but because the filmmakers, or more exactly the producers, were afraid the audience would be bored. There is a sense of an ending to the film, and there should be, because a work of art, as opposed to life, has a clear shape, but in the meantime the screenwriter and director have run out of ideas. They cannot drill to a deeper layer in the relationships that have been formed. And the producer begins to complain that the product he has in hand is good for only sixty or seventy minutes, but what happens after that? So then, instead of developing new aspects of the existing conflict, they spread a layer of glue on the story to attach an additional plot – ghosts arise, long-lost relatives come to visit, painful family secrets are exposed, or one of the characters gets cancer. No, this is not the same old deus ex machina of the Greek plays, a god brought down from the skies with a butcher's knife to slice through the complications that the characters can't manage to resolve. This is actually an additional plot, connected to the other one with crude, implausible threads, to please the distributors of the film.

"Outstanding. A sharp diagnosis." Moses applauds. "And in my early films, you say, you found no tendency toward a double plot."

"Not yet. The plot line is clear and unified, though very simple, maybe a bit primitive, but not doubled in any way."

This young and handsome Spaniard — I like him a lot, thinks Moses. He is thoughtful, honest, open, and it will be possible to get information out of him that the sly little priest shrouds in secrecy.

"Let's have another cup of coffee and see if there's some double plot on the buffet, and have a taste of that. Then we'll go to the museum, and perhaps again to the cathedral. When I arrived I said to de Viola that we'll have plenty of time here, but the plenty will too soon be over."

"Three days in a city like Santiago de Compostela is a quick trip, but if your time is running out, my time will make it better."

2

MOSES GOES TO get his jacket and finds the room is dark, except for a bedside lamp by which Ruth, relaxed in her nightgown, is leafing through a booklet of photos of the city.

"Good thing you decided to go back to bed."

"Only because you said last night that uncivilized sleep isn't restful."

"Precisely" — he is gratified that she remembers — "which is why you need to rest before the exhausting encounter with two films we made in our childhood."

"Exhausting?"

"Because it's harder and harder for me to understand what we made then and why."

"Hard? For you?"

"Even for me. Because, as you know, for me the plot is not enough, not in my films or in the films of others. And in those first screenplays, the real power was not in the story, not even in the strange situations, but in the sharp dialogue that he . . . Trigano . . . wrote. That's where his wild imagination really shone."

Only rarely does he explicitly mention in her presence the man who drove her away, and her face catches fire, and she seems about to respond but thinks the better of it and returns to the photo brochure.

"You still have a headache?"

"Who told you I had a headache?"

"The Spaniard, the teacher."

"Aha."

"So how is it?"

"Going away . . . Soon it'll be gone."

"I'm sorry I told you to postpone the blood test."

"And I'm sorry I mentioned it."

"Why?"

"Because I have no intention of letting anybody take my blood ever again. So don't be sorry. I'm healthy."

"Of course you're healthy," mumbles Moses, sensing the old resentment. It was imprudent of him to take her to the retrospective before clarifying in advance what would be screened. The gap between past and present would likely be painful for her. He glances at *Roman Charity* and notices that the little light above the picture is off. Did the bulb burn out, or did Ruth find the hidden switch? He still resists directing her attention to the painting. She should make the connection on her own.

"As a matter of fact," he says, "the handsome young man, our escort Bejerano, an intelligent and honest man, told me that he didn't get around to telling you that despite all the years that have passed, you still have the allure that was evident in yesterday's films."

"Why didn't he get around to it?"

"Because all his talk about the double plot drove you away from the table."

"Why should it drive me away? Your recent films are filled with double plots and I tolerate them anyway."

"Double plots in my films?" He laughs to mask the sting. "In what sense? Tell me."

"Not now." She switches off her bedside lamp. "We still have plenty of time together here . . ."

"Not that much," he mumbles, and puts on his jacket.

A freezing wind gusts through the huge, empty square.

"Thanks to your Israeli presence," says Rodrigo, "we have been blessed with perfectly clear skies."

"But very cold days," Moses adds.

"That's not a bad thing. Cold and dry sharpens the thoughts; rain and snow dull them."

Rodrigo suggests going first to the museum situated beneath the cathedral. Not a large museum, nor in his view an important one, but since it is included in the schedule, best to get it over with before it is flooded with tourists. And instead of making another visit to the cathedral, he suggests taking advantage of the sunny morning and going to the promenade on the far side of the Old Town.

Is this teacher, wonders Moses, trying to save him money? For he stubbornly argues with the museum director, demanding that he not make the guest of honor and laureate of the retrospective pay for admission. Moses quickly takes out his wallet and pays for them both. The museum director offers, perhaps by way of compensation, to show him around, but Moses declines. He who pays to get in deserves an exemption from the erudition of an enthusiastic guide.

Rodrigo is right; even at first glance, the sculptures are mediocre and the paintings boring. No need to impersonate art lovers strolling through the exhibits. Moses picks up his pace and makes for the exit. "Already? Your visit is over?" The museum director is dismayed, and even as Rodrigo tries to apologize, Moses turns and asks him if he happens to have heard of *Caritas Romana*. He has found a reproduction hanging in his hotel room but without the name of the artist. And with his hands and lips he acts out the scene of the old man and the bare-breasted woman.

The museum director has heard of this motif in Renaissance art but does not exactly remember the story behind it. Perhaps the reproduction is on loan from the museum archive and listed in the catalog.

"The museum exhibits pictures in the hotel?"

"We have dozens of reproductions gathering dust in our storeroom, so it makes sense to lend them for a nominal fee to the Parador, which routinely rotates the pictures for the sake of bored chambermaids, or regular guests who are pleased to find something new each time they visit. Yes, there are still people who are not indifferent to the pictures hanging by their beds in a hotel, even when they stay for only one night."

"True," says Moses. "Like me."

He hurries Rodrigo to the square and gladly accepts the suggestion that they go to the promenade for a view of the cathedral on a clear day from another, more distant vantage point. They walk briskly through the alleys of the Old Town, passing squares and fountains and gates, arriving at a grassy expanse with a broad promenade from which the cathedral, in all its sculpted glory, may be seen. Above it, like the veil of a floating bride, hover wisps of morning fog that the bright sunshine has yet to dispel. Farther along the promenade, in a pleasant little garden paved with white marble, stand two stern-faced women arm in arm: one in a fiery red coat with a folded black umbrella in her hand, staring ahead with steadfast grimness, and her companion, a flamboyant woman in a headscarf and shiny blue robe, looking sideways and extending her hand toward the sky as if asking a question. Their thin, straight legs are firmly fixed to the pavement with bolts, needing no further means of support.

"What's this?" asks Moses.

"These pieces are left over from a whole sculpture garden that students from the art college set up years ago as a kind of fantastical secular response to the seriousness of the cathedral and its statues of the saints."

"But who are these figures?"

"They are called the Two Marys, but they are not saints. If you keep walking, you'll see another sculpture on the bench."

Indeed, a few steps farther on, sitting upright with legs crossed at the edge of a public bench, is the figure of a skinny, gray-haired intellectual with a long pointy beard, clad in a gray suit, peering intently into the far distance through oversize eyeglasses.

"What's he made of?"

"Mostly rigid plastic. Like the clothes of the Two Marys."

"And he manages in the cold and the heat?"

"Does he have a choice?" jokes Rodrigo. "Go on, feel him . . ."

But Moses declines to reach out to the weird intellectual.

A group of students, boys and girls, sit on a nearby lawn with books and notebooks, apparently studying together for an exam. Some of them spot Rodrigo and rush over to greet him. "Yes," he explains to Moses, "they are my high school students, that's actually my main job." And as he banters with his students, he does not fail to introduce them to an important foreign film director who has fond memories of the days when he, too, was surrounded by students.

An Israeli retrospective at the archive of the film institute? Yes, they think they may have heard something of it. The sight of the youngsters chatting with a beloved teacher spurs the suspicion that flickered at the museum. Trigano? Who else could have informed the Spanish archive about early Israeli films? Who other than the scriptwriter is still loyal to those ragged old movies? The cameraman is dead, the soundman left the country, the editors dissolved into other films. Only the writer could try to augment the value of his forgotten work in a faraway film archive, thus also tarnishing what his director had later done without him.

But how did the films get here? Did Trigano ship them over, or bring them himself? The possibility that his scriptwriter had preceded him here as a pilgrim captures Moses' imagination, so much so that the former collaborator who tore their partnership to shreds hovers in his mind's eye alongside the kings and saints arrayed in the heights of the distant cathedral.

Does this explain the mischief of the little priest, who every morning sends him a different escort with a new list of films? Trigano doubtless told him about their breakup and advised him to conceal his visit and also not to tell the director in advance what they planned to screen in the retrospective, lest he refuse to come.

The students have returned to the books and notes they left on the grass, except for two fawning girls who find it hard to leave the handsome young teacher.

Yes, Moses is ready to believe that with a bit of tugging, the thread in his hand can be woven into a fuller hypothesis. For if the writer brought the films himself, he also helped with the dubbing. All of this in secret, so that Trigano could construct a hidden reproach to the man who rejected him.

The teacher eventually succeeds in breaking free of the two girls, and he hurries to apologize with a sigh that is also one of satisfaction.

"May I ask you a personal question?" says Moses.

"By all means . . ."

"Are you married?"

The young man's laughing face reddens.

"No . . . but it's probably time."

"Because I was also like you, a young teacher in the upper grades of high school, and though I wasn't as handsome as you, I still felt I was a constant topic in the thoughts of my students."

Rodrigo laughs. "It's also a teacher's job to nourish the imagination of his students."

"May I ask something else?"

"Please."

"Was there a visitor recently here at the archive, an Israeli?"

Rodrigo doesn't remember any Israeli. But Moses persists. "A man around sixty, thin, dark skin, named Shaul Trigano. He wrote screenplays many years ago."

The Spaniard closes his eyes, plumbing his memory. But for naught. Trigano is a name clearly accessible to the Spanish ear, and yet, no, he doesn't remember any Trigano.

But Moses has a feeling that even if the Spaniard doesn't remember the name, he knows who he is, so he presses on and tries to portray the wanted man, picturing the young Trigano in his mind and improvising an up-to-date character, blending all possible changes visited by time since last they met.

The Spaniard turns away and lowers his gaze in one final effort, but he remains faithful to his earlier response. No, there was no Israeli recently at the institute, though of course he cannot claim to know everyone who visits here.

3

As moses enters the hotel, the desk clerk points to an old woman who is waiting for him. This is the art history teacher enlisted from a neighboring city; she has arrived early. Though she is long retired, she is pleased to oblige the desk clerk, her diligent student, who has proven that after all these years he has not forgotten her. Moses introduces himself, overcome with feeling for this sprightly old lady with the intelligent face and snow-white hair. For a moment it seems his mother has sprung from the film screened the day before and come back to life to educate him.

Carefully he takes her wrinkled hand, fragile as a sparrow, and briefly explains his request and its background.

"Would you like to go up to your room to see the picture, or should we ask that it be brought down here?" she says.

He hesitates, but decides for the room. If the picture was removed from the wall, defects might be discovered in the frame or glass that would have to be fixed before it could be re-hung by his bed. He would also feel uncomfortable hearing the explication of a risqué painting in the hotel lobby, amid the guests coming and going. But as they step out of the elevator on the fourth floor, he suddenly realizes he should warn Ruth of their arrival, even though the visitor is an old woman. He knocks on the door and waits, then inserts the key in the lock.

The dark room looks the same as he had left it, disorderly and unventilated, stuffy with the smell of sleep, and Ruth is wrapped in her blanket like an embryo. This is strange, even worrisome. Sleeping this long is rare for her. Without turning on the light he kneels by the bed and gently touches her face, to wake her and let her know that a visitor is joining them, an art expert, who has meanwhile slipped into the room with feline agility and now faces the reproduction, turning on the little picture lamp affixed to the wall.

The dim light is enough to awaken the sleeper, who opens her eyes and requires a moment to recall where she is. In confusion, she smiles at her companion, who returns an embarrassed grin as he gestures at the old woman with the magnifying glass, scouring the picture for the signature of the artist.

"The picture? Why?"

"To explain the background of the painting to us . . . the story behind it . . . who the old man is, and why he is nursing at the breast."

"The old man?"

"The prisoner, the one kneeling on the ground."

"The prisoner?"

Has that memory vanished entirely? Can it be that no chord was struck as she stood and stared at the picture that morning, then went back to sleep? Had she truly banished from her mind her little artistic mutiny, to erase the humiliation of abandonment by her lover? Or was she only pretending, to test Moses? With genuine puzzlement he studies the actress, the outline of her breasts beneath her thin cotton nightgown inspiring both compassion and desire. "I'll explain later," he whispers, "but say hello, because this woman is an art expert who has made a special trip."

The actress is bewildered and amused at the sight of the expert whom Moses has parachuted into a room cluttered with clothes and blankets, but she doesn't get out of bed, merely props herself up, turns on the reading light, and nods a greeting to the elderly white-haired woman, who gives a little bow in return. From the gleam in her eye it appears she has already identified the artist.

"Matthias Meyvogel," she declares, "no doubt about it. Seventeenth century, born in Zeeland – not New Zealand – a Dutchman who worked in Rome; very little is known about him. From the painting he would appear to be a great admirer of Rembrandt, from whom he copied the sitting position of the prisoner Cimon, and the strong light on his naked back –"

"Just a minute, madam," implores Moses, still unnerved by the expert's resemblance to his mother, "please slow down. You say 'Cimon,' as if I'm supposed to know who that is, but first of all, what is the act of charity here? And in what way is it Roman?"

"Oh, do forgive me, it didn't occur to me that you had never heard of *Caritas Romana*. For it is a truly wonderful and important story that has inspired dozens of writers and artists, if not hundreds."

"An Italian story?"

"Not Italian, Roman. Rome is greater than Italy, and the original story comes from ancient Rome, one of the thousand stories published in A.D. 30 by Valerius Maximus in his collection *Facta et Dicta Memorabilia* – in other words, 'acts and sayings that must be remembered.' The story is about a young woman named Pero who fed her father from her own breast."

"Her father? The old man, this prisoner, is her *father?*"

"Of course, he's only her father," the art historian says to calm the Israeli who thought the suckling man was a stranger. "He is Cimon, and he was sentenced to die by starvation, so his daughter came to him in secret and nursed him so he wouldn't die. In the end, the jailers caught her, but they were so impressed by her daring and unique devotion that they had mercy on the father and set him free. That's the kernel of the story, which inspired many paintings back in ancient times. For example, when they dug Pompeii out of the ashes of Vesuvius, they found a fresco with this motif. Valerius Maximus himself admitted that such paintings were more powerful than his story. People stop and stare in amazement at this picture – they cannot take their eyes off it, they see it come alive. Even you, sir, a citizen of the twenty-first century, were so agitated by the painting that you sent for me."

"But is this a copy of an original painting from ancient Rome?"

"No, surely not. The story enticed many important painters over the centuries, and each one expressed it in his own way. Rubens, who painted it at least twice; Caravaggio, Murillo, Pasinelli, and a great many others before them and after."

"Before them — you mean the Middle Ages?"

"No, in the Middle Ages the motif almost disappears, but it was revived and flourished during the Renaissance and Baroque periods."

"Maybe because of the overt eroticism."

"Precisely so. In the medieval period, they questioned the honesty of the compassion and mercy of the daughter nursing her father. Perhaps she was exploiting his misery, in an oedipal fashion, I mean . . ."

She bursts into hearty laughter.

"Oedipal?" Moses chuckles. "What did they know in the Middle Ages about the Oedipus complex?"

"They didn't know the term, but they felt the essence of it, the same longing. After all, the truth does not need a label in order to be real. Therefore the eroticism tangled up in this act of kindness deterred, and perhaps frightened, the artists of the Middle Ages, as much as it aroused artists of the Renaissance and Baroque and later, into the nineteenth century. Yet each one dealt with the erotic aspect in a different fashion, depending on his personality, his natural inclinations, and his courage vis-à-vis his surroundings."

"For instance?"

"In many paintings, the artists made sure that the daughter looked off to the side, so as not to see the face of her nursing father, out of respect for him or out of shame or not to reveal other motives, his and perhaps hers too."

"Hers?"

"Hers too. Why not? We are talking about human beings who are alive and complicated, not figures made of cardboard. But in some other paintings, such as the one hanging here, or one by Rubens, for example, one sees that Pero is unabashedly studying the face of the old man she is nursing. It all depends, of course, on the father's situation."

"In what sense?"

"If he is depicted as feeble and dying, she is allowed to look at him directly, because it is clear to the viewer that his approaching death neutralizes any erotic intent on either side. The daughter may therefore permit herself a gentle gaze, or even support the head of the dying man. But when the father is strong and muscular, as in your painting, or one by Rubens, she must be very careful. Look, for example, sir, at Cimon here. Despite the baldness and the beard, I wouldn't take him for more than fifty, and a man like that is able to desire and take pleasure, is he not?"

"Why not."

"And therefore, when such men are being nursed, it is important that they be tied up, either their feet or, usually, their hands, like the man in your picture."

"My picture, my picture." Moses laughs in protest. "Please, dear lady, it's not mine, it belongs to the hotel."

"Of course it does, but while you are staying here, this fellow is hanging beside your bed. If his hands are tied behind his back, it means the artist wants you to know that the erotic possibilities of the situation are limited, or at least under supervision, and therefore the merciful gaze of his daughter, as depicted here, may be construed as pure, even though one can never really know the line that divides compassion from passion."

"That says it all, señora."

"Excuse me, sir, but might I inquire as to your profession? They did tell me over the telephone, but at my age I easily forget things that are not directly connected to my field of interest."

"I am a motion picture director. And my companion here in the bed is a wonderful actress, a veteran of many of my films and those of others."

"Very pleased to meet you, madam," says the expert, and again bows politely, wedged between the bed and the wall. And Moses makes a mental note that this image — a hotel room in faint light, strewn with blankets and clothes and an open suitcase, with a tiny old lady who resembles his mother speaking to a woman in a flimsy nightgown lazing under the covers — needs to be fully re-created in one of his future films, perhaps even his next. And again the question flashes — is it possible that Trigano was familiar with a painting on this theme?

"As I was saying," the art expert continues, "these are very delicate issues."

"Very delicate," agrees Moses, "and also complicated."

"And in Caravaggio's marvelous painting *The Seven Acts of Mercy*," the expert carries on, "as with Perino del Vaga, who influenced Caravaggio, the daughter nurses the father through the bars of his prison cell, and thus, even if the man is strong and active, he is nevertheless neutralized. A magnificent painting like Caravaggio's can even hang in a church. But in most renderings, the *Roman Charity* enables the daughter to be in closer contact with the father, sometimes to touch his head and shoulders, and in bolder paintings to expose her beautiful shoulders and bare the non-nursing breast. Such things generally occur only on the condition that the father's hands are bound, although, for example, in the painting by the American artist Rembrandt Peale, early nineteenth century, only one of the father's feet is attached to the wall by a long chain, whereas the hands are free, and one of them touches the thigh of the daughter, and they both look aside fearfully, as if to check whether someone can see them, and such a thing might justifiably raise all sorts of suspicions and speculations. Yet there are artists who, to dispel any suspicion, gave Pero a baby, to demonstrate that she is indeed, first and foremost, a nursing mother, and she includes her poor father as a second child, and only as a child."

"The baby is her alibi," says Moses, beginning to tire.

"Precisely, sir, you got it exactly."

Moses turns with a smile to Ruth, still recumbent in bed, her hair scattered on the pillow, her pretty eyes glistening with tears that express her thanks for the cautious yet elegant way her companion chose to revive a banished memory that never vanished.

"But I am obligated to tell you," expounds the expert, suddenly raising her voice, "that there are painters who gave themselves unbridled license. They preserved the heart of the story but shamelessly, gratuitously stripped not just the miserable father but the gracious daughter of clothes, thus taking a story of compassion and kindness to a most disgusting place. It's best I not burden you with any additional names, but you know as well as anybody that art has no boundaries."

"None, as perhaps it should be . . ."

The old woman tilts her head with mild disapproval and forges on.

"In any event, a moral artist places the act of kindness at the center, adding the erotic touch only to deepen compassion and devotion, not to contradict them, and certainly not to replace them. There needs to be a proper balance among the elements: the man, the father, his age and his physical condition. And if the man, the father, is in good shape, the binding of his hands and feet, that is to say, the extent to which he is immobilized, is crucial. So too with the nursing daughter: What is she is looking at? How does she expose the feeding breast? How much of her body is unclothed in the painting? A balance among all these should give us a human picture that is also a moral one. All this is quite apart from the quality of the composition, the perspective, the finish of the details, and the colors."

"And this picture, my picture, the hotel's picture, maintains this balance, in your opinion?"

"Yes, all in all it is a worthy painting; the compassion and kindness are clear."

Moses' head is spinning. He fears the expert will not let him go, leaving him little time for a proper lunch. He takes her hand, warmly expressing his gratitude.

"Thank you, thank you, from the bottom of my heart, you are a marvelous teacher. You have provided a superb summary of the story of Roman Charity in such a short time, and if more questions arise, I can surely find the answer on the Internet here at the hotel."

"Oh no," she cries, "please, no, not the Internet. It is full of mistakes and foolishness. Anywhere but the Internet, please. If you need more details, sir, I am at your service. I have plenty of time. And although I am older than you" — she blushes, a mischievous twinkle in her eye — "I can still, like Pero, feed you and your companion additional information."

4

FOLLOWING A FAST lunch in the cafeteria, the Spaniard steers his guests to the small screening room. The crowd has shrunk. "See," remarks Moses with bitterness, "people have grown weary of my immature films and quite rightly prefer a nice winter siesta. What can I say, my friend, I fear I will leave this retrospective deflated." But Rodrigo dismisses the complaint. The smaller audience stems from scheduling conflicts, not disapproval. He recognizes in the audience a number of wise and sensitive people, and the quality of the attendees makes up for their dearth. He escorts Moses onto the small stage.

But a few "wise and sensitive people" do not compensate for the thinness of the crowd. Besides, the director cannot shake off the suspicion that this retrospective was engineered by Trigano to compel him to defend the writer's fantasies. Can he even remember the film they are about to show? Did it have a well-defined plot? What he recalls is a static, dreamlike atmosphere; a short, vague, hallucinatory film. A rocky desert crater in winter, filmed at night in freezing cold. He whispers to his young escort, who is ready and waiting to translate: "Believe me, I don't have much to say." But Rodrigo, who has not yet seen the film and has heard only a brief description from the archive director, whispers back: "If so, perhaps explain the historical context, say a few words about the function of the army reserves in Israel, for although we are located in a famous barracks, we have not been at war for seventy years."

Moses complies, folds his arms on his chest, closes his eyes, and retrieves the distant sixties. In a deep, low voice, he describes to the Spanish audience a period that now seems almost like a time of peace: no terror attacks or assassinations, battles or revenge operations. A small democracy in the Middle East, still in its infancy. Jerusalem divided but serene. The army dormant. Peaceful Galilee towns populated by obedient Arabs, and the country's borders marked by little tin signs.

And as he talks he notices, in one of the half-empty rows, Ruth shaking her head in disagreement. But Moses keeps at it, swept up in his private idyll, insisting on days of peace and stability, a period that has passed and will never return. It is from this point of departure that he asks the small audience to understand his antiquated film, for only a hibernating army can give rise to peace. And as Rodrigo struggles to translate, stumbling over the last sentences, Moses distractedly leaves the stage, motioning to the hidden technician to turn off the lights.

Only as the first images appear does the director realize that the color has vanished from his memory. He was sure this film was shot in black-and-white, and here it is in color. "Did you remember," he tests the woman by his side, "it was in color?" "Of course," she answers at once. "I loved this messy movie, I still think it's one of the decent films you made, even if it went nowhere."

"*Decent?*" He is thrown off by the word. "What do you mean, *decent?*" "In other words, modest," she whispers, putting a finger to his lips to hush him as the first bit of dialogue is spoken. Moses studies her with affection. The morning sleep did her good: color has returned to her cheeks, and the spark to her eyes. The link he imposed on her memory between *Roman Charity* by their bed and the film scene she refused in Jaffa seems not to trouble her. On the contrary, it revives her spirit. Will we, he wonders, in the limited time remaining here, find passion as well?

After three dubbed films he is used to the Spanish. Without understanding a word, he at least finds it natural on his actors' lips. Ten men about forty years old, from cities and towns, factory workers and teachers and clerks, leave their families to go to an army camp and sign for weapons and equipment, because, after assuming they'd been forgotten, they were called up for reserve duty. With practiced hindsight, Moses zeroes in on the film's weakness. The color erects a barrier between the realistic opening and the fantastical and hallucinatory things to come. Too much detail in the scenes showing the reservists leaving their homes, saying goodbye to wives and children, getting their equipment, telling jokes. A film that seeks to convey intimacy with soldiers who abandon their mission and spend long days in deep sleep must, from the start, go with shades of black, white, and gray alone, the colors of dream.

Sluggishly moving onscreen are older men, heavy and balding, who have not made peace with the reserve duty they have been dealt. Slack-shouldered and befuddled, they shed civilian clothes and put on old uniforms, examine with revulsion the gear and weapons from the past war, and shake years of dust from army blankets, and the director wonders if in these opening scenes, one can already see the seeds of his obsessive attention to detail. He recalls that he intended to ask the actors to improvise freely before the camera, drawing on their experience as reserve soldiers. But Trigano stood firm, fiercely defending his script: Only what is written will be spoken, with nothing added.

Was the quick transition from colorful city scenes to the monotonous yellow desert detrimental to the film? In a very long shot, the small truck carrying the reservists looks like an ant inching into a pothole on a heat-bleached road. It cautiously makes its way down the slope of a small crater to an ancient Nabataean ruin, which the cameraman and set designer came upon when scouting locations. To convert it into a military installation whose nature and purpose no one could guess, they wrapped it in shiny silver sheets, adding a profusion of colorful cables that suggested a giant prehistoric beetle. To ensure the site's safety and security, the reservists get down from the truck and go to work, unloading cartons of field rations, setting up the water tank towed by the truck in a patch of shade under a desert bush. Since their longtime commander is late to arrive, a replacement is designated at the last moment, a minor bureaucrat in civilian life who spreads a blanket on the ground and goes to sleep.

In light of the film's failure at the box office and the disappointment among more than a few of the director's friends, Moses now asks himself why he had not insisted that the screenwriter strengthen the film with a solid plot, beyond the provocative allegory of slumber at a secret military installation. But now that history has debunked the illusion of peace, a group of soldiers who slumber with a clear conscience in front of a vital military installation is a strong image, at least for the director who considers it anew at a screening in a distant land.

Moses insisted that the reservists in the film all be amateur actors, and he recruited them himself from local drama clubs, preferring men who had served in combat units and knew their ways, so their sleep would make a strong, realistic impression. Right now they're examining the installation, which they must guard without ever being told what it is, and as they ponder its purpose they also prepare for their first night under the stars and light a campfire.

It's quite likely, Moses muses, that some of these amateurs, who were then ten or fifteen years older than he was, have since died, and those who are still alive may or may not remember the bizarre movie that must have frustrated them when it became clear that the script afforded no gripping conflict or complex situations, no opportunity to hone their acting skills, that it merely demanded their presence, day after day, night after night, in front of a camera that absorbed their slumber. Like actual reservists, they left work and family, agreeing to go down to the desert without pay for a few days of shooting, and now they were asked merely to act fatigued. He and the cinematographer had tried to cover up the feeble plot with flames and flying sparks and faces flickering in the silver cover of the installation, along with unforgettable shots of the desert by day and by night. Will this audience appreciate their beauty?

Moses attempts to assess the reaction of the few viewers scattered among the rows of seats. True, he does not yet hear whispering, coughing, or fidgeting, but he assumes the audience will be indifferent to this film and perhaps hostile. He steals a glance at Ruth, whose eyes are fixed on the screen in anticipation of her entrance as an elusive Bedouin woman, dressed in black and wearing a veil, spying on the sleeping soldiers. After Ruth's impressive role as a deaf-mute in *Distant Station*, Trigano was tempted to bestow a new disability on his beloved, making her lame or even blind, but Moses vetoed it and they compromised on a veiled Bedouin woman who slips through the night like a ghost.

5

THE BOND BETWEEN the scriptwriter and his beloved grew stronger during the shoot in the desert. Since they knew each other from childhood, their relationship had earlier resembled love between cousins, but after the success of *Distant Station* they came to believe that their partnership also involved an artistic mission, and the fact that a former teacher had made it a reality heightened their self-importance, and their love as well. And so, during the filming of *Slumbering Soldiers*, Trigano never once left the location, yet he made sure not to intervene in the directing or cinematography, for he knew that everyone, by the terms of the agreement, would be faithful to his script. But at night, when cast and crew rolled up the silver sheeting and went to sleep inside the ancient Nabataean structure, the screenwriter and actress would disappear with their sleeping bags behind a nearby hill, their laughter echoing within earshot.

But the little screen at the film institute doesn't feature broken memories, only an old movie driven by its own obsessions. The melancholy moon, whose countenance Toledano managed to capture on the silvery cover of the installation, whitens the faces of the reservists, grown men who nibble the leftovers of their meal before spreading their sleeping bags on the ground and zipping them closed in a way that makes it possible for the camera to move from soldier to soldier. Even the guards who are to patrol the premises are too lazy to leave the campfire. Their conversation dies down, their eyes gradually close. And then, at the top of the crater, appears the thin silhouette of the Bedouin woman, who moves silently as if moonstruck. And for the first time in the film — which so far has been free of background music — the sound of a flute, which from now on will accompany the performance of the veiled woman in black.

"Even now," whispers Moses to Ruth, who is entranced by her night-walking character, "I can't understand how I was talked into directing such a movie. How I agreed to build a whole film around the idea of sleep, of slumbering soldiers yet."

"I also didn't understand how he managed to drag you into this one. I was easy, I was ready to play any foolishness that came into his head. I had total faith in whatever he wanted. Look how I'm running barefoot over rocks and thorns for the three of you."

"The three of us?"

"Not just the two of you — Toledano also insisted that in all the night shots I go barefoot, even when my feet weren't in the frame. It's a good thing that among the guys you brought was a nice older man, a former army medic. Every night after the filming, he would help me take care of the cuts and scratches. All you cared about was my savagery."

"Savagery?"

"Yes, Shaul intended that I not be some pathetic Israeli Bedouin trudging by the roadside, but someone strong, wild . . . Sometimes, you remember, he would call me Debdou, the name of the Moroccan village I came from with my father. He would also insist, in jest or seriously, that my family had traces of foreign blood. The jaw, the height of my tall father of blessed memory, and especially the yellow-gray color of my eyes he thought could come only from a foreign Sahara tribe, because that color didn't exist among the Jews . . . That's how he would talk, the lunatic."

And she suddenly bursts into loud laughter.

Looks of disgust and fury are directed in the darkness at the creators of this slow and impenetrable film. This time of his own volition, Moses scurries a few rows behind.

A foreign tribe . . . He laughs to himself in his new seat. I never grasped the extent of Trigano's wishful thinking. There's truth to her claim, that the chance to realize his assorted fantasies about the girl he loved was what got him into writing film scripts to begin with. So this is not just some pathetic Israeli Bedouin woman . . . He insisted the young nomad be free, not dependent on anyone, able to wander about, perhaps as a figure of reconciliation, between enemies who in the 1960s had begun to realize they were trapped in a vicious circle of bloodshed.

It's now clear to Moses that the soldiers' reckless slumber serves to protect their sanity from crazy adventurism. Like the sleep of the railroad supervisor in *Distant Station*, the slumber that spared the midget god from giving the stationmaster a clear answer — earning the acclaim of perceptive reviewers — maybe the prolonged sleep currently onscreen will also be praised, for people believe that slumber oscillates between nothingness and creativity.

Moses remembers that in those far-off days Trigano had a theory: that the energy of the young, industrious state fanned the hatred of its neighbors and fatigued the Jews who came from Arab lands. That might point to a connection between the sleep of the stationmaster in the previous film and the collective, addictive, reckless, and aimless slumber of the military men in this one.

Now and then one of the soldiers wakes up, wriggles slowly from his sleeping bag, goes for a snack or drink or to answer nature's call, and on returning shoves aside his gear and weapon with such force that it suggests not only the rejection of military duty but erosion of the core of his identity. The Spanish mumbling between the soldier and the guard, who opens his sleepy eyes for a moment, sounds softer at night, if not more intelligible. Whatever they may be saying, Moses knows that the desert, with its shifting colors and sunsets and wailing winds, is meant to overwhelm the reserve soldiers in the absence of their longtime commander.

And so, in this brazen, pretentious script, the vacuum of authority may be filled by a young Bedouin woman, a powerful persona cloaked in black. Now she draws close, approaching the campfire, daring to come near the secret installation itself; the sleepy reservists, who had earlier perceived her as a fleeting reverie, now tolerate her veiled presence fully.

Each night she comes to the camp and with gentle silence wins the trust of the guards, who have no idea what she wants but enjoy her exotic female company and as family men are protective of her honor. Sometimes she brings along a black child, and sometimes an old woman trails behind her. One night she is accompanied by two sturdy men, who keep their distance. The veiled young woman, who only at night visits soldiers who also sleep by day, lays bare the prevailing anarchy.

As the filming progressed, the cinematographer and director came to appreciate the hidden mysteries of the veil, the concentration of female eroticism in those yellow-gray eyes. Moses' gaze wanders in the hall to the aging Berber, and when he locates her a few rows in front, her head slung back, he is reminded that this movie ends badly. How could he have forgotten the reversal in the second half, a truly dramatic twist with not a trace of a double plot and a conclusion whose meaning depends on what one makes of the secret installation.

Moses recalls that after he read the first draft of the screenplay, he kept interrogating his former student about the symbolism of the installation. Trigano avoided an answer. The installation does not need any meaning, it can stay fluid and elusive, open to different and contradictory interpretations, somewhere between hope and despair, past and future.

Moses lowers his head and closes his eyes. He remembers agonizing over the meaning of the installation and worrying that its symbolism was diluted by vagueness. At night, after the day's shoot, while the crew and the extras were absorbed in backgammon or card games, Toledano would offer creative, half-serious opinions about the installation to lift Moses' spirits. Assume it's a storage for nuclear waste, or an archive of top-secret documents, or a cache of illicit biological material that could wipe out humanity, and you'll feel better. Once, he even suggested Moses imagine that hidden inside the installation were the ashes of the Golden Calf that was burned and ground into powder after the biblical Moses received the Ten Commandments — ancient vestiges of a failed identity. Entangled in practical problems, the director was unable to undertake such flights of abstraction. This was a desert production at the bend of a dry gully in the belly of a small crater, and it was not easy to bring in provisions and maintain a system of communications. Moreover, they had to provide security for the sleeping soldiers and the crew that staged and filmed their sleep. Because across the border with Jordan, a real enemy lay in wait, and because bands of fedayeen were known to infiltrate the area, the military authorities agreed to send an occasional patrol, and the actual young soldiers were fascinated by their elderly lookalikes lounging idly in front of a camera.

It was in those days that they first drew on the support of Yaakov Amsalem, a likable fellow of North African extraction, a wholesaler at the Beersheba produce market and lover of cinema who later went into real estate. Amsalem believed in Trigano's ideas and even saw moneymaking potential, and he not only supplied fresh food but also volunteered to work as an extra.

Moses spots him on the screen, a beefy man in a rumpled army uniform. It was hard to film him as a sleeper, because his bubbly personality limited his capacity to lie still before the camera. Instead he happily took responsibility for tending the campfire, proving himself an able wood gatherer. Toledano instructed him to bring twigs that produced a purplish smoke, which imparted a devilish quality to the soldiers. Right now, such a haze fills the screen, and Moses again closes his eyes to intensify the memory of the smoke. Slowly, he sinks into the old, sweet fragrance of soft branches burning, their purple smoke painting the screen of his eyelids.

6

WHEN HE OPENS his eyes, the smoke and the campfire and the installation and the soldiers have disappeared. The desert too has faded, and night is replaced by a strong afternoon sun as an airplane lands at the tiny airport of Tel Aviv. In a quick series of shots, the commander comes into view, a vigorous man about fifty with graying hair who projects authority as he returns in his private plane from a business trip abroad. Moses smiles to himself as he recognizes the head of the village from *Distant Station*, and he suddenly recalls the name of the actor: Shlomo Fuchs, known to everyone as Foxy, no longer among the living. Yesterday he convincingly collaborated in plunging a passenger train into an abyss, and today he will play a more complicated part that entangles him in a hasty killing.

His wife does not seem at all happy to have him home, as written in the script or perhaps as embellished by the actress. The moment he enters, she hands him the reserve call-up notice that arrived in his absence, as if urging him to perform a duty to the nation before he begins to pester her and impose order in the household. After a quick lunch with his grown children, the new protagonist does not further impede the plot; he readies himself to go down to the desert and join his soldiers.

The montage is brisk but believable. In his bedroom he puts on his uniform and straightens his officer's stripes. From under the double bed he pulls out a submachine gun and a kit filled with black magazines, and he is ready and able, as always, to go to battle.

It was the cinematographer and not the writer who called for the commander to drive himself to the desert in an army jeep with no doors or roof, enabling the camera to follow him from far and near, emphasizing the loneliness of the authority figure as he aims to end the anarchy. As close-ups of a determined brow and silvery locks tossing in the wind are intercut with long shots of a green jeep meandering among desert cliffs, the commander nears the remote crater, and Moses can feel that the jeep's journey in daylight and darkness, taking no more than a minute of screen time, has aroused expectation in the hall, mingled with vague trepidation. But he also remembers how Toledano tortured them for hours to get that one pure minute, how he repositioned the crew again and again around the jeep, which at one point broke down, and how he kept switching lenses and angles, waiting for changes in the light and movements of the clouds, all to make his visual dream come true.

The jeep descends silently, headlights off, into the crater, where the installation flickers with reflections of a dying campfire. The commander does not confront the peacefully slumbering guards or try to wake his troops, but rather strolls through the little encampment lost in thoughts and plans, surveying the surrounding cliffs and making mental notes of lookout points, a suitable location for a firing range, hillsides for combat exercises, an open space for lineups. It is only when he climbs on a rock to find a place for his soldiers to practice digging trenches that he catches sight of a thin black figure watching him from afar.

The one soldier he finally wakes up is the bugler, who henceforth will accompany him with staccato blasts. All of a sudden the slow, quiet film is filled with loud speech and urgent action. Commands, shouts, complaints, laughter, and cursing whose rapid dubbing in Spanish reminds Moses of Italian movies about World War II. On top of guard duty, training exercises, and nighttime lineups, the screen is gradually dominated by the relationship between the older commander and the young Berber.

Despite the discipline and order imposed by the commander, the young woman continues her visits, as if she too has a stake in the installation. And despite the commander's strict order to banish her, she manages to outwit the guards and slip close again and again. But unlike the guards, who were indifferent to her presence and never bothered to interrogate her, the commander grows increasingly angry over her nightly appearances, and since he himself has no idea what sort of installation he is guarding, he assumes that she knows nothing about it either, that her stubborn visits at night are only meant to demonstrate that she is an equal partner of the Jews, an ally in ignorance. The commander decides to eradicate this presumptuous partnership at its root.

Trigano's intention to end the film with the killing of the young woman worried Moses. If you have a mature citizen, a family man and successful businessman, called up for a short stint of reserve duty and thrust into a situation of no clear and present danger, he said to Trigano, it will take an extreme directorial feat to convince an audience that his murderous rage is believable. But Trigano would not give up on the death of his Berber. Only after their final breakup did Moses understand that it was probably the writer's great love for Ruth that impelled him to drag her in his scripts into situations of loss and humiliation, so the evil realized on the screen would return to real life drained of vitality, which was his way of protecting her. Meanwhile, between scenes, a unique friendship developed between the two lovers and Foxy, whom the scriptwriter and the actress fondly dubbed the "killer officer."

With a pang of discomfort, Moses watches two members of the audience slipping sheepishly out of the hall. True enough, he wasn't sure whether to stage the murder at night or by day, or whether the girl should be aware of the threat or remain proud and aloof until the moment she died. And the fatal shot — should it be at close range or from far away? Should she die theatrically, or should he make do with a modest bloodstain on her garment? Trigano began to make suggestions, but Moses objected to his interference and in the end banned him from the filming of the scene. "Just as I don't hover over your desk when you're writing, I don't want you standing behind the camera while I'm directing," he told him firmly.

Did the cinematographer's fervor for Ruth also render the director suspect in her lover's eyes? The cameraman and his assistant pleaded with Moses to keep the scriptwriter at a distance, as "his wiseass intellectualism will only trip us up." But in the Spanish screening room, in the company of maybe a dozen foreign viewers, Moses can suddenly feel the pain his young collaborator suffered when he was prevented from witnessing his loved one's murder.

"We'll tie you up at dawn on a cliff," said the cameraman to the actress, "but in your death you'll be even more beautiful than in life." Indeed, on the day before the filming, the cinematographer climbed onto an east-facing cliff just before sunrise to check the light from every angle. The following evening, he sent his assistant and the soundman up with the equipment. In the dead of night he led the two actors and the director to the spot, and there applied makeup, his own concoction, to the actress and waited for the glimmer of dawn to illuminate the contours of her face, which would appear uncovered for the first time when the impact of the bullet to her heart knocked off her veil.

All the scenes leading to this one had already been shot: the repeated expulsions of the Bedouin woman from the installation, the rebukes and warnings, including a forced march back to her family's encampment. Her father had warned and threatened her and would have also tied her up, except he knew she would escape and return to the Israeli watchmen, believing that she too belonged at the secret installation.

The final pursuit of the Bedouin girl by the officer had been filmed over and over, in daytime and at night, leaving only the final showdown on the rim of a cliff—a respectable citizen, an angry and exhausted commander, versus a young and delicate but strong-minded woman, whose joyful laughter now heightens the screen. Moses knows this laughter was not in the original script but was born of his inspiration. Laughter meant to trigger the rage of the officer, who apparently imagines that the woman is trying to seduce him and fears that he might succumb to the passion of this desert creature. He pulls the pistol from his pocket and fires in the air, but the laughter, free and young and mocking, demands another bullet to silence it, and a third bullet so the actress, persuasive and credible in her pain and collapse, will not rise again.

When Trigano saw the scene in the editing room, he had to admit that it had gone well. The sunrise, enhanced by artificial lighting, gave a mysterious greenish tinge to the bloody confrontation, with the young actress dropping to her knees before breathing her last. "You produced a glorious absurdity, like Camus in *The Stranger*," Trigano complimented the cinematographer and director while still resentful over being barred from the set. He of course knew about Toledano's deep feelings for Ruth, who was their shared childhood love, but he never regarded him as a true rival. Now, for the first time, he suspected that his former teacher's heart might be joining them.

But the movie doesn't end there. It goes on for another twenty minutes, which had been erased from the director's memory. For the script is determined not to let the officer get away with it, but requires him to cover his victim with stones, dismantle his gun, and throw the pieces into the abyss, and only then to return to his soldiers and snuggle into his sleeping bag. And since the wandering girl had an independent way of life, it takes several days for her family to notice her absence. In the meantime, the killer officer has tightened the disciplinary screws on his soldiers, concocting new military chores and tedious ceremonies. A flagpole is erected and a flag raised to the sound of the bugle. At the pre-dinner lineup he reads out passages from the Bible in a clear, charmless voice, as if giving orders, and if he thinks someone isn't listening, he tosses pebbles at him. After the meal he sings long-forgotten Zionist songs, accompanied by a harmonica-playing soldier. And though at the morning lineup every soldier is checked for unshaved stubble, the commander has grown a beard, so when two military policemen arrive looking for him, they need to check the photograph against his face more than once before slapping on the handcuffs and putting him into the same green jeep that he, the authority figure, had driven down to the desert.

The director, watching his long-neglected work, is duly impressed by the precise mix of haughtiness and insanity on the prisoner's face. Was this expression a product of scrupulous directing, or did it arise from within the actor? Or could it be the fading of the original print, which sat abandoned for many years in an anonymous drawer? But Moses well remembers the closing scene and is still proud of it. The installation twinkles in the light of the dwindling campfire, while the guards have all returned to their deep soldierly slumber.

7

THE APPLAUSE IS guarded but lasts long enough not to qualify as insulting. When the lights go on, one member of the audience gets up from his seat, turns to Moses, makes a two-fingered V for victory, bellows a brief *Bravo!*, and flees the hall. Yes, better an abridged reaction than a tiresome ritual of Q&A, says Moses to himself, but Bejerano insists on proper procedure and rises to invite the director to the stage to fulfill his duty at the retrospective held in his honor.

Moses sighs discreetly and heads down the aisle. He spots Ruth, her eyes teary. He hugs her warmly, strokes her hair. "See," he says with affection, "we gave you a nice powerful death back there. Believe me, that kind of scene makes it worthwhile to transfer the movie to DVD so Israelis too can appreciate what we did with primitive equipment forty years ago."

She nods and grasps both the director's hands, squeezing hard. Does she feel a new threat, is that why she is so upset about her death scene? As he gently works free of her grip, an old man gets up, skinny and hunched, clad in a black suit and red bow tie. This is Don Gomez, explains Bejerano to Moses, a distinguished member of the faculty who years ago served as dean, a theoretician of cinema whose articles are published in important journals. And because the Israeli film has prompted new thoughts, Don Gomez asks his young colleague for permission to come to the stage and say a few words.

Moses approves the request at once. The straightforward and independent reaction of a theoretician is preferable, in his view, to any other discussion. He gestures grandly to the elderly teacher, who removes his hat and goes onstage while Moses stays with Ruth, holding her hand to calm her, asking that Rodrigo translate.

Translation is not simple. The erudite old man has many thoughts, not all of them germane to *Slumbering Soldiers*, and he takes advantage of the right of first response to deliver a learned lecture to his assembled friends.

Rodrigo tries at first to translate faithfully the complex thoughts of Don Gomez, rapidly expressed in a hoarse voice tinged with pathos. But the limits of his English become quickly apparent, and he gives up. "Leave it be," says Moses, "listen to him and tell me if his overall position is positive or negative." "Absolutely positive," the young Spaniard hastens to assure him. "He was very impressed by your military installation and the system of symbols it generated, and he also appreciates the courage it took to make a film with such an airy plot, free of dramatic effects." "In that case" — Moses settles into his chair — "I have no further need of translation. For a veteran like me, the main thing is a friendly review and not the reasons that justify it."

8

ONLY AT 5:30 are they liberated from the hall. The scholarly old man lost track of time, and the discussion heated up and ran on forever. Meanwhile, Pilar came in to inform Rodrigo that the plane from Madrid carrying Juan de Viola's mother and brother has been delayed and that the screening of the film based on the Kafka story would be postponed for two hours at least; the guests should rest in the office of the director of the archive.

"Why don't you lie down here," says Moses to his companion, "on the sofa; my head is spinning from our crazy movie, I need to walk it off. Also, tomorrow night we'll be on our way back to Israel, and it's still not clear to me what this institute is and how the archive works, I need to sniff around a bit. Lock the door, or you might be surprised by some young filmmaker eager to confess to his priest."

Again, he yearns for that Berber girl who has come back to life, and he embraces her gently, runs his lips lightly over her forehead and neck, and says, "Just know you were and still are an extraordinary actress" — and quickly goes to hunt through the halls. He cannot find the men's room and heads outside into a huge parking lot. Winter clouds have darkened the late afternoon, so he doesn't fear for the good name of his native land as he urinates between two cars, casting his gaze skyward. Soon the rain will wash away the little puddle, leaving not a trace of his visit. In addition to the white lines marking the parking spots, he notices, there are blurry lines painted on the asphalt, long and diagonal, yellow and red — traces of bygone drills of infantry soldiers or armored corps or artillery. He will ask de Viola what happened here during the civil war. The Spaniards have indeed become a peace-loving nation; they have blithely converted a military facility to an arts institute. When we filmed *Slumbering Soldiers*, Moses wonders, did we actually believe that our wars would someday be over?

He marches along one of the red stripes. A cold wind pelts his face with drops of rain, but he soldiers on to the middle of the field, stands there at attention, perhaps at the spot where the base commander had surveyed his troops, and imagines he hears the roar of the ocean. But the strong wind chases away his illusions of grandeur and he has to retrace his steps.

He returns to the institute by an entrance that leads to a lower floor, where he finds the postproduction labs he visited yesterday, the big editing room with the latest equipment, and the sound studio, with happy voices inside. *This must be where they dubbed my films,* he thinks. Carefully he opens a door and finds a room with two projectors and recording equipment and two technicians managing them. At a round table sit young people with script pages in their hands, among them two Asians, an older man, and a young woman. The dubbing director, perched in a high chair and orchestrating the activity, greets the visitor and identifies him by name.

"I didn't mean to interrupt," mumbles the director, pleased to be recognized. "I just wanted to know if this is where my films were dubbed."

"Here, Mr. Moses, there is no other place. I hope that the voices we transplanted into your characters sound right."

"Definitely."

"These are our actors, students at the institute. And the gentleman there is a famous screenwriter from Vietnam, Mr. Ho Chi Minh, and the lady is his interpreter."

"Ho Chin Lu," corrects the writer, rising from his chair.

"Of course. For the next month we will be preparing a retrospective of Vietnamese films about love affairs between men from the North and women from the South, and vice versa, from the time of their endless wars."

"Interesting and also important."

"Amazing films, difficult and painful. What can you do, wars provide great film material."

"Damn wars," snaps Moses.

"Of course. But they must not be forgotten."

"No doubt," mutters Moses, and draws closer to the dubbers. "When you dubbed my films," he says to the group, "was there an Israeli here to advise you?"

"Your screenwriter."

"In other words —" says Moses, his heart pounding.

"Of course, Shaul Trigano. About a year ago he was here in the studio for quite a while. He explained a lot of things, acted them out, made us laugh. A sharp man. Very original."

"So Trigano was here?"

"It wasn't you who sent him, sir?"

"No, no . . . the idea was all his."

"A blessed idea . . . We were very taken by your early films . . . especially the one based on the Kafka story."

"*In Our Synagogue.*"

"Did Kafka really write this story about Jews in Israel?"

"About Jews in general."

He roams the floors and corridors until he finds the room Ruth was supposed to have locked herself into. Its door is open, and lights and voices welcome him. De Viola has brought the guests from Madrid, opened a bottle of red wine in their honor, and all of them, Ruth and Rodrigo included, are laughing, glasses in hand. Moses bows slightly to the mother, Doña Elvira, a beautiful actress, age ninety-four, who has come to grace the retrospective with her presence, joined by her younger son, Manuel, a tall Dominican monk, about forty-five years old, a golden cross dangling on his white robe.

"Welcome to our abode." He greets Moses in the classical Hebrew the Dominican order encourages its monks to study.

"What's this?" Moses addresses the mother. "Religion has conquered your family?"

"What can one do" — she sighs — "today, religion conquers all."

Juan laughs.

Wine is poured for Moses and he clinks glasses with everyone, takes a sip, and turns with a smile to the director of the archive. "They just told me in the lab that Trigano was here a year ago and that he helped with the dubbing. But if he is the hand behind my retrospective, why conceal it from me?"

"Because he asked us not to tell you."

"Why?"

"Because he knew you would not want to follow him here."

"Why wouldn't I?"

"You do know how much he hates you."

"Still?" Moses sighs heavily. He turns to Ruth, who averts her eyes.

"Still . . ." whispers the priest. "And believe me, my dear Moses, that we, who do not wish to be emotionally involved in your conflict, are nonetheless grieved by any strife between brothers."

four

IN OUR SYNAGOGUE

1

"In point of fact," Moses tells Juan de Viola in confidence, "when first I saw the list of my films you had selected, I suspected the ghost of Trigano behind this retrospective. But in the wake of our breakup, I've come to regard him as a failed artist, and it was hard to imagine that his faith in his early screenplays was so strong that he would go to an archive at the far edge of Spain to dub them in a foreign tongue."

"As a distant descendant of Jews exiled from Spain — that is how he put it," says Juan de Viola, "it was important to him to learn some Spanish and supervise his works in Spain."

"Faith in the immortality of one's art," continues Moses, "even if unfounded, is understandable, but is it possible that he convinced you to hold a retrospective to force me to come and defend his delusions?"

"No, Moses, the opposite is true," insists the director of the archive. "After we dubbed the films, including the one that disappeared from your official filmography, we asked Trigano if it was worth organizing a retrospective around them and inviting the director to reconnect with his old style."

"And what did he say?"

"I would rather not repeat what he said."

"I've put that loser way behind me, he can no longer upset me."

"Funny how you define each other in a similar way."

"Meaning what?"

"A failed artist," whispers Juan, "that's what he calls you. A director whose earliest achievements were not his own."

Moses' eyes narrow. He looks around to check if the scathing diagnosis was overheard in the room.

"A failed artist?" He laughs scornfully, resting his glass on a corner shelf. "That's how he defines a man who has made so many successful films after breaking off with him?"

"And what if he said it?" The priest hurries to soften the blow. "If he is worthless in your eyes, why take what he says seriously? We here, all of us, at the institute and the archive, refused to accept his opinion and were keen to mount this retrospective. The four films we have seen in the past two days confirm that we were not mistaken."

But Moses is overcome by gloom. He casts a baleful look at the sanctimonious little clergyman who has slandered him slyly yet again.

"Then why did you invite *me*? You could have done with his explanations of the films."

The director of the archive is quick to answer.

"The writer can explain the intention, but only the director can justify the result."

Moses takes his glass and refills it from the wine bottle on the desk. Silence has fallen in the room, as if to lay bare his humiliation. Doña Elvira, sitting on the sofa wrapped in Ruth's blanket, smiles brightly, and her younger son, the Dominican, sitting beside Ruth, gives Moses a supportive look.

With his glass filled to the brim Moses returns to the director of the archive and says pointedly: "I don't know of any film that was dropped from my filmography."

"The one we are about to see, *In Our Synagogue*."

"That film?"

"Here," says the priest, pulling from his pocket a familiar wrinkled page with Moses' picture. "It's not mentioned here, unless it's under a different name."

Moses straightens out a crease in his Internet biography.

"It's true, this film is missing for some reason, but why would its name be changed? It's based on a Kafka story of the same title. It was Kafka's aura that enabled us to let a small wild animal join in prayer."

"Join in prayer?"

"Be present at all times in the synagogue," Moses clarifies. "It's a film I am proud of in every way, and if it was dropped from my filmography, it's one more proof that the Internet is full of mistakes and nonsense."

"Exactly." The priest sighs. "But the public perceives it as an omniscient deity that demands our confessions. In any case, I'm pleased that you stand staunchly behind this film, because to be frank I was a bit wary and decided to show it by invitation only, to people for whom Kafka is a holy name."

"What were you afraid of?"

"Apart from the fact that I didn't find it in your filmography, I also didn't want to find Jews in the audience."

"There are Jews in Galicia?"

"You never can tell. There are crypto-Jews everywhere."

"And what if there were Jews in the audience?"

"They might be offended by the participation of such an animal in the worship of God. We don't need any protests."

"The animal is not a participant in anything," says Moses flatly. "It's a free and independent animal. A metaphysical animal."

"A metaphysical animal? Is there such a thing?"

"In any case, that's how I tried to portray it."

2

IT IS SUGGESTED to have dinner early, before the screening, lest the animal dampen the appetite, but in the end they stick to the original schedule. The length of the film is finite, but dinner can last indefinitely. Moreover, the elderly mother, weary from her flight, would prefer to see the film while she is still lucid.

The screening room is actually the archive's recording studio, with the control room included to provide extra space. The screen is small and made of fabric, which rustles slightly in the drafty room.

Juan de Viola introduces the invited guests by name and occupation, the first being the same elderly teacher and theoretician who had, an hour before, with courage and generosity, decorated *Slumbering Soldiers* with commentary that might transmute a film left for dead into a forgotten masterpiece. The rest are teachers at the institute, vaguely remembered from the previous day's luncheon, along with a few young people, advanced students. All told, Moses counts twenty strong, crowded around a one-time movie queen who has accomplished her life's work and now devotes her time to contemplating the works of others. Beside her sits her son the monk, avidly translating Ruth's words into modern Spanish for his mother, and the latter's words into ancient Hebrew for Ruth.

Juan asks Moses if he would like to say a few introductory words. Moses hesitates. Dinner is being prepared, and introductions, which invariably prompt reactions, would delay the meal and cause the cooks to burn the food. Better the movie should stand on its own — strange, inscrutable, provocative — and if it incurs opposition, the expert theoretician will again offer his interpretation. And yet the insult, "failed artist," pecks away at him, so he reconsiders, and although the lights have gone down he stands up and strides toward the screen. "Just a minute," he says, "perhaps it's worth saying a few words before the actual film obscures its good intentions. But there's no need to turn up the lights, I can talk about a film in the dark." And he invites the Dominican monk to translate his Hebrew into Spanish, so he can express himself more precisely and succinctly.

Manuel at his side, the screen behind him, he faces the silhouetted audience and the projector, its little red switch awaiting action.

And there is Moses defending not only himself, but also the screenwriter who borrowed a burning coal from a literary genius.

"We in Israel became aware of Kafka in the fifties, in Hebrew translations of his novels and stories. In those years of ideological intensity, there was something refreshing in his symbolic, surrealistic, absurdist works, which seemed disconnected from time and place and wrapped in the mystery of a writer who died young, in the stormy, chaotic years between the World Wars. After a while, Kafka's diaries and letters also began to appear in Hebrew, and we found detailed, intimate revelations about a secular Jew who grew up in a traditional home and whose complex identity was bathed in metaphysical yearning. But as opposed to those who interpret every line of his writings in light of his private life and sexual struggles and celebrate every Jewish detail exhumed from his biography, there were many readers, myself among them, for whom Kafka's cryptic, radiant works transcended the specifics of his personality and inhabited the realm of the universal.

"Trigano, my screenwriter, was drawn to Kafka as a student in high school, when I was his teacher of history and philosophy, and found him to be a steady source of ideas and inspiration. One day he discovered, perhaps in a French translation, a little-known story of Kafka's, one not yet translated into Hebrew. It was impossible to detach the story from Jewish identity or familiar experience, since the author, who often put clever animals into his stories — monkeys, dogs, mice, even a cockroach — this time, with ironical zeal, placed a small animal, a creature both calm and frightening, into a Jewish synagogue where the narrator himself is one of the worshippers; an animal whose silence, for once, adds new dimension to the riddle of Jewish existence, which is forever a threat unto itself. It is a strange story, unusual even within the corpus of this great writer. In this story he seems to relinquish his anonymity and deliver in first-person plural the testimony of a small Jewish community, in whose synagogue this old creature had lived for many years, an animal that carried inside it a rich Jewish historical memory and perhaps also the gift of prophecy.

"Here, ladies and gentlemen, is how the story begins. I still remember the opening by heart. 'In our synagogue lives an animal approximately the size of a mongoose. It can often be seen clearly. It allows people to come no closer than a distance of two meters away. Its color is a bright blue-green. No one has ever touched its coat, so nothing can be said about its fur.' What exactly drew my scriptwriter to this story, I don't know, but I was swept up in his enthusiasm. A small symbolic animal in a narrative film seemed like a worthy adventure for a young director who believed that Kafka's genius would protect him.

"Kafka's story, however, has no narrative line, only the description of a situation, of the relationship of the worshippers to the animal, a relationship that continues from generation to generation. For according to the story, the animal is older than the synagogue and has a secret hiding place inside it, but the noise of the prayers prompts it to dart out of hiding — not to interrupt, but out of anxiety. It knows the noisy prayers are not directed its way, but it remembers something from the past, or is perhaps afraid of the future. In any event, to broaden its angle of vision, it sometimes hangs from the copper curtain rod of the holy ark or, more often, grasps the lattice that separates the upper women's gallery from the men below and looks down. But unlike the men, who remain indifferent to it, the women worshippers are afraid of it, yet also attracted to it, and they even compete for its attention. Here we have another charming Kafkaesque paradox."

Moses stops, hesitates, wonders how and why he got carried away by the details of a story that grows sharper in his memory. In the darkness he can make out the sparkle of his listeners' eyes, but he has no way of judging their attention, so he poses a question to Juan.

"Can I go on? Do we have time?"

"There's time, Moses, of course" comes the loud reply. "This is an educational institution, not a movie theater."

"In that case," the director continues, "to adapt a short and static story into a full-length film we had to do two things. First, create a plot with conflict and crisis; and second, choose an animal, one we could manipulate. The story supplies few details about the animal, apart from its remarkable longevity, its size like a mongoose's, and its color, which might be natural or possibly a product of the dust and plaster of the synagogue. And since we could not produce a Kafkaesque animal, we naturally enough decided on an actual mongoose, though not an elderly one, hoping it could be trained. We painted its fur, as you shall see, the color of the synagogue wall, in keeping with the story, but added a few thin gold stripes as a mythological touch. For the benefit of the Israeli audience, we had to transplant the synagogue from the sad, fading Diaspora, unaware of the looming European catastrophe, to the new Jewish state, repository of Jewish hopes."

Manuel translates rapidly, with great enthusiasm, apparently enjoying the opportunity to show off the Hebrew he learned in the order. Moses is so swept up in his introduction that it seems there will be no time left to show the film.

"To construct a plot, you have to choose a protagonist. Of course, it was possible to put the beadle of the synagogue at the center of the film, because it is he, more than anyone else, who maintains regular contact with the animal, especially at night when the animal is active and the synagogue is empty. But to render the story more meaningful, we preferred to make the rabbi the main character. We imagined a rabbi who had arrived in Israel with his flock from a distant Muslim land and established a synagogue where they could combine the old and the new. Then it turns out that a little animal, old and stubborn, had got there first, and its hideout is so ingenious that only if they destroy the building and put up a new one can they get rid of it. This, in short, is the issue: Do they destroy the synagogue, which was created with great effort and whose congregation may have scattered by the time it is rebuilt, or do they try to discover, in the sad, absurdist spirit of Kafka, some sort of coexistence between the worshippers and the animal? This is the heart of the matter, and I think I've already run on too long."

He tries to disappear into the audience before the translation is over, but the hoarse voice of the theoretician stops him, adding a detail that perhaps escaped the filmmakers and that Kafka himself was probably unaware of. In ancient Egypt, the mongoose was considered a noble and holy animal, perhaps owing to its ability to trap and kill poisonous snakes. It was therefore entitled to be embalmed along with the Pharaonic families.

Moses is delighted. "Thank you, thank you. We didn't know about ancient Egypt, and perhaps Kafka didn't either. In any case, the historical dimension you have added to the animal can only deepen the understanding of our complex film." And he motions to the projectionist to start the screening.

3

MOSES TRIES IN vain to recall the name, or at least the provenance, of the actor who played the rabbi in the film. He doesn't appear in the credits because he had refused to have his name listed; during production, the animal was filmed separately and inserted in the editing room, and when the actor saw the final picture, with the full dialogue between him and the animal — whose role in the film transcended comedy and was anything but marginal — he complained that the animal had insulted him and demanded that his name be removed.

By contrast, Moses well remembers the origin of the animal and even the lovely name given it by the soundman: Susana. One of Amsalem's porters stalked her for a few days in the desert near Beersheba, trapped her, and brought her to the set. She was a large mongoose with a long hairy tail and proved to be timid, as in Kafka's story, though at this moment, as she fills the screen and looks out with big red eyes, flashing her thin, sharp teeth, she makes a terrifying impression. To accustom her to the camera and to learn her habits, the director and cinematographer would visit her cage, feed her, talk to her gently, and play with her. They filmed her mainly at night. The porter, who became her trainer, would attach to her neck a transparent plastic leash, invisible on film, and tug it carefully, so her moves would seem natural and willful, to lead her from the holy ark to the grille of the women's gallery and back. A few days later, in the editing room, they would include her among the faithful at prayer, generally filmed in daylight.

But who played the rabbi? Moses can clearly see him in his mind's eye even before he appears on the screen. A middle-aged man, tall and thin, in a black suit and hat, his dark eyes blazing. Might Ruth remember who he was? Was he just some amateur who happened to be around or a real actor?

Trigano, in his loyalty to the neglected south of Israel, originally situated the synagogue in one of the forlorn immigrant towns, but Moses was sick of the arid landscape and insisted on moving the synagogue to the seashore, near the home of the cinematographer. A dry, simple story needs to be irrigated with images of water, and the sea looks wonderful on camera at all hours of the day.

The first part of the film is preparation for Kafka's parable. Members of the community are scattered among various synagogues but are nostalgic for the ritual flavor of their birthplace near the distant Sahara. And so they decide to establish a synagogue of their own. Lacking money and permits, they take over an abandoned building not far from the sea and pirate their electricity and water from a nearby nursery school. One day, a group of the men goes for evening prayers to the big synagogue in Tel Aviv, and at the end of the service, they steal from the ark two small Torah scrolls, then mask their identity by removing the red velvet Ashkenazic Torah covers and putting the scrolls into the round wooden cases typical of Sephardic communities. Only then do they send a delegation to a laborer planting trees by the roadside, their former rabbi, and implore him to serve again as their rabbi and cantor.

And as the rabbi makes his entrance, so too does Kafka's creature. On the very first Sabbath, the longtime resident of the building shows up during prayer. The animal's agility conceals her cowardice, and the congregants are cowed by her fearsome appearance. They can't turn to the municipal authorities to provide professional animal trappers, lest it be found out that the synagogue is hooked up illegally to the electricity and water of the nursery school. So the worshippers, young and old, decide to deal with the animal themselves.

Here the screenwriter dipped his pen into Kafka's story and added conflict and confrontation. In one camp are devout worshippers who demand the place be forcefully purged from the unclean beast, and in the other are the moderates, led by the rabbi, who wish to establish coexistence with the animal, in the spirit of Kafka. The film overflows with speechmaking and yelling, whose details Moses can't remember and doesn't try. He remains fixed on the rabbi, hoping to find a clue that will help him retrieve the actor's name. Given his age then, he is probably no longer alive, but, dead or alive, the man has captivated Moses, and he tries to locate him in his memory. The actor dazzles him not merely with the excellence of his acting, but also with his delicate, fragile physicality. His face is dark and gentle, and his big black eyes shine with wisdom. For a moment he looks familiar. It seems the author from Prague, Kafka himself, has leaped out of his short story and turned into the rabbi of the film. *How could I have let go of such a true actor?* Moses despairs. *I could have cast him in many complex roles in my later films.*

4

HE GETS OUT of his seat and ducks down, dodging the beam of the projector as he makes his way in the dark to Ruth, then steers her away from the hall. "Who is the rabbi? I mean, who is the actor?" he pleads. "What was his name? How did we find him?" Although she too is impressed by the actor, whose performance invests grotesqueness with true spirituality, she cannot identify him either. "Did Trigano bring him to us?" "No," she says. "If Trigano had brought him, I'd remember."

"What about Toledano?"

"Toledano?" She fondly speaks the late cameraman's name. "Maybe . . . because he would sometimes find you actors who were naturally gifted. But you can ask him only if you run into him in the afterlife."

"Afterlife," he says. "That's a new one for you."

She hesitates a moment, then breaks free and returns to the screening. But Moses doesn't hurry back in. He walks around, looks at his watch. Tries and fails to open the door leading to the parade ground. Attempts in vain to hear the roar of the nearby ocean. Finally, lest he be accused of deserting his own work, he returns to the studio but remains standing by the rear entrance, monitoring the audience's attention from behind.

The foes of the animal have invited to evening prayers an irate ultra-Orthodox Jew, who is frightened as the creature stares at him from atop the holy ark. He demands that the synagogue be purified of the abomination and consecrated again, threatening the congregants with excommunication if his ruling is not heeded. It's easy enough to invoke religious law, but as a practical matter, it is impossible to expel the animal without killing her or destroying the synagogue, and the rabbi, who during the week continues to work as a laborer, refuses to harm her. At night, secretly and alone, he tries to discover her hiding place and to persuade her gently to leave his synagogue.

Thus begin nightly conversations between the rabbi and the mongoose, the rabbi talking and the animal responding with her eyes. He leans toward her now, falling onto his knees to beseech her, trying to cajole the animal to leave the synagogue and go into the big natural world that awaits outside. Actually, he speaks only to the camera, and his hand reaching to touch her fur is stroking the empty air, while the animal listening to him speak is not a free being capable of escape but a creature held in place by the invisible plastic leash, attentive to the lens of the camera that evokes from her big, sparkling eyes the elegant sadness of one who understands the rabbi's request to leave his synagogue but who cannot allow herself to abandon the Jews to their fate.

Moses, standing in the rear, cannot see the faces of the audience. Two or three have left, and two others are whispering. There are also a few nodding heads, perhaps dozing, but the heads of the de Viola family, the old lady and her two sons, remain upright as, toward the end, the film gathers momentum.

The congregants, despite their love for the rabbi, abandon the synagogue, one by one. Someone takes the stolen Torah scrolls, another dismantles the holy ark, still another disconnects the electricity and water, and they all go in search of a new place of worship.

The building gradually reverts to a ruin, and the camera captures the waves licking its foundations. From time to time a few hikers visit the site. A pair of lovers spends a night there. The rabbi, still working with a hoe, no longer plants trees by the roadside but has been sent to dig wells in the hills. Toledano's camera has apparently broken free now of both writer and director, following the rabbi who has lost his congregation as if his character holds the key to Kafka's riddle. The film ends with a moment of rest for the laboring rabbi. He sits down among the rocks to eat his meager meal and watches as a large mongoose battles a snake. Thus hope is born from a strange, dark, and absurdist film, which Kafka could have barely imagined.

5

THE LIGHTS GO back on but are dimmer than before the screening, as if to allow people to make a getaway without revealing their reactions. But Moses is not interested in reactions. Yes, this is an immature film that was imposed on him, and it's just as well that it was dropped from his filmography.

He stands in the corridor waiting for the mother and her two sons and Ruth, who is with them. The theoretician walks by and shakes his hand firmly. *If he happens to be a member of the prize commit-*

tee, Moses thinks, *I'll be going back to Israel empty-handed.* Manuel fondly grasps the director and says in Hebrew: "May your hands be strong, you have done a great thing — you have forced Kafka to be optimistic." Juan reinforces his brother's words with a nod and invites his guests to sit awhile in his room before dinner, the final item on today's agenda.

But Moses doesn't want a dinner where conversation will inevitably make its way to the film just screened. "No," he says apologetically, "attending a retrospective is harder for me than making a film, because I've lost control. If you want me clear-headed at tomorrow morning's ceremony, please liberate me from this last supper and enjoy the company of my companion. With the aid of such an accomplished translator she will surely be able to explain anything that needs explaining."

They readily agree to his request and quickly arrange his transportation, which makes him suspicious. By ten o'clock he has arrived at the Parador, where he is surprised to find the lobby empty save for three guests, whose boisterous laughter suggests their intoxication. He suddenly realizes that his fear of negative criticism has condemned him to go to bed hungry, and tomorrow's generous breakfast will not compensate for the splendid farewell dinner planned by the priest and his staff. He asks the reception clerk, a pretty young woman, if food might be available at this hour, which is after all not terribly late. She is sorry, the dining hall is closed, the cooks have gone home. But she herself could prepare for him something light.

"Cold and simple food will satisfy me, señorita."

She leaves behind the math textbook that she had been immersed in. Before long she brings to his room a bottle of wine and a loaf of black bread with a large hunk of goat cheese. Moses sits in front of *Caritas Romana*, lustily chewing fresh bread and cheese, whose pungency he offsets with slugs of wine straight from the bottle. He removes his shoes but not his clothes before getting into bed.

He glances at his watch; it's past midnight and Ruth has not returned. There is of course nothing to worry about, she is under the aegis of two men of the cloth, but he keeps his clothes on, so if his presence is needed he can be prompt and presentable. He switches off the bedside light and turns over, like turning a page, in hopes that all his worries will vanish. But the new page in the book of sleep is more unsettling than the last one. For when he next opens his eyes he is startled to find the room lights dim, and himself naked under the blanket. By his side lies Ruth, quiet and content, leafing through the menu of the closing dinner.

"Tell me," she says to the man awakening beside her, "what scared you so much about the film that you passed up a great meal?"

He pulls the blanket closer. He feels his head is glued to the pillow.

"The truth? This time I was afraid of real anger."

"Anger over such an old film?"

"All of them are my children" – the director sighs – "even the weak and the pathetic ones. Kafka wrote a story about that, in the first person, called 'Eleven Sons,' and the most miserable son is the one he loves best, though he would not want to entrust his life to him. Indeed, Kafka felt most of his works were flawed, but he did not destroy them and instead deposited them with a friend, asking him to burn them after he died. But the friend refused, and rightly so. If Kafka truly wanted to burn his works, he would have done so himself."

"But why did you think it would arouse anger? You know, the old man, the theoretician, gave his own little interpretation."

"Good or bad?"

"An interpretation I didn't understand. Any interpretation is good, no?"

"What else happened at the dinner? Why was it so long?"

"Spaniards are night people. They don't get up at seven in the morning to listen to the news."

Moses laughs. "And the food? It really was special?"

"A fabulous meal. Heavenly. What you missed tonight you'll never have a chance to eat again."

"And they talked about me?"

"Because you could do without them, they did without you. The cultural attaché from the Israeli embassy phoned from Madrid to apologize for not coming to tomorrow's prize ceremony."

"So there'll still be a prize?"

"If that's what they promised you."

"Maybe, between a fabulous course and a heavenly course, you remembered who played the rabbi?"

"I tried, but I couldn't remember. I also can't figure out how we lost track of such a compelling actor."

"Maybe he'll surprise us in the last movie tomorrow."

"No, he won't be in tomorrow's movie. That one I remember in every detail and will never forget."

"Meaning what?"

"Juan told me which film was picked for the screening before the ceremony. Believe it or not, it's *The Refusal.*"

"*The Refusal?* Interesting."

"And this time they kept the original name."

"Trigano wouldn't give up on this one, would he?"

"Even though you gave it a different ending . . ."

"Only for your sake . . ."

"*Partly* for my sake."

She turns off the remaining light.

In the darkness he feels the blanket on his nakedness, and presses on.

"Who took my clothes off?"

"You did. You took them off before I ever got back, but apparently you were woozy and lay here naked, with no blanket. I had to move you over and cover you. But that went smoothly. When you're asleep, you're a darling, easy to control."

6

FROM THE DEEP well of time floats the face of a young schoolgirl, shaking him from slumber. The question of why she, the girl from north Tel Aviv, of all the characters in tomorrow's film, is the first to burst into his memory will not let him rest, urging him out of bed. It's four in the morning; the winter dawn is slow to arrive, yet he succumbs to his waking state. Stark naked, but trustworthy and careful, he checks on his companion, who is sleeping peacefully, then gathers up his clothing, gets dressed, puts on his coat, and pockets his passport and some paper money, but he leaves his hearing aids and wallet on the night table. Taking with him the pilgrim walking stick, he slips silently from the room.

"If my metaphysics tire you and hurt your pocketbook," Trigano told him after even the little art house in north Tel Aviv refused to show *In Our Synagogue*, "and you think our collaboration could use something more emotional and popular, the next screenplay will be about the travails of a young woman, and to give it an epic dimension we'll start with her childhood. But to do that we need to find a girl who looks like her."

Moses decides to take the stairs down, because if anything should go wrong with the elevator, who would come rescue him in the middle of the night? The stairwell is unlit at this hour, but the stairs are comfortably carpeted, and on the walls curving around them hang pictures, unintelligible in the darkness.

In the hotel lobby, two people doze in a corner in sleeping bags. Strange. Are they young backpackers who arrived late at night, discovered that the room they reserved was given to someone else, and were granted permission to sack out here and wait till morning? The cubbyholes behind the front desk are all empty of keys. The young woman who had brought the wine and cheese to his room is still on duty, and her face, fetching earlier that night, is now ever more radiant and unique. *If I were called upon to direct a movie in Spain,* thinks Moses, *I would come back here and get the inexperienced reception clerk to play a small part in my film, maybe the part of a reception clerk. Even if her appearance in the film totaled just a few seconds, her beauty would be preserved in the archive for generations.* He feels an urge to introduce himself to her as a film director and tell her that she may be unaware of her own beauty, but he resists. At that hour, such a compliment from a stranger could be construed by a young woman as harassment. Besides, could she believe that the old man standing before her is still active as an artist, planning for the future?

"I see you haven't made much progress tonight in your math," he ventures, indicating the equations in the open book.

"Chemistry." She sighs with a winning smile and a pair of dimples.

"Chemistry?" He sighs back sympathetically.

"And you, Señor Moses, are hungry again."

"No, not at all." He can still taste the goat cheese. Neither does he crave the hotel's Internet access, but he does have a yen to walk around and would like to know if the city is safe at night for a foreigner, who to be cautious has left his wallet behind, taking only his passport.

"Best to leave the passport with me," advises the desk clerk, "and take instead the business card of the hotel. Also leave the walking stick and take an umbrella, because it's cold and rainy outside. But the city is holy at night too, and if you get lost, the cathedral will always lead you back to the hotel."

Beside the cubbyholes hangs a colorful woolen scarf, long and thick, and he asks with atypical audacity if it belongs to her or was left behind by a guest.

"Both."

"Meaning?"

"Somebody forgot it, and I use it on cold days."

"If it's a scarf without a permanent owner, perhaps I could use it to keep warm in the cold?"

She hesitates. She is probably aware of her own allure and senses that the elderly guest with the little beard and stubbly cheeks would like the feel of her, but she takes down the scarf anyway and hands it to him. "And if I'm not here when you get back," she says, "leave it for me," and she writes her name for him on a slip of paper.

Unabashedly, as if the desk clerk has turned into a character in a movie now filming in Spain, he takes the scarf — which on closer inspection is a bit tattered – wraps it around his neck, and inhales its scent. He walks out of the hotel and likes how the damp milky fog shifts the shape of the plaza and hides the palaces, makes the cathedral appear to be floating. Recalling that the alleys of the Old Town lead to the promenade and the paved garden nearby, he steps up his pace and strides confidently to his destination.

In recent years, Yair Moses has been on friendly terms with death, which sometimes talks back, either in muffled tones or a shriek, and on the strength of this friendship he is not afraid to wander alone in remote places, even in a foreign country. Now too he is undaunted by the echo of his lonely footsteps. The Old Town is quietly sleeping, its plazas desolate save for a single shop with the lights on, where a large woman with wild hair arranges souvenirs on the shelves. For a moment, he wants to stray from his path and go in, but the gentle patter of rain on his umbrella is too pleasant to interrupt. And the moon, which on the first midnight had welcomed them with its glow, lingers beyond the clouds and fog as a faint patch of whiteness, perhaps to be unveiled before the dawning of day.

7

THE OLD TOWN of Santiago is not as large or confusing as the Old City of Jerusalem, nor is it surrounded by walls, so the Israeli navigates it with ease, crossing a bridge over a gully and arriving at the promenade he had visited the day before with the young instructor. He has not come for a night view of the distant cathedral from this angle but rather to have another look at the sculptures that the art college students had installed in the park. First he examines the two angry middle-aged Marys holding on to each other, their spindly legs bolted to the ground. Now, with nobody else around, he knocks on them to ascertain what they are made of. Bejerano had interpreted this sculpture as a secular challenge to the marble sculptures of the cathedral and thus decided they were made of plastic. But now, as Moses drums his fingers on the coats and smooth faces of the two women, he can feel a sturdy material, some alloy more durable than the young man had suggested. Serious women such as these two would not stand a chance in a public park, exposed to wind and rain and mischievous children, if they were made of simple plastic.

He moves on, heading for the skinny intellectual sitting on a park bench to find if he's made of the same stuff as the women. But from a distance it would appear he has acquired a friend, as if in the past day a new sculpture was installed beside him.

Moses slows his gait, his heart pounding, but the silhouette has heard his approach and stands tall – a heavyset homeless man, wrapped in a sheepskin cape, who emits a growl or a curse and vanishes into the darkness.

Just like the movies. The director grins and takes the freshly vacated seat beside the bareheaded, cross-legged intellectual who peers at the world with boundless curiosity. Moses gingerly runs his hand along the stiff scarf that covers the man's neck – or is it a long frozen beard? – feels his close-cropped head, and tries to remove his big round eyeglasses, but they are welded to his ears. There is no doubt, he confirms, those art college students cooked up serious material. Secular characters meant to challenge saints carved in stone require a solid foundation.

The rain has stopped, but the breaking dawn sharpens the cold. He wraps the tattered woolen scarf tight around his neck and closes his eyes, again reaching out to the girl who unsettled his sleep. He suddenly worries that he may not see her tomorrow, that she ended up on the cutting-room floor. It's hard to be certain.

Toledano, who had known Ruth since kindergarten, considered himself best qualified to find an actress who could play her as a child. He scouted a few drama clubs at community centers and found the candidate in an upscale neighborhood of Tel Aviv. He managed to convince her father, a high-ranking army officer and war hero, to permit his young daughter to appear in a few scenes in the film, whose content was still mostly unknown even to the cameraman himself.

Despite the very different background of the young girl, she bore an uncanny resemblance to Ruth, not only in her facial features and expressive eyes but in her dark skin tone and the timbre of her voice.

Trigano's cerebral screenplays had not previously called for children, and Moses wondered if he'd be able to direct an inexperienced girl playing a difficult part, but Ruth, excited by the cinematographer's choice, took the girl under her wing and promised to coach her.

He insists on not waiting till he sees the film to find out whether the girl beating on the doors of his memory, the forerunner of the film's heroine, has remained in the final cut. He demands that his memory supply him an answer right away. That innocent girl would come to the filming chaperoned by her father, who worried that something edgy might be required of his daughter. It wasn't simple to direct a young, unseasoned amateur under the watchful eyes of her father in brief scenes intended to give clear signals of a relationship with her teacher that was somewhere between love and enslavement. Ruth kept her promise and did her share. She helped to choose articles of clothing that were right for the girl's character, and she showed her how to ignore the camera as well as her father's steely gaze, which disconcerted the cast and crew.

The Refusal was relatively well received by audiences and was even able to recoup a respectable fraction of its cost, but the fight that broke out during the shooting of the final scene, and the subsequent breakup with Trigano, distanced the film from the heart of its creator, and after it had made the rounds of theaters he was quick to deposit it in the Jerusalem film archive, in the knowledge he could always see it again. But years went by and he never did, and now his screenwriter had gone back to the film and brought it to the Spanish archive so they could transfer it to digital format and dub it in a foreign tongue.

With no warning, the moon is freed from the last tuft of a stubborn cloud, and the skies are bathed in lunar brilliance that reveals secrets of the night. Moses can see now that the homeless man who relinquished his seat is not far away, leaning his head on the shoulder of the Mary with the outstretched hand, waiting for the director to abandon his post beside the intellectual.

The two exchange sharp glances and Moses realizes that he read the fellow wrong. The tall, athletic man with a beard and bushy eyebrows, who wishes to retrace his steps and reclaim the bench, is not a homeless vagabond or beggar but a lone pilgrim who arrived not as part of a group but on his own. By the looks of the cape, the unruly beard, the woolen leggings, and the knapsack, he is a true believer who chose to come to Santiago on foot, on a long and difficult path. But Moses, who sometimes talks with death, is not afraid of a man holding a large, thick staff with a huge clam shell affixed to the top — an authentic staff, not the kind for sale in souvenir shops. *If he wants to harm me,* he says to himself with a smile, *maybe I deserve it,* and he stands up and gestures graciously at the place no longer occupied. And if he were invited to make a movie in Spain, he would include, regardless of the plot, a pilgrim like this to walk around in silence before the camera.

8

DURING HIS NOCTURNAL outing, there's been a change of personnel at the front desk, and he returns the scarf not to the young chemist but to a stern middle-aged clerk, who hangs it on its hook and discreetly points to a man sitting by the closed dining room door, leafing through a newspaper. Moses recognizes the teacher of cinematic theory, embalmed in his black suit. Apparently he has agreed, or perhaps requested, to serve as the escort of the Israeli director on the last day of the retrospective. But Moses decides to postpone his encounter and slips back to the attic.

He takes off his shoes in the dark, quietly, so his footsteps will not wake the sleeper, and, remembering that the closet door squeaks, he drops his coat on the floor. But the eyes that opened as he entered do not close.

"You're awake?"

"More or less."

"Since when?"

"Since the time you left."

"But I was careful."

"I'm not awake because of you."

"Really? Why not worry over me?"

"You don't need worrying over. Anyway, where were you?"

"I walked around a little, to get away from this place. Past the Old Town there's a promenade and sculpture garden of clever local characters. Rodrigo showed it to me yesterday, and tonight I had the urge to feel them so I could tell what they were made of."

He sits down on the bed, and cautiously, in the darkness, reaches for her hand. He counts her fingers one by one as if to be sure none is missing.

"If I didn't ruin your sleep, what did?"

"Thoughts."

"For example?"

"For example, the film today. *The Refusal.*"

"You too? Funny, because ever since you said it would be closing the retrospective, I've been trying to remember what we did there. Do you remember it well?"

"Yes. It's the first film that centered on me alone from beginning to end."

"Even before the beginning, from preadolescence, from the childhood of the main character."

"Childhood?"

"Childhood, girlhood. The young amateur we brought in who played you as a grade-school student. For some reason I couldn't stop thinking about her tonight. I'm curious to see how I created your precursor."

"You won't see a thing."

"Why?"

"Because you cut all of her scenes from the final film."

"Oy," cries Moses in sorrow, "she was cut in the end?"

"You claimed at the time that the film turned out too long, and the producer was demanding cuts, so without asking or notifying anyone you took out all the early scenes in elementary school and began with my graduation ceremony."

"Your graduation?"

"I mean the heroine's."

Moses feels a need for self-defense. "I wouldn't have cut it shorter just for the producer. There was surely some other reason, which I don't recall at the moment. Trigano was sharp and clever with dramatic stories told in a limited time frame but was less convincing when it came to giving a character a strong background, like inventing a childhood for you that would add depth to what happened to you later."

"To me?"

"I mean the heroine. But that girl, who in the end wasn't in the movie, keeps me up at night like a ghost. What was it about her that I want so much to see? Was she especially attractive? Did she really look like you?"

"Toledano, who discovered her, thought she looked like me as a schoolgirl, and there were people in the crew who saw a resemblance, but for me it was hard to see, which is natural. But she really was an impressive girl, smart and ambitious, and I invested a lot in her. In any case, you never had the patience to work with little kids or teenagers. There's also something about you that seems to scare them."

Moses is amused. "What about me could be scary?"

"When you are next to the camera, fixated on your goal, you're not aware how alienated and hostile you become toward anything unconnected to the film. Although toward that girl, as I remember, you were a little more patient, maybe because her father the colonel was always at the rehearsals and shooting. That's why you didn't dare yell at her. Or maybe because you also thought she looked like me.

Or because back then, every so often, you were a little in love with me."

"I'm always in love with you. Sometimes a little, and sometimes more. But what was her name?"

"Ruth."

"Ruth?"

"It was because of her that I added her name to my old one."

"Because of her? Why? You never said you changed your name because of her."

"I intended just to add it, but her name, the new one, swallowed up the old one."

"Why because of her?"

"Because I was happy that a real Israeli like her, from a good, established family, was picked to represent the childhood of the heroine who gets into such trouble. Therefore, after you dropped her from my film, I decided to compensate her by adopting her name."

"Compensate her for what?"

"For the fact that until the film's premiere, she didn't know she wasn't in it. And that you didn't see fit to inform her, and I didn't know."

"You didn't know because you never, in any film, wanted to get near the editing room and always waited to see yourself in the finished film."

"Because it was hard to watch how you and the editors would cut us up, destroy our continuity, then paste us back together. And therefore, at the premiere, as I recall, not only she but I was astonished to see that you had dropped all the scenes of my youth."

"Again yours. Not yours. The heroine's."

"No, mine too. Because I liked it that you chose such a perfect girl to portray me in my childhood."

"What do you mean, perfect?"

"Perfect. Rooted. A real Israeli. Salt of the earth. Well connected. Because in those days I thought . . . and now too, really . . . I know that we — Trigano, Toledano, the lot of us — would always somehow stay a bit in the margins, so I was happy that you gave me a little sister, so to speak, a twin who could strengthen me."

"Again you?"

"Me in the film."

"What is this, the movie gets mixed up with reality for you?"

"Sometimes. And not for you?"

"Never. The boundary between reality and imagination is always there for me."

"Because you never dare to stand in front of a camera, only behind it, because only from there can you be the one giving the orders."

9

THE ROOM IS still dark and neither one can clearly see the face of the other. He holds her hand, separating her fingers one by one and pressing them together again, filled with desire for the actress whose childhood memories make her voice tremble.

"She, the little Ruth, came to the premiere excited, and confident too; we all praised her acting during the filming. And you didn't even bother to inform Amsalem that you had cut her out, and he sent her numerous invitations to fill up the theater. She arrived happy, surrounded by her family and girlfriends. At first I thought you'd changed the sequence and would go from present to past in flashbacks, but the film went on and on, and no trace of her. You simply erased her. And now you have the gall to say that you can't recall if she's in the movie or not?"

"I honestly didn't remember. I honestly hoped to see her."

"You won't. You wiped her out. That's why she comes back at you like a ghost. To take revenge."

"Revenge for what?"

"Until the last minute she waited to see herself. And when the film was over and the lights came up and the congratulations began, I saw her sitting frozen in her seat, her father consoling her. But when I came over she was crying bitterly – she wanted to be an actress, she wanted to play my childhood me, she felt she'd played her part well, and now it was all lost. And though I had no idea how to explain to her what happened or why, she took it all out on me, as if I were complicit in eliminating her from the film. Her heart was broken, and mine broke along with hers."

"You're breaking hearts left and right, but after all is said and done, what happened? This wasn't the first or last time that more than a third of the material was cut in the editing process."

"Not so simple. I held her deep inside me while we worked on that film, and despite Trigano's difficult script I led myself to believe that I was a natural extension of her, not of the girl in the movie, of the real girl I knew. I knew her family too, and I was even in their home a few times. You should know that when it came to that crazy scene with the beggar – it was because of her that I ran away."

"Because of her?"

"And I didn't even know that you intended to cut her from the film."

"I didn't know either. But where's the connection? Why her?"

"Because if she is me when I was young, and I am her as an adult, if she saw me on the screen in that sick scene Trigano scripted – and you standing there, demanding that I expose my breast and force a filthy old beggar to suck milk meant for the baby taken away from me – if she were to see that onscreen . . . As I faced that scene, I thought of her, the young actress, this pure and intelligent girl, and I thought how shocked and disappointed she would be, she and her whole family, when she saw this repulsive scene, and she might say to herself, Why did I get involved with this film in the first place? What possible connection could I have with such a disturbed woman?"

Moses speaks softly, as to a person who is ill: "What are you talking about? About characters in a film or about human beings?"

"Both."

"Both? How does one mix the two up?"

"One does, if one lives the right way."

"So in order to protect the ego of a spoiled, ambitious child from a good family, you ran away from the camera and killed our entire scene? And I even defended you. Maybe dropping that girl from the film was a good thing," he says and regrets it immediately, considers how to soothe her, when the room phone rings. The reception clerk timidly informs Moses that the professor from the film institute is awaiting his presence in the lobby. "It's okay, I'm awake," Moses assures him, "I'll be down soon."

But instead of going down, he undresses, gets under the warm covers, tightly holds on to the real character, and kisses her as if asking for forgiveness and absolution. But as Ruth, surprised, yields in his arms, the phone rings again, the reception clerk announcing that the professor is now awaiting him in dining room.

"Damn," grumbles Moses, trying to tighten his embrace, but Ruth pushes him away gently and says, "Go. I didn't understand a word of what he said at dinner, but I felt he was making an effort. Don't disappoint him."

"And what will I understand? He speaks only Spanish."

"Sometimes it's better for an artist not to understand the interpretation of his art."

10

THE DINING ROOM is still empty of guests, and Moses spots the theoretician right away. The man in his black suit sits at a table near a window slightly ajar, with only a carafe of coffee before him. Moses walks over briskly, apologizes for his tardiness, hoping to receive in return a simple "Good morning" in English.

But at this breakfast there is to be no English. So, thinks Moses, *if another monologue in Spanish is in store, I may finally be able to eat a full meal in peace.*

The Spaniard escorts his guest to the buffet, and the meal is full indeed. The theoretician of cinema recommends traditional dishes of the region of Galicia, apparently providing details of origin and history. Moses, as someone who attaches aesthetic importance to food in his films, dares to broaden his palate, filling his plate with foods that in the past repulsed him.

So starts the breakfast. Two waitresses attend the two guests, one talking and the other one eating. The theoretician consumes nothing but black coffee, and when Moses raises an eyebrow to ask why, the theoretician sighs and interpolates bits of his medical history in his interpretation of film.

Now, with the teacher sitting across the table and not in an audience, Moses can get a good look at him. Don Gomez is actually his junior, but his hair is sparse, and the redness of his eyes suggests a chronic malady or sleepless nights. His black suit is shiny from use, and threads dangle from his jacket in place of two missing buttons, suggesting the absence of a spouse or close friend to look after him. Ink stains on the fingers of his right hand indicate an intellectual who is still fearful of computers. If he were asked to make a film in Spain, Moses would invite not only the reception clerk and the pilgrim to go before the camera but also this man, to talk for thirty seconds about anything he wanted. He appears to have considerable acting talent, able as he is to carry on in a resonant voice to a man who doesn't understand his language. And when Moses hears the names Kafka and Trigano repeated again and again and sees the Spaniard sketching in the air with his little hands the *animal* and *sinagoga* and talking about *servicio militar* and the *desierto*, and from there to the *tren* and *accidente*, it is clear that this scholar has delved deeply into his early works and is attempting a grand synthesis of them all. Guests now entering the dining room acknowledge with a curious smile the teacher's histrionic performance. With great appreciation Moses sees Ruth entering. This means she had not sought to be rid of him when she shoved him out of bed, for here she is now, giving up her lazy morning to join in and help him endure the unintelligible.

Before she sits down with them she helps herself to a little bowl of dry cereal and pours in some milk.

11

AT ELEVEN O'CLOCK a student from the film institute arrives at the Parador and escorts the two guests to the municipal auditorium, for there, and not at the institute, will be held the screening of the last film in the retrospective of the early work of the Israeli director, for which he will be awarded a prize. Is the prize only for that film? Is it a consolation prize, Moses wonders, or an award of merit? Or a prize to encourage new projects? He is taken with the grandeur of the municipal auditorium, full of fine paintings and sculptures representing generations of connoisseurship. The screen, made of a sheer grayish fabric, hangs at the rear of the stage, failing to conceal adequately the colorful fresco behind it.

The invited guests, about a hundred in number, are a varied lot. Alongside a few dignitaries in dark suits sit teachers and students from the institute, and behind them elderly men and women from a local old-age home, some holding canes; the back rows are filled with municipal workers, clerks and secretaries and traffic inspectors, and Moses believes he recognizes a few of the whistling and pot-banging sanitation workers.

"You have certainly gathered a diverse crowd," Moses says to Juan, who is quick to separate the two Israelis. He suggests that Ruth sit beside his mother, in the second row, and directs Moses to the front row, next to the mayor, who nods a friendly hello.

"Yes, for such ceremonies one must fill the hall," Juan says apologetically. "The value of the prize is diminished if the applause is feeble."

"Believe me, my dear Juan, the prize is important to me even if its value is merely symbolic."

"But this prize is not symbolic, it's real," protests the priest, "even if it is awarded for films that are symbolic. Did the cultural attaché of your country not inform you? This is a prize of three thousand euros, and had my mother not been enlisted to contribute, the municipality, which suffers a continuous deficit, would have been hard-pressed to provide the sum."

Moses turns red in the face. "Very generous of you, and moving. But I wonder if this is an award for merit, a consolation prize, or an award to encourage new projects."

"Anything is possible," says the priest. "When my mother gives you the envelope, she will explain the intention of the prize. She has told me nothing about what she plans to say."

A light goes on in front of the screen, and Don Gomez Alfonso da Silva, small and grave, takes the stage.

"This is a serious man," whispers Moses, "and though I don't understand what he says, I feel he speaks of me with generosity and appreciation."

"With generosity, and also with anxiety about the continuation of your work. Last night he watched your film by himself and got so deeply involved, he woke me up and asked to be allowed a few words before the screening."

"Meaning I don't need to give an introduction?"

"We'd be glad if you didn't, because we don't want to wear out an audience that is mainly not professional with too much intellectual talk."

"Fine with me," manages Moses, embarrassed.

"But in your words of thanks you can explain yourself at length in your mother tongue; my brother Manuel has volunteered to translate."

"It would please me to speak in Hebrew. Anyway, what is your theoretician saying now?"

"He sees *The Refusal* as a transitional film in which the director relinquishes radical symbolism in favor of popular psychology."

"Popular? Not really . . ."

"Don't be too upset. Don Gomez is truly erudite; over the years, he was married to three different women, and each wife sharpened his thinking. These women came from different parts of Spain, and today he mingles various dialects in his speech and invents original expressions and images that amuse the audience, especially the old people. See how they laugh and enjoy him."

Moses wearily leans his head on the back of his chair. The sleepless night is taking its toll. He closes his eyes and calculates the number of hours that remain before the return flight to Israel.

12

WHEN THE ISRAELI lifts his head and opens his eyes, he finds that Don Gomez has faded into darkness, and projected onscreen is young Ruth, dressed in her high school uniform at her graduation ceremony. This film, like its predecessors, is dubbed in Spanish, but as opposed to the others, in which actions and locations were the principal elements, contextualized by the dialogue, here the drama develops mainly by means of long verbal exchanges that deepen the relationships among the characters. Moses remembers the draft pages of the screenplay, written in crowded longhand by Trigano, where speech followed speech, with no provocative slumber in a desert crater or moonstruck hallucination in a remote village. The characters in this film interact at a kitchen table, or in a corner of a neighborhood café, or in a bus station at the edge of the city. At the end of the film, the main character does not find a dramatic location to give birth to her child but chooses a small illicit clinic near the produce market in south Tel Aviv.

"So how can we infuse your story with the mystery you crave so much?" Moses had wondered aloud after he read the draft. But Trigano was unperturbed. "We'll look for that mystery in our next film, but now, after our defeat by Kafka's elderly animal, we must invigorate our image with a simple human story, for which we might find actors funded by the Ministry of Immigrant Absorption."

And indeed he found them, and after many years they reappear on the screen of the auditorium of the municipality of Santiago de

Compostela: a man and a woman, both about forty, who play a married couple, both teachers. With great affection they embrace the young graduate, singing her praises to her long-suffering, working-class mother, a resident of the south of Israel, who reverently tucks her daughter's precious certificate in her handbag.

The state paid the salaries of the actors playing the teachers and also provided a handsome grant to the production. Trigano tailored the fictional characters to the real ones. The pair were actors in the Hungarian theater, husband and wife, who escaped to Israel in the late 1950s after the failure of the Hungarian revolution. Their Jewishness was somewhat dubious, particularly the wife's, whose facial features and tall stature testified to remote Asiatic ancestry. Trigano used to call them "the two Khazars given us for free by the Ministry of Absorption."

But where were these Khazars today? Where had they gone, how had they aged? They were a good deal older than Moses. But now in the dark, on the limp screen by the gorgeous fresco, they are young and active as they portray bits of their own biography.

As two artists who arrived in the country from behind the Iron Curtain, they enjoyed special treatment and spent considerable time in a Hebrew-language program to train them for performance in Israeli theater. But their Hungarian accents proved to be a formidable obstacle, and even the expert in pronunciation assigned them had a hard time inculcating emphasis on the proper syllables. True, in humorous skits, such an accent was an asset, especially when juxtaposed against speakers with the lilt of Arab lands, but the pair considered themselves serious stage actors and expected to play dramatic and tragic roles in the Jewish State. The Ministry of Absorption tried to find them employment at government expense in movies, where the soundtrack might be manipulated to impart the right meter to their Hebrew. To make it easier for Moses to cast the two in the new film, Trigano invented for the actor the role of a history teacher, turned his wife into a teacher of art, and instead of two refugees from the communist regime they were made into Holocaust survivors whose time in the death camps had rendered impossible their hopes for a child who would bring them consolation.

This is the point of departure for the drama that develops between the pair of teachers and the pretty and gifted student, daughter of an underprivileged family, to whom Trigano awarded the same scholarship he had received as a youth. And not just the scholarship. He also saw fit in the screenplay to grant his girlfriend the matriculation certificate of which she was deprived when he convinced her to drop out of school and become an actress in his films. And because, when the time came, he also persuaded her to declare that she was Orthodox in order to avoid military service, he made it up to her by turning her into an outstanding soldier who becomes an officer. All these compensations, which he showered upon her in his imagination to atone for his domination in real life, were still not enough for him, so he resurrected her mother, who had died in childbirth, and it is she who now fills the screen, a widow dressed in black, listening to the two Khazars who try to ingratiate themselves with her so she will not obstruct their secret plan.

"How is the teachers' Spanish?" Moses whispers to the director of the archive sitting beside him. "Is it correct?" "Not really," he answers. "Trigano asked that their dubbing be given a foreign accent and the grammar sabotaged a little, and a Polish student who studied here last year showed the dubbers how to do it without making them sound ridiculous." Indeed, the foreign accent and mistakes provoke no laughter in the municipal auditorium, which was also the case when the film was shown in Israel. From the start, the artful acting of the Khazars creates a mood of uneasiness.

The plan of the pair of teachers, the Holocaust survivors, is becoming clear. They've picked out the gifted student and try to convince her, as the film progresses, to give birth to a child they can adopt. After her graduation, they continue to cultivate their loving relationship.

Moses admits that the two played their parts professionally. In effect, they portrayed themselves and even subtly steered him and the cinematographer to bring out the best in them. It was no wonder that they were praised by critics and audiences alike, but after the partnership collapsed, there was no chance of persuading them to work again with Moses. Their loyalty was to Trigano.

In any case, the Spanish sounds alien to the spirit of his film. Some echo or other in the dubbing studio has amplified the artificiality of the speech. He removes his hearing aids, takes out their little batteries, and replaces them in his ears as plugs, to muffle the sound.

The Refusal is a quiet film, centering not on the two teachers but rather on a strong, impressive young woman whose inner journey is complicated but credible. This time Trigano created a worthy character. He gave his girlfriend not only fortitude but moral fiber and sent her to serve in an army base not far from Jerusalem. On weekend leaves, she chooses not to make the long trip to her mother's home in the south but to stay with her former teachers, who have given her a room of her own in their apartment.

This is a drama of subterranean currents with lengthy close-ups, but still, the story unfolds steadily toward its goal. These two teachers know their student well, and from the time she arrived, in the tenth grade, a gifted girl from a poor town, they spotted her as a means to their own happiness. They are aware of her strong points and vulnerabilities, and cautiously, quietly, over breakfast and dinner, they will try to chart a path to her heart and to incline her toward granting their wish. They tell her about the war, show her pictures of the European world that was destroyed, photos of relatives and children lost. In precise, restrained language, without excessive pathos, they confess their barrenness. And the soldier, now an officer, slowly guesses what her former teachers want from her, pretending she doesn't while giving them hope.

Step by measured step, the story Trigano devised for his loved one moves ahead, doled out gradually, with no sharp turns, building the tacit agreement, repellent and scandalous but with a mission — to provide a child to those whose world was destroyed, a descendant who will not disappoint them, because they have faith in the Israeli womb that will give it life. This absurdity, in the skillful script, wins the approval of the lonely widow, the mother of the heroine, who accepts that her gifted child, before starting a family of her own, will bring happiness to others.

And so, in this old film, on a makeshift screen in the auditorium of the municipality of a foreign city, a young woman officer still serving in the army becomes pregnant. But now Trigano changes the game. She is not an innocent and confused girl who falls prey to the desire of others but a self-confident, sensual young woman who, to mask the identity of the father, switches lovers promiscuously. The passing of seasons, one of Moses' directorial specialties, is rendered in the slowly bulging belly of the young woman.

Trigano demanded the right to oversee the proper development of the pregnancy. He did not rely on the costumer or the makeup artist. In the breaks between filming he would lovingly rest his head on the soft pillow taped each morning to Ruth's belly. But, unlike Trigano, the military authorities are not overjoyed. They advise this valued officer to terminate the pregnancy, but she refuses and so is discharged from service. And instead of accepting the adoptive parents' invitation to move into their home and enjoy their care until the birth, she rents an apartment on the scruffy southern edge of Tel Aviv and waits there for her delivery date.

At this point, the mighty Israeli landscape enters the picture. Moses is struck by how Toledano's old camera managed to wrap wind, waves, and sky around the heavily pregnant woman as she walks on the beach. Here begins the turnabout in her mind, a reversal that Moses had to convey with few words and many silences. Slowly the meaning of the mission she has undertaken becomes clear to her: even after the child is handed over to its adoptive parents, she will always, as its mother, be tied to it. And not only to it, but to them. She, too, will have to bear the burden of their memories.

From now on, a new, painful recognition comes into focus, devised by Trigano for the ending of the film in keeping with his personal ideology. In Jerusalem, the two future adoptive parents are preparing for the imminent birth, their anxiety mingled with excitement, retaining an obstetrician and a veteran midwife, splurging on overpriced baby gear to pamper the newborn, while in Tel Aviv, the heroine is in touch with a local agency and is offering her unborn child for immediate, anonymous adoption.

And so, when the hour arrives, with no one by her side and without a word to anyone, she disappears behind the iron door of a semi-legal clinic, a door whose color Toledano requested be changed from green to blue.

Moses feels the suspense among the Spanish audience as the birth, filmed in a studio, draws near. Trigano demanded that this time he not be barred from the set and that he even take part in the directing. But the childbirth scene was cut out in the editing room, where it seemed crude and inconsistent with the spirit of the film. Ruth had screamed and writhed more than she'd been asked to, and the blood did not look realistic. The transfer of the newborn to the social worker was filmed in a real hospital, in the maternity wing. The infant, who was a week old, was loaned to the production by the sister-in-law of the soundman, but only on condition that she play the social worker receiving the child for adoption. And though the woman had never stood before a movie camera, she played her role so naturally that Ruth broke uncontrollably into real tears. Who knows better than Moses about all the fake tears he got out of her in subsequent films. He is amazed how genuine and pained was her weeping in this one, so much so that the screen seems to tremble.

He turns around to find Ruth and sees that Doña Elvira, the experienced actress, also appreciates the dramatic quality of this crying and holds Ruth's hand as if to congratulate and console her.

From here the film carries on to the end, but not to Trigano's stormy ending. The pale new mother will not open her coat and undo her blouse in a gesture of generosity and despair. She will not breastfeed the aged actor from the National Theater. She will just keep walking and head to the beach.

Moses had to improvise these last moments of the film on the spot, and he made do with an atmospheric ending. The young mother is distressed not only over the child she has given up, but by the disappointment she has caused her two beloved teachers, the survivors of hell, who so believed in her, and she begins walking slowly but steadily along the beach, and when she vanishes in the distance, the audience in the dark is meant to believe that she is secure in her newly acquired freedom.

13

"The hour is late and the municipal workers must get back to work," whispers de Viola to Moses amid the robust applause in the room. "Let's try," he suggests, "to make the ceremony short. There's been more than enough talking at your retrospective."

"Indeed."

While the credits roll, employees of the mayor's office bring a small table, cover it with a green cloth, place two chairs behind it, and set up a microphone and next to it a pitcher of water and two glasses. The names keep parading down the screen, albeit in smaller and smaller letters. People stand and stretch and start to chat, but the projectionist has yet to stop the film. And Manuel, picking up a signal from his brother to get things moving, steers his elderly mother in small steps to the table, where a city official shoves an envelope into her hand, at which point the director of the archive nudges Moses from his chair and invites him to the stage.

But on the makeshift screen, with remarkable persistence, continues the recitation of gratitude to all manner of institutions, large and small, and to private individuals, and artisans and drivers, restaurant owners and cooks, all of them engaged, often unknowingly, in the creation of this film. *See,* Moses says, congratulating himself, *even in an early film I had many partners, overt and covert, who supported my art.*

Doña Elvira speaks softly in Spanish, with Manuel translating line by line into formal Hebrew, and Moses gets the gist: The prize is not large, but it is presented with appreciation for a director who at the beginning of his career was unafraid of the absurd and meta-physical and allegorical, and we all know, going back to Luis Buñuel, how hard it is to inject authenticity and warmth into abstract ideas and wild, surrealistic dreams cloaked in a shaft of light cast upon a screen, and we thus owe a great debt to those courageous enough to take this difficult path.

Moses kisses her on both cheeks and offers a brief response:

"During my long life I have participated in any number of retro-spectives of my films, in my homeland and abroad, but I know that these three days in Santiago de Compostela I shall remember till my dying day. Yes, Doña Elvira, beyond the manifest reality lurks a dark abyss, and we must rip open the screen and look straight into it, for only then will we know how best to handle what is known and appar-ently understood. But we must not become addicted to it, for then despair will sap our strength. Therefore a prize is also due those who loyally stick to the familiar and day-to-day, to draw from it joy and consolation."

And Moses again warmly embraces the elderly actress, who whis-pers to him: "Your film touched me and made me think, but why was the ending so vague and empty of meaning?"

"The ending?" Moses smiles.

"Yes, the end. The very end."

"The end," Moses explains, "is always a compromise between what was and what will never be."

five

CONFESSION

1

No DOUBT, thinks Moses, sticking the envelope in the inside pocket of his jacket, *this was a far-reaching retrospective, and if the Spaniards drew pleasure from the vertigo they caused me, I earned my prize.* He watches Doña Elvira, who has chosen to lean not on her son the monk, whose robe billows mischievously down the marble stairs, but on the arm of the Israeli actress, who makes sure the fragile Spanish lady does not trip on the hem of her long dress.

After her feet land safely on the rain-spangled pavement, the legendary actress does not let go of the helpful womanly arm but asks Ruth to come with her to an antique store in the Old Town. Don't worry about my mother, Manuel assures Moses, who briefly wondered if he too should not escort the prize giver to the Old Town. Everywhere in Spain people know who she is and attend to her. And he invites Moses to accompany him to the library of the cathedral to browse through one collection or another of the many treasures amassed over the centuries.

Moses politely declines the invitation. The "plenty of time" promised him on the first night was an overstatement, but nonetheless, because of his age and habits, he would prefer to take a quick nap before the long flight ahead. But he promises the Dominican that this is not a final farewell to St. James. He intends to come back, perhaps as the guest of a more balanced retrospective that does not ignore the best of his works. Or he might come on a private visit and bring his eldest grandson. In short, he jokes, he will not rush to relocate to the World to Come before returning for another look at the mighty cathedral.

At the reception desk he is reminded that checkout time has passed and he needs to vacate his room. But when he gets to the room he sees that departure has begun without him. Two African chambermaids are inside, wielding a noisy vacuum cleaner, stripping the bed, preparing to scour the bathroom. When they see him, they freeze in place, then return to work as if a light breeze had blown through the room and not an actual guest whose belongings and those of his companion are strewn everywhere. Moses infers that his presence will not prompt them to leave, so firm is the decree to ready the room for the next incumbent. He points to the door and indicates with three motions of his outstretched hands how much time he will need to get organized — a mere thirty minutes. But they brazenly reject his request, agreeing to one hand only. Five minutes, not more. He holds firm — thirty minutes, not a minute less. But the two, who seem amused by the sign language they've improvised with the old man, bargain as if every minute were made of gold. At the end they settle on twenty, and the two women entwine their twenty dark fingers together, to avoid misunderstanding.

"*Yalla*, bye," he says as he hurries them out, a fine fusion of East and West, presumably intelligible to anyone anywhere. The two women leave, laughing, taking the sheets and towels with them, as well as the soaps and lotions, lest there remain in the room any temptations to slow down his exit.

He looks sadly at the naked mattress, stained with ancient stigmata of other men, and the room filled with cleaning materials, the vacuum cleaner hose uncoiled like a snake — an afternoon nap a lost cause. The splendid harmony of the attic, which impressed him so on the first night, is shattered. He has to start packing. First he puts his own clothes and other belongings in his suitcase, and then, absent his companion, he takes charge and carefully folds the clothes she wore during the retrospective, plus items, more numerous, that she didn't. He carefully wraps up her boots and shoes, making sure to isolate in a plastic bag everything destined for the laundry. He takes special care with cosmetics and perfumes and small makeup implements. He does not resist the temptation to ferret through the side pocket of her suitcase, in case the results of her blood test have wandered there. But there is nothing medical in the pocket, only maps of European cities and brochures from hotels, along with *My Glorious Brothers*, an old historical novel Ruth intends to adapt as a Hanukkah play for her drama class. Once the two suitcases are by the door, he looks under the bed, not in vain, as her slippers have migrated into the darkness.

Had he been more focused and assertive in his desire, he reflects ruefully, he could have taken with him a sweet memory of this room, but the hidden hand of Trigano that had raised old works from the dead had surprised and confused him to such a degree that on the final night, it felt as if the former screenwriter were watching him as he slept. In any case, he has decided this is the last time he will bring Ruth to a retrospective. If she wants to ignore her illness and destroy herself, let her. He is not the man who can stop her.

His hearing aids detect faint tapping at the door, but he ignores it, gets up for a final look at *Caritas Romana*, now that he has come to understand the story of the bold and beneficent daughter who breastfeeds a father dying of hunger.

There is persistent knocking at the door, but the agreed-upon twenty minutes have not elapsed. It is hard for him to part from what might have been but was not. And in the sunlight generously pouring through the window he approaches the reproduction and interprets small details he had not noticed before — the calm and contented facial expression of the nursing daughter, whom the Dutch painter had chosen to depict not as a frightened and bashful girl or a wild and defiant young woman but as a mature individual whose serene demeanor signifies confidence in her bold act of grace, perhaps because the infant that had endowed her with milk may not be her first but one of many she has brought into the world, and she knows from experience that she is not depriving or neglecting it if she also feeds its unfortunate grandfather.

But is the grandfather really unfortunate? Apart from the baldness at the center of his head — which the daughter's steady hand maneuvers, bringing it near or distancing it, so his lips will not demand more than their due — he really does seem like a sturdy man in his prime. Although his hands are tied uncomfortably behind him, his naked back is straight and strong. No, this is not a pathetic person or an innocent victim, Moses decides, but a suspicious old character, convicted by law and serving his sentence, and if, after the gift of nursing, his jailers let him go, he will likely do further harm in the world.

The knocking on the door gets louder. The twenty minutes have passed, and what was agreed in sign language does obligate him. He puts on his coat, takes the walking stick, and opens the door. "*Yalla,* bye." The African women burst into laughter, having brought as reinforcements two gray-haired bellhops. One loads the suitcases on a small cart and heads for the elevator, the other walks over to *Roman Charity*, takes it down from the wall, and hangs in its place a picture of pears and dark grapes.

Moses observes the switch uneasily and hurries after his suitcases. At the reception desk he asks if he has any outstanding bill and is told no, the city council is taking care of all expenses, whatever they may be. He then decides to exchange his prize check for cash so that in Israel he won't need to share it with the bank and the state. To his pleasant surprise, in this city of believers, honor is instantly given to a check signed by the mayor, and it is cashed into notes of many colors.

"When my lady companion arrives," he cheerfully tells the desk clerk, "please tell her that our room is vacant and her bag packed, and that she is to wait for me here."

2

HE GOES OUT into the square, walks amid its chains and palaces, and finds the plaza flooded with new groups of tourists gathered around tour guides who point with sticks at the cathedral, investing every statue, tower, and alcove with significance. Moses checks his watch to see if there is time to revisit the cathedral, as he will almost certainly never have occasion to come back.

He ascends the steps and finds the great church on the verge of religious ecstasy, with the scent of incense merging with stately organ chords to announce the mass. Pilgrims flow into the pews, some kneeling, crossing themselves, and murmuring, others staring at the ornate altar and waiting for someone to navigate their faith. The confessionals on both sides of the sanctuary are occupied, and near them wait men and women who surely believe that confession in such a historic place upgrades their piety. *Too bad*, thinks Moses, *I didn't act on Pilar's suggestion to try a brief confession with the director of the archive. When will I ever get another chance?*

He asks someone who looks like an official beadle of the church to lead him to the library, where he finds Manuel de Viola standing at a lectern and leafing through a hefty volume.

"They evicted me from the hotel," he says to the monk, who is delighted to see him. "So I came to bid farewell to the cathedral, since at my age, who knows if I'll be able to come back. But why the crowds? Have I stumbled into a special holiday?"

Manuel knows of no holiday that Moses has stumbled into and thinks it is mere coincidence that several organized tour groups have arrived all at once and are attempting to perform in a few hectic hours the entire pilgrimage ritual that in the past took weeks and months. But it's quiet here in the library, and he can show the Israeli director something of the priceless collection.

The guest is disinclined to spend the minutes he normally spends napping immersed in antique drawings. He would not, however, object to fulfilling a wish that arises every time he visits a church — to be closeted just once in a real confession booth and confess whatever comes to mind to an unseen authority. And would not the confessing of a non-Christian person, a disbeliever in divine providence, be an interesting experience, not only for the giver of the confession but for the receiver as well?

"You wish to confess?" The Dominican's eyes light up.

"To try it, to get a taste of this ancient and venerable practice. In churches in Israel it's hard to find a priest who is not an Arab, or at least a supporter of Arabs, and therefore the confession of an Israeli Jew is likely to get tangled in a political debate that would undercut its simple humanity." As an artist, Moses has been wary of trying psychotherapy, out of concern that it would burrow too far into his meager unconscious and extract childhood lies and secrets that even in old age spur him on and nourish his creative work. For the psyche is a nest of vipers: you pull out one snake, and its friends are dragged along with it. But a short confession, offered by chance in a foreign country before boarding an airplane, might restore his soul.

"A fine wish for you, but hard to fulfill. If my brother were here, he would be happy to be your confessor."

"Then why not you, Manuel? You strike me as trustworthy and attentive, and besides, there's little chance we'll ever meet again. So let's do a confession in Hebrew, as in the early days of Christianity, and I'll concentrate on my professional sins so as not to interfere with our friendship."

"Ah, my friend," Manuel says with a clap of his hands, "I am a monk, not a priest, and I cannot grant absolution to anyone."

"Absolution?" Moses is taken by surprise. "I don't need absolution, nor do I believe in absolution that does not follow an act of atonement — which no one else can perform in my place."

"If you want just confession" — Manuel smiles — "let's sit down at the table, and please, speak slowly."

"No, no, not here," objects Moses, "what I want is a confession in a real booth, tiny and dark, with a curtain and grille, opposite a hidden face that enables total freedom. But now, as I walked through the church, I saw that the booths were full and the lines were long."

Manuel promises to try to find a suitable confessional on the lower floor, for everyone who comes to Santiago is something of a pilgrim, and it would be a shame if Moses returned to his homeland with an empty soul.

Manuel goes out to look, and Moses regrets embroiling such an amiable fellow in his scheme, a man of goodwill, if a tad disorganized. The flight to Barcelona is four hours from now, and the airport is not far away, but because the bags are ticketed to Israel, they are suspect by definition and must be checked well in advance. Meanwhile, Ruth will return to the hotel and be worried by his absence, so he decides to wait for only ten minutes, and if Manuel has not returned, he will leave him a note of apology next to the open book.

It is a volume in Latin, printed in the early nineteenth century. Its text is minimal and illustrations plentiful, some in bright colors and others in black-and-white. Portraits of priests and bishops and cardinals in decorative vestments, each according to his role and rank — apparently clergymen who served in the cathedral, which appears in faint outline in the background of each picture. Inserted at times among the men of the cloth is a man of temporal power — a patron or prince, or a tall gaunt knight wearing a helmet and sword with a small goatee, perhaps a distant relative of Don Quixote. And now and then, a band of armed soldiers, clad in billowy riding pants, preceded by a handsome young man tooting a hunting horn. Less often, he happens upon a well-fed noblewoman reclining in the parlor of her home, or a thin, sad young woman sitting on a horse, and on the next page a portrait of just the horse, and beside it a tall dog, gazing purposefully into the distance. Moses turns the pages drowsily, looks again at his watch. The desire to sit in the confession booth seems childish and unnecessary. Really, why bother with reality? In his next film, he can stick a confession scene in the script and tell the set designer to reproduce a booth, with a curtain and grille, so that during production, between takes, the director can enter it at will and confess to someone he deems worthy.

The sound of rapid footsteps. The door opens and the radiant face of the monk appears. A confessional has been located on the lower floor, actually the personal booth of the local bishop, intended for visiting priests and monks who wish to confess to him. Manuel has received permission to admit the foreign confessant, but so as not to provoke a theological controversy, he has not disclosed his non-Christian identity, though he does not fear its exposure, since his life's mission is to be a subversive monk: this is the new word he uses to guide his actions. In Madrid he received a special dispensation to assist immigrants and refugees of dubious identity and illegal foreign workers, among them even pagans. His heart is gladdened by the mere possibility of taking confession in Hebrew from a Jew who denies the existence of any God, so he has now decided, on his own authority, to violate another principle: though he is not a priest but just a monk, he is prepared to grant absolution, and he announces this so Moses will feel free to confess with complete openness.

Moses laughs. He doesn't need absolution.

And why not? It will be given even if not urgently needed now. Moses can save it for the afterlife. Dominican absolution in a bishop's booth in the historic cathedral may come in handy in the World to Come, should he discover that it exists.

They descend more stairs, passing the tomb of Saint James, where pilgrims crowd for a touch of the sacred stone, and continue through a maze of hallways to a quiet chapel with a dark booth in the corner. But Manuel's subversion is not complete. Because he is unwilling to have the aged confessant kneel before him, he turns the tables — he opens the booth, moves aside the red leather curtain, and gently seats Moses on the chair of the priest, while he kneels to hear the confession from behind the lattice.

3

To confess for the first time in his life in the depths of a magnificent cathedral just prior to a flight back to Israel is very naughty, downright anarchic. What's not yet clear is what to confess to.

He decides on a brief, symbolic confession, a training confession, so that if he ever wants to stage such a scene in a movie, say a detective flick or a comedy, he can boast to the actors that he's directing from personal experience.

The booth in the bishop's chapel is unlike the booths Moses has seen in churches. This one is plush, almost luxurious. The curtain is made of leather and not cloth, and the inside walls are also upholstered in leather, as in a recording studio, to muffle the voices as much as possible. On the seat lies a plump leather pillow, and, remarkably enough, the screen separating the confessor and confessant is not metal but is also made of leather, punched through with holes, so it seems as if myriad eyes are peering from the other side. The overbearing scent of the leather, redolent of the sweat and tears of generations of sinners, makes Moses a bit nauseated, as if he were trapped inside a hippopotamus. But Manuel's voice is soft and courteous.

"Here I am listening to you, Moses, you may say whatever comes to mind."

"Thank you, Manuel. My confession will be short and to the point. Also, I don't want to keep you too long in that uncomfortable position."

"Please don't think about me. Think about yourself."

"Do you remember the film screened this morning at the municipality before the ceremony?"

"A most interesting film."

"Do you know what your mother said about it?"

"Verily, she praised it."

"In fine words, but noncommittal, and she had strong reservations about the ending, thought it was vague and meaningless."

The darkness of the chapel intensifies that of the confessional, and the eyes of the monk disappear intermittently from the grille, but his voice expresses regret. In recent years his mother has been disappointed by all endings of films, plays, and novels; she even rejects the final scenes of older, classic films, surely for a personal reason: her own approaching end. Moses is in the company of respected directors and screenwriters and should not take her words personally.

Moses smiles and pauses before continuing.

"But this time, Manuel, your mother is right. This morning, having seen the film for the first time in many years, I understood the weakness of the final scene – it does not relieve any of the tensions that have built up."

"If so," says the voice behind the screen, with relief, "you are not angry with my mother?"

"Rather than getting angry over justifiable criticism, a serious artist should be angry with himself."

"But in those days you were a young beginner, so why be angry with yourself?"

"Because the evasive ending of the film did not come from inexperience. The film had a different ending, a truer one, but I rejected it."

"Ah . . ."

What am I doing in this grotesque and suffocating darkness? Moses asks himself. *Maybe I should leave it at what's been said and go back to Ruth?*

Except the Dominican, yearning to grant absolution, holds on to the confession so as not to lose the confessant.

"And if you had the right ending, why did you give it up?"

"The actress was frightened, and I, instead of calming her and letting the screenwriter, her lover, convince her to play the part he wrote for her – I supported her refusal. You probably want to know what the original ending was."

"But of course!" replies Manuel, excited.

"You remember the film: the heroine hands her baby to a social worker, who hurries off so the mother will not have time to regret her action and change her mind. And instead of aimlessly walking, lost in thought, to the beach, the heroine was to have left the clinic and wandered the streets – then, lost and guilt-stricken and exhausted, she would spot an old beggar on the street corner, approach him, toss him a few coins, and ask him to forgive her for what she had done. When she realizes the old man has no idea what she wants of him, she would suddenly throw open her coat, unbutton her blouse, take out her breast, and compel or seduce the beggar to suck the milk intended for her infant child. That was the scene I canceled."

"Alas," murmurs Manuel, but he regains his composure and consoles Moses, tells him not to flagellate himself. Sometimes life is more important than art.

"What makes you think I'm flagellating myself?"

"Is it not the regret over canceling that scene that makes you seek confession?"

"No, I have no regret, only a desire to understand. And in this retrospective, I've come to understand that I didn't cancel the scene out of consideration for the actress but because of the opportunity to sever the connection with the one who conceived of it. I did it in order to distance myself once and for all from this strange and alien spirit that had hypnotized my work in the early years."

"Señor Trigano . . ." Manuel pronounces the name.

Moses is alarmed. "You know him?"

"Only his name."

"How?"

"My brother spoke his name."

"And what did Juan say about him?"

"Not much . . ."

A long silence.

"And?"

"He depicted him as a private person trapped in his own thoughts . . . a unique soul, but hardened by pride."

"What else?"

"My brother admitted to you that it was Trigano who initiated the retrospective in your honor. If, as you say, he is now an alien spirit for you, why do you feel guilty about severing your partnership with him?"

"And why," Moses says half seriously, "is it necessary to talk about guilt in every confession?"

"There always needs to be a little guilt," replies the monk apologetically, "a minor sin, a tiny error . . . because if not, why have absolution?"

"But I told you, I have no need for absolution. Your brother Juan has a keen eye for people. If I had succumbed to the ideas and fantasies of that man, I would have slid to a place of no return."

"Slid?" The Spaniard tastes the Hebrew word.

"Slipped . . . sunk . . . descended . . . entangled myself in revolutionary, pretentious stories intelligible only to the cognoscenti, which would have brought me to the point of surrendering my directing to Trigano too."

But the Dominican, troubled that his confessant shows no regret, now tries cautiously to cross the thin line between the professional and the personal, to deepen the confession.

"If you wished to distance him," he ventures, "perhaps it was because you wished to get closer to the woman so she would be under your wing alone?"

"The opposite . . . the exact opposite," Moses answers, after a brief silence. "Like everyone in my crew, I had strong feelings for her, but we all knew that she and Trigano were soul mates. So when he broke with me, I was sure he would take her with him. I wanted him to, but he punished her and me, left her to me as a character for whom I had to take responsibility."

"A character?"

"I mean, not as a woman, but as a character."

"As a character?" The monk strains to understand. "A figure that resembles another figure?"

"Yes, a character."

"As a character of whom?"

"Like a character in a book, a novel, or a character in art," fumbles the confessant, "characters you see in a stained-glass window. A character who is herself, but not only herself."

"You mean symbolic? Who symbolizes others?"

"Not necessarily. Not always others. Also not an archetype. A real person, an individual, but one who has something else around her . . . a frame of sorts . . . a halo . . . an emotional aura . . . as in a dream. After all, Trigano also brought her to us as a character. A character from whose very existence a story flows. So when she rebelled against him, and he gave her up and left her to others, to me, he handed her over not as an actual woman but as the character of a woman."

Deep silence from beyond the grille. Just the muffled moan of organ music drifting from above.

"Yet when he left her, he punished himself more than he punished you," the monk suggests to his confessant.

"His art was more important to him than his loved one."

"And she?"

"She?"

"Or you?"

"I?"

"Has she stayed with you since then as a character alone?"

"As a woman, she had friends, and still does."

"Just friends?"

"I mean, also lovers . . . they come and go. She even had a son by one of them."

"And you?" Manuel dares to step over the fence that has utterly collapsed.

"Not to be tempted by her solitude, I hurried to get married. Besides, her spirit isn't a good fit with mine, she comes from a wilder place. But I couldn't abandon a character who sought a place in my work."

"Only the character?" Manuel continues to probe.

"If this is hard for you, we can switch languages . . ."

"No, no," protests the monk, "you cannot imagine how the He-brew lifts my spirit. But I ask that you help me out with another example."

"Take, for instance, the portraits and drawings in the book you were leafing through when I came into the library. You weren't look-ing only for random individuals from the past out of a desire to learn what it was like then, how it looked; you searched for characters . . . something abstract that would leap out and touch you, something the artist exposed in people who sat for him. Something they embody."

"You mean their roles?"

"The role is one way the character is embodied. But it is possible to move it from role to role, from situation to situation, from film to film, period to period, family to family. And yet we can discern its unchanging essence, which goes beyond a style of acting, more than the mannerism of an actor — do you understand?"

"I am trying, Mr. Moses, but it's not easy."

"That's right, it's not easy to understand the dreamlike dimen-sion that makes a certain person into a character. For example, the woman I was married to didn't understand the nature of the connec-tion that I maintained with the character the screenwriter left me with, and although during our entire time together she was confident that I never stopped loving her, she ended our marriage."

"Even your wife didn't understand."

"Perhaps she did understand, but she did not want to reconcile herself to what she understood."

"Because of the beauty of the character?"

"Her beauty? Is she still beautiful?"

"Yes, very beautiful. And you should know that the gaze of a monk, for whom the beauty of a woman is forbidden even in his thoughts, is pure and accurate. Since the separation from your wife you have been alone?"

"I am alone, but not lonely, I am surrounded by people."

"And the character?"

Moses is pleased that his confessor feels comfortable with the concept. "The character continues to turn up in my films, but sometimes also in the films of others . . . by her wish and mine too. We are free people . . . not dependent on each other. She is her own person as am I, even when we sleep in the same bed."

"Yes, my brother told me he put you both in one room."

"And though he surely didn't tell you everything he was told about me, you understand that my confession is innocent of sin, and therefore, Manuel, absolution is unnecessary."

Manuel's eyes vanish from the grille, and the rustling on the other side indicates that he is rising to his feet. Has Moses' refusal to accept absolution disappointed him so much that he has decided to bring the confession to an end?

Moses glances at his watch. No, time has not stopped. Ruth is doubtless asking herself where he's disappeared to. He reaches for the cord to get free of the booth, but the curtain fails to move. "Can you get me out of here?" he implores, and Manuel slides the curtain and opens the gate.

"Thank you, Manuel, this was an unforgettable experience," says Moses, his head spinning.

But Manuel has turned gloomy and he neither responds nor smiles, as if he has uncovered a defect in the Israeli's confession. He grasps Moses' arm, and carefully, as if the director were feeble or disabled, helps him climb the spiral stairs that ascend to the nave of the church.

4

THE MASS IS in progress. Surrounding the high altar are seven priests in elegant vestments conducting the service in various languages before a devoutly silent throng. And because Manuel and Moses enter from behind the altar, they cannot make their way through the worshippers without disturbing the holy rite.

"What do we do?" whispers Moses. "I can't delay much longer, Ruth is surely worried about me."

"The character?" The word slips silently, ironically, from the lips of the monk, who turns Moses around and leads him through a maze of rooms and dark stairs to a heavy wooden door. He opens the bolt and delivers Moses into the small square where the angel stands, pointing with his sword at the Jew fleeing the cathedral.

"From here you will easily find your way back to the hotel," says Manuel in a cool, oddly severe tone; he does not invite a farewell handshake but merely presses his palms together, then turns on his heel and disappears behind the heavy door.

I disappointed him with my inflexibility, thinks Moses. *Was it so hard for me to accept his absolution with an eye to the future?* And he hurries from the little square to the great plaza, which is empty now.

Waiting by the hotel is the car that will take them to the airport. The driver, a directing student at the institute who has volunteered for the job, opens the trunk so the director can confirm that the three suitcases and two pilgrim walking sticks are securely there.

"But we have another few minutes, no?" asks Moses. "Just a few, not many," says the student.

Tranquillity has returned to the hotel lobby as people have gone off, some to rest, others to pray, and from afar he espies the ethereal figure of Doña Elvira sitting alone in a corner, bathed in the soft light of a bright winter's day. He rushes to her but finds her sound asleep. A shriveled, motionless old lady, breathing so minimally it seems that air flows through her with no effort of her own. He checks to see whether Ruth's bag and coat are beside her, but doesn't find them. He goes downstairs to the rest rooms. After urinating and rinsing his face with cold water, he goes to the ladies' room, opens the door a wee crack, whistles the first notes of a tune, their longtime signal, to indicate his presence, and waits for the response. But no whistling from within completes the melody. He stays in the doorway, and, not to be suspected of sinister intent, he whispers her name and whistles the tune to the end. When one of the booths opens to the sound of rushing waters, and a big strong cleaning woman emerges brandishing a green brush, he withdraws at once.

We have some time, the airport is not far away, he reassures himself, and he returns to Doña Elvira, who has not changed position but who now has her eyes open. She smiles and invites him to sit by her side. He is careful not to create the illusion that he has time for a real conversation, so he remains standing as he tells her about the confession taken by her son in the bishop's private booth.

The mother is not surprised by her son's misdeed.

"You made a mistake, Mr. Moses, by agreeing to confess to a monk who is not authorized to receive confession, and if Manuel also granted you absolution, you should know that it counts for nothing."

"I didn't ask for absolution," he says with a smile, "and I don't need it."

But Doña Elvira continues her complaint. "Lately he has been playing around with the principles of his monastic oath and looking for needless provocations. The Dominicans will end up tossing him out of the order, and he'll come back and live with me and be even more dependent on his mother."

Moses is touched by the candid and endearing complaint. "But my confession to Manuel is not a provocation, for I, as you recall, am not a Christian or even a believer, just a person."

"Not a Christian?" For a moment she seems confused, but her memory quickly recovers and locates the proper identity of the Israeli director. Yet she does not give up entirely. "Not a Christian, but why not a believer?"

"Because that's how God made me," declares Moses with a triumphant look and a shrug of helplessness, "and I have neither the power nor the authority to change His will."

She laughs. "Then come sit with me," she says. "But first get me a blanket."

"I'll sit for just a minute," he says and covers her shoulders with the blanket that lies folded beside her. "We should already have left for the airport, but Ruth has disappeared."

Doña Elvira shrugs.

"She didn't come back with you?"

It turns out Ruth went on her own in the Old Town, to look for more presents.

"And you came back on your own? When was that?"

"Less than an hour ago."

"But she knows that we are supposed to leave at three for the airport."

"And what time is it now?"

"One minute to three."

"If she knows, why should you worry?" says Doña Elvira serenely. "In this city she is safe."

"Why should I worry?" he challenges the old lady, as if he had entrusted her with a little girl, and he rushes to the front desk to see if there is a message for him.

But no message has been received.

He leaves the hotel and, skipping down the few steps, goes out into the great plaza, then hurries across to the first alley of the Old Town and stops. What now? Where to look?

She does have her passport and plane ticket with her, and she knows the time of the flight, and he has a fleeting suspicion that she is deliberately late, that she wants to part from him here at long last, this place where Trigano's spirit has come and gone. As though the confession he has just made has risen from the depths of the cathedral and drifted to her in the Old Town, and she knows that there will be no role for her anymore in his work.

He goes back to the hotel. "What's going on?" the student asks. "We're late, and there's traffic on the road to the airport." Moses leans on the car. "We'll wait a little longer. My actress seems to have a hard time saying goodbye to this wonderful place."

"If she doesn't get back," says the student, "we have to remember to take her suitcase out of the trunk."

"You're right." He grins at the future director and points to her suitcase, feeling vaguely vengeful. "Take it out now, and one of the walking sticks, and put them over there, and before we leave we'll ask the porter to take them back into the hotel." Suddenly he adds,

"If you want to be a movie director, you ought to practice trips to the airport, because in every film today there's at least ten minutes of driving to or from an airport."

The student laughs.

It's three thirty. *No*, he tells himself, *this is no mistake or forgetfulness, but a deliberate act.* She knows how anxious he is about time, knows about his punctuality, his sense of responsibility. However, the two of them are independent souls. Even when they are in bed together, they are like two actors supervised by a director and cinematographer and sound and lighting people.

"That's it, we should go," he says to the student as he finally accepts her absence. "Let me just leave her a message at the hotel."

When he returns to the car he can see in the distance, in the waning afternoon light, the missing woman strolling through the great square.

"I thought there would be another cathedral farther down, so I kept going," she says.

He gazes into her eyes.

Many times he told Toledano, and subsequent cinematographers he worked with, to point the lens straight into her eyes, to reveal, from within her yellow-green irises, the inner world of the character.

six

PUTTING THE OLD HOUSE
IN ORDER

1

THE TAXI DRIVER seemed to recognize Moses' companion, and the director gave him her address only, as if it were his as well. But when they reached her building in the Neve Tzedek neighborhood, Moses said to the driver: "Hang on to my suitcase and walking stick until I get back. I have to help the lady, no elevator."

"You need a hand?"

"No, thanks, I can manage."

They climb the stairs slowly, turning on the timed stairwell light three times. The director lugs the suitcase up the stairs, slides it along the landings, and when they get to the fourth floor, he doesn't leave Ruth until her door is opened and the apartment light switched on and he is sure that the world left behind three days ago has remained intact.

"Should I help you turn on the main valve?" he asks at the top of the stairs as they enter her apartment.

"No need," she says, "I was too lazy to turn it off."

"You want to get flooded again?"

"What can I do, it's so hard to reach."

Since the founding of the neighborhood at the end of the nineteenth century, the apartment has been renovated many times, but its main valve is still buried deep in a kitchen cabinet, requiring getting down on one's knees and crawling to reach it.

"That's enough." She hurries him off with a slight laugh. "The driver will think you ran away and left him with a stick and an empty suitcase."

The timer in the stairwell has gone out again, leaving only backlighting from the apartment. On the flights from Santiago to Barcelona and then to Israel she slept peacefully. Before landing she added color to her cheeks with new cosmetics purchased between flights, so her face is radiant. And the passion that was blocked for the three days quivers inside the man who stands before her.

"One last thing . . . one more . . ."

"No." She presses a finger to his lips. "No need for another test. Believe me, I'm healthy. And if I die, it won't be your fault."

He puts his hand on her forehead to feel her temperature, then his lips, to double-check, and holds her close. She smiles and kisses his eyes and forehead. They stand this way for a moment, embracing in the stairwell. Once he was taller than she was, but he has shrunk with the years and their height is now the same. Finally she enters the apartment and closes the door after her, but he lingers a bit by the adjacent apartment, its door decorated with colorful stickers. This is the studio where she gives acting classes to children. *Despite everything,* he comforts himself, *there's always something pure and lovely between us. We've accomplished something rare.*

The driver's head rests on the steering wheel in sleep so deep that Moses needs to knocks on the windshield to wake him, gently, so as not to scare him. The driver rubs his eyes vigorously, as if to tear away not just cobwebs of sleep but the remnants of a dream, and he gapes at Moses as if he were a new night rider with no baggage who happened into his cab.

"On TV there's someone who looks like her."

"That's her," Moses gladly confirms, "she's the one."

When they get to Moses' high-rise, the driver wants to be paid for waiting time. "But why?" asks Moses. "You waited for me all of five minutes." The driver checks his watch and also the meter. "You're right, I'm sorry," he apologizes, "the dream confused my sense of time." "Which dream?" The passenger is curious, but the driver is not about to disclose his dream to a stranger.

On the twentieth floor, in darkest night, in a beautiful apartment acquired with the profits of the film *Potatoes*, Moses can see Tel Aviv, wreathed in buildings and billboards, twinkling beyond a wall-to-wall window, and only a hint of faraway surf signals to the traveler that nature still exists in his home city. He turns on the main tap and the heat, puts the prize money in a drawer, and sheds his clothes. He stands in front of the window, a glass of wine in hand, and tries to estimate which floor the crosses would reach if the cathedral of Santiago were placed alongside his apartment building.

He goes into the bedroom and raises the blinds in the east window to enjoy the view from his bed of the distant lights of the Judean Hills. His thoughts during the two flights did not let him doze, but now he is determined to devote himself to deep sleep.

The extras in *Slumbering Soldiers* were fast asleep when asked only to impersonate sleepers in front of the camera, but the artist returning home, exhausted by a demanding retrospective, still tosses from side to side. *I so pleased the Spaniards with the strange sleeping in my old films*, he grumbles in his big, comfortable bed, *that they laid claim on my sleep too.* The heart that soared at the edge of the West seems to require a sleeping pill back in the East.

But not even the pill puts him to sleep, and he tries, to no avail, to reimagine the thwarted passion and relieve it on his own, so he gets out of bed to unpack his suitcase and put away his things. Yet sleep will not come, and he glumly opens his e-mail, does a lot of deleting, listens to a voice message from his ex-wife, and then, as his eyelids begin to droop, he shuts down the channels of communication, closes the window blinds, burrows his head deep into the pillow, and whispers, "Sleep, that's it, now you have no choice."

And Sleep not only succumbs to the director but grows stronger and sweeter from hour to hour, and when he wakes up for a moment to scurry to the toilet, he knows he will find Sleep again, awaiting him loyally in the bed he left behind. Nonetheless, in the mist of consciousness hovers a vague irritation. No, this time it's not the spirit of the screenwriter who secretly engineered his retrospective. Moses now, to his surprise, feels strangely fond of Trigano. Something else, insignificant but stubborn, is nibbling at his slumber. Again and again he returns to his film *Circular Therapy*, urgently needing to know if the three of them, he and the cinematographer and the set designer, really did succeed in splitting his parents' home into three different houses with three separate front doors or whether he imagined it in Santiago out of faulty memory. But who remembers, and who cares? Toledano is dead, the set designer is forgotten, and why should Ruth remember? Sleep does not cancel the question but quiets it for the moment as it sweeps him into the abyss he desires.

2

BUT WHEN SWEET nothingness dissolves into a flicker of consciousness, he is frightened by the glaring eye of the clock on the wall. Can this be the right time, or has the clock broken in his absence? He raises the blinds and again finds night, only now the world is rainy and foggy, and the glowing advertisements sputter in the murk. Can it be that nearly twenty-four hours have passed since he went off to sleep?

He puts on lights and turns on the heat and heads for the kitchen to prepare himself a meal, which might rekindle the appetite trumped by the fatigue, and amid the cutting and mixing and boiling of water, he remembers how Susana disappeared in the middle of filming and the general panic over how to find a replacement, until Amsalem's Bedouin found her hiding under the carousel in the playground and with threats and enticements wooed her back to the synagogue so she could do her job. In Kafka's short story, the animal is old and has an

amazing memory, whereas their mongoose was young and inexperienced, nervous, and devoid of memory and vision. A staffer from the
biblical zoo in Jerusalem, recruited to coach the film crew in handling the animal, was impressed by how they'd already half trained
the feisty young thing and suggested that at the end of the shoot they
turn her over to his zoo, where her artistic experience might inspire
other animals.

During the years of his marriage, Moses regularly shared the
kitchen duties and became quite skilled at preparing dishes not requiring special expertise. Ever since he and his wife parted ways,
although he has mostly eaten in restaurants, he has broadened his
repertoire. So now, full of food and fully awake, he waits for dawn
so he can tell himself, *I'm back to my apartment and my routines*, in
the meantime activating the washing machine and again checking
e-mail, this time not with an urge to delete but with a desire to be in
touch. New correspondents have not appeared, apart from Yaakov
Amsalem, who congratulates him on the Spanish prize and has an
idea for a new film.

Why does every little far-flung prize get publicized in Israel? Can
it be that awards from abroad muffle the injustice and corruption at
home? *Amsalem, my friend*, he is quick to reply, *congratulations are
unnecessary. This is not a prize but a tiny investment in the next film.
So please, keep it quiet, so as not to wake the dormant taxman.*

He reconnects the telephone, which immediately signals that a
message arrived during the big sleep. Again, his ex-wife, who in the
clear and civilized voice he has always loved also offers her congratulations on the prize. If such a private woman has heard the news,
there's no other choice but to declare it to the revenue authorities.

On the kitchen table lie leftovers of the big dinner; he can't bring
himself to look at them. He shoves them in the fridge, washes dishes,
and tidies up, but doesn't consider going back to bed, so in advance
of his normal schedule he showers, shaves his cheeks and trims his
goatee, puts on clothes and shoes too, to feel he is indeed getting
back to daily life. He rotates his cozy TV chair to face the big win-

dow, and while witnessing the first stirring of neighbors he pulls a screenplay from the ever-mounting pile on his table to see if some hidden spark might twinkle within.

But there seems to be no spark for now, and soon the script drops to the floor, and he, a lone spectator in an awakening world, snoozes. And the snoozing grows deep enough to dream, about cautious descent on broad stairs, following his ex-wife who supports her aunt, a big blond woman confined to a wheelchair before her death but who now, in the dream, has returned to life without a wheelchair, and she slowly, propped by his wife, goes down the stairs of a high school or college. He hurries after the two women, poised to catch hold of the aunt and steady her should she fall backward.

The educational institution is built on several levels on a hillside, like the high school in Jerusalem where the dreamer was a student and later a teacher, until he became a director. And the aunt, although limping, walks downstairs with determination, neither slipping forward nor tripping back, landing safely at the ground floor, where her niece leads her to the cafeteria, its walls lined with books, finally relieving Moses of his supervisory obligation. Free at last, he looks around for other stairs and finds a narrow flight, its steps ugly and pocked, leading down to a deserted cellar. He flings from the top of the stairs a bag filled with dirty laundry — underwear, socks, shirts — and as the bag flies downward, he regrets his recklessness; he has a washer and dryer at home, so why ask an educational institution to do his dirty laundry, which isn't labeled with his name? But he can't undo what's done. The bag has disappeared, and he has to accept its loss. He retreats from the stairs, opens a wide glass door, and finds himself gazing into a green gully.

A pinprick of light on the eastern horizon beyond the bedroom window. The rain has slowed down, the fog has lifted. If the long sleep had such a drowsy epilogue, it means the Spaniards had not deprived him of sleep but given him some of their own. Has his retrospective really ended? Not knowing if the cameraman of *Circular Therapy* had been able to split his family home in three still bothers him. He moves the laundry from the washing machine to the dryer, puts on a windbreaker, and takes, as he heads for his car, the walking stick.

3

BY THE TIME he gets to Bab-el-Wad he has to battle with the sunrise. Last night's rain has cleansed the world, and the rays of eastern light glinting from the Judean Hills grow stronger in the purified air, blinding the driver. From time to time he lifts a hand from the wheel and shields his eyes to see the road. But since traffic is thin at this early hour, and he knows the way, he arrives safe and sound at the scene of his childhood – a stately Jerusalem neighborhood, conquered when the state was established, where a mossy, mysterious leper hospital was joined eventually by the residences of the president and prime minister. He parks his car near the imposing Jerusalem Theater, not far from the house where he grew up. Here, now, he completes his retrospective for himself alone. It was nearly twenty years ago that he sold the small handsome stone house, and he has not visited it since nor passed by, so he is prepared to find changes and additions, even a second story. Yet at first glance, everything is as it was. The same big, black iron door separating two exterior stairways, the same mailbox. The huge ceramic flowerpot that appeared in *Circular Therapy* stands on its base atop the fence and has changed its color. The house was purchased from him after his father's death by a young couple, both lawyers, whose names are on the large mailbox. Do they still live here, or is the house rented to someone else? They had intended to add another floor, but it turns out that what was good enough for his parents was good enough for them, or else they failed in business.

Winter stillness in the street on a cold Jerusalem morning. The hour is early; his entering the garden to check camera angles would look strange. He returns to the car and fetches the Spanish pilgrim's staff – a white-haired man with a walking stick will cut a friendly figure even before his intentions are clear. The morning paper has been stuck in the mailbox; he can wait till the owner comes out and ask his permission for a visit in the garden to verify an imaginary reality. But the owner tarries, and waiting in a cold empty street is an undignified waste of time. He opens an adjoining gate and enters a yard, which stood empty throughout his youth until a four-story apartment house was built there. On a narrow path alongside the stone fence separating the two properties, he walks around his parents' home, and after cutting through a tangle of bushes, he reaches a corner from which as a child he enjoyed secretly watching his parents on the patio. Despite the hour, there is a risk that someone at a rear window may wonder about the unfamiliar old man standing in a far corner, so he huddles in the bushes, gets down on his knees, and grabs the edge of the stone wall, his eyes fixed on his former family home to calculate whether Toledano and the set designer with ingenious trickery had indeed managed to turn one house into three.

Why is he hanging around here? If a whole day could disappear so easily, why try to reconstruct so distant a reality? Wouldn't it be better to stop struggling with an unreliable memory, even if the retrospective comes to an end with an open question? But he is a Jerusalemite to the marrow, able to rest his head comfortably on a stone wall as the vine on the stones caresses his face with a fragrant tendril, and his walking stick, its tip planted in the ground, steadies him as he gazes at his parental home.

At last the door opens. An old dog comes out of the house, begins sniffing among the plants and bushes. Slowly, in widening circles, the dog progresses toward Moses but, oddly, exhibits no excitement or wonder, not a growl or a bark. Moses clucks at him gratefully, and the old dog just perks his ears and wags his tail, then urinates and turns his head loyally toward his master, who has followed him outdoors: an elderly man in a bathrobe, with a little beard like Moses' and a similar body type. The man takes down several wet items from the clothesline, then goes to fetch the newspaper. He does not hurry back inside but pauses on the doorstep, shielding his eyes for a better look. Can it be that in the back corner of the adjacent property, amid the bushes, is a male figure that resembles him? Now a woman appears from the house, skinny, with a mane of white hair and a watering can, and she begins dousing plants that were sheltered from the rain. Although twenty years have passed since the sale, Moses recognizes the woman lawyer who had bargained with him stubbornly over every detail. In light of this recognition, he is also sure now of the identity of the other man, also a lawyer, her husband. If he is right, the couple have not only maintained his old family home as it was, with all its defects, but also remained true to each other. Have they clung to the house because of its proximity to the president and prime minister, or because they believe that the enigmatic Belgian consulate, which dominates the top of the street like a secular cathedral, enhances the beauty of their own house?

In any event, concludes Moses, a talented if tragic cinematographer like Toledano could certainly have produced three different houses from this one. He might even have placed his camera here, in this very corner, and with delicate shifts left and right, up and down, convinced the audience that in each scene, the main characters were entering a different house in a different area. But was all this done merely to save money in a low-budget film, or was there also a symbolic intention, which only the screenwriter could explain?

The two lawyers summon the dog to the warmth of their home, but before entering, the animal turns its head toward Moses and emits a brief bark, as if to say: *I smelled you, don't you dare cross the fence.*

Yes, here at Moses' family home on a cold Jerusalem morning, his retrospective is finished, and now it's time to return to routine. As he approaches his car parked in front, he sees that the doors of the theater are wide open, and the lights in the lobby are on. Young people in coats and scarves mill toward a makeshift counter to waken themselves with coffee and bagels. Someone recognizes him from a distance and calls his name. They are actors and singers and dancers, here for the dress rehearsal of a musical play for children to be staged during the Hanukkah vacation.

"A play? By whom, about what?" Moses asks.

"Based on *Don Quixote*, adapted to an Israeli setting."

"More *Don Quixote*?" sniffs Moses. "Enough is enough, no? The eternal hero."

Other actors recognize the director and flock to him as bears to honey. Among them, a tall young man with a little beard who will apparently dance the part of the Knight of the Sorrowful Face. A few of them have heard about the prize and congratulate him. "Small prize," he says, thinking, *That does it, I'll have to declare it, but I can reduce it by deducting my expenses, maybe Ruth's too.*

A young and pretty actress, who years ago studied in Ruth's class for children, brings him coffee and a bagel and asks what he's doing in Jerusalem at such an early hour. Preparing for a new film? What's it about? Has the cast already been chosen? Would he like to watch their rehearsal? No new film, just some vague ideas. He is too tired to attend the rehearsal. When the musical begins its run, he will bring his oldest grandson to see it and his sister too, Moses' little granddaughter.

The group is called inside, and the lobby empties quickly. Moses gets ready to move on, but the cafeteria worker who is collecting the dishes says, "What's the hurry? Finish your coffee."

4

HE KNOWS THAT Hanan, the husband of his ex-wife, gets up late in the morning; at night he usually works on his music. To avoid exchanging pointless pleasantries with his successor, Moses phones Ofra during morning hours.

"I just got back from Spain and I'm returning your call," he says to her on his mobile.

"How are you, my dear?" she asks.

"Doing my best."

"I was so happy about the prize."

"Be only a little happy, it's a tiny prize."

"In any case, it's encouraging. They gave you a retrospective too."

"A strange retrospective, drilling deep down. But you didn't leave me a message because you wanted to encourage me."

"Why not? Absolutely. But also to clarify something about Itay's bar mitzvah."

"Clarify what?"

"Not on the telephone, Yairi — let's meet this evening."

"Where?"

"At home."

"Not at home. You know I don't like being a guest in an apartment that used to be mine."

"You're not a guest. You are always the former owner and not a guest. And besides, Hanan is abroad and I'm alone."

"Alone? Even worse. Better we should meet elsewhere."

"Why?"

"Remember what happened a few years ago when we were alone in the apartment? I hassled you and lost my self-control and it ended in an ugly scene that hurt us both."

"But that was years ago. You've gotten over me since then. I'm a woman of sixty-three."

"Sixty-four."

"Almost. And you're pushing seventy."

"I'm already there."

"Then why get worked up about an old lady like me? You especially, always surrounded by beautiful actresses."

"No beauties," he growls, "it's all fairy tales from the tabloids."

"Perhaps not beautiful. But good, talented women who undoubtedly like you. Come on, this time let's meet at home. It's important to me, and you'll control yourself. And I will too. Apart from Itay's bar mitzvah, I have a few things here that require a good eye and smart advice."

"Like what?"

"No, not on the phone. Come. Early in the evening. For an hour, no more."

"Even an hour will be hard for me."

"It won't be hard. I promise you. We've both told the whole world that we've stayed good friends."

"True. Which is probably my mistake."

The first sounds of music waft from the theater to the lobby. Little by little, they interweave with the delicate lilt of a woman's voice. Dulcinea. He smiles to himself, briefly tempted to drop in on the rehearsal, maybe discover new acting talent, but then decides no, give the play a chance to take shape, and if the reviews are good take the two grandchildren to see how *Don Quixote* can be revived in the twenty-first century. He walks out into the plaza and is blinded by the strong Jerusalem light. Conversations with his former wife are painful and exasperating; each time he feels a longing for her. He should not have given in. Following such an invasive retrospective, a meeting in close quarters with the wife of his youth, in their old apartment, will most likely be distressing. To his dying day, he will not be able to decide if his divorce was necessary. Years have gone by, and she has remarried, and he even likes her husband a little, a middling musician, younger than she is by three years, who still dreams of writing music for one of the former husband's movies.

He starts the ignition, pulls away from the curb, and the car phone rings. It's Amsalem, who has read the e-mail warning and pledges not to talk about the prize with anyone, but anyway, how much was it?

"Not important. Not much."

"Every shekel counts. Don't be embarrassed."

Moses names the amount, and Amsalem is shocked. "That's not a prize, that's just a symbol," he tells the director. "To fit the symbolic films you screened for them. With an amount like that, you sure mustn't let the state stick its fingers in."

A few years back, Yaakov Amsalem turned eighty, but he is still alert and forceful. Even though he kicks in only 3 percent of the production budget, mostly by providing food for the cast and crew, he considers himself one of the producers, a partner among partners. He walks on the set freely, demands from time to time to look through the camera. Above all, it's important to him to pepper the director's brain with the basics of human existence. Actually, he was the one who proposed the idea for the potato film, which was a surprising hit. Now he feels the time is ripe for a new film, and he wants to be in on it.

While driving out of Jerusalem, Moses tells him about the retrospective and mentions that Trigano had contrived it from behind the scenes. Amsalem has, in fact, lost touch with the man who ushered him into the film business, but he remembers Trigano's old screenplays, which he had thought overblown, until Israeli reality began to catch up with them. Yes, odd that after many years, with some words he'd picked up from Ladino-speaking neighbors, Trigano finds this archive in Spain, at the end of the earth, and they honor him. And it's just like him, Trigano, to ignore the director; why should he forgive him for an old insult? Back in those days, Amsalem knew the uncle well, the brother of Trigano's mother, an unsuccessful wholesaler in the produce market but a decent man; he didn't live much longer than Trigano's father but while still alive devotedly helped raise the boy. Hasn't he told Moses about the uncle before? Trigano loved him. He was a sweet man and had a good singing voice, but when he got emotional, he would stutter. Despite the stutter, he served as a cantor in the synagogue, if only at afternoon prayers, when the place was all but empty. The congregants loved him but feared the stutter would prolong the prayers and so would prod him to go faster. Who knows, maybe it was because of his uncle's stutter and humiliation that Trigano invented that little animal, which would run around the synagogue and make a mess.

"Susana."

"Yeah, Susana," says Amsalem with a booming laugh. "Susana, that's right."

"But Trigano didn't invent her, he borrowed her from a story by Kafka."

"Kafka? Who's Kafka?"

"A world-class writer, and even you, Amsalem, who dropped out of grade school should know who he is and remember his name."

"If you say so, I'll remember."

"There are many animals in his stories, all interesting. By the way, I wonder what your Bedouin did with the animal after we finished shooting."

"Do I know? He set her free, or ate her, or gave her to his dogs."

"Because in ancient Egypt, and I learned this only in Santiago, a mongoose was considered a holy animal, embalmed just like the Pharaohs."

"So maybe the Bedouin embalmed her, and when you come to see me in Beersheba on Saturday we can make a pilgrimage to her grave."

"Who says I'm driving to Beersheba on Saturday?"

"It's important not just for me but for you too. Come for lunch, and we'll give you a room to rest in after the meal, so you won't miss your nap. It will take you an hour at most from Tel Aviv to Beersheba on a Saturday, and there'll be some interesting guests, a young couple, special people, who might help us get the next film going. Enough, friend, get over it, the retrospective is behind you, stop picking at it. We're not young, and if we still have a little energy left, let's look forward and not back."

5

MOSES DOES NOT ignore the admonition of the veteran producer, even if the man holds only a 3 percent share of his films. Instead of going straight home, Moses visits his small office, to see what the world wanted of him in his absence. His secretary congratulates him on the prize, and he decides not to snap at well-wishers because of its small size but instead just nod humbly and offer polite thanks. Not much is new in the small office, which gets bigger during every new production but in between films only keeps the embers burning. He gathers up anything that seems vital, fills a plastic bag with screenplays and also novels and stories that seek adaptation to film. Finally he adds a few DVDs of short clips sent by actors or cinematographers who wish to impress him with their work. Then he invites the secretary to lunch to find out what's new among his competitors.

When he gets back to his apartment, he removes the laundry from the dryer and folds it. He inspects the bed sheets that swallowed up a day of his life and decides to wash them too. For a moment he weighs whether to phone Ruth, but he chooses to leave her be, not to plant any false expectation of a new role. *We've had more than enough of that*, he thinks while making his bed with fresh sheets. After a short nap, he sits down to surf the Internet. He easily locates the story of Roman Charity and, despite the warning of the elderly expert, clicks on a bonanza of images of the daughter and father, whose essence was ably captured in that quick lecture by his bed at the Parador.

Now he takes a look at a few clips from actors and cinematographers, and at the same time, barely straying from the screen, he looks at script synopses, some no longer than a single page. As a high school teacher he perfected an efficient technique for checking homework and tests that resulted in instant evaluation of their quality. And because the world of film inspires many people to float glib ideas and fantasies on the assumption that others will make them work, he has learned how to skim and select, without fear that something good will elude him. So when Ofra phones as evening falls, to confirm their meeting, he looks with great satisfaction at the heap of discarded pages at his feet and says: "If there's no choice, I surrender to you as always, but only for a short time."

He sees Ofra at family events or social gatherings, where relatives and friends look on with approval and relief at their easy and amicable interaction. What had belonged to him he either took or discarded, and if some forlorn bit of mail insists on going to the address he left fifteen years ago, it's fine if it waits for him with his grandchildren. As a matter of principle he is unwilling to be a guest in his former home, and when he sees the red mailbox he himself had installed many years ago at the entrance to the building, a fragment of his name still lingering there, he feels demeaned. The Spanish retrospective has apparently sapped his resolve. Amsalem is right when he says he should stay away from her. He eschews the elevator and slowly climbs from floor to floor, to see which of the old neighbors still live in the building. But when he gets to the fourth floor, he stops on the last stair. The thought that the wife of his youth awaits him alone in his former apartment arouses tension and trepidation.

It appears that Ofra has seen him from the window, for she opens the door before he reaches it. Yes, she too is surely emotional and confused and perhaps regrets insisting that he come over. Not looking at her directly, he mumbles hello, pulls her close, and plants kisses on her forehead and cheeks, so she'll be intimidated from the start and not entangle the soul that is still tied to hers.

Disaffected but oddly satisfied, he observes his former domicile, which looks even sadder and messier than the last time he was here. Ofra grew up as a spoiled only child, and her parents would clean up her clutter with patient love that they bequeathed to her first husband. But now she must deal with not only her own chaos but also that of her husband, the artist, a musician who apparently believes that chaos stimulates creativity.

To make room for a grand piano, the harmony of the living room has been violated. The sofa was shoved in the wrong place, and a computer and printer are permanent guests at the dining table. Old newspapers, so hard to part with, are stuffed under the coffee table, which is decked out with plates of savory cookies and dried fruits. But when Ofra offers him coffee, he insists on making his own, to prove to her and to himself that till his dying day, he will not be thought of as a guest in a home that rejected him. Embarrassed, she tries to prevent him from entering the kitchen, and with good reason, since the disarray in the living room is but a pale prologue to the anarchy of the kitchen. He switches on the electric kettle with the cracked handle and chooses a yellowish cup he once loved, but its cleanliness is suspect so he takes a glass mug instead and waits for the water to boil. And she stands beside him, small and tense, smiling uneasily; her face is properly made up, but her hair, gone gray, is not dyed well, or maybe she has stopped dyeing it. The coffee jar is not in its assigned place; she has to find it for him. "You still don't sweeten your coffee?" she asks softly. "Never," he says and opens the fridge where, amid the scary proliferation of staples and leftovers, he sees not one milk carton but three. He will not ask the lady of the house which is the most recent but will check the expiration dates and then whiten his cup with the milk of his former wife.

In the meantime, her embarrassment has turned to affection. She beams as she watches the liberty he takes in her home, as if her former husband's immersion in her chaos gives her hope. Her warmth almost tempts him to comment on the gray hair — is it laziness, or overstated feminism? — but he doesn't. She is not his. And though the decline in the appearance of the woman who left him should perhaps gratify him, it actually pains, frightens him.

In the living room, she congratulates him again on the award, and in keeping with his decision, he is not quick to dismiss its value but rather smiles and thanks her. Next she shows interest in the retrospective and is happy to hear that Ruth went along. "How is she?" she asks. "She is not well," he says, "neglects her health." He mentions her refusal to repeat the blood test. "This is not okay; you have to convince her," demands his ex-wife. "Why me? She has a son." "You know what he's worth," she reminds him, because she knows Ruth's story inside out and retains personal and family details long after he has forgotten them. He tells her about his encounter with his earliest films; she remembers them, of course, that was how they met, he would call on her at the National Library to help him select music for them. "There still may be some prints around here," she says, "look in the storage room." "No" — he recoils — "there's nothing of mine still here."

She has invited him over to talk about their grandson Itay's bar mitzvah, scheduled for early spring. Itay and his parents decided to eliminate the big party and make do, after the synagogue ceremony, with a lunch for close family, perhaps on the assumption that Ofra and Moses would be writing the big gift checks anyway. Neither Galit nor Zvi has the energy for a big party. Zvi is still waiting for tenure at the hospital and takes on many shifts, and Galit's salary, despite her tenured position, is the salary of a technician.

"Why, then, should they take on the burden of a big party with many guests? Because Grandpa promised to make a little film of it?"

"I suggested it once, with good intentions. Anyway, I'm a lousy cameraman."

"I didn't know it was possible to be a successful director and a lousy cameraman."

"Anything is possible. So what's your question?"

"Well, they were wondering how to make Itay happy with something real, not just being called to the Torah; in other words, to give him a truly enjoyable experience, and nowadays among his classmates there's a trend of taking a bar mitzvah trip to Africa, so Galit and Zvi thought that a trip like that would be a wonderful thing for him, and for his sister and for them."

"Of all the continents, it's Africa they choose for the transition from childhood to maturity," he remarks.

"They're not thinking in educational terms. They're thinking about an enjoyable trip in the outdoors, the animals and scenery. A trip to clear the head a little."

"Itay's or theirs?"

"Everyone whose head needs clearing."

"But why Africa? If they're passing up a party and taking a trip abroad, they should go to Europe. Give the boy a little culture. Show him cathedrals, museums, historical sites. Connect him with something aesthetic, not some lion or monkey that he could see in the safari park in Ramat Gan. And believe me, such a trip wouldn't hurt Galit and Zvi either, two people who spend their lives cooped up in a hospital."

"There's plenty of culture here, without Europe."

"You really think that?"

"I don't know what I think, but that's their wish and it should be respected. If you want to persuade them to change their travel plans, by all means, do it, but whatever happens, you have to help them."

"With what?"

"I don't know how big a present you were thinking of."

"That's an odd question."

"Why? Is it a secret? It'll come out sooner or later."

"Two thousand shekels, something like that."

"Perhaps you could increase it a little, help them with the trip? It's an expensive trip."

"Increase it? Thanks to our divorce, Itay will get two presents from us instead of one, from his grandpa and from his grandma."

"He gets two presents but has lost a natural connection with a grandpa and grandma who are together."

"Not my fault."

"It is your fault. But let's not get into that now, please. Let's keep up the good mood."

"Good mood. Fine. How much are you planning to give?"

"Three thousand. I have a small savings account I can go into. It's not for Itay, it's for Galit and Zvi, who are dying to get out in the world a little."

"To Africa."

"Africa is also in the world."

"All right, I'll try to increase it."

"You did just get a prize."

"Enough." He raises his voice. "The prize is none of your business."

"Sorry, I'm sorry."

"And I still hope that I have permission to try to persuade them to change the itinerary from Africa to Europe."

"Permission, sure. She's your daughter and he's your son-in-law. So they, at least, have to listen to you."

He hears the scornful tone in her voice and turns a cold eye on the grand piano that wreaks anarchy in the living room.

"Tell me, was this piano here the last time I was?"

"There was a piano but not a grand."

"Aha," he says. "This piano turned the nice living room we had into a music warehouse."

"Which is exactly what I wanted to talk to you about, and which is why I wanted you to come here."

She stands up and points to the wall separating the living room from the hallway, and asks if he recalls whether it's original or part of the renovations they did when they moved in.

"It is original," he declares, "we didn't add any wall here. Why do you ask?"

"Because Hanan thought it might be a good idea to tear it down to expand the living room."

"For an even bigger piano?"

"No." She laughs. "This is the biggest. So it can move around here more easily. If we take down this wall, we can add the hallway to the living room."

"You won't be adding a thing," he says, pleased to contradict her. "This is a retaining wall – if you take it down, you'll bring down the upstairs apartment, and Schuster will sit in your living room."

"He doesn't live there anymore."

"Or a different neighbor."

"You sure?"

"Ask a contractor or architect, why me?"

"You planned the renovations."

"That's why I know what I'm talking about."

"So what then?"

"Why tear down walls when all you have to do is reduce the chaos you've created here?"

"How?"

"Move the piano near the window, with the wing in the corner."

"It won't fit in the corner, there's not enough room."

"Says who?"

"That's where the armchair goes."

"Which one?"

"The pink one."

"What's it doing there?"

"It has sheet music on it."

"Let's remove it from there, and you'll see that the corner will be happy to accommodate the entire back of the piano. There's all this space going to waste."

"Wait a second. It's hard for Hanan to write music facing the window, the view distracts him and takes him where he doesn't want to go. He writes, you know, very abstract music. Not romantic."

"So he should close the window and shut the blinds."

"He won't have air."

"He should write his music blindfolded."

"You just want to find fault."

"No, but I am curious about the self-indulgence."

"It's not self-indulgence. It's art."

"I'm also an artist, and I was never self-indulgent."

"True, in that sense you were an easier husband."

"So listen to me now too. In the living room, the solution is fairly simple. Your chaos makes me furious. I got so dizzy in your kitchen, I can still feel it."

"You're exaggerating."

"I'm not. When I left, the place was orderly. Now it's this insane warehouse."

"Because you didn't teach me how to be neat."

"Teach? You didn't want to learn. You relied on me for everything."

"Because you didn't force me to be neat."

"Was that possible?"

"Not force. But educate. You didn't have the patience to educate me."

"That's true. I loved you too much, so I gave in to all your weaknesses."

"So do you have an idea how to restore order?"

"Come, give me a hand. We have a chance since he's not here. And believe me, I'm doing it for you. For some reason I still have a little bit of love for you."

She blushes with an old, dreamy smile; she knows that he still loves her. She gets up to help him remove the computer and printer from the dining table, collect the cables, move the stack of musical scores from the armchair to the bedroom, and return the chair to its former place. He then releases the piano's brakes and rolls it toward the window, carefully easing the closed wing deep into the corner, and on his initiative, without asking the owner, he places a vase on top to create, in his words, a melodious nook.

Her face is flushed now from the joint effort and the physical closeness with her former husband. And she is amazed how, with simple common sense and without tearing down a wall, he has successfully retrieved some of the beauty and order of the living room. "Don't worry," he says, "Hanan will get used to his piano's new location. And in general," he sermonizes, "artists who agonize and think that if they pamper their muse she will repay the kindness don't understand that serious muses hate indulgence and self-indulgence."

"Hanan is not self-indulgent," she insists, defending the husband who is three years her junior. "He's just in a difficult period."

"In my difficult periods, I did not create this kind of chaos all around me."

She looks down. "You did worse things," she whispers, as if to herself.

"It only seemed that way to you, because you didn't understand that a director is different from artists who work alone. He has personal responsibility to the characters realized in his work."

"She was not a character," she mutters, "she was a woman. But let's drop it now, please. So many years have passed."

"Yes, years have passed."

And he remembers how this refined and fragile woman tried to hit him when he admitted he had betrayed her and how he forced her to make love, but it was the last time.

"You want me to help you straighten out the kitchen?"

"No," she says nervously. "You've done enough. Thanks."

Silence. He knows she would be grateful if he left her alone, but settled now in the pink armchair, the stack of music gone, he finds it hard to go.

"Even though so many years have passed," he says, "you'd be surprised to hear that I sometimes dream about you. Perhaps hoping that, if not in reality, then in a dream, you'll finally be able to understand what my art is about."

"You still dream about me?" She sounds concerned.

"Once in a while."

"And what do you dream? What are you doing to me in your dream?"

"I am not doing anything, just looking. This morning, after I heard your voicemail, you suddenly appeared to me in a little dream, that's why I agreed to come here."

"What did you dream?"

"That you were going down the stairs, a lot of stairs."

"Where?"

"I can't remember, but stairs, as you know, are not just stairs but also an erotic symbol, one that I sometimes use in a film when I want to tighten the bond between the hero and the heroine."

"First time I've heard such a theory."

"It's true, ask Hanan. If he's an intellectual, he's surely heard of it. But don't worry, in my dream you weren't alone. You were with Aunt Sonia, so nothing very erotic could be going on."

"Aunt Sonia?" She giggles like a child. "Nice that you brought her into your dream too."

"I didn't bring her, she came on her own, and not in a wheelchair — you both walked down slowly, you supported her and took care of her, and I was behind watching carefully, so if she fell I would catch her."

"At least in dreams you are a generous person."

"But now, telling it to you, I think I understand the dream. I think I brought her to protect you from the yearning I still feel for you. A pure and noble longing for, say, the big, beautiful birthmark on the back of your neck, above the spine. You couldn't see it, so I had to bring you news of it now and then."

Her eyes are closed. She sighs. Her face is weary. Wrinkles unfamiliar to him have been added in the years he hasn't seen her. But when she speaks there's a soft irony in her voice.

"I see that you still can't get away from the retrospective."

"Maybe. Is that a sin?"

"No sin. But you promised you would restrain yourself."

"I'm not restrained?"

"Not really. The retrospective is still affecting you."

She speaks without anger, without fear, relaxed and calm, her legs resting on the coffee table. She seems no longer in a hurry to have him leave.

And the sting of separation pierces his heart once more, he rises from the armchair, not heading for the door but approaching her, and he asks, with a smile, "I'm not entitled to a little reward for moving your piano and finding room for the wing and reducing your chaos?" She eyes him with gratitude. "What if for a second I took another look at your beauty mark, the one that you can't see but that I loved from the moment I discovered it."

Like an actress obeying her director, she slowly leans her head to expose slightly the nape of her neck, and he cautiously turns down the collar of her sweater, finds the spot, dark and oval and a bit worrisome, and brings his lips close and touches it with the tip of his tongue, and then puts the collar back in place and says firmly, "That's it, I'm out of here, and don't think I won't try to talk Galit out of the barbaric idea to celebrate our grandson's bar mitzvah among monkeys and lions."

6

ON FRIDAY EVENING Amsalem again insists Moses come down to Beersheba. "There'll be a few people at lunch we can persuade to invest in the new film, but they need to see who and how you are." "Instead of seeing me," replies Moses, "tell them to see my latest films." "No," objects Amsalem, "these are plain folks with too much money who know nothing about film but understand people, and so they want a sense of the dreamer before they start to fund his fantasies. Besides," he adds, "my sister-in-law will be there, and she recently got divorced."

"How old is she?"

"Forty-five. But I'm not thinking about her for you. I'm thinking about a young man with a baby, which I have a feeling would make a great story that hasn't been seen before."

"Everything has been seen," says Moses, and gives him a tentative promise predicated on various conditions: how he feels, the weather, visiting grandchildren. But the next morning, as he lazes in bed with the newspapers, the producer again calls and tries to coax him to come. "A storm is coming," protests Moses, "let's postpone the visit till next Saturday?" "Only in Tel Aviv is a storm coming," says Amsalem. "In the south the skies are blue, and the new highway will zip you to Beersheba in under an hour."

Although the investments by the Amsalem-Tamir Company have never exceeded 3 or 4 percent of his films' budgets, the wholesaler's loyalty and faith inspire the director's affection. For Amsalem, as opposed to the production companies and public film funds that support his projects, has a fundamental folksiness. The scent of the fruits and vegetables that made him rich stayed with him even after he broke into real estate, and despite his advanced age, he has lately begun wearing his hair in a small braided ponytail. Although Amsalem also disconnected himself from Trigano, Moses does not forget that it was the screenwriter who brought them together, and even if Trigano is gone from his life, the connection he left behind is not forgotten.

He phones his daughter to persuade her to switch Africa for Europe before he increases his bar mitzvah gift. She is taken aback. Though the Africa decision has been made, and they plan to order the tickets next week, she is willing to hear why Africa is anathema to her father. "Come, let's talk about this in person, Abba, without Itay or Zvi. Not this morning, because people will be here. Tonight we'll be at a concert. But tomorrow morning, at the hospital, I have a break between ten and eleven, and we can sit undisturbed in the cafeteria, and I'd also like to hear about your retrospective and the prize that Imma told me you got in Spain."

"A small prize. Negligible."

"The main thing is they honored you."

He knows his son-in-law is touchy about his intervention in family matters, so he welcomes the idea of a private meeting at the hospital, especially because she could — he realizes — do an ultrasound of one or another of his internal organs and tell him what's what.

The storm has not yet hit, but the darkening sky has further dulled the city's spirit on this quiet Saturday, and he decides to trade the drizzle of Tel Aviv for the dazzle of the desert. And indeed, in one hour flat, following precise directions he receives en route, he finds himself looking for a parking spot amid the many cars circling the vegetable magnate's villa.

Amsalem did not mislead him. Among the guests, merchants and middlemen and contractors, are some who are interested in his films, but first they want to get to know the director and learn where he's heading in the next one. Before long he is sitting in the middle of a massive living room, sipping from a glass his host keeps refilling with a superior wine, providing answers to curious questioners who blend artistic naiveté and practical guile. Now and again unruly youngsters of various ages surge to the buffet, help themselves to the rich spread of savories and sweets, then lope back outside to play.

"So what's the next picture?" asks a guest, whose financial worth Amsalem has already confided to Moses. "What's cooking on your front burner?"

"The pot is still empty," Moses says frankly, "and the fire's still out." He senses at once that he has made a mistake, for an artist who complains that the muse is snubbing him encourages people to shower him with suggestions and ideas, true stories or ones concocted on the spot. And when they see that Moses' attention has faltered under the torrent of ideas, they press the host to bring a sheet of paper so they can write their names and phone numbers, should the director want further details. And Amsalem, old and experienced, who knows and loves his friends, is weighing his inclination to meet their request against the need to rein them in, and summons a boy, who sits alone sadly in a corner, rocking a baby carriage, to bring him paper to write down the names of those who do not want to be forgotten.

But the boy ignores the call and stays at his post. Instead, a most charming woman advances, her hair gathered in a colorful scarf. This is Amsalem's sister-in-law, younger sister of his second wife. Moses had met her and her husband among the many people the producer invited to "his" films. Now he makes room for her beside him, and the holy Sabbath notwithstanding, she diligently writes down, in an oddly childlike hand, the names of those wishing to breathe life, and possibly money, into the dying ember. Can it be that the recent divorcée, pretty and sweet, her perfume pleasantly enticing, is why Amsalem insisted on getting him down here today? For if Amsalem had allowed himself, after the death of his first wife, the mother of his children, to marry a woman twenty years younger than he, why should Moses, ten years younger than Amsalem, not follow his example?

The sign-up is complete. Moses folds the page, sticks it in his pocket, promises to get back to them all, and invites the lovely scribe to join him at the buffet. As he piles food on the plate that the woman, Rachel Siko by name, has handed him, he takes the liberty to inquire where she lives and what kind of work she does, and naturally about her children, who, despite her religious proclivities, turn out to be but two in number, and still young. The older one, Yoav, celebrated his bar mitzvah not long ago, and he is the pale lad rocking the baby carriage in the corner and casting a longing eye at the buffet. Whereas the daughter, Meirav, who according to her mother is a ten-year-old beauty, is running around with the other kids. Moses listens politely and concludes that the children are too young; any permanent relationship is out of the question, only friendship. But the woman keeps talking about herself, fixing her radiant eyes on the listener, and with bold, near self-destructive candor, she tells him that in addition to her two children she has a grandson, seven months old.

"Grandson?" He tilts his head to make sure his hearing aid picked up the word correctly.

"Yes, a grandson. There in the carriage, with his father."

"His father?" he asks. "Meaning your husband?"

"Not my husband, my son. Yoav, the boy sitting there."

"The boy?"

"Yes, the young man sitting by the carriage and looking after his son. He is his father."

"His father . . ." whispers Moses.

"Yes. And that's the story my brother-in-law and I were thinking to propose for your next film . . . unless you're already set on a different one."

As Moses casts a horrified look toward the corner of the enormous room at the callow youth who sadly rocks his baby, he drops his plate, which shatters at his feet. But his conversation partner quickly calms him with "Mazel tov!" and bends over to pick up the pieces.

So, he wonders, fetching another plate, was it because of that bizarre story that Amsalem insisted he hustle down to Beersheba, or because of the woman telling it? Or both?

7

BUT THE STORY is interrupted, for Amsalem's wife has enlisted her sister to help in the kitchen. Now Moses can recover and serenely amass his lunch upon his plate. He finds a seat at one of the small tables in the garden, and while eating he tries to decide who among the swirl of children racing around the empty swimming pool is the young beauty who became an aunt before entering junior high. An older couple, residents of Sderot, sits down at his table. They came to Amsalem's house as a Sabbath respite from the rocket fire from Gaza. "But don't the rockets," asks Moses, "reach Beersheba as well?" Yes, they confirm, but only occasionally, with longer warning time, and besides, those who live outside of rocket range have not invited them to visit. They know who Moses is, Amsalem had invited them to the premiere of *Potatoes*, they loved it, even cried a little at the end. They have a big fruit and vegetable store in the produce market of Sderot and were pleased to see a story developed from such everyday material. The film he made was simple and realistic, they inform Moses, which is why it was so touching.

The boyish father enters the garden, carefully bearing a tray with plates full of food, as the grandmother, carrying the baby, scouts for a shaded table for the little family. Moses wants to join them but fears offending the greengrocers at his table. He signals to Amsalem, who circulates among the tables holding two bottles of wine, red and white. As red wine flows into his cup, the director whispers to the producer:

"Is this a true story or some fantasy of your sister-in-law's?"

"Of course it's true." Amsalem is insulted. "I wouldn't have dragged you down to Beersheba on a Saturday for a fantasy. You don't lack for fantasies in Tel Aviv."

"Where's the baby's mother?"

"You want to hear the whole story from my sister-in-law?"

"Give me the bottom line."

"The baby's mother is no longer here. I mean, she left Israel."

"Who is she?"

"Was. I mean, still is. An American girl."

"Actually American?"

"Also Jewish. Half, actually. From California. She came here with her father, who is a professor, geology or zoology. He came for a year to the desert research institute. She's a year older than Yoav, but they put her in a lower grade because of the language. Even so she had problems, especially in Hebrew and Bible classes, because she knew next to nothing about being Jewish. But just so you know, Moses, I got to know her through my wife and sister-in-law, and she is a well-developed girl, both physically and personality-wise. Intelligent and cheerful, but neglected. Her father was always out in the desert doing his research, leaving her in an empty house, which became an open house where the kids, her group of friends, would hang out and have a good time, including our Yoav, whom she really liked. Just look at him, at the table over by the tree, a fine-looking boy — see? I'll introduce him up close."

"Why introduce?" Moses gets nervous.

"For the story . . . for a movie, maybe."

"Wait . . . what is this? You're going too fast . . . who said I want this story for my film?"

"Why not? It gives you a slice of life. You know there was a story like this in England? But there the youth are wild and violent. They were on television, two kids more or less the same age as Yoav who had a baby. The girl was big and heavy; the boy, the father, was like a little bird, a skinny English type, cultured . . . You didn't happen to see it?"

"No, Amsalem. Wait . . ."

"I'm telling you. Believe me. If we don't hurry with our movie, the Brits will beat us to it."

"Let them. What's going on? Why are you rushing?"

"I'm excited about the subject, the possibilities."

"Like what?"

"I don't know, problems of youth, too much freedom, permissiveness, alcohol . . ."

"But not here, not exactly. I still don't get it."

"What don't you get?"

"Why they didn't terminate the pregnancy."

"Because this girl was essentially alone here, without her divorced mother, for whom the daughter was out of sight, out of mind, and with no family to understand what was happening. Her father, the professor, neglected her, spent too much time in the desert. By the time they realized she was pregnant, it was already late. Meaning that an abortion would have been too risky. So we all said, It's not so terrible, let her give birth, then we'll give up the baby for adoption. That's what we all decided."

"All of you were involved?"

"Yes, all of us. It's such an unusual story, also from a family perspective. Though there were surely other boys who had slept with the girl, it was clear that our Yoav was the father. He was crazy about her, head over heels, and he took responsibility, though his father warned him to stay out of it. But his mother, my sister-in-law, defended her son, so her husband gave in."

"And then what?"

"She gave birth . . . the delivery was not easy, she lost a lot of blood. For a minute there it was life-threatening, she was such a young girl. But at least her mother, who turned out not to be Jewish, came from America to be with her. But right after the birth, she and the zoologist and a sharp lawyer forced the girl back to America, so if the baby was adopted, his mother would not be able to stay in touch. So the baby's American identity gets lost, but maybe when he grows up he can reclaim it."

"Why wasn't the baby put up for adoption?"

"Because the boy, the father, Yoavi — that's the point — suddenly says he doesn't want to give it up. If the baby stays with him, he believes, eventually the girl he loves will come back to him. Come back to her baby. In the meantime, he's been trying, unsuccessfully, to stay in touch with her."

"He loves her that much . . ." whispers Moses.

"What can you do? His whole life is ahead of him, and he's caught up in this love for that crazy American girl. Now that she's in America, he can't get over her, and the love just gets stronger by the day. Meanwhile, he's raising a baby with his mother. And who is this Yoav? Just a kid; he had his bar mitzvah two years ago. A real tragedy for him . . . So, Moses, we should let the English have a story like this? Why not grab it?"

"Why is it important to grab it?"

"As an educational film for our youth. To warn them. The Ministry of Education and also the Welfare Ministry could invest in it . . ."

Moses rests his head on his hand, takes a sip of water. He is uneasy with the transition from a tragic personal story to possible investment by a government ministry.

"Let's talk later," he says to the producer.

"Don't worry," says Amsalem, laying his hands on the shoulders of the greengrocers, who have listened raptly, "these are good friends, why shouldn't they hear the story?"

The two nod their agreement.

"By the way, how was the roast beef?" continues Amsalem. "Want some more?"

"No," says Moses. "If I want some more, I'll help myself. You're making me dizzy."

"I don't know why you're dizzy — I suppose too much retrospective made you oversensitive. Have more meat before the cake and dessert. And before you go back to Tel Aviv, rest in the room I reserved for you. I know your siesta is worth more to you than all your friends."

8

MOSES GOES TO the buffet, takes a fresh plate, and again inspects the meat dishes. But the story of the young mother has upset him and he puts the plate back, takes a bowl, and surveys the colorful desserts, then puts the bowl back, takes a red apple, sticks it in his pocket, and makes his way to the garden. The mother and son are sitting under an olive tree waiting for the little sister to finish her ice cream. He stops, puts a hand on the girl's head, and bends over to look at the baby in the carriage. The tiny baby, light-skinned, flutters his hands. Moses touches the white scarf wrapped around his head. The father, tense, watches him, but Moses smiles and says, with the confidence of a veteran grandpa, "A sweet baby, but does he let you sleep?" "Not all the time," says the boy, "in fact, hardly ever." Moses takes a closer look at the boy. He is not much older than his own grandson, but he has already known a woman and sired a child and seems mature, serious. And Moses looks with warm encouragement at the young grandmother, whose allure has only grown in the sunshine. "Yes," he says, "your brother-in-law told me the rest of the story, and I must admit, it is a truly unusual story."

"That's why we thought," interjects the boy, "that my story could be the basis for a film of yours . . . with some changes, obviously."

Moses is stunned by the clear willingness of the boy to turn his sin into a film, as if art could atone for his disgrace. Careful to say nothing hurtful, he mumbles softly, "Yes, maybe . . . but to make a decision I need more details. Like how your classmates have reacted, what they think about what you did or what happened to you . . ."

"At first they didn't believe it. Then, when they saw it was real, they were scared, they didn't want to get near her or me, and after the birth they were even more distant. It wasn't so much them as their parents, they made us and the baby sound contagious. It was like a boycott. But now it's not a boycott, now some friends, especially the girls, come to see the baby and want to help. They bring me assignments from classes I missed, and they volunteer to diaper him or give him a bath. Not just girls . . . boys too . . ."

"Wonderful," says Moses, who is devising a scene in his mind, boys and girls getting a bath ready for the baby. "But what does your father say about all this?"

Silence falls. The boy's face darkens.

"His father doesn't say anything," says his mother. "His father abandoned his son, abandoned us all."

"Abandoned? Why? Religious reasons?"

"Religious? Why religious?"

"No reason . . . I thought . . . because I understand you are a bit Orthodox."

"We are traditional, and if you are traditional you decide for yourself what is forbidden and what is permitted."

"Beautiful, that's how it should be," declares Moses, getting carried away. "I noticed that despite your lovely headscarf you allow yourself to write on Shabbat."

She seems confused. "Not just write . . ." she whispers, stopping there, not spelling out what else she does on the Sabbath.

"In any case, why did the father abandon the son?"

"From the start we had agreed that the baby would be given up for adoption. Because Yoav's father is positive that the girl, the mother of the baby, won't be coming back."

"And you believe that she will," volunteers Moses.

"I don't know . . . But how can I not respect the love and loyalty of my son? Would it be right to dismiss his hope that because he is taking care of their baby, she might come back — to him, or even just to the baby?"

The youth gazes at his mother in gratitude, as if this is the first time he is hearing such a strong and clear statement of her support for him.

"And you still don't believe that this story in our hands can be turned into a marvelous film," mutters Amsalem, who has been standing behind them.

"I'll understand once I've thought it through."

"Bravo!" shouts the producer. "Get some rest and do some thinking."

Amsalem steers him through the crowd to a little room connected to the house through the kitchen, tucked into a rear courtyard and exposed to the arid desert air. A little office of sorts, where Amsalem sequesters himself with account books and documents, most of which he does not care to make public. "The real accounting room," as he calls it, is furnished with a desk and computer and shelves, and also a big reclining armchair where one may nap while the real and true accounts balance themselves.

"You want a blanket?" the host asks the guest. "Or should I turn on the heat?"

"Both," says the director, "though I don't want to fall asleep, just get refreshed."

"Even if you sleep a little it wouldn't be so bad. It's more comfortable here than under my truck."

"In the days when I would rest under your truck during the shoot I thought it was a way of reviving brain cells that had died that morning. Then I discovered that what dies doesn't come back to life. If you can, please, have somebody bring me coffee, black, Turkish, strong, of the kind your first wife of blessed memory knew how to make."

"The second one also knows. I wouldn't marry a woman who didn't know how to make good coffee."

"She does seem like a wonderful woman. Her sister too. Though she is slightly odd."

"Not odd, stubborn. She injected something religious into the argument with her husband over the baby, got God involved. I said to my wife, Get her off God, but my wife didn't succeed. We also tried to convince her to give the baby for adoption but we couldn't. She knows the mother won't be coming back to Israel but is afraid to ruin the boy's hopes and doesn't realize that meanwhile, the baby is robbing him of his youth. Tell me, Moses, the truth: Isn't this a good story?"

"Slow down, you're overexcited. So far it sounds like a Bollywood picture."

"Maybe the basic idea. But if we got a clever screenwriter, a bit crazy, like Trigano, he would upgrade the film from India to Europe, stir the pot and spice it up, maybe even have the lovesick and desperate boy threaten to harm the child, not seriously, but as a way of getting his loved one back."

Moses closes his eyes.

"What made you think of Trigano?"

"No reason. You didn't mention him when you told me about Spain?"

"I might have. You still in touch with him?"

"Not at all."

"Now, for God's sake, be a good host and get me some coffee. And let's call a time-out."

"As you wish. But do me a favor, don't touch anything here. It's all organized so that if one piece of paper is moved, I'm a dead man."

9

THE HOST IS gone and a sweet silence fills his bookkeeping hideaway. Beyond the barred window, a view of skies as blue as if painted by a child. The power of the desert, thinks Moses. Eighty kilometers away you have rainstorms, and here, pure clear skies. Though the little room is warm, he has no intention of falling asleep, and while he waits for the coffee to revive him, he wraps himself in a checkered woolen blanket, eats the apple he stashed in his pocket, and studies the portrait of the king of Morocco hanging over the desk where Amsalem performs his tax evasions.

He is so accustomed to afternoon naps that despite his decision to rest and not sleep, his eyes snap open only when Amsalem's sister-in-law, the young grandmother, enters, pulling the baby carriage while balancing a tray of coffee and cookies, the sounds of robust Israeli singing accompanied by accordion trailing behind her.

Moses suspects she took the coffee delivery upon herself so she could continue narrating her family story, but she surprises him with a strange request — she would like to leave the baby with him in this room. The young father wants to unwind a bit in a soccer game with the kids, and she would like to join the group singing in the living room, to lift her spirits a little, and if the baby starts crying he can call her. After all, Moses once had grandchildren this age, didn't he?

"Four," he proudly declares, "with more to come, I hope."

"Good, then." The woman smiles.

What's good? He is baffled by the rather presumptuous request for him to babysit this problematic child — perhaps to tempt him to make a film that will alleviate the indignity. But he smiles kindly, helps the attractive woman find a suitable place for the carriage, and takes charge of the pacifier, making it clear that he will seek help at the first signs of yowling.

"Thank you, Yair." Suddenly they are on a first-name basis. She hurries back to the singing, he closes the door after her. Before checking on the uninvited guest, he gulps several small cups of hot coffee. Now, wide awake, he takes a close look at the baby whose name nobody has bothered to tell him.

The baby is awake and gives the director a quiet, knowing look. Is the blue-black color of his eyes a joint venture of America and Israel or something temporary, likely to change? Moses considers whether to stick in the pacifier right away to head off a scream, or wait for one patiently so he can put a quick end to babysitting and restore the child to his grandmother, who didn't leave him milk. He offers the baby the pacifier, and the little one hesitates before accepting it as consolation for the breast that had gone all the way to America. But even as he sucks at it avidly, he maintains a curious gaze at the unfamiliar old man who might make him a character in his next film.

Moses knows from experience that the pacifier will not prevent a round of wailing, nor will smiling or making funny faces. He leans over and picks up the baby in his arms, amazed how light he is.

He takes him to the window, to the vista of the gleaming desert in the noonday sun, carefully holding the child's head lest it fall back, though he seems already able to hold it up on his own. The baby is quiet. Moses points at the blue skies stretched over the desert, and the pacifier falls out as the child gapes with wonder. A new, urgent idea crosses the director's mind, and he replaces the baby in his carriage.

The baby, disappointed, produces a slight wail of protest, a clear enough sign for Moses, who will not do battle with any child. He picks him up again and carries him through the kitchen, its air thick with the smell of leftovers, to the front yard, looking for the young father, who is indeed there, a boy among boys, excitedly chasing a ball, and Moses suddenly laments the lost childhood of this lad trapped by love, and he retreats to the house with the baby in his arms and sternly scans the group of singers, and as he searches for the young grandmother, she hurries toward him, takes her grandson, and says, disappointed: "What happened? So fast?"

"Nothing I could do; you didn't leave any milk, and besides, I have to be going, because I'm paying another visit on the way back."

10

IT'S STILL EARLY afternoon, and Moses asks Amsalem, who escorts him to his car, if he remembers the location of the wadi where *Slumbering Soldiers* was filmed. Amsalem remembers, for it was he who supplied fresh food during the shoot. "It's no more than forty-five kilometers from here, and the road has surely been improved."

"It's been more than forty years," says Moses, "so find me the place on the map. When I saw the film in Spain I got all nostalgic for the Nabataean ruin we turned into a secret installation."

"Let's hope it hasn't been razed."

Moses takes out an old map from the trunk and follows Amsalem's thick finger as it moves from the Ohalim junction by the Ohalei Kedar prison, to the Nokdim junction by Ramat Hovav, to the forest of Nahal Secher, to the Negev junction, then heads left from there to the old oil pipeline road that passes at the foot of Hyena Hill to the vicinity of Yeruham and then straight to the Big Crater, where it plunges down to Wadi Matmor. "This is where we made that crazy movie," says Amsalem.

"Matmor?"

"Or maybe it was Hatira. When you get there you'll remember, or just ask any Bedouin. If I didn't have guests, I would gladly drive you, but since you're already in Beersheba, why not go there? The roads are empty on Shabbat and the police don't go there, you can speed down and back in an hour."

Given such encouragement, Moses heads south and not north. He drives the route of Amsalem's finger and finds that the late-afternoon road is indeed empty, taking a holy Sabbath nap. Here and there, an old pickup truck emerges from a distant Bedouin encampment. Sometimes Bedouins cross the road, raising a hand in greeting or just wanting to hitch a ride.

Yellow dominates the desert scenery, dotted here and there by reddish bushes and green shoots, encouraged by infrequent rain. The mountains in the distance look like a giant accordion, their foothills arranged like loaves of dough awaiting a blazing oven. The view is joined by the whistle of a new wind, which thickens the haze and fans the road with a fine coating of sand.

At the Negev junction he is uncertain about the turn onto the oil road; he slows down and looks for a human being who can assure him he is not lost. A small group of Bedouins, men standing and women sitting, are gathered by the shell of an old bus stop. He pauses for them to confirm the route, which they do, and they also take an interest in his destination. Wadi Matmor or Wadi Hatira in the Big Crater. Does any of them know the place? And if so, does anyone know if the old Nabataean ruin is still there? They pass the question back and forth, and finally a dark skinny man pushes his way to the car window and swears he knows the wadi and the ruin and is able to guide the driver there. But why?

"Just to see it."

"And to stay?"

"No, just to look."

In that case, the Bedouin offers his services as tour guide, but for a fee, since it is a long way. "Long?" Moses is apprehensive. "How long?" He waves the map. "Long," insists the Bedouin. Long for him, for he lives not far from here. "A hundred shekels," offers Moses. "A hundred each way," counters the Bedouin, "you also have to come back." Moses closes the window and shifts into drive. "Let's go, a hundred shekels, final price." The Bedouin knocks on the window. "Okay, a hundred and thirty, final price."

Does he really know the place, or is he just pretending? It's too late, though; the Bedouin hops into the front seat and signals to three veiled women, dressed all in black, to get into the back seat. "Only one," shouts Moses, lifting one finger, regretting the whole business, "only one!" The Bedouin starts to bargain. "Two, only two." "No." Moses holds firm. "Not two, only one. We are coming back. The others can wait for you here. One woman, or none at all."

The Bedouin considers this and finally gestures to one woman, the smallest, who like a quivering bird squeezes into the back seat with her bundle, only her eyes visible, sparkling in the rearview mirror.

Meanwhile, the day has darkened, with a big cloud drifting from the north and devouring the sun. According to Moses' calculation there are only twenty kilometers to go, and though it's early winter, and the days are shorter, there'll be enough light for the round trip.

They drive along the old pipeline road, filling up the gas tank on the outskirts of Yeruham, and silence reigns in the car, but the eyes of the Bedouin woman scorch the nape of the driver's neck. The Bedouin man indeed knows the way, and as soon as they begin their descent into the Big Crater and turn onto a dirt road, Moses recognizes a few bits of the route traveled by the officer in the open jeep on his way to impose law and order on the sleeping army unit. Dusk falls more quickly than he expected, and when they arrive at the spot where the Nabataean structure ought to be standing, darkness prevails throughout the Big Crater, except for beams of light that reach out to them from a watchtower near a double roadblock. Three reserve soldiers, who in their uniforms look like extras from his old film, except they are alert and tough and armed. They stop the car and order its three occupants to get out and stand in a line.

Before them is a sizable military base, well guarded, where no soldier sleeps without permission. Tents and buildings surround an inscrutable installation with an iron dome, which thrills the director in its resemblance to his original vision. Except the real installation is ten times bigger. Is this just a facility intended to provide early warning to the nearby nuclear plant, or is it a new reactor?

There is no one here willing to disclose the secret even if he knew it. In fact, it is the unexpected guests who are suspected of knowing something and coming to sniff around. They are requested to identify themselves. Even the woman is not exempt from reaching into her robes and producing her identity card. Moses tells the soldiers about the film that was shot here decades ago and is curious whether an ancient Nabataean ruin might have been swallowed by the facility at this base. His question is ignored; no one has heard of the film, but they still express respect for a director who proudly lists the names of two of his recent films. Yes, one of the guards has heard the titles.

If you've come to make a new movie here, we're ready to be in it, they joke, and call their commander, an officer wearing a knitted skullcap, who considers what to do with the improbable visitors, deciding in the end to release the director and detain the Bedouin for further questioning. As for the woman, she can do whatever she wants.

Moses is upset and fights for the release of his tour guide. "What do you want from him? What did he do? He helped me get here. Besides, we didn't go into your base, we're in a public area, open to all citizens."

The commander calms him down. "Don't worry, we just want to get to know this man a little better." "What's to know?" screams Moses. "You can see, he's an ordinary innocent person I happened to meet." But the commander again calms him down. "Every person holds a surprise. No one is out to harm him. In the morning he will surely be set free. Meanwhile he'll get food and lodging, but someone who understands Bedouins needs to find out how and why this man happened to take you to this place, and to clarify what he knows and what he doesn't know. A few small questions before we let him go."

As they take the man away, he remains composed and impassive, and he says to Moses, "No big deal, don't get upset, I know them, this is nothing. But take the woman with you and bring her back to the place you took her from, and from there she can make her own way. Now, pay me what we agreed."

Moses compensates for the inconvenience by paying him double and checks whether the woman, whose identity and status remain unclear, may sit in the front seat beside him so he doesn't get lost. "No need," says the Bedouin, "from the rear she can tell if you are going the right way."

11

THOUGH IT IS not yet five in the afternoon, they drive in total darkness, the headlights revealing one dirt road, which takes them to the main road. In the darkness of the back seat sits not an actress but a real woman, a slender Bedouin whom a husband, brother, or uncle has left unsupervised, and she is relieved to drop her veil and gaze brightly at the world. Moses studies her delicate face in the rearview mirror and inhales her scent but is wary of speaking to her. Finally he dares, almost shouting: "Do you know a little Hebrew? You learned a little Hebrew?"

"A very little," she answers in singsong, suddenly adding, "next to nothing."

Maybe she knows more Hebrew than she lets on, he says to himself, but would rather concentrate now on the glittering lights of the world than be cross-examined by an old Jew. Yet Moses feels an urge to talk to her for the few kilometers they will be together, so he asks if she belongs to the al-Azama.

When she hears the Jew mention the name of the strongest and most famous tribe in the area, she flinches. "*La* al-Azama," *no*, and hastily wraps her face in her veil. "Al-Jarjawi." She defiantly pronounces the correct name.

He decides to back off and leave her foreignness free of interpretation. And from then on the ride takes place in silence, till he feels the woman's light touch on the back of his neck, as the time has come and this is the place. "Here?" He is bewildered, for the place is entirely barren. "Here, here," she asserts with utter confidence, and even before the car comes to a complete halt the rear door opens, and she escapes with a moan that might be Arabic or Hebrew, her dress flapping till she vanishes in the darkness.

The storm in Tel Aviv has abated, but the street is carpeted in twigs and leaves plucked by its force; water runs along gutters and collects in puddles. He turns on his apartment lights and heat and listens to his voicemail, but no one needs him. He looks at his e-mail but is too weary to answer or delete. He has an urge to surprise Amsalem with the real installation that sprang from the ruins of Trigano's creative vision, but he resists. *First I have to digest the truth myself before I share it with anyone else.* He takes off his clothes for a shower and feels the scent of the Bedouin woman whispering to him. Has she reached her encampment yet? Or did she take advantage of the ride to join up with another tribe?

Slowly Ruth assumes her character, a temporary Bedouin in the small screening room of the Spanish archive, veiled and laughing, until she is shot by the commander. "Debdou," he says to himself, Debdou, and the unfulfilled passion of the hotel room shoots through his body. He goes to the shelf that holds the twenty movies he has made since Trigano left him and pulls out the film that might be the only one he is still able to watch. He puts it in the video player and finds the scene he desires.

The film is not one of his best known or most highly praised, but it does have some strong scenes. Ruth was about thirty then, eight years after the break from Trigano, still finding her own way. In this scene she played a young woman waiting in a hotel room for an older married man who has expressed interest in her. The scene wasn't long, not more than a minute, but once it became clear to her and the audience that she was waiting in vain, Moses had her remove her clothes and get into bed naked, then wrap herself in a sheet.

They had to reshoot the scene three times to get the right camera angle, the right light, and the precise mood. This was not the first time that Ruth had bared her body to the camera, and she usually did it easily and calmly. But in this scene, sadness and loneliness shrouded the breathtaking nudity. Maybe it was the small, neglected room contrasted with her beauty, or maybe the pensive, disappointed gaze directed at the camera.

In the studio, made to resemble a hotel room, Toledano and the soundman were with him. But because the scene was supposed to take place mostly in silence, Moses decided to remove the soundman and do the sound himself, thus making it easier for Ruth to undress. But Toledano, who had been in love with Ruth since childhood, grew more excited by the moment, as did the director, and thus it happened that the nudity, lasting no more than ten seconds, shimmered with intense eroticism even after Ruth was wrapped in the sheet.

Now the Bedouin woman disappearing in the darkness blends again with the actress of his film, and he himself stands before her naked, for he knows that he wants and can bring relief, and he does.

seven

VIRTUAL MAPPING OF
THE HEART

1

THE FOLLOWING MORNING, when he's sure she's awake, he calls to ask how she is.

"You again?" Ruth is surprised to hear the voice of someone who has just spent three nights beside her in the same bed without incident. "And I thought you wanted a little time off."

"Time off for what?"

"Time off before I get the news that there won't be a part for me in your next film."

He is uneasy. "That's an original way of putting it, but it's not so; in fact, there might be a part for you after all in my next film. The concept is barely in gestation, but when I think of it I also think of you, not as a fictional character but as a real character."

"What do you mean by that?"

"In other words, not as an actress but as an assistant director. Because the main roles would be for young people, boys and girls. And who's got more experience than you in teaching acting to children?"

"Assistant director?"

"Not just an assistant, but a partner. You would decide how it would appear in the credits of the film. That's a long way off, though.

Meanwhile, I'd like to visit you sometime at your studio to watch you direct children, to get a feeling for how far one can go. This has to be a daring film. And as you know, I have used children very little in my films."

"What's the story?"

"Too early to say. I told you, Ruth, for now it's just a seed in my mind, or more correctly in Amsalem's mind. He invited me to a party at his villa in Beersheba on Saturday, where he let me in on a strange drama taking place in his family."

"What happened?"

"Slow down, let me go at my own pace. Not on the phone, and not in a hurry. I'd like to visit your studio, see the kids and how you direct them, then we'll think together."

"It's a small studio. Three kids at most in a class. But if you insist" — she sighs — "how can I refuse."

"You can't refuse me, and see, I haven't said a word about blood tests."

"Wise of you."

"Why? You took them?"

"I didn't take them and I won't. See, you're at it again."

"I'll say no more."

"Good."

"Not good, but I'll say no more. Meanwhile . . . I have a story for you. An amazing story."

"The retrospective brought you back to life."

"Not life, just curiosity. Yesterday, at Amsalem's, at the edge of the desert, I was thinking about *Slumbering Soldiers* and had an urge to see the crater where we filmed it. And guess what: Amsalem not only remembered the place, but encouraged me to hop over, because it's not so far away on today's roads. So I said to myself, What have you got to lose? It's a chance to complete the retrospective, when will you next be going south? You remember how during the shoot we would take the shiny tarp off our installation and go in there and cook, sing, play games?"

"It was a fun production."

"Exactly, that's why I went back there. On the way, not to get lost, I picked up a Bedouin with one of his wives. It was almost dark by the time we got there – and you won't believe it, imagination turned into reality: a military camp, reserve soldiers, but no sleeping soldiers, very much awake they were, so awake they didn't let us go in. Nevertheless, and this is the whole point, beyond the roadblock, in the distance, in the twilight, what do I see? An installation."

"The installation?"

"The same one."

"The same one?"

"With a dome on top, like in our film, but bigger, a solid dome, maybe something connected with the nuclear reactor that isn't far away, something meant as a warning. And the soldiers, like in the film, they may not even know what they're guarding. I said to myself, How wonderful, our hallucination turned into reality, back then we had a touch of prophecy –"

"We? You?" Her sudden outburst cuts him off. "You know it all came from him . . . from Shaul . . . from Trigano."

"Trigano started it, planted the first seed, but we were partners and believers who made his hallucination come true. A crazy story, no?"

"Maybe for you, not for me. Even when we were children I could sense he had these intuitions, almost like prophecy, that in the end made him arrogant, rigid, even cruel . . ."

"Exactly." Moses picks up her words. "Rigid and cruel, and he paid for it."

"We all paid for it, not just him. But let's not go there now. Just tell me about our building, the original one, the Nabataean or Turkish one . . . did you find it?"

"No. It got dark, and they didn't let us into the camp, and they practically held us for questioning, because they couldn't understand why we were there in the first place. So I didn't push it. In any case, when the army takes over a wadi, what's going to be left of an ancient building?"

"It's buildings like that, the truly ancient ones, that they take better care of in this country. But enough, Moses, I have to get up and get going."

2

THAT SAME MORNING, he drives to the hospital to persuade his daughter, before it's too late, to divert the bar mitzvah trip from Africa to Europe.

He waits for her, as arranged, in the hospital cafeteria, but Galit phones and asks him to come up to the ultrasound and CT department, because her schedule was switched. "You came all this way, Abba, so let's spend a little time together and try to understand why Africa annoys you. I warn you, though, you can't convince us to change our plans, but we can make a date for dinner at our house."

Despite her precise directions, he gets lost amid wings and departments, finally arriving at a locked door with a red light flashing above it. Given no choice, and disinclined to absorb someone else's radiation, he waits for his daughter on a bench in the corridor, squeezed among patients waiting for tests and patients waiting for test results. He has never been here before, for it was only two years ago, after working for years in private clinics, that Galit was given a senior post in the ultrasound and CT institute of this major hospital. Though he is proud of her promotion, he remains disappointed that she quit her medical studies midway because of her pregnancy and hasty marriage to a fellow med student, whom she supported while he completed his studies. During the first years of her marriage, her father tried to coax her to finish medical school, even promising regular financial assistance, but to no avail. With all her family responsibilities, she finally gave up on medicine and settled for the technical side of things, and perhaps to justify that concession she quickly had another baby. And though she is successful in her work, and perhaps even loves it, Moses believes that it was her parents' divorce that prompted her to hook up in her youthful prime with a fairly unimpressive man and thus fix what was broken in her childhood home.

Is this another reason he's trying to persuade her to change her mind in such a marginal matter? Will the shift of a bar mitzvah trip from Africa to Europe serve as a small corrective for a missed medical career? As he sits and waits patiently for a ceasefire in the radiation warning, a gurney with an elderly woman on it comes rolling his way, steered by a male nurse who stops, places her medical record on her stomach, and leaves her lying alone. The sprightly old lady sits up and inquires if Moses is waiting for tests or for results.

"Neither; I'm waiting for my daughter, who happens to run this clinic."

The old lady's face brightens, and she refers to Galit by her full name, adding the title of Doctor, then praises her to the skies.

"Your daughter is so patient, sir. This is the fourth appointment I've had with her for a CT of my heart."

"Fourth? Why is that?"

"It turns out"—the old woman winks—"that I have a naughty heart that goes wild and makes their machine crazy. Their new scanner can't decide what's truly going on, but your wonderful daughter, the director, hasn't given up."

"Yes," confirms Moses with satisfaction, "even as a child she was stubborn and thorough."

"And a good thing you let her be stubborn. What do you do, sir? Are you a teacher?"

"I was a teacher in the old days, but now I am a film director. An artist."

"An artist . . . how unusual. Here she is."

The red light has gone out, and his daughter, in a white coat, a sheaf of papers in hand, rushes to hug and kiss her father. "You dropped in on a crazy day," she says apologetically, "they keep sending me emergency cases. But you're here, so let's go inside and chat a bit."

She takes him into a room where the new machine, a great white cylinder attached by cables to wall sockets, is installed alongside a bed, on top of which electrodes and wires are bunched. Beyond a glass wall is a console of computer screens that monitor the mapping.

Galit introduces her father to the other technicians, who greet him cordially. Then she sits him down in a little room and says, "Before you start complaining, tell me about Spain. Was the retrospective in your honor alone, or were there actors and cinematographers along with you? In the newspaper it said that only you got a prize."

"Galiti, my dearest, forget the prize, it's not important, and it's small besides. If you want, I'll tell you all about this strange retrospective when I come for dinner. Now is not the time, you're in a rush, and I made a special trip to convince you to go to Europe, not Africa."

"Why is this so important to you?"

"It's a matter of principle. And I'm not talking about your decision not to have a party."

"Really, Abba, you shouldn't get involved in any of this. A party is a pain in the neck that makes nobody happy. Think about it — who gets invited anyway? You and Mother have no mutual friends anymore. So who do we invite? The medical staff here, people we see all the time at the hospital? There'll always be someone insulted because he wasn't invited. And believe me, it's a pain for those invited. Once upon a time, a guest brought a book to a bar mitzvah and it was considered a respectable gift; now everyone has to bring a check that covers the cost of the meal. Isn't it enough for you that he should say the Torah blessings in the synagogue, followed by a lunch for the close family? Then we'll go to Africa to forget about the world."

"That's exactly the point. What I came to discuss. Why forget the world and not remember it? You asked me about Spain, and we were in a truly spectacular place, Santiago de Compostela."

"Where is that?"

"In the northwest corner, within earshot of the ocean."

"So?"

"There's a magnificent cathedral."

"So you want us to go there for the cathedral?"

"I didn't say there in particular. Anywhere. Europe is full of cathedrals, filled with culture. Great museums, historical sites; this is a chance to give Itay something rich, and you too, you too . . ."

"He can see all these things on television or the Internet, why travel all that way?"

"Animals, darling, also roam all the time on TV and the Internet, and if he wants to see them in real life, he can go to the safari park in Ramat Gan, or the biblical zoo in Jerusalem."

"We're not going for the animals, Abba, but for the quiet and the scenery. It's being out in the wild that we want, the opposite of the civilization that suffocates us here."

Moses notices how much his daughter has come to resemble his mother. The sharp gaze, the rapid, self-confident manner of speech that's warm at the same time.

"You and Zvi think" – Moses tenses – "that you are profoundly civilized because you can operate all sorts of medical machinery. I'm talking about art, about music, pictures, myths that will enrich you and offer my grandson another aspect of the world as he begins the transition to adulthood."

"No rush, Abba, he's not entering any adulthood. Today the kids stay kids until the age of thirty."

"Your mother asked me to increase my gift, and I gladly agreed, but I'm asking what for? Why spend money on lions and elephants?"

"Also on breathtaking scenery."

"Yes, but after his army service he will no doubt travel to India or South America to see the scenery and primitive people. But right now there's an opportunity for a shared cultural experience with his parents. Something of value that will stay in the family's memory. By the way, there's also breathtaking scenery in Europe."

"But it's hard to get to it. In Africa, you get off the plane straight into nature and you don't have to go looking for it. No, Abba, I understand what you mean but it won't work. The two of us are tired and run down and we simply want to relax in the heart of nature. Besides, all of his classmates have traveled or will travel to Africa, and he can't be the one who only went to Europe. What will he talk to them about? And believe me, an African trip is also expensive, and if you increase your gift, it'll help. By the way, when did you eat breakfast?"

"This morning. Early."

"And since then?"

"Nothing. I was waiting for you."

"Very good. If you ate more than three hours ago, I have an idea. I can put you through the scanner and do a virtual mapping of the heart."

"The heart?"

"Yes, why not? When did you last have your heart checked?"

"I don't remember . . . I didn't . . ."

"I'm sure your heart is fine even though you're far from young, but in any case, so you won't be able to say you took the trouble to come here for nothing, we'll do a complete mapping of your heart, and you'll leave here reassured. And we too, of course."

"How long does this kind of mapping take?"

"No time at all, twenty minutes. And it doesn't hurt. We'll inject some contrast dye and see what's happening in your heart. Come, Father, come, give me your hand . . . a little sting, that's all . . ."

Galit talks to the technicians, and they happily agree to scan her father. But first they have to get his signature, because the test is considered experimental. After Moses gives his consent, they lay him down on a gurney, attach four electrodes to his upper back, and connect his ankle to a blood pressure machine. Then the daughter maneuvers the father twice through the scanner, each time giving him different breathing instructions, once to hold his breath, then to pant like a dog after a long run, and between the scans, and between the breaths, she circles back to the retrospective in Spain and asks if he was alone or if someone was with him, and he mentions Ruth, and Galit knows about the woman who caused her parents' divorce. "Are you still with her?" she inquires matter-of-factly, without bitterness. "Not really," he answers quickly. And when the scanning is completed and he is freed of the electrodes, he says, "You can't imagine how much you've come to resemble my mother." "Is that good or bad?" she asks apprehensively. "It's good," he assures her, "all good."

He is sent out to the hall, and the elderly patient, still waiting, with her medical history on her stomach, looks at him malevolently. "So, they did end up checking you," she says. "Not really," he tells her, "I came to see my daughter and she insisted on scanning my heart." "But why not wait your turn?" complains the old woman. "You're right," he admits, "I didn't wait my turn, but what can you do, she's the director." He moves away to a bench at the end of the hall, and as he waits for the results, anxiety grips him, draining his energy, and he closes his eyes, and his head drops back. But a hand touches him gently, and there stands his son-in-law, father of his grandchildren, in a white coat, a stethoscope around his neck. He leans over Moses with a warm smile and hands him the results of the virtual mapping of his heart, with his signature as the cardiologist.

"What is this?" Moses is nervous. "What does it say?"

"Read it for yourself . . ."

CTA of coronary arteries

The examination was conducted on a new 128-slice Cardiac CT scanner as part of a clinical trial with the consent of the examined.

In the course of the examination two scans were performed:

One of the entire chest with low radiation and no injection of contrast dye.

The second a CTA of the heart with the injection of 70 cc Ultravist 370.

In the course of the scan the heart rate varied in the range of

75 beats per minute and a good imaging of the heart and coronary arteries was obtained.

The heart is of normal size. No pericardial fluid detected.

Minor calcification in mitral valve annulus.

The organs scanned in the upper abdomen are free of gross pathology.

Calcium score of 186 corresponds to 52nd percentile of subject's age group.

Upper aorta with circumference of 35 mm.

Left-dominant coronary artery system.

Eccentric calcium plaque in the anterior area without significant stenosis.

No evidence of defective myocardial perfusion.

Summary: Non-occlusive sclerosis as described in coronary arteries.

"So?" asks Moses, but now without anxiety. "So" — the doctor pats his father-in-law's shoulder — "you won an extra prize, a retrospective of a healthy heart, so you can keep going wild with no worries."

3

IS THE IMAGE of a free and hedonistic person attached to him by family and friends alike solely the product of his ambiguous relationship with the character abandoned by his former screenwriter? Or does the art of cinema, where directors are always changing characters, locations, and plots while working closely with actors and crew, create the impression that the loneliness of a director cannot be genuine or painful, since he is always surrounded by people? Not even his family members can imagine the depth of his solitude or the magnitude of his misgivings amid his cast and crew. And can he be fairly described as unrestrained if he has no real authority over the character he drags from film to film? For Ruth has made his visit to her studio conditional on getting some idea of the new film, and only after he gives in and tells her, albeit in general terms, is she intrigued enough to set a time for him to visit.

For Hanukkah, she has suggested to one of the schools in south Tel Aviv where she runs drama clubs that they not settle for some banal holiday skit about the little cruse of oil that lasted eight days but stage a real play about the Maccabees based on a fine novel by Howard Fast, *My Glorious Brothers.* The school's principal was concerned that the lofty language of the Hebrew adaptation might prove too difficult for many students. However, when Ruth explained that many years back, in a school in the desert town of Yeruham, she herself as a girl had acted in *My Glorious Brothers*, and that even though the parents and children were new immigrants the play was received with awe and appreciation, the principal gave her approval, provided that the play run no longer than fifty minutes.

And so, for several weeks now, Ruth has been coaching the Maccabees at the school, occasionally inviting the lead actors to her studio to polish their performance. She would not, of course, think of inviting Moses to the school, but if he wants to attend the individual coaching sessions, he can come, on two conditions — first, that he not introduce himself as a movie director, as that might generate false hopes; and second, that he not share his comments, positive or negative, with the students, only with her.

He has often visited her apartment in Neve Tzedek, to discuss a new role or as a loving friend who happened to be in the neighborhood, but she has never opened her studio door to him, even though it is across the hall from her flat. More than once, when he inquired about her sources of income and expressed interest in seeing the studio, she refused. "It's a mess and you will not find what you're looking for." "But what am I looking for?" he would protest. "I only want to know you better." And she would persist in her refusal: "What you know is more than enough."

But today, in hopes of being a partner in his new film, she will open the door of her studio to him and let him observe her work. In so doing she forces him to go without his afternoon nap and get to her place before the students arrive, and she repeats the stipulation that he must sit on the side and not intervene and, most important of all, not introduce himself as a film director.

The studio is not nearly as small as he had been warned. It's a fair-sized room, with an adjacent kitchenette used for storage. Though the room has only one window, it's large and faces the sea, admitting mellow afternoon light. True, there are lots of costumes in the studio — some that she and other actors had worn in his films — alongside props meant to stimulate the imagination of children: masks, swords and spears of tin or wood, toy guns and hand grenades, all stuffed into the kitchenette. She seats him beside a tiny bathroom partitioned by a curtain, near a white tunic worn by the cantor in *In Our Synagogue*.

"To hide you completely would be dangerous," she says, "because if you sneeze or cough it will scare the children, but for once in your life, try to minimize your presence."

Before long, three students pile into the room, two boys and a girl, quickly removing their coats and overstuffed backpacks, dumping them in a heap in the corner by Moses. He smiles at them but is careful not to say a word. Ruth, contradicting her own instructions, introduces him as an old friend, a famous film director, who has come to observe the rehearsal.

Predictably, the kids, for whom film is the pinnacle of all the arts, are excited, and one of them, a dark-complexioned boy of about thirteen, wants to know the director's name and film credits. Moses, with a sheepish smile, lists a few from his retrospective, but Ruth interrupts and says, "That's enough, kids, let's get down to work." The two boys are apparently of Middle Eastern extraction, but the girl's coloring suggests the Far East. A tall, slim Asian with a finely sculpted face and big slanted eyes — perhaps she's the child of foreign workers who put down roots here, or a member of some tribe from deepest Asia that qualified as Jews under the Law of Return. Their drama teacher has them perform a few warm-up exercises to loosen their bodies and wake them from the torpor of their school day, and then she seats them on a bench to refresh their knowledge of the text before they perform the scene.

The boy who took an interest in Moses plays Simon the Hasmonean, the main character, and has mastered his lines of dialogue. The girl, who is called Ruth in the play, is still a bit shaky in her part, but the traces of a foreign accent in her delivery add to her charm and beauty.

He will need to get her name and address, decides Moses. Even if she had no dialogue, a close-up of her marvelous face would captivate the audience.

A nighttime conversation ensues between Simon the Hasmonean and the girl who courts him, while the other boy, Judah Maccabee, sits still on the side, staring at the young lovers.

RUTH: Simon, where art thou?

SIMON: Who calls Simon?

RUTH: A moonstruck lad like you, sitting and dreaming of a lovely lass — were you bored, Simon?

SIMON: I feared that jackals had broken into the corral. It is not proper, Ruth, that you sit here with me.

RUTH: Why? Why is it not proper that I should sit with you, Simon, and is it not a lion you wait for and not a jackal?

It is three hundred years since a lion has arisen in Judea.

You never smile, you are never amused, is this not so, Simon, son of Mattathias? There is no one unhappier than you in all of Modi'in — in all of Judea — in all the world. Methinks I would give the best years of my life to see a lion leap hither and swallow you up.

SIMON: That is most doubtful . . .

RUTH: There was a time that you liked me, Simon, or did I just imagine it . . . Each time I came to Mattathias' house, my heart asked me — will Simon be there? Will he look at me? Smile at me? Speak to me? Touch my hand?

SIMON: Not four days have passed since Judah went away.

RUTH: What?

SIMON: You heard my words.

RUTH: Simon, what have I to do with Judah? Simon, what troubles you? What harm have I done to you? You are a block of ice, not only with me, with your father and Judah as well!

SIMON: And for no reason?

RUTH: I do not know for what, Simon.

SIMON: When you went out with Judah, before he left —

RUTH: I do not love Judah.

SIMON: And he, does he know this?

RUTH: He knows.

SIMON: But he loves you, I do know this, I know my brother Judah, every gesture, every look of his eyes, every thought of his heart. All his life he has received what he has wished. I know his accursed humility —

RUTH: And for this you hateth him.

SIMON: I do not hate him.

RUTH: Simon, Simon, Simon son of Mattathias, Simon of Modi'in. Many are the names I have called you in my heart. My Simon, ah, how wise you are, yet such a fool. It has always been only you for me, and I dream that one day you will love me. Even if you do not love me, I will live near to you. So that you will look at me, speak to me. Am I not even worthy of this?

SIMON: And Judah loves you.

RUTH: Simon, is Judah the purpose of your life? Have you nothing else in your world except for him? Judah took me in his arms and I took pity on him. I am not his and not another's. Simon son of Mattathias — there is but one man to whom I could belong.

SIMON: You took pity on him? You took pity on Judah?

RUTH: I took pity on him, Simon, do you truly not understand?

And here the director stops them, as impassioned and excited as if she herself has poured out the love-talk of two ancient youths into her small studio space. And the visitor is pleased by the ability to turn stilted and archaic dialogue into flowing, living conversation, and despite the caution not to react, he cannot hold back and claps his hands.

The two youngsters smile. But the third one, serious and gloomy — Judah Maccabee, who morosely listened to the others speak, a rejected lover before he even enters the play — casts a cold eye at Yair Moses, who stands up as he tries to recall in the mist of memory where and when he encountered such a serious gaze.

4

BECAUSE HE WOULD never consider using a toilet meant for children and concealed by a curtain, he hints to his hostess that he would like to enter her apartment. And she gives him the key and asks in a whisper: "Will you manage by yourself?" "Of course," replies the guest. "What kind of question is that?"

He does know the apartment well. Past the living room is a charming bedroom, in which a few years ago he sometimes spent the night. Not much has changed. Colorfully upholstered sofas and armchairs with scattered pillows cheerfully complement framed posters on the walls of films she had appeared in.

Admittedly there is something tacky about an apartment whose walls are covered with street ads, yet the occupational narcissism doesn't detract from the aesthetic of the flat, especially since its owner anticipated that Moses would not miss the chance to get inside and made sure to tidy it up.

Before returning to the studio to see how the children manage the lovers' dialogue scene, he sinks into a favorite armchair and pours himself a glass of cognac from a bottle he brought here years ago. He looks around at the familiar walls and at the table. Among various papers is a new, unfamiliar drawing, a charcoal portrait of Ruth as a young woman, almost a girl. Clearly this is not by a professional artist but by a barely trained amateur, whose pencil made one eye a little bigger than the other and raised the forehead too high. The actress's smile in the portrait indicates the artist knew her well. Maybe the results of that first blood test are also on the table. If he showed them to his son-in-law, Zvi could tell what was ominous and what wasn't. But he doesn't touch anything. There was a time when he felt at home in this apartment, but that's over. The gaze of Judah Maccabee, the boy who had not spoken a word, flashes in his mind's eye. Can it be? Or was it just an illusion?

Ruth enters to see what's taking him so long.

"I felt weak, watching your young actors . . ."

"Well, get over it. Because now they want you to watch the rehearsal. I knew they would get all excited over a film director. Even in the most out-of-the-way school in this country, everybody wants to be a star."

"Excuse me, but I'm not the one who revealed my identity."

"That's true. But someone had to explain to them why an old man like you suddenly materialized in the studio, and I couldn't think of another identity for you. But what made you tired?"

"You just said I was old. Also, I missed my afternoon nap. Nice to see how patient you are with children. Though don't you think you ought to simplify the text a wee bit for them?"

"Simplify how?"

"Cut back the 'where art thou' and 'hateth' and 'hither.' I'm afraid the audiences of kids will get lost in the stilted language."

"Don't be so sure. Most of the students from south Tel Aviv come from traditional homes and their parents take them on Shabbat and holidays to the synagogue, where they are exposed to such words."

"What about that boy?"

"Which boy?"

"The third one, the silent one, Judah Maccabee."

"What about him?"

"He hasn't said a word. He doesn't have any lines?"

"Not today. I invited him to suffer in silence witnessing the love that grows between his beloved and his brother. To bring him closer to despair so he convincingly performs his death in tomorrow's rehearsal."

"It's wonderful how you work as director. You seem to have learned something from me after all."

"Maybe, a little."

"By the way, doesn't that boy remind you of someone? That look of his . . . the way he stares . . ."

"You mean Trigano."

"Exactly." Moses is agitated. "I was afraid to say anything . . ."

"Afraid?"

"I don't know . . ."

"When I started to work with them I did notice a certain resemblance, and I checked whether there was a connection. Didn't find any. Though his grandfather came to Israel from the same region. But in the course of working with him, the resemblance got blurrier. He's a complicated child, not easy, uptight . . ."

"What's his name?"

"Elisha."

"I didn't dare to say he reminds me of Trigano, it's been so many years since I've seen him."

"Yes, there is something . . . You're not imagining it."

"You see, I'm not yet completely senile. Let's go back to the studio. I'm eager to see you directing that scene. Will you ask the kids to touch physically, or does their love remain hanging in the air?"

"Kids today touch each other with ease. With love and also violence. Aren't you planning some serious touching in your next film?"

"Don't put the cart before the horse."

5

IN THE STUDIO, the two students have shed their clothes and are dressed in white robes. Elisha continues to brood in his corner, warming his hands on a cup of tea. But the drama coach gets him on his feet and tells him to put on a robe too.

"Why?" he complains. "You said that today I'm here only to watch."

"Yes, watch, but not as an outside observer. If you're dressed like them, you'll participate with your body and not just by looking and inflame the jealousy in your heart at both brother and lover. This will help build the character you'll be playing tomorrow."

The boy shrugs, skeptical, but goes to the corner, picks out a big embroidered robe, puts it on over his clothes, and returns to his place.

Ruth stacks pillows by the window and seats the Hasmonean lad on them, gently angling his head to the sky, and she asks the girl in love to remove her shoes, stand barefoot in the corner, and call in a whisper: "Simon, where art thou?"

The scene progresses, and regresses, and Ruth doesn't just instruct but demonstrates the gestures and expresses the feelings, moving from character to character. She knows the script from memory, she is free to act and explain at the same time, and toward the end of the scene, after Simon's heart acknowledges his love and succumbs, she asks the boy and the girl to draw closer, to touch and stroke, to put a head on a shoulder, and encourages them to venture a gentle kiss on the forehead and cheek. The children are embarrassed. "Ruth," they protest, "the kids will laugh at us; we know them." But the coach dismisses their concerns. In her youth, her school had put on *My Glorious Brothers*, and when the giggling began, the principal stifled it at once.

The day wanes and grayness descends, auguring rain. But Ruth still does not turn on the light — she takes advantage of the darkness to deepen the feelings of her actors. The visitor in his corner is fascinated by real and imaginary intimacies between the two youngsters and glances at the sorrowful doppelgänger of the young Trigano, who closely studies his two friends to cultivate pain and despair for tomorrow.

She is deliberately tormenting and abusing that boy, he thinks, a strange, fleeting thought.

When the rehearsal is over he is careful not to applaud, and his mind has already wandered to Amsalem's idea. Can the story of the sudden parenthood of two children be told with psychological realism, or does such deviant subject matter need a different key, and if it does, who will find it?

The young actors in their white robes move about the dark studio like ghosts. Moses feels they are looking to him for a reaction, but he smiles and keeps silent. The next rehearsal is scheduled for tomorrow, and the students get dressed, put on their backpacks, and say goodbye.

The actress collapses on the pillows by the window.

"Nice work," praises the visitor, "you give me hope."

"Hope for what?"

"For the new film, about the children who suddenly become parents."

"Why a movie like that?" she says with eyes closed, her face pale.

"Why not? It's a contemporary drama, in the spirit of the age. A period that's full of sex and violence among kids."

She opens her eyes, looks at him.

"That's the spirit of the age?"

"That's what they say, that's what I hear."

Silence. He tries again.

"It'll be like your *Glorious Brothers*, only a different kind of glory, more like infamy."

"That's what you and Amsalem are plotting?" A shadow of derision in her voice.

"And what do you think?"

She doesn't answer. She is exhausted, can't keep her eyes open, and he knows she'd be happy if he just left, but he wants to stay, go back into her apartment.

"Let's go out and eat. . ."

"No, I'm dead, I'm going to bed, and don't you dare mention the blood tests."

"Not another word. May I invite myself to the next rehearsal? I want to see pain and despair in Judah Maccabee, that little Trigano. You seem to be picking on him."

"Could be."

"Please let me drop in on the next rehearsal?"

"No, Moses, I'm sorry. You could tell the kids were excited by the presence of a film director. You're confusing them with possibilities that kids acting in a school play don't need. If you want to see the final results, you'll have to come with all the parents."

"Which parents?"

"The parents of these children and their grandparents too. Why not? You have a grandson their age."

He nods, says nothing. As darkness pervades the studio, he recalls the musty smell of the confessional booth in the cathedral. There, behind the leather lattice, opposite the monk who spoke to him in ancient Hebrew, his heart opened wide. He had forgotten to tell the monk about the time he nearly married her. He didn't, and not because he feared the revenge of Trigano, but because he was afraid of shackling himself to a character who would appear and reappear in his work. But that happened anyway, without his marrying her.

He stands up, absent-mindedly reaches for the pointed walking stick he bought her in Santiago, approaches the woman sprawled by the window, and says: "They were like a dream, the three days in Santiago."

"How so?" She is surprised. "I remember every minute of the retrospective they put on for you and, actually, for me too."

"Of course," he affirms warmly, "it was a retrospective for us both."

"Why a dream, then?"

"Because our three nights in one bed passed by like a dream."

"The dream was yours, Moses, and in a dream you have no right to get near me."

"Why? Because you saw the rape scene in the wadi and your old anger came back?"

"Not anger, disappointment," she explains. "I understood that with the savage violence against the deaf-mute girl you made Trigano's darkest fantasies come true. So I was disappointed in you, in the young man you were then, a teacher and educator who was prepared to throw away his values and surrender to someone else's story – to hand over a young woman, barely an actress, to an actor who used the camera as an alibi for his lust. And Trigano, who was at your elbow the whole time to protect his script, was pleased with your submissiveness as a director, which encouraged him to go to extremes with me in his screenplays from then on."

He turns around, puts on his jacket, and goes back to Ruth, who has wrapped herself in a light blanket as if determined to stay on her pillows and not return to her apartment lest Moses try to follow.

"So if you were right, if the retrospective in Spain was not only mine but also yours, let's go down together to the abandoned station and see what became of our railroad tracks."

"Why?"

"Why not? The old border is gone, and the Arab village Toledano annexed with his camera is now under Israeli control. We can get a new angle on the place we shot the film."

"Why do you care?"

"Because we have to finish the retrospective before we can start thinking about a new film. And that's why you have to come with me. Down there in the desert, in the darkness, I was alone with the Bedouin and his wife, but this time we'll be there in daylight, we'll walk by the tracks, and even go down in the wadi where I failed you as a human being."

She perks up, but tugs the blanket tighter.

"Could you find your way around after so many years?"

"Between your memory and mine, we'll manage. Besides, we do have a map."

"But when? I work every day."

"We'll go Saturday. First thing in the morning."

"If it's important to you, I'll come. Though that young girl's pain could come back."

He grins. "We'll explain to her that we needed that scene for the sake of the story, that in actuality, no harm was done."

"*You* explain that to her. I'm not so sure that *she* will understand."

"She will understand. That deaf-mute that Trigano brought to the film was clever."

A little smile flickers on her face, heartbreakingly pale in the darkness.

"One more thing, and don't get angry."

"No . . . not that again."

"One short sentence. Please."

"Very short."

"If you're sure there's nothing wrong with you, don't do another blood test, but why don't we just remove your name from the tests you did and show them to Zvi, my son-in-law, so we can rest assured."

She says nothing. Closes her eyes again.

"For example," he says, advancing his case, "I happened to visit Galit at her radiology clinic and she, on her own initiative, took the opportunity to do a virtual mapping of my heart, and now I can relax."

"And you weren't relaxed before? Your heart is so relaxed it barely works."

"Relaxed, but for no good reason. Now I have confidence in my heart, I can let it get more emotional. So you too, with one quick peek by an understanding eye, can maintain your serenity."

"I don't need an understanding eye, and that's final." She is fuming. "You promised one short sentence and you've already come up with five long ones. Goodbye."

6

MOSES' ROAD MAP is plainly outdated, giving no indication that Israeli control over the Jordanian village conquered in the Six-Day

War has more recently been transferred to the Palestinian Authority. After the two enjoy a scenic drive on a fine Shabbat morning, winding on a repaved road from the Ayalon Valley into the terraced hills south of Jerusalem, in the company of cyclists serenely climbing or coasting below snowy puffs of cloud, they run into an army roadblock at the turnoff to the village. And though the barrier is splintered and essentially symbolic, Moses honors it and waits. A female police officer and male soldier come out yawning and rumpled and ask: "Where to?"

He gives them the name of the village, and they ask what he plans to do there. And though the director would like to tell the security forces about a retrospective that began in Spain and aims to end here, the car behind is honking, and they wave Moses through, warning him that Israelis visiting this village do so at their own risk.

"Should we go on?" Moses wonders after passing the checkpoint. "Is it worth the risk just for one more look?"

"Turn back now?" scolds his companion, her cheeks ruddy in the mountain air. "What's to be afraid of? If the Jerusalem train doesn't stop here anymore, the only way to the station is through the village, and from there we can look down into the wadi. If not now, when? Once you're immersed in the next picture, you'll forget the retrospective. And life is short."

"For whom?"

"Not just for someone with a problematic blood picture, but also someone who discovers his heart is fine and capable of emotion."

For a moment happy laughter fills the car.

He gently touches her hair. Since Santiago she is linked in his soul not only with the characters she acted in his early films but also with the bare-breasted young woman nursing her own father. And though he still believes that all shades of her character have been exhausted and that even her remaining fans and followers would be wary of his giving her a new part, he fears that if he doesn't, he will lose her forever.

After a few kilometers, they reach the sign pointing in Arabic and

Hebrew to the village, and he deliberates whether to be content with an overview from afar or to snake down a steep, narrow old road into the belly of a village that was turned from foe to friend in the editing room. Positioned not far from a sleepy Jordanian guard post, Toledano's camera captured houses, alleys, courtyards, and animals, and sometimes villagers, who in the editing room were annexed into the Israeli film and became involuntary collaborators in the daring allegory of a nightmare screenplay. Might they run into trouble at the entrance to the village? For if the village is no longer under Israeli occupation, it will surely assert its sovereignty.

He pulls over to the side and goes out in search of a secure lookout. But Ruth, protesting the undignified vacillation, stays in the car.

A portentous cloud glides above the village, filtering sunbeams that cast a golden glow on homes and olive groves. From what he can tell, the village has grown over the years, and though he can locate the wadi and see the tracks, he can't find the little railroad station.

"So what if it disappeared?" says Ruth when Moses again suggests skipping the descent into the village. "The tracks are still there, so is the wadi, and anyway, what are you afraid of? Do the Palestinians care about you? And if they ask what it is you're looking for, they'll be glad to hear that we once included them as partners in an art film."

He puts a hand on her shoulder. Ever since he watched her work with the young actors, he can't get her out of his mind; he is worried, he wants to be good to her. And so, despite the fear of entering a place where safety cannot be guaranteed, he starts the car and heads slowly down the narrow road, braving half-filled potholes. And what was once simulated appears now in full force — a square and a well, a donkey tethered to the rusty remains of a car, chickens pecking peacefully, and also a gleaming, late-model motorcycle parked beside a top-quality tractor, with a satellite dish on every house. The locals, mainly women, look at the Israelis with no particular interest. As the two walk down to the tracks, escorted by a barking dog, the clouds sink lower and the air thickens.

But here they face a clear border. A high fence separates the village and the tracks. It is strange that in the past what was porous between enemies is now a firm barrier between neighbors.

In any case, what happened to the little train station? They ask a young Palestinian who sits on the steps of his house reading the sports section of the Hebrew paper *Israel Today* and learn that a few years back the villagers used the building stones of the station to expand their homes. "But until the new tracks are laid between Modi'in and Jerusalem, doesn't the train still pass by here?" "Passes but doesn't stop," explains the young man, "and on Shabbat doesn't even pass." "So how can we get down to the tracks and walk a bit in the wadi alongside?" "It's not possible and also not permitted," says the Palestinian, "because it's a border fence, so we have a bit of independence. But for you," he adds with a sly smile, "since you belong to the other side, I'll show you how you get into Israel without a passport."

He folds up the sports section and leads the actress and the director, pilgrim stick in hand, down an alley and then another, to a field of green alfalfa. Reaching what looks very much like a fence, he grabs the border with both hands, shakes it hard, and opens a wide entry.

"Well done," says Moses, "but please close it in a way that we can open easily on our way back. Better yet, if you could wait for us here, we're only going for a short walk, to retrieve something from the past."

"Okay, I'll wait for you," agrees the young man, who seems amused by two older Israelis eager to take a Sabbath-morning stroll on a desolate railroad track near his village. "But to get back into Palestine" — he grins — "you'll have to undergo a security check and pay a fee."

"We'll pay the fee" — Moses chuckles — "on condition that you not budge from here."

The young man finds a big rock, sits down, and opens the sports pages. Meanwhile the director and the actress make their way single file along the tracks, first he in the lead, then she, stepping on the gray concrete railroad ties, trying to find the spot where the imaginary train plunged into the imaginary abyss. But it's not so simple to reconstruct a reality that was imaginary to begin with, and the actress trips and the heel of her shoe gets stuck in a gap between the rail and one of the ties. Moses quickly grabs her and sets her aright, pausing a second before kneeling to pry out the shoe and fit it back on her bare foot. Holding her in his arms, in the here and now, he can feel the tenderness of the woman who took part in so many of his films. And even as she smiles at him with gratitude, she wants to be released from his embrace. Perhaps she suspects that it's not her the old director desires, but rather the lithe, dark young woman whose lover had demanded she portray the character of an inscrutable deaf-mute.

"So what are we actually doing here?" Ruth asks.

Moses finds it hard to explain his urge to reconnect with the shooting locations of his early films. Does he just want to get the feel of them, or does he want to repair them?

"Can they be repaired?"

"It's impossible," admits the director. "But one can try calming the old anger."

"Not anger, just disappointment."

"And even if just disappointment," he insists, "disappointment hurts no less." This is why he has brought her here, to soften the disappointment.

"To soften it? How?" Her eyes flash mild disdain.

Maybe, as they walk near the village that is again beyond the border, she will understand why *Distant Station* could only have ended with a scene of violent rape. Even a foreign audience in a distant land was sympathetic to the film.

"The sympathy of the audience doesn't compensate for the humiliation of the actor."

"Hold on. I didn't write the screenplay, I only interpreted it."

"An extreme interpretation, far beyond what was only hinted in the script."

"But Trigano was there with us and could have restrained me."

"He couldn't, because of the agreement that you could change nothing in the script once it was done and that he would not meddle in the directing once it began. His hands were tied."

"Tied even when I, as you claim, degraded you?"

"Fine, maybe the agreement didn't stop him, maybe that was just his excuse. But understand this: your creative partnership with him was thanks to your normalcy, your sense of proportion, on the assumption that you, as director, would impose credibility and restraint on his wild imagination, that you would calm the disquiet raging inside him, clarify the symbols that raced around in his soul. But then, as we're filming the last scenes of *Distant Station*, he suddenly sees that your flexibility is not so simple. That it has a different mindset, broader margins, than he expected. He understood that the bourgeois values you brought from your Jerusalem were less stable than he imagined and that normalcy could also be violent and cruel. That's why he didn't want to interfere with the rape scene. He liked the idea of going to extremes with you . . . to dare more. With me, or through me . . ."

"With you. Mainly with you." Her words have moved him. "We all knew how close a bond he had with you."

"It wasn't just a bond, Moses, it was much more than a bond, much more than the love of a man for a woman. Love wasn't enough for him. It had a purpose beyond itself. To turn me into a symbol, into a character."

"A character?" he says disingenuously. "In what sense?"

"A character," she continues confidently, "a character who, because of her own uniqueness and regardless of the part she is playing, is able to force people to think a little differently about the world. And despite what happened in *Distant Station*, I took it upon myself to be a character, not just because of Trigano, but because I saw that you were on his side, supporting him and loyal to him. But when you both sent me out into the street after I handed over the baby, and you expected me to force an old dirty beggar to nurse from me, and you degraded me in front of the girl who was me in the past, I felt that if I didn't stop, the two of you would push me even farther. Because love that tries to go beyond a woman and make her into a character, a symbol, is a love gone wrong."

They keep walking carefully along railroad ties. Moses listens in silence.

"That's why I tried to stop the momentum of the final scene. I wanted to test *your* reaction."

"You only tried?"

"Yes, I only tried. But instead of offering a solution – perhaps promising that through the camera work you would inject some compassion into the scene to shield me from the weirdness – you simply switched sides and joined my refusal. You canceled the scene so fast that neither I nor you had a chance to reconsider."

"I was quick to support you, to protect you."

"Yes, but the support was so ferocious that it insulted Trigano, wounded him."

"Because of his pride, his delusions of grandeur. He was sure my 'normalcy' would defer to him and accept everything he fed you."

"You were ready to do that scene. That was not the point."

"Then what was the point?"

"You created in him, and in me as well, an impression that you supported me because you wanted me for yourself, wanted to take me away from him. But you didn't really want me – you certainly didn't love me then."

Moses kicks a small stone. "That's true."

"So you should have appeased him, suggested a compromise, calmed my anxiety, most of all. You could have tried harder and found a way to remedy the scene that was scaring me. Why didn't you try to make peace between me and him? You were the director, you were the strong one. You were the native Israeli, you controlled the production. You should never have allowed him to cut off ties with you and with me. But you wanted to exploit the argument to be rid of him once and for all, so you wouldn't have to keep dealing with his crazy ideas."

In that case, he realizes with a shudder, the picture of *Caritas Ro-*

mana by the bed at the Parador had hit a deep nerve after all, though she hadn't said a word.

"Yes," he confesses, "I did want to break away from him, or at least keep my distance for a while. I was afraid he was leading me down a blind alley."

7

THEY HEAR DISTANT buzzing, the sound of a saw or a lathe, but it gets louder, closer, and the walkers on the tracks, who assumed they were protected by the Sabbath from any trains, freight trains included, are surprised as a little yellow railcar barrels toward them from around a bend, shrieking like a bird of prey. Moses grabs Ruth by the arm and pulls her aside. "You can't even rely on the chief rabbi in this country," he grumbles.

The two exchange a grin as an old man in coveralls, bald and heavyset, brakes the railcar and hollers: "What's going on? How'd you get here? This isn't a hiking trail! Get out of here or I'll call the police forces." It's hard to pin down his nationality; he says "police forces" as if he's a bi-national with double protection. Moses jests, "Is it not the Sabbath, sir? You want us to inform the religious authorities that Israel Railways rides on Shabbat?" Except the railroad man doesn't get the joke. He climbs down from the railcar and waves his hands. "*Yalla, kishteh,* scat," he commands in three languages, then gets back in the car, blows the whistle, and heads for the coastal plain.

The young Palestinian, their border guard, is still immersed in the sports section. He sees the two approaching and takes his time getting up and going to the breach in the fence. Moses hands him a hundred-shekel note with a smile and says, "Here's the fee, you can skip the security check, because we're at peace with each other." The young man fingers the unexpected bill and yanks open the border with two hands, singing, "Peace, peace, there is no peace." He invites the Israelis for a cup of coffee, included in the entrance fee. "Why not?" The director is enthusiastic. "We have time."

Yes, Moses wants to prolong the Sabbath excursion. Especially since from the neat, pleasant living room, there is a fine view of the route of the Israeli railroad tracks till they vanish around a mountain bend. He sips the excellent coffee and tells the young man and his wife about the film of long ago.

They are amazed to learn that an Israeli feature film was shot near their home before either of them was born, and they relish the mischief of the cinematographer who crossed the border and stole their village, but they are unsettled by the plot, the act of terrorism that Israelis perpetrate on their own people for no reason, without politics or war.

"This could actually be true?"

"Yes, that's what we thought at the time," says Moses, "with no political conflict, just out of human loneliness and emptiness."

The hosts nod in agreement. Yes, they know people like that. In their village too.

"In any case," says Moses, pointing at Ruth slumped wearily in an armchair, "she is to blame, she's the one who incited the villagers, she bewitched them with her beauty." And he details the deeds of the deaf-mute girl in the old film.

The hosts are excited. There is a deaf-mute woman in the village today, but she is old now. If the Jews would like to meet her, they can bring her.

"Why not?" says Moses. The chance to burrow into another retrospective tunnel appeals to him. But his companion motions him to stop. She's worn out. It's time to go.

The Palestinian sees them to their car and asks hesitantly if the film was a hit. His wife, who works in a law office in Bethlehem, thought that the village might be entitled to a share of the profits.

Moses laughs. "Are you mad? You're talking about profits from a film made more than forty years ago."

"Why not?" says the young man. "What's forty years? Our account with you has been open for more than a hundred years, and will surely last a hundred more."

Ruth gets into the car. Moses waves his hand dismissively and gets in too. But as Moses turns the key, the Palestinian opens the door on the driver's side. The sunlight on his face uncovers a spark of enmity.

"The movie did well with the critics, but at the box office we only had losses," Moses says, attempting to reassure him. "But tell your wife that if we're opening accounts, we can also sue you for losses you dealt us a hundred years ago."

8

MOSES SUGGESTS THEY continue on to Jerusalem, but Ruth objects. "Enough," she says, "for me the retrospective is over, and I urge you to end yours too. In any event, please take me back to Neve Tzedek." She emphatically pulls a familiar lever, moving her seat to make room for her legs. Then she unpins her hair, leans her head back, shuts her eyes, and turns off.

She is ill, no doubt about it, he thinks as he glances away from the road at her face, which seems distorted by pain.

Is she asleep or only pretending? He's not sure, but in any case he refrains from speaking and pilots the car smoothly on the open Sabbath roads. Light rain taps the windshield as he navigates the narrow streets of Neve Tzedek, and carefully, so as not to startle his passenger, he stops quietly in front of her place and waits for her to wake up. The redness in her eyes indicates that her sleep was real and deep. She sees her building, straightens her seat, and says with a smile: "You're a good driver."

He gets out of the car too, though it is clear he is not invited in. It's hard for him to part from her because of the sudden hostility she displayed toward him. So he drags out a few extra minutes and asks about the new portrait of her he saw on her table. Who drew her? How did it come about?

She hesitates, then whispers: "Toledano."

"Toledano?" Moses is taken aback. "I didn't know he drew."

"As a hobby. Without telling a soul. Mostly he drew portraits of friends based on photographs. Sometimes he would make miniature drawings of scenes he had filmed."

"Wonderful." Moses snorts. "He never so much as hinted to me about it. It's as if the art of cinematography wasn't enough for him, he needed to supplement it with another art."

"Yes, it came to light only recently."

"He never told you . . ."

"Hid it from me too . . . from everyone, used to draw in the film lab."

"How did this portrait suddenly get to you?"

"His son David gave it to me."

"David? Really? The family stopped boycotting you?"

"The boycott was only his wife. Against me and also you, and basically the rest of us. She blamed me for his accident, but she was also angry with you."

"Very angry, because I didn't keep you away from him. As if I were able to do such a thing. Tough woman, a wounded lioness, wanted no contact at all. Even at the cemetery, at anniversaries of his death, she demanded I stand on the side, till I got tired of it and stopped going. So how did the anger suddenly come to an end, what happened?"

"It didn't end, it never will. She found herself a husband, a French Jew, newly religious, and left the country with him; the two sons decided to sell the apartment and get rid of everything in it. That's how they found the drawings, including a few portraits of me, of others too."

"In that case," says Moses eagerly, "there might have been a drawing of me. We were close, after all, had a strong common language, especially in the films you were in."

"That's true."

"So what do you say? Get in touch with the son, with David, before he and his brother get rid of the rest? I've seen children who throw away hundreds of pictures and entire libraries after the parents die, with no emotion. If Toledano drew a portrait of me, I would be curious to know how he saw me. It's curious, all the movies he shot, including some marvelous artistic images, that his camera wasn't enough. Apparently it's hard for a truly artistic soul to be content with one medium."

"Apparently so."

"I loved him too," Moses says, "I loved him and respected him, though his desire and love for you were sometimes ridiculous."

Her face reddens. Her jaw tightens.

"Ridiculous? What do you know? It was a love from childhood, pure and genuine. It was a pity I couldn't reciprocate."

"A pathetic love."

"Not pathetic, tragic . . . What do you know about such a love?"

"Sorry, I apologize . . . You could be right. I didn't know what went on between you."

"Nothing went on. Feeling, just feeling. Precisely what's so hard for you to fathom."

They stand in a narrow street in Neve Tzedek. His car is holding up traffic. Someone honks. Moses says, "Wait, wait, don't run away," and he gets in the car and moves it onto the sidewalk, goes back to Ruth.

"Listen," he says, "you must have his son's address or his phone number. I'll call him."

"You don't have to call him. He's invited friends to his mother's apartment Saturday night to give away possessions and pictures. If there happens to be a portrait of you, I'll take it."

"Why would you take it? I'll go there myself."

"Why do that? You're not part of their crowd — people from Yeruham in the Negev, from the town in Morocco, friends from school. I'll be glad to take it for you, if there's anything to take."

"I'll go there myself . . ."

"Don't. It's a private gathering, I'm sorry I mentioned it. David specifically did not invite you."

"What does that mean? Why does he care if I come?"

"He doesn't care, but –"

She can't find the words, but he understands.

"Trigano will be there too?"

"Maybe . . . Toledano did a number of portraits of him."

"So what?"

She backs away against the wall of her building.

"Say something . . . what's going on? You're hiding something from me? In Spain we slept in the same bed. What's happening to you?" He seizes her hand. "Did Trigano say he'd come but only if I wasn't there?"

"Something like that . . . not because of me, I have no contact with him, you know that. That's what I gathered from David when I asked if I should tell you about the evening. He said best not to, it would be bad if Trigano ignored you, or walked out. In any case he thinks these amateurish drawings by his father won't be of interest to anyone."

"He thinks!" His shout bounces off the walls of the narrow street. "Who's asking him to think for me? And who is this son anyway? What does he do in life?"

"Don't get angry. David is a sweet and gentle boy. He finished the army, and like his father, he's a photographer, of stills, not film."

Moses is carried away with new, unfamiliar rage.

"I don't care what he does or whether he's sweet and gentle, he shouldn't decide what does or doesn't interest me. His father was my loyal and true partner, not like that madman, so don't you say a word to anyone. If I decide to come, I'll come. You know me. But please, give me the address."

"Same one."

"Where? Still down in Bat Yam?"

"Rishonim Street," she says feebly. "I don't remember the number."

"Doesn't matter, I'll recognize the building, I was there many times."

9

SATURDAY'S LIGHT RAIN was prologue to strong winds and rainstorms. After the skies had calmed, the temperature plummeted and bitter cold rattled the world. *Yes,* he said to himself, *the cold weather will chill our minds and freeze stupid delusions.* He puts on a heavy coat and an old wool cap and takes the pilgrim staff he has grown so fond of, and guided by memory alone, he finds Rishonim Street in Bat Yam, south of Tel Aviv, and a parking spot not far from the apartment house. For a moment he questions whether he should take the walking stick, then decides, Why not?

In the old times, on an evening prior to a day of filming when Toledano needed to take care of his boys, Moses would come to his home to plan the next day's work. He can see right away that not much has changed here over all those years.

The noise of the gathering on the second floor can be heard at the entrance to the building. The apartment door is open, and the guests, mostly childhood friends of Toledano, some of whom have come from the south for the occasion, are not here to divide up the loot, which in any case is meager, but to look for portraits of themselves or of friends who have died, to exchange memories in a half-empty apartment thick with cigarette smoke. It seems to the director that since his last visit to his cameraman's home, the shabby apartment has grown shabbier. There's a big pile of coats, scarves, and hats near the front door, but Moses refrains from adding his coat to the pile and is above all wary of leaving his pilgrim staff unguarded, lest someone should think it had belonged to the late cinematographer and take it home as a memento.

The apartment is dim. There are few light bulbs and they are weak. It appears that Toledano's widow had neglected the flat long before she hooked up with the Jew who took her overseas. But the dimness actually heightens the merriment of the crowd as they look at dozens of portraits and other drawings tacked to the bare walls in neat rows by Toledano's two sons. From afar Moses notices big drawings of Trigano side by side, and Trigano himself — with a short haircut, wearing a khaki shirt and a red vest, straight-backed and thin as ever — holding a large candle and inspecting the portraits of himself, exchanging words with David, the elder son, whose silhouette resembles his father's, though the father was taller.

Most of those present are middle-aged men and women, younger than Moses, some standing, others seated or reclined on straw mats apparently brought in for the gathering after the furniture was disposed of. Despite the physical discomfort and refreshments consisting of salted snacks, there is palpable fellow feeling among the invited guests, who pour into plastic cups the remnants of alcoholic beverages left behind, colorful liqueurs from old bottles.

Moses knows none of the people seated in one far corner except for Ruth, who is heavily made up and wreathed in the smoke of longtime admirers. A few guests recognize the director, and as the walking stick in his hand suggests a disability, efforts are made to clear him a path.

He anxiously scans the walls for a portrait of himself, but in vain. He does find a few graceful charcoal drawings of scenes he directed, but the figures are only the actors. The director and cinematographer and soundman are nowhere to be seen. Nonetheless, he does not despair of finding himself, if not as a separate drawing, at least as a member of a group portrait. Toledano's work with charcoal pencil is remarkable for both its precision and simplicity, for in lieu of complex detail he often made do with a line or two that wondrously conveyed the image. In drawings of Ruth, her hands or hips are portrayed only tentatively. He finds that Ruth, like Trigano, is featured in many drawings, but as opposed to Trigano, who stands and eagerly examines his pictures, Ruth is indifferent and huddles in the corner with friends, a glass of something yellowish in hand.

Moses is certain that Trigano is aware of his presence. Presumably incensed that despite his request his archenemy has been invited, he is trying simply to ignore his former partner rather than insult him in public.

But it can't be, Moses fumes, *that he will continue to ignore me af-*

ter sending me to the far reaches of Spain to defend his screenplays. He grabs Trigano's shoulder to show that he demands to restore, if only for a moment, the connection broken more than thirty years ago.

As if no hand has touched him, Trigano turns to the young David Toledano — who is embarrassed by the encounter that was not supposed to happen — and asks him to take his portraits down from the wall, since he would like to leave.

The director tugs at the red vest of his former scriptwriter and says, "Hello. I have regards for you from Santiago de Compostela."

Trigano's dark eyes have sunk over the years into their sockets, and his forehead has grown with his receding hairline. A strange smile materializes on his lips when he sees that the director will not desist. And with an unfocused glance to the side, he hisses: "You insisted on coming anyway."

"Yes, why not? Toledano was my cameraman even after you left me."

"True," says Trigano, looking straight at him, "and yet he didn't draw you."

"How do you know that?"

"I've already been through the other rooms. You can relax, you're not hanging here."

"Why relax?" Moses is perplexed.

"Because who knows how your portrait might have turned out."

"How did yours turn out?"

"See for yourself. Each one is different. Supposedly we were good friends for a time, but I seem to have remained a riddle for him. See how he kept drawing me over and over, obsessively."

"And Ruth too."

"Debdou? Fine, in her case it's obvious. He was fixated on her till the day he died. So it's only natural that he'd pursue her not only with his camera but also with a pencil. But you, despite everything, didn't stir his soul at all."

"As opposed to your soul."

"I broke away from you and blotted you out for good."

"You're sure about that."

"I don't even have to check."

"But you unsettle my soul."

"So why not settle it with another crappy movie?"

The noise level in the room has lessened. It seems some have paused in their conversations and are following the unexpected encounter. Moses is afraid Trigano will not be able to hold back and will let fly an insulting remark that will kill any chance of talking further. With the authority of a teacher, he grasps the arm of a rebellious student and leads him to a corner.

"I want to talk to you."

"About what?"

"I have things to say."

"On what subject?"

"Not here. Let's meet."

"I'm busy, I have no time. I teach in several places. I have many students and I sit on many committees. Let's wait till summer vacation."

"Summer vacation is a long way off. I want a short meeting. That's all."

"It's hard for me to make time even for a short meeting; moreover, you're unwilling to tell me what it is you want from me. Write me a letter, you can do it by e-mail, and I'll see if there's any point in a conversation."

"E-mail? Are you crazy? I want to talk."

"So give me your phone number, and during the Passover break, or on Independence Day, if I have time, I'll try to call you."

"What, Independence Day? Forget Passover. You dragged me all the way to Spain, and now you want to run away? I need help, Trigano."

Trigano shrugs. "Really, I am busy. I teach at three colleges, advising students, supervising their work. Once a week I go down south to Netivot and stay the night — I have a film workshop at a community center there."

"Then I'll come to you in Netivot. At night."

"Netivot? There's rocket fire there from Gaza. Do you have a death wish?"

"What do you care if I die? But before I die I demand a talk. The retrospective you so honored me with is not over."

eight

SUPPER WITH YOUR FORMER SCREENWRITER

1

YOU PLAN TO arrive in Netivot before dark, to locate Trigano's studio more easily. If he is so insistent on estrangement from you, it's best to show him that you've come not merely for your own personal agenda but to reconnect with his thoughts and imagination and be, if only for a short while, the student of your student.

In light of your recent road trips, you no longer trust the map you have in hand, so you buy a new one at a gas station. Its user-friendly design promises that this time you won't get lost.

"Any rockets been fired at the south?" you inquire of the young man filling up your car.

And though this Israeli Arab appears indifferent to rockets not aimed at him, he says that so far as he knows, rockets are more likely to fall on the Jews at dinnertime. But it's clear to you that he's not familiar with the intentions of his fellow Arabs across the border in Gaza, since on the way down, long before dinner, there were radio reports about rockets falling in open fields. If so, you hope that the daily quota will have been filled before you enter the fire zone.

You are pleased to note that Netivot is no longer a peripheral village but an actual city, its status and prestige enhanced by the rocket war of recent years. Shops are still brightly lit and streets full as dusk falls, and everyone you ask knows the way to the community center. But you have arrived early. And since it would be humiliating if Trigano barred you at the door, it would be better to slip into his darkened classroom while a student film is being screened. So you sit down on a bench in a wooded park a stone's throw from the community center, and though your hunger rumbles, you ignore it, preferring to break your fast with the scriptwriter, who as you recall is in the habit, like a Muslim during Ramadan, of eating hardly at all in daytime and enjoying a big meal at night. If you've made the trip down south to unravel an ancient hostility, it would be good to invite him for a generous meal, at your expense, conducive to relaxed conversation.

Sitting in the little cluster of pine trees, complete with a glimmering pond of goldfish, you watch with wonder as a multitude of night students, arriving no doubt from around the region, young and old, mainly women, park their cars side by side in the lot and go to classes and workshops at the center, which in the evening turns into a community college. Now and again muffled explosions are heard in the distance. And though a senior citizen who has sat down beside you on the bench dismisses those as "ours" and not "theirs," you, the cautious Tel Avivian, head for the bomb shelter in the community center and are relieved to discover that the film workshop is held in the basement.

You wait awhile before sneaking into a large classroom, and you find a seat in the back row. Considering all the silver hair sparkling in the light of the projector, you will not stand out on account of your age.

You don't yet see the man, but his voice is clear and confident, and it seems that since you parted ways his Sephardic accent has grown more pronounced, possibly to connect better with his students. The big old projector rattles in the middle of the room, presenting an amateur production shot on film, not video, perhaps to attune the budding directors to genuine shades of color. Judging from the conversation, this is apparently not the first screening of this film, since there are references to comments previously made and scenes viewed earlier. Sometimes, without turning on the lights, the teacher asks that the projection be interrupted in order to discuss fundamental issues — aesthetic, technical, or moral — and the conversation flowing in the dark indicates that the teacher can identify his students by their voices. As Trigano pinpoints weak spots and describes missed opportunities, you close your eyes and are propelled back in time, to the entrance of the Smadar Cinema in the German Colony in Jerusalem, where after the second show a student usher stands excitedly delivering his opinion of the film his mentor has just seen.

The screening is over and the lights go on, but Trigano has not yet spotted the new arrival. While reels are changed in the projector, an older woman in a headscarf and long dress stands before the class and delivers a few introductory words about her short film, an imaginary and experimental story, as she defines it, about a religious family that decides unanimously, after careful thought, to become secular. She and her husband play the leading roles, and relatives and friends play secondary roles and serve as extras. Despite the cast members' doubts, they were all swept up by the story, and as it turned out, the imaginary heresy in front of the camera was so pleasurable it was hard to let it go and get back to reality.

The lights go down, and on the screen an unprofessional film unfolds, confused and choppy, but also bold and entertaining, and the Orthodox amateurs portraying their newfound irreligiosity play their parts with conviction and élan. All eyes are drawn to the leading character, a beautiful religious girl who lures her family to a bacchanal on the beach, and even the neighborhood rabbi who tries to hold the family is forced to give in and ends up splashing in the sea as the ultimate heretic.

As credits and acknowledgments sail down the screen, cheers

break out in the classroom, and you join in. Trigano, grinning with emotion, stands up to embrace the artist with the headscarf, who in real life recoils from his male touch. And now, as he surveys his students with pride and affection, he notices you, an auditor in the back row, and his face turns dark.

2

AT THE END of the session he has to face the fact that there's no escaping the old man who waits for him in the now-empty classroom.

For the moment, just a handshake. There is a tremor in physical contact renewed after an eon.

"You really stay the night here?" you wonder. "Because if the area is quiet, it doesn't take long to get back."

"Even when it's not quiet, it doesn't take long," he says dismissively. "I took on this workshop in Netivot because we have a son in the area, in an agricultural moshav, with a foster family. So after my class I have a chance to be with him at night, and in the morning, before he goes to work."

"This is the boy . . ." You hesitate as you recall distressing knowledge, forgotten in the passage of time.

"Yes." He interrupts the hesitation and defiantly pronounces the name of his eldest child, Uriel, who years ago found a good home with a family in the moshav nearby, where he works as a packer of fruits and vegetables.

"How old is he now?" You are curious to know the age of the mentally disabled son, to measure the toll on his father.

"He's twenty-one."

"He's not your only son," you say, as if to reassure yourself.

He throws you a sharp look.

"Uriel has a brother and a sister."

"And they?"

"His brother is in the army and his sister is in high school."

"Oh, nice. I didn't know."

"It's not the only thing you don't know."

"Of course. It's been years. But you too . . . about me . . ."

"A lot less than you think."

"We'll see," you say, rising to the challenge. "But what I did know about you, I remember. For example, that you postpone your main meal to the evening. If that's still true, let me take you out to a good dinner, assuming there is a decent restaurant in Netivot open at this hour."

His smile suggests that the personal detail preserved in your memory might overcome his hostile preference for a quick exchange of words in an empty classroom.

"You have no choice." You continue to provoke him. "If you went on a pilgrimage all the way to Santiago to renew ties with me, you'll have to hear me out patiently in Israel."

"I didn't go to Santiago to renew any connection with you," he objects. "I went to deposit some of my films in the archive, to save them from oblivion."

"But since I happen to be a collaborator in these films, you dragged me out there too, whether you wanted to or not. And because of you they organized an odd retrospective for me, which came with a little prize at the end, if you can believe it."

"I had no part in your retrospective." The voice echoes firmly in the empty room. "And you didn't deserve any prize for films that were my ideas, whose value you doubted. But what can I do, Moses, if people from a civilized country, no less sensitive and discriminating than you and your friends, recognize the quality of my work and are interested in preserving it in an archive, to learn from it? But I have no interest in you. If I wanted to reconnect, why go all the way to Spain, when here in Israel you're open to everyone and running around everywhere?"

You concede the point with a smile.

"And in general," he carries on, "from the time we split up, I never had the slightest desire to get near you again, especially when I hear about the inferior quality of your movies. But what can I do. You force yourself on me."

"Indeed, what can you do."

"I asked David, Toledano's son, not to invite you — after all, Toledano didn't draw a single picture of you. But you invited yourself, told me you needed my help, which I don't believe you really do. And no matter how hard I tried to escape, or at least delay, you insisted and chased after me all the way here — so, please, Moses, a *meal?* Let's talk here right now. It's nice and quiet. Talk, but make it quick, what more do you want from me?"

Up against such harsh language, it might be best to preserve your dignity and walk out now, but the fatigue and hunger fortify your self-control. Beyond your former scriptwriter's insults and anger hovers the image of the disabled son, deleted from your memory, inviting clemency for the father who does everything in his power to hurt you.

"Come, Trigano," you say, your hand on his shoulder. "Even so . . . not like this . . . not standing, not in an empty classroom . . . I came to you hungry and thirsty, with goodwill, so, please, let's sit someplace more reasonable, and the minute you tell me it's enough, I'll get up and leave."

But he customarily eats his evening meal at the moshav, with the family that cares for his son.

"And you can't include me?"

"Not sure the place would suit you."

"Why not? Where is it?"

"A few kilometers west of here, near Netiv Ha'asarah, on the Gaza border. But don't worry, *they* won't kill you tonight."

For a moment you freeze at the malicious spark in his eyes. Then you burst into laughter.

But he isn't laughing. He gathers his papers, puts on a windbreaker and a white, wide-brimmed hat, and turns out the classroom lights. He bids a warm long farewell to the security guards and leads you outside, to the empty parking lot, bathed in the yellowy light of a full moon. "Follow me in your car," he barks, "and I'll explain later how you get back north. Make sure not to lose me, especially at turn-offs to back roads."

"Just a minute" – you grab his shoulder – "it's not my job not to lose you, it's your job not to lose me." And he stares at you, startled for a second by your powerful grip.

After the city lights disappear he leads you down narrow, desolate roads, where only military vehicles pass now and then, with dimmed lights. Though he could easily shake you on the road and be done with an unwelcome guest, he is careful not to lose you en route. He slows down at traffic lights so you can continue together when they turn green. He waits for you at the turns, signaling in advance at each one. And because he knows well the way to his son, he takes a few shortcuts, including dirt roads, heading west the whole time toward a horizon intermittently brightened by a silent flash, perhaps lightning freed of thunder, or a missile bearing its payload. And though he stays in the area merely as a guest for the night, you have faith that he too has learned to distinguish between "ours" and "theirs." But when a flare goes off in the distance, with a boom that mimics the drumbeat on your car stereo, you are surprised to see him stop at once, jump from his car, and point at the sky, and when he sees you don't under-stand, he pulls you from your seat to a ditch at the side of the road and shoves your face hard in the ground, and then a second blast, stronger and closer, shakes you both, pebbles land on your head, and when the air regains its composure, it exudes a sweetish smell of gunpowder.

When Trigano gets back on his feet you are still lying in the ditch, and you say facetiously, "What happened, *habibi*? You promised me that *they* won't kill me tonight."

He finally breaks into the old smile, the wise smile of the dreamer who won your heart the first time you met him. Yes, he confirms, not *they*. Something else. Wait and see. He brushes the dirt from his clothes and lights a cigarette; you are still in no hurry to get up. Curled amid weeds and stones you inhale deeply the smell of the earth you have not been this close to in years. Trigano may have guessed that you enjoy this moment of weakness, because he doesn't offer you a hand but blows smoke and regards you with an ironic gaze, as if to say it's good that the director who betrayed him should grovel at his feet.

"I don't understand" — you hold on to a rock and get up slowly — "I was told that they always fire in early evening, not at night when everyone is home near a bomb shelter."

"There's no system. They fire when they feel a longing, and longing as you know cannot be controlled. It comes and it goes."

"Longing for what?"

"Longing for fields and homes that were taken from them in 1948, and maybe also longing for our greenhouses and canneries, our nursery schools and pretty houses with red-tiled roofs we shoved in the face of the refugee shacks. They want us next to them again, so they can envy and hate and take revenge, and not only in their thoughts. Like frustrated children they fire stupid rockets that barely scratch us, to entice us to return and be at their side again."

"But we won't go back and settle there."

"I hope not. Not to stay, at any rate. Enough of the goddamn partnership."

His tough talk seems to be about more than Palestinians and Israelis. Meanwhile, out of nowhere, reserve soldiers appear, looking for the rocket's point of impact, and when they see two men standing calmly beside cars, they shout, *Yalla*, this isn't the border with Tuscany, not a good place to hang out.

Not long thereafter you are stopped at a checkpoint at the entrance to a moshav called Na'arut, and from the strange and tormented faces of the youngsters surrounding your car, you understand this to be a whole village full of foster families. For a moment, as the barrier lifts, you are inclined to waive your entrée to the moshav and forget your wish to restore the connection with such a proud and difficult man. But your concern for the character who refuses to acknowledge her illness awakens a strange desire for a new film, and you push on.

3

"HE WAITED FOR you all evening but finally caved in and fell asleep. You want us to wake him?" The speaker is a thickset farmer surrounded by a pack of silent dogs licking his boots.

This is a good-sized farmhouse at the edge of the settlement, giving out onto fields and hedged by fruit trees, with a cowshed and goat pen and chicken coop in a muddy barnyard.

"No, don't wake him," says Trigano, "I'm staying the night anyway, but he will leave right after supper." He introduces you politely as "an old teacher of mine, who left his students for the film business." The farmer, a man of your own age, looks you over sympathetically and says, "But if the teacher should change his mind, we'll find a bed for him."

"He will not change his mind," says Trigano.

"Of course not," you confirm, bending over to the friendly dogs, who sniff and lick your shoes and trouser cuffs, and suddenly you have an idea: accept the farmer's offer and stay the night to pursue the dramatic meeting. You can tell that despite the circumstances that forced Trigano to turn from an artist into a teacher, his vitality is undiminished, his wit and originality intact. If you get access to him and show compassion for his suffering, reconciliation will become more possible.

In the doorway waits the mistress of the house, a farmwoman around forty, built as solidly as her husband. The permanent look of wonder in her eyes and her slow movements suggest that she herself may have been cared for here and over the years worked her way up to caregiver. Your admiration for this place grows stronger by the minute and you greet her with a slight bow, introducing yourself by name and profession, apologizing for your unexpected visit.

As you cross the threshold you realize that this farmhouse is essentially a live-in clinic. The living room is now a dining hall, and on the walls, like pictures at an exhibition, flicker small screens with TV programs for youngsters and the not-so-young. Some of the residents gaze at you with longing, others huddle as if a cold wind has sharply blown in. Puppies trot from inner rooms and gather in eerie silence, as if their vocal cords have been plucked out.

"Uriel is sleeping," the woman says, repeating her husband's words. "He waited for you but caved in. Should we wake him for you?"

"No, no need," says Trigano, hugging her, "I'll be here till morning. Where should we sit? In the kitchen?"

"You said you were bringing a guest, so we set you a table in the arbor, and if it gets cold, we can light a stove in there."

"The arbor is wonderful, and we'll see about the fire."

"How do you control all these dogs?" you inquire of the farmer.

"They control us."

"How many do you have?"

"We stopped counting. Don't worry, they're not all ours. Dogs from the area invite themselves over to feast on our leftovers. This little bastard," – he snatches a little white wiry-haired dog and waves it in the air – "is a regular guest who comes every night from Kibbutz Re'im for his supper." He squeezes the dog lovingly before tossing it back to the pack.

Trigano is at the table, tearing hunks from a big loaf of bread. The farmer hauls out an electric light with a long extension cord and hangs it in the Italian honeysuckle that luxuriates in the arbor.

"Do you remember our first short film?" you ask Trigano.

"About the husband who masquerades as a dog."

"Is there a print of it anywhere?"

"A few years ago I looked for it."

"For the Spanish archive?"

"No, long before I knew such an archive existed, I wanted to show it to my students, to demonstrate how best to direct animals. You were not half bad with dogs, navigating intelligently between symbol and reality, and you succeeded, the devil knows how, in getting that dog to express the jealousy and despair of the cuckolded husband. But perhaps this came naturally to you," he continues with a grin, "because during the shoot you would boast that in your previous life you had been a dog."

"Me, a dog?" You turn red and laugh.

"That's what you said, in your previous incarnation. Or maybe that you would be a dog in your next incarnation. I don't remember exactly, but the fact is those incarnations helped you develop an intimacy with that dog, who was quite unusual."

"A street dog, we got him from the animal shelter. But you gave him a name in the script?"

"Nimrod."

"Nimrod, right." You laugh again. "A smart dog but a bit disturbed."

"After the filming you latched on to him, kind of adopted him, until you got tired of him and he ran away from you."

"He didn't run away, he was run over."

"Ah, run over, you didn't tell us that." Trigano tries to catch you out. "Maybe you were ashamed to admit that you abandoned a loyal actor."

"First of all," you calmly reply, "he was not privately owned but a dog belonging to the production, and second, I didn't latch on to him, he latched on to me. It's amazing though that you remember what I told you more than forty years ago."

"Yes, Moses, you'd be amazed, almost every word of yours."

From the tone of the answer it appears that tonight, the weight of your every word will not apply in your favor but be turned against you. Therefore, you keep quiet and stare at a pair of ducks that waddle into the arbor and are applauded by the vigorous tail-wagging of dogs awaiting the remains of the meal. Vegetables fresh and cooked, spreads and dips in many colors, fried fish, and mysterious aromatic meat.

Your own appetite has faded, despite your self-imposed fast since noon to ensure full participation in the meal. The fork falters in your hand, its small morsel dropping back into the plate. The lighting set up by the farmer exaggerates the shadows, with the moon now out of view. And you don't know whether the man who eats silently opposite you is expecting you to say something or waiting for you to go away.

How to begin?

"You know that at my retrospective in Santiago they screened *Slumbering Soldiers*? They changed the name of the film and called it *The Installation*."

"Yes, over there they typically change the names of films."

"At first I thought it was a meaningless title, but —"

"It's not meaningless."

"That's right. It's a good title. I understood that only after I got back to Israel and had an odd urge to go check out the places where we shot those early films. I even went to the desert, to the crater."

His dinner knife halts in midair. "To that same wadi?"

"It was hard to find. The landscape had changed. New roads were carved out, and at first I thought the cliffs were different. But I didn't give up, and I saw from a distance the location where we squatted for three weeks."

"Why only from a distance?"

"Soldiers, guards, they didn't let me get close. Now, would you believe, there's a similar installation there, sealed off, big and very real. As if our wild imagination had created a reality."

"*My* imagination."

"Yours, that's right, but also the cinematographer's, and the set designer's, and the lighting designer's, and even the director's . . . Go check it out for yourself."

"There's nothing to check. It's not my first metaphor to have turned into reality. What was the point of the metaphor? That a state that turns into a military installation instead of being a living, breathing homeland doesn't deserve soldiers who want to protect it. In the end they will disrespect it and fall asleep."

"Yes, I understood that then."

"Allow me to question that. True enough you were captivated by my fantasy, but you didn't fathom the deeper meaning that drove it. Not only in that film, but in others as well. I assisted with the dubbing in Spain, so the films would stay faithful to the proper pitch of dialogue, and I realized how many hidden symbols in my screenplays you, the director, were unaware of, even though they proved to be accurate predictions."

"Really?"

"Of course," he insists, "and not because of narrow-mindedness but because of the narrowness of your vision, for just like today, you were incapable of deviating from your social background, transcending your safe and steady environment to connect with the outlook of someone like me, who came from the margins of society."

"Nonsense, Trigano. I was the one who took care of your story, the continuity of the plot, the credibility of the characters, the proper flow of cause and effect. How can you say I didn't get the hidden meaning of a work in which every scene was my doing?"

"Because you couldn't identify with a rebellion that sought to undermine fundamental values you grew up on and held holy. In the Spanish archive I took another look at your mother. Behind the weak and lonely old woman she was supposed to be in our film, one can sense a tough and self-confident personality, a high-ranking administrator in the Treasury Department."

"State comptroller's office."

"Better still. But already then, during production, I could detect the rigid value system this Jerusalem lady had imposed on you. Even after you switched from being a son to being a director, you didn't shake free of your loyalty and submissiveness and were careful to protect her honor —"

"Not so," you interrupt, "you are wrong — out of pure hatred for me. At the archive, where I didn't understand a word of dialogue, I noticed other things, important things, beyond words, and contrary to what you think, I was brought to tears to discover how far I had gone to belittle my mother, all because of the script, and how generous she was in humiliating herself."

"Really," he says sarcastically, "to tears? You are actually capable of tears?"

"Only if they're real."

"The moment has come, Moses" — he leans in close to your face — "for you to understand that your reality, then and now, is shielded and pampered. What you consider humiliation is a pale shadow of humiliation. What you didn't understand as a young teacher you certainly won't understand now, at the end of your career. But it's not the past that makes you chase me here."

"Not only."

"Anyway, why aren't you touching your food? Go on, start eating, or there won't be any food left. And if you think the food here isn't clean because of all the animals running around, I promise you not a single dog is allowed in the kitchen."

"It's not the food, Trigano, it's you . . ."

"Me?" He laughs. "You still get upset by what I say or don't say? At your age and position in life the time has come to be indifferent to the person who gave up on you long ago."

"What does it have to do with my age?"

"Because on the road, when the missiles landed and I shoved your head into the ground, I saw something in your ear. What was it? Cotton?"

"A hearing aid. I have another one in the ear you didn't look at."

"In that case, let me give you some advice. If people like me annoy you, pull out the gadgets. Believe me, I'd be happy if I had access to such simple disconnection."

You put down the knife and fork. Fold the napkin and sit up straight. For a second he seems unnerved.

"Thanks for the advice, Trigano, good of you to dispense it at no cost. I'll give it serious thought. Meanwhile, point me to the toilet."

4

A HARD FEELING. The hope over renewed contact is subsiding. Trigano was not an easy person when young, and over the years he has grown more complex and bitter. Is he taunting you so you'll get up and leave, or does he want to open an old account, want you to stay? It's past eleven, and you find yourself crossing the main room, now empty. The screens on the walls display a newscaster from Israel Television who oddly resembles an American president. In a maze of corridors and rooms you find three bathrooms, all in use, the residents now being readied for bedtime.

"If you really need to, you can come in," offers a female caregiver who is bathing a grown youth in a tub. "I'll step out, and the boy won't mind." You smile your thanks but retreat; it still matters to whom you expose yourself. But as urgency mounts, you hurry outdoors, toward the fields. In a patch purplish in the night, past a vegetable garden planted with large cabbages, between tall, tousled bushes not recently pruned, a big-boned horse stands still, regarding you with the sad look of a philosopher as you unburden yourself before him with tremendous relief.

When you return to the arbor table, you find a reddish soup that arrived in your absence and Trigano slurping his with gusto.

"You found what you needed?"

"Everything was occupied, so I went out to the field."

"Well done. Best that a man hang loose under the starry skies."

"And next to a quiet horse."

"A mule, not a horse," Trigano corrects, "his name is Sancho Panza, and he pulls the children around the moshav in a cart."

"I see that you're also a good friend of the animals."

"I try."

"How long has your Uriel been here?"

"Almost four years."

"And your wife doesn't visit?"

"She comes once in a while, but for her, the visit is harder."

"Who is your wife?"

"A woman."

"I hope she's not a secret."

"Every woman is a secret, my wife as well. Years ago she was a student in a class of mine. Toledano met her before he died. From the time Uriel was born, she was totally devoted to him — he became the focus of her life at the expense of his brother and sister. Our whole family became disabled. But since we moved him here, she was liberated from her obligation or her guilt and she found herself another mission."

"Is she also involved in film?"

"No, God forbid, she has no connection with art. She is a healthy soul, with a stable mind."

"And what's her new mission?"

"Tell me, Moses," he snarls, "does my wife really interest you, or are you sticking to small talk because you're afraid to get to the point?"

He's right. Going in circles and trying to soften his hostility by showing interest in his life doesn't merely fail to draw him closer but apparently alienates him further.

"I came to talk about Ruth."

"Why not eat something first? You said you came here hungry."

"I want to talk about Ruth first."

His face darkens; he looks to the side.

"I want you, Trigano, to help me save her."

"I don't believe you came down just for her."

"For her and maybe a new film."

"Look, Moses" — he sounds serious now — "you went to all this trouble for nothing. I warned you that there was no point in our meeting. But you're stubborn, so I'm telling you again flat out, I can't give you anything because I don't want to give you anything."

"Don't give, just listen. I want to tell you about Ruth."

"I put her out of my mind a long time ago."

"Be that as it may, she was your childhood sweetheart and for years your lover and partner. Look, my wife and I also split up years ago, but I never refuse to listen to her and I care about her."

"Your wife is your wife, and my lover is my lover. There's no connection. But before you go on, put something in your mouth, the people here will be insulted if you don't touch a thing."

"You're right. I don't know what's going on. I'm sort of nauseous. I lost my appetite."

"The place turns you off?"

"Not the place. You . . . you're tough."

"You haven't heard anything yet."

"I want to talk to you about Ruth."

"Make it fast. The night is short and I'm tired."

"She's sick and doesn't want to admit it."

A little smile crosses his lips, as if he is pleased by the news.

"Sick with what?"

"I don't know what the illness is, but I sense it and I'm almost sure. Her doctor has been pestering her to repeat some blood tests, which apparently were bad, but she decided to ignore them."

"Just like her to ignore them, not because she's afraid of the results, but because she believes that ignoring a problem makes it go away. Wait a minute, what does 'I sense it' mean — you're living with her again?"

"No, definitely not. And I never did. I don't know what you know or others told you, but after you left her I didn't want to live with her. What I felt was a responsibility toward her, an obligation to the character we used, we built, we believed in — you first and foremost as the creator, but also I as the director, and also the cinematographer and the others who worked with us. So when you left, she had to have protection, or call it what you will. Because who knows better than you the world she came from? That world could offer no cure for the breakdown you caused her. And if I hoped that Toledano's love would win her over and free me from her, I turned out to be wrong."

"Because she found him too feminine."

"Feminine? Why? Do gentleness and patience have to be feminine? I don't agree."

"You can agree or not, but even in kindergarten Debdou needed someone manly, someone cruel and hard to please, because only then could she feel she had earned his love."

"Someone like you, for instance . . ."

"For instance."

"And someone like me?"

"You're a dubious case; the narcissism in someone like you, so sure he is an artist, erodes manhood over the years, and even if he runs to the toilet and manages to control every drop, his manhood needs more validation than that."

And he laughs.

"I came to talk about Ruth," you repeat patiently. "She's ill and needs to be convinced to let us at least find out what the illness is."

"But if you don't live with her, why are you investigating her illness?"

"Even if I don't live with her, I can still tell she is deteriorating. You should know that I brought her along to my retrospective."

"I knew that."

"Who told you?"

"De Viola told me you asked that she be invited."

"You're still in touch with him? You have no more films to deposit with him."

He ignores your question.

"There, in Santiago," you press on, "during the three days of the retrospective, I saw new symptoms. Weakness she had trouble overcoming, chronic fatigue. Sometimes watching herself on the screen she dozed off, and in *Circular Therapy*, it took her a while to recognize herself. We were staying in the same room, I could see this up close."

Temperatures rise in the arbor. "Yes," he says. "I know that room."

"Not exactly a room."

"Right, an attic they reserve for guests of the municipality, with wooden beams and a window that faces the plaza at the rear of the cathedral."

"Exactly," you say uneasily. "With a stone angel waving a sword or a spear."

"A sword, not a spear."

The revelation that the former scriptwriter had slept in the same room, and lain in the same bed, strengthens the hope that the intimacy, rebuilt and reimagined, could lead to reconciliation.

"I was not considered an honored guest, nor did they give me a prize, or a fee for coaching the actors," continues Trigano, "but they did treat me to a nice stay at the Parador."

You very nearly bring up the *Caritas Romana* hanging on the wall, but you resist, so as not to awaken ghosts.

"By the way," you add, "this wasn't the first retrospective where they made a false assumption and housed us in the same room. And the bed, which you surely noticed was big and wide, was still not so big for a man not to sense what the woman lying beside him was feeling."

You mean to hurt him, in the hope that causing him pain will bind him to you, that jealousy might diminish cynicism.

He looks you in the eye now, seriously.

"Look, Moses. I regret I agreed to bring you here, because you are about to insult a woman who is important and dear to me."

"Which woman?"

"Have you not noticed that the farmer's wife is also in treatment here?"

"So?"

"That's why you have no confidence in the food she cooks."

"No, why do you say that? Your confidence is more than enough for me."

"But you told me you came here hungry, and if I read correctly in an interview you gave to some newspaper or other, in your recent films, which of course I didn't see and don't intend to, you make sure that the meals are real, long and full of detail, and that the characters relate to what they are actually eating —"

"You read correctly."

"So there mustn't be a gap between art and life."

"You think so?"

"Sometimes." He laughs.

"I have nothing against this meal," you say, snatching the wisp of goodwill that suddenly surfaces between you. "Here we are, sitting opposite each other at the dinner table, and if I were here not as a guest but as a director, I could stage an attractive scene lasting a minute or two. I would ask the cinematographer to pan this unusual arbor and try to capture the velvety darkness enveloping its greenery, and from there I would encourage him to zoom in among the plates and bowls on the table to convey precisely the lively colors of the food. From time to time, I would want to spice the dinner scene with a few quick takes inside the kitchen and the dark rooms of the patients, so some fear and mystery can trickle in. That would underscore the dramatic tension between the skinny, younger man who crackles with hostility and disdain while gobbling the food ravenously, and his interlocutor, an emotional old man who pokes his fork into one dish and another but doesn't eat a thing. This contrast alone, without a word spoken, as in a silent film, would build tension that requires a payoff and gives the producer hope of filling the theaters."

He listens attentively but doesn't smile, not even a little. "Because the producer is what matters," he mutters.

"And all this," you say, sticking to the scene, "comes before we get to the heart of the matter. Reconciliation between a teacher and a student after many years."

"No reconciliation. And I'm not saying another word until you put something in your mouth."

"In that case," you counter, "I'll start with the red soup, if it hasn't got cold."

"It's tomato soup that was cold to begin with, and spicy."

You dip your spoon into the fragrant red puree dotted with white specks, bring it to your lips, swallow a spoonful and then another, and suddenly your mouth is on fire and the spoon falls from your hand.

"Great soup. Don't worry," you tell him, like a child to his mother, "just resting. I can't help it if my excitement at seeing you kills my appetite."

"You, Moses, still get excited?" He reverts to mockery.

"Excited, and confused."

"Confused? The one who should be confused here is me, as I picture the two of you in a bed I slept in. My heart is calm and cold — though I know where you want to lead me, there's not a chance that I'll go there. Anyway, objectively, don't you think it's pathetic to travel on a winter night to a dangerous area looking for a man you haven't seen or talked to in many years, all to tell him about the imaginary illness of a woman who has become meaningless to him?"

"It's not an imaginary illness, believe me, Trigano, it's real."

"In what way real?" He reddens. "In that she refuses to play along with the patronage you offer?"

Finally. You knew that Trigano could not conceal indefinitely the root of his pain and jealousy, and you try to maintain a gentle and patient demeanor.

"Again you misinterpret my protectiveness, or call it what you will. Because as I told you, it began as professional care and not personal, and if at times it involves the closeness you're thinking of, it happens naturally in the course of working together. Which is why there are always boundaries."

"Nice and decent, but not true."

"True . . . believe me."

"Okay, why not? Really, what do I care how you interpret your patronage and what you do with her and what you don't do." But he is still angry. "A scene of two adults, lying in the same bed, and the man senses, without any attempt at touching, just from the edge of the bed, the hidden malady of the woman. I wouldn't buy such an absurd premise even in a work of literature."

"Not even in symbolic stories like yours?"

"They have nothing to do with this."

You change the subject and tell him about the first night, about *Distant Station*, which the Spaniards turned into *The Train and the Village* — how astonished you were to discover that the village girl at the center of the plot was a deaf-mute.

"And you forgot that?"

"Evidently."

"But the critics at the time singled out the deaf-muteness as a daring and original element in the script. It was the only way the villagers could support a diabolical plan without incriminating themselves. Her disability created a twilight zone where meanings were confused and outcomes were blurred. Like linguistic obfuscations created by sly politicians to fool the masses and manipulate them at will."

You acknowledge the powerful originality of the deaf-muteness in this film but give yourself some credit too, as the director who was able to elicit from the wild, confused gesticulations of a young woman a strange, alluring eroticism.

"Yes" — he is caught up in your words, eyes blazing — "yes, both I and the Spaniards who did the dubbing could feel it when we worked on those scenes. A strange eroticism floating in the studio . . ."

"In Spain Ruth told me about your sister, who was her model for the character."

"You didn't know about my sister?"

"You never mentioned her. Maybe you were embarrassed by her."

He averts his eyes.

"Maybe . . ." he says. "In those years I avoided exposing my personal life."

"Is she still alive?"

"No. She couldn't keep going after my mother died."

"I'm sorry . . ."

He says nothing. Regards you with caution. The thread of conversation has snapped, and he wonders what you're after.

"I'm afraid of causing you pain," you say, almost in a whisper.

"Cause me pain? How?"

"You surely remember the final minutes of the film, when she is dragged into the bushes. I was amazed to see how savage and violent it was, how far I let it go, even compared to movies today. I was filled with compassion for the living character, the real one, sitting beside me in the hall."

He tenses in his chair, his eyes narrowing, his hostility entangled in the web of your story.

"Yair Moses, I have no interest in an account of your feelings or your lust."

"You're wrong, this is not about my lust but about her illness, which is why I am here. You wondered how I could sense her illness if I don't live with her — well, when we got back to the Parador after the screening, she crashed, fully dressed, in her coat and boots, onto that big wide bed, and sank into an unhealthy long sleep. It was as if a dead woman were lying at my side. I took off her clothes and her boots, knowing that she couldn't feel me. And then, though I had never, ever forced myself on her, not even a light touch, I held her feet and covered them with kisses — just her feet — and by the heat and dryness of the skin I could tell she was sick."

A strange, evil smile distorts his lips. He gets up as if possessed, then calms down. Pours himself some wine, and pours some in your glass too. He sips it slowly, ceremoniously, looks at you as if you are someone he is seeing for the first time.

"Your lips are that sophisticated?"

"Apparently . . ."

"Maybe your loneliness, Moses, has bent you completely."

"Maybe."

"So why don't you tell me what really brought you here, so we can say goodbye?"

"A simple request. Pick up the phone and tell her you found out, from me or whoever, that she is neglecting her blood tests, and this is of concern to you — you can phrase it however you think is right — because, though many years have passed since you parted, you still care, and though you are certain, or you hope, that the test results will be reassuring, in any case it's better for the truth, any truth, to come out earlier rather than later."

"Bottom line?"

"Bottom line, you're asking her to get another blood test, if only for your sake."

"For *my* sake?" He stretches out the word, as if shocked and insulted. "For my sake?"

"Yes, for your sake. That way you might convince her. And if you want, you can add 'in memory of our old love.' I leave that to you."

"Our love?" he retorts in a hoarse whisper, as if you've invaded a vipers' nest.

"Yes, your love. I still remember its intensity and its joy. That's why she'll listen to you. You've remained an authority figure for her. Every time your name comes up, I can feel the awe she has for you. More than awe, admiration. I am asking you to talk to her . . . preferably in person, but it could be on the telephone. If that's too hard for you, write her a letter. There's nothing easier."

"That's enough!" He raises his voice. "You don't expect me to believe you came here for her."

"For her, but also for myself and for you."

"She does have a son . . . a grown man. Why don't you talk to him?"

"Because he's the alienated, childish hedonist type, and it never dawned on him that he should be taking care of his mother. He has no influence on her at all . . . Believe me, Trigano, there's a good reason I took the trouble to come here."

He gets up, walks a few paces, then comes back and stands facing you.

"Listen carefully: No chance! Never! Not by phone or in writing or any other way. You should know that this request is repugnant and insulting – it's as if all feeling has gone from the world."

"But it's feeling I'm talking about."

"These are synthetic feelings, created in films like yours so the producer can massage them any way he likes, not real feelings that torment a man until his dying day."

"His dying day?"

"Yes, Moses, even if your puny imagination cannot grasp it, I must not get near her, not even talk to her from afar, so I don't burn her and myself out of sheer rage and hatred."

"Even now?"

"I don't count the years, time doesn't affect me. Look, quite a few years after I broke up with her – I was already married – I went to see one of your films, whose title and content I have since deleted from my memory. You gave her a supporting role, and in one scene, I wonder if even you can recall why, maybe as an added turn-on for your kind of audience, you put her all alone, at twilight, in a hotel room where she was supposed to be waiting for someone who didn't come, or was late, and she slowly took off her clothes and wrapped herself in a sheet and lay alone in the bed, and her face wore sadness that I'd never seen before."

"I think I can locate that scene for you."

"No!" he screams. "Don't locate anything for me."

"To explain –"

"No, shut up," he shouts, "don't locate and don't explain and don't interrupt, just shut up, or else I'm going to leave you here to the dogs."

His face is twisted in pain. You are not offended but smile uncomfortably.

"Someone told me about the film," he says, caught up in an angry memory. "Or I may have seen her photograph in some ad, and in a moment of weakness I said to myself, *Let me see what became of her, that Debdou,* and I went in and sat in the dark, I didn't even tell my wife I was going to see the film. And as she lay there on the bed, naked and wrapped in a sheet, I wasn't thinking about the cinematographer, the lighting man, the soundman, or the director in the room, only the loneliness and pain looking straight at me, and all at once my passion for her came back, I had a erection from longing and sadness, and I climaxed, and I rushed out of the theater, wet and wounded. I then understood that if I wanted a life, I had to make sure this connection remained broken forever, until the day I died. Perhaps now even you, Moses, can understand why I don't care whether she's a real or imaginary invalid or how her blood tests turn out. Actually, and this is the truth, I also don't care whether she lives or dies . . . So don't ask anything from me. She betrayed a deeply rooted relationship, she broke a covenant. You also betrayed me, because when I asked you to be the director of my screenplays, I believed that the screenplay was not just one element among many but the highest purpose of the film. And suddenly you betrayed me. Except you didn't owe me anything. She betrayed the calling I created for her; my art was born from her and for her. In primary school, in fact in kindergarten, I picked her out as someone who could make a daring dream come true. Not because of her beauty. Believe me, it wasn't because of her beauty. Her beauty was a passing, temporary detail of my vision. I felt the absurdity she radiated, the surrealistic mixture within this ragamuffin child of an old rabbi who brought her to Israel from a village at the edge of the Sahara."

And at this moment, as if on cue, the dogs under and around the table get up, stretch, and vigorously wag their tails.

"And so you will allow me, Moses, not to believe that you came to see me only because of her. I don't remember you as someone who cares about other people. There's always a back pocket in your mind, and in the pocket there hides a slippery frog that will soon jump at me. Do you want to shift the caregiving responsibilities to me, because you no longer have a role for her?"

The agitated dogs drown out his voice, barking and howling for dear life.

5

THE MOTHERLY FARMWOMAN comes with the news that Uriel has woken up and is asking for his father. "Should I bring him to you, or will you go to him?" "He should come here," says Trigano, "let him sit with us awhile. Dress him warmly."

"We'll also get Shaya to light the stove. But I see, Trigano, your teacher doesn't like my cooking."

"The food looks so beautiful," you say in your defense, "it's a shame to ruin it by eating."

"Ruin it, please," she pleads, "that's what my food expects from people, otherwise only the dogs enjoy it."

You laugh. "Yes, of course, soon. I'm just so emotional meeting with my student, whom I haven't seen for over thirty years, I forget to eat."

"If you haven't seen each other for that many years, you couldn't have met Uriel."

"That's right."

"It's a good thing he woke up, so you can see this special boy before you leave. I'll bring him, and you should put some food in you. If you don't like your tomato soup cold, I can make it boiling hot."

"This soup is just fine. See, I'm going to eat it now."

"He'll eat, he has no choice," promises Trigano, who puts on his white hat. "If he doesn't eat, we'll keep him here as a patient."

The dogs trail behind the woman as Trigano moves chairs to make room for his son.

You dip the spoon into the thick red liquid and play with a wild idea: Should you ever be tempted, in your old age, to make a horror film, you can trick the killer in the last scene and serve him a red soup mixed with blood. You are saved from the soup by the dogs who dart excitedly between the father and son, who arrives in a wheelchair. Uriel is a small young man in army work clothes. A knitted cap flops on his head, hairs are plastered to his forehead, his eyes are innocent and blue, bright with yearning for his father, who rushes to hug him and wheel him to the table. "Abba, Papa, Daddy, Papi, Babo, Père," gushes the son, the drool from his lips absorbed by a bib tied round his neck.

"Uriel, I'd like you to meet my old teacher."

"My old teacher," parrots the son, quickly specifying, "*sabba, nono, opa*, grandpa."

You rise to embrace the boy. "Yes, Uriel," you say, "I am also a *sabba*," and the young man is excited to discover a grandfather. His legs are splinted in some sort of Inquisition-style apparatus that helps him control involuntary movements and be aware of his body, but his arms return your embrace, and with great affection he kisses your hand, not letting you go before resting his head on your chest. "*Sabba*," he repeats with warmth and wonder, a mischievous glint in his pure blue eyes, the glint there once was in the eyes of your screenwriter.

"That clear blue he got from his mother," you both state and inquire as you gingerly free yourself from the lad's embrace.

"Not from his mother. From the blue skies that stretch above the desert of his ancestors," his father says, either joking or provoking.

"What is it? Brain damage?" you ask cautiously.

"Yes, to a degree."

"From the birth, or from the pregnancy?"

Trigano takes off his hat and looks at you strangely.

"Earlier, Moses, before the pregnancy."

"Meaning?"

"Meaning . . . meaning . . ." he repeats scornfully, "meaning, there are moments, call them delusional, but at the same time very real, when I regard my son's injury as an extension or a consequence of the injury you caused me."

"That's absurd!"

"You know and remember that everything that you think is absurd, I think has value and meaning. Yes, you too, indirectly, are to blame for what happened to this child."

"I am?" You recoil.

"That's right, but you won't understand what you've just heard and you're better off not trying. There's just one thing you'll take away from this in any case. You'll understand why I avoid you, and why, when you force yourself on me, as you are doing now, it's torture."

"Such a thought is not only absurd, it's despicable, total madness."

"Exactly, madness." He happily seizes the word. "You're right, total madness, sweet, private madness . . . superfluous madness but nonetheless real . . . madness that commands respect. But enough. We'll stop now. They're bringing us a stove."

The old farmer pushes a jerky baby carriage containing an old oil stove, its flame already burning, and a woolen blanket. "I came to warm you up a little," he announces. And while Trigano wraps his son in the blanket, the farmer shoos the dogs away from the table to make room for the stove.

"If the feet are warm," he declares, "the whole body is warm." He collects dishes from the table and puts them in the carriage and scolds you: "You, sir, the teacher, will come to regret you didn't eat. Soon our neighbors might send us a little red alert, you'll have to drop everything and run to the shelter."

In a whirl of emotion your heart aches for the wounded creature wrapped by his father in the blanket, now resembling a newborn with his flattened drooping head, and you rise, stand up straight, and make a strange little speech to the farmer:

"Yes, your wife already chastised me, but I beg for more time. I am paralyzed by the meeting with this man, a former student, the most brilliant and original of all my students, which is why I chose him as my partner at the beginning of my career, until he ripped asunder our partnership in a ferocious argument, which we are trying to arbitrate now. Please tell your wife not to give up on me."

And upon concluding your speech, as the astounded gaze of the brilliant student impales your back, you exit the arbor with head held high and stride through the main house, across the big living room with the little screens sporting a seventies singer in black-and-white, down corridors where breathing and snoring blend with the sound of sighs, and though the toilets are vacant, you prefer a visit to the old mule out by the big cabbages, now that you know the mule's name, and he cocks his head with curiosity as you urinate, slowly and thoroughly, and the subversive notion enters your mind to get in your car and leave, for surely a soldier can be found at a nearby junction who will be happy for the ride and point you in the right direction.

6

THE HONEYSUCKLED ARBOR, all lit up, looks from a distance like a purplish installation with a perforated dome. Two big dogs hunch over a small trough, politely dividing its spoils, the leftovers from Trigano's dinner. And within the arbor Trigano is patiently feeding his son soft rice scooped from the tomato soup. Has he guessed your thoughts of escape? For he gives you a friendly, open look, as though he shed his anger the minute he slammed you with his absurd accusation.

"What's this, Trigano," you joke, "these dogs were trained in table manners?"

"When they are castrated they are well-mannered," he answers, "but do sit down and start eating. There is culinary pride here, so it's important to the lady of the house that accidental guests eat and praise her."

"I have praised her. By the way, does Uriel usually need to be fed, or is this a treat on a special night?"

"A treat, but I'm helping. He knows how to eat, but needs a bit of prodding."

"What kind of work does he do here?"

"He works in the packing house of the moshav, sorting fruits and vegetables. He has a good eye for potatoes and onions, sees what will go bad quickly and what will keep longer. They're so happy with him, they even give him a small salary, right?"

"Two hundred shekels," Uriel burbles cheerfully.

"Is treatment here expensive?"

"The state will subsidize anyone willing to get treatment in a place close to the border."

"That doesn't eliminate anxiety for his well-being."

"Obviously. On the other hand, the caregivers here are good and dedicated, and there are plenty of bomb shelters."

The whole time, he keeps feeding his son, who opens his mouth wide like a baby bird and tilts his head from side to side, his eyes fixed on you, listening to your conversation. You flash him smiles but don't speak to him, for you are afraid of saying something that will embroil you in an answer you won't understand. It turns out your smiles disturb him; he tugs at his father's ear and whispers at length, in choppy bursts, and his father nods his head vigorously to signify both understanding and agreement.

"What's he saying?"

"He's worried about you, wants you to stay here. He says we should make a bed for you."

"Ah, Uriel, how good of you to be concerned about me."

"Yes, from the care and love that he gets from everyone, he has learned how to give to others. By the way, apart from the wadi of *Slumbering Soldiers*, did you look for any other locations from those films?"

"Yes, my parents' house. But I looked only from the outside, to figure out how we managed to turn it into three separate houses."

"And that's all?"

"No. I also took Ruth to that Jordanian village Toledano annexed and we went down to the railroad station and the tracks and the wadi of the train wreck. Because when I saw the film in Spain, it seemed like the station wasn't a real one, that we built it, like the installation in *Slumbering Soldiers*."

"No, it was a real train station."

"Right, but today you won't find it. The people in the village took it apart stone by stone. But the stretch of track built by the Turks is alive and well. And the railcars are still running, and the train to Jerusalem still crawls by but doesn't stop. You see, Trigano, in the twenty-first century, your international express is still an Israeli fantasy."

"Which makes it doubly powerful."

Silence.

"Did you also go to Kafka's synagogue?" He snickers.

"It's gone. You tore it down in your script, no? But I have faith that the old animal found herself another synagogue, where she still runs around between the ark and the women's section. But the women of today aren't scared of her."

Now at last you share a laugh.

"When I saw that mongoose on the screen at the Spanish archive," you go on, "I was impressed all over again by Toledano's talent for catching her at exactly the right moment."

"Don't dismiss your own role in taming the shrew," Trigano says with a thin smile. "You do have a talent for directing animals. Maybe that should be your true calling in the few years you have left, a director of animals."

"It's too late," you say, keeping your cool. "I'm too old to start a new career, especially without Toledano's help. He could have become an important cinematographer, had it not been for Ruth driving him crazy."

"He drove himself crazy."

His son listens, smiling, as if sensing the irony between the lines.

You pour yourself some wine and stare at the food still left on the table, weighing where to begin.

"At the film institute, when I saw the Kafka movie," you say, "I asked myself why you picked that story. Even though it's an abstract Kafka story, with no defined time or place, it's still about an old synagogue in Eastern Europe, in a very old community drenched in memories of pogroms and foreshadowing Holocaust terror. By the way, who played the rabbi? A wonderful actor."

"Really wonderful."

"How did he end up in our film? I never saw him again anywhere on the screen. It wasn't you who brought him in?"

"No, I don't think so . . ." He's avoiding the question.

"There were moments he looked like Kafka himself."

"Maybe he was Kafka himself," he says, not smiling.

"Another thing, why did you move the animal to an Israeli synagogue? I tried to explain the intention to the Spanish, but I don't think I succeeded."

"Why do you struggle to explain to other people things you yourself don't understand?"

You patiently ignore his words and continue.

"And you had no desire, after you dubbed our films, to visit the places where we shot them?"

"One place. I go there sometimes, but you forgot about it long ago."

"You mean —"

"That's right. A green iron door by the old port in Jaffa. The gate of the pitiful clinic."

"There I didn't go."

"Why not? It's the door I go back to. Sometimes it suddenly changes color, then returns to the original."

"The door did stay in the film. You see the heroine coming out of it sadly after giving up the baby for adoption. Only her scene with the beggar Yehuda Gafni was canceled."

"And you insulted him too, and profoundly, when you canceled that scene."

"What could I do? He was pissed off because I took away a steamy scene where he was to suck the breast of a young woman."

"No, Moses. Please. Don't reduce everything to your own level. That was an important scene that you didn't understand, and don't even today, and you had no problem dropping it so cavalierly, not asking permission from the one who invented it."

"Please" — you are angry now — "don't twist what actually happened. It wasn't me. The woman you had such a deep connection with is the one who was disgusted by the scene you wrote for her. I am not a director who is prepared to crush the heart of an actor to satisfy the disturbed imagination of a writer."

"And in all the movies you've made since, you of course never imposed any kinky situation on your characters."

"I tried not to. But today, the actors are swept up in the mood of the times and have grown daring and uninhibited, so they pull me to all kinds of places."

"After you killed the scene and fired the actor, I went to his house to apologize. You know what he said?"

"No."

"He didn't say a thing. He just cursed you."

"I'm not surprised. Though he actually should have cursed Ruth, not me."

"No, just you." Trigano tightens his lips. "You were the one in a hurry to ruin it all, never giving me a chance to talk her into it."

"But how could you do that? Didn't she lock herself in the truck and refuse to look at you?"

"That was none of your business. She was mine, not yours."

"Yours? What do you mean? Private property?"

"No, no. You saw, I could relinquish everything private and personal I had with her. What I mean is that I created her character, shaped it from within her, gave it substance and motivation and words. And if at the end of the film she rebelled, then what the hell drove you to get between us? Why didn't you let me stifle her rebellion?"

"*Stifle?* There's an awful word."

"Then find a nicer one. You knew how important that woman was for my work."

"But if that's the meaning of *mine* for you, then she was also *mine*, and as a director I had to protect her credibility as an actress."

"Stop piling up excuses. You simply used her rebellion to take her for yourself."

"Not guilty. And the many years have proven how wrong you are. I didn't want her for myself, and even if I did, I wouldn't have dared tear her away from you. But the two of us, you and I both, had no idea what her rebellion was really about. It was not on account of the sick scene you wrote for her, but because she feared the reaction of the girl who played her young character in the film."

"What girl?"

"You forgot? In your original script was a girl who played the heroine in her childhood. You wrote her a few scenes in school, her youth group, her teachers' home. We had nearly ten minutes of her already edited, but then, who knows why, we decided to cut her out."

"You mean the girl Toledano found?"

"Who looked like her."

"She didn't look like her, couldn't have looked like her. The resemblance was all a fantasy of Toledano's. I remember her. The general's daughter, north Tel Aviv. From the self-styled Israeli aristocracy. A little female Moses."

"Female Moses?" You're shocked.

"Forget it. Yes, I know who you mean. In fact, I suggested cutting her out in the editing."

"Ah, you . . ."

"Don't you remember? Not just because the film got cumbersome. She was a mistake from the start. She didn't belong there. I remember her well. A shallow little spoiled Moses type."

"Again Moses? What is this? Have you lost your mind?"

"What do you care."

"Her name was Ruth."

"Ruth? No way. I mean, I don't remember."

"But that was her name. It was out of guilt toward her that Ruth decided to take the girl's name for herself. During production, it was Ruth who coached her and invested time, as if she had discovered a little sister. She was so happy that a real homegrown Israeli would play her as a child and perhaps upgrade her own identity. So when it came time for the last scene with the beggar — and at that point she didn't yet know we were cutting the girl from the picture — she was afraid that if the girl saw this rough scene, it would frighten her away. That's the real reason for her rebellion. She didn't want to disappoint the girl."

"To disappoint the girl?"

"Exactly."

"How do you know all this?"

"She told me, in Spain."

"Aha." He laughs triumphantly. "If that's the real reason for the havoc this woman wreaked all around her, it's clear why she didn't have the nerve to tell me herself. And if this was indeed the reason, then thank you, Moses, for coming down here."

"Thank me? Why?"

"Because now I can truly be at peace."

"At peace in what way?"

"Knowing it was good and right and necessary to make that final break with her. Because that sort of concern for her image, for what others would think of her character, would have made it impossible for me to keep taking her to places I wanted to go. It's good that I broke with her. Sooner or later she would have ruined me."

You feel how worked up and confused he is, but you don't let up, you plunge headlong into the storm to defend yourself.

"Think anything you like, be at peace or not, that's your business, but one thing is clear: I didn't reject a scene you wrote in order to separate you two."

At first he seems hesitant, slow to answer. He has stopped feeding his son, who sits in his wheelchair with mouth wide open, waiting.

"Yes, I admit it," he finally answers, "I made a mistake. You have no love for her, there is no genuine connection between you, and even if you sometimes sleep in the same bed, you have no influence on her. You had to come all the way to a man like me, who hates you and considers you worthless, to influence her in such a small matter."

"You see?"

There is suddenly a hope that this trip, to a danger zone on a winter's night, might not be in vain after all.

"Yes," he repeats proudly, "I made a mistake. Back then I wasn't strong or clear-eyed enough to end my partnership with you, so I took the excuse of personal jealousy, instead of realizing the fundamental difference between you and me and accepting the fact that you didn't have it in you to be a true partner, a partner over time, in the vision that burned inside me. But you can take comfort, Moses, that after the break with you, I also began to understand that it was not just a matter of your own blinkered vision, but something bigger. When I looked for somebody to replace you, various other collaborators but similar to you, Moses, from the same species of human that people here describe with that expression I hate, 'salt of the earth' — in other words, dedicated and responsible Israelis, progressive in their minds and logical in their thinking — I saw that this salt of the earth was sick of its saltiness and especially repelled by the saltiness of others; people like me, for instance. At the same time, those whose backgrounds and natures were ostensibly similar to my own were still wallowing in resentments and paralyzed by perennial feelings of deprivation that kindled a vague yearning for the grandfather trilling the old prayers or the grandma feeding them stuffed peppers. So I gave up writing scripts for good and started teaching. I want to try to plant a few of my own seeds in the mental furrows of random Israelis, in the hope that over time, something different might grow here. Yes, after I became a teacher myself, I was able truly to forget you."

"And Ruth too."

"I told you. A glimpse of her in a movie poster could get me worked up for days, but all in all I felt sorry for her, for the path you were taking her down, and I didn't want to punish her in my heart.

That way I could respond to a loving and understanding woman, who gave me three solid children. First and foremost Uriel, my special son, who nullified her once and for all in my heart."

"But he doesn't nullify me."

"What nullifies you are the movies you make. And if I needed any further proof that leaving you was the right thing to do, I understood it in Spain. Three years ago, when I sent our old films to the archive in Santiago, I received to my surprise a warm letter from Juan de Viola, who invited me there to coach the Spanish actors in the dubbing. I came to watch the films scene by scene, line by line, and I was able to see that your quick surrender by the green door was not an accident, and not out of sudden pity for a panicky actress. It happened because your powers are limited and the salt-of-the-earth Jerusalemite was looking for something sweet. In retrospect I saw that even when you tried your best to direct my artistic passions, you didn't understand what you were directing."

"That's insulting."

"Not so fast. It's pointed at not just you, but me. Yes, me. You were not the only one who did not fathom what I was striving for; I myself was confused. Fantasy and surrealism blurred my thinking and I didn't always realize where I was."

"And what were you striving for, do you think?"

"To strike out against metaphysical terror. To reduce its authority. Not to attack religion as such, the rituals and prayers, all that small stuff, which do no harm so long as they give people comfort or provide structure for anxious souls. But those souls must not be dragged into the fear of something hidden and invisible, of a God who is abstract, jealous, and aggressive. I directed my arrows at God. Against the awe of God's majesty. I thought that if I was incapable of destroying that supremacy, I could at least play tricks on it, make it hazy, mock it, put it to sleep, expose its wickedness, its instability, inject into it elements that contradict its holiness — pagan, absurd elements — put strange animals beside it. Because maybe even then, as a young man, I felt that the rational identity of the salt of the earth, his hedonistic secular culture, is basically a thin, brittle crust that at a time of crisis or conflict crumbles before the terrifying power of transcendence."

"And it was there of all places, in the dubbing studio of the archive in Santiago, that this epiphany came over you . . ."

"Which has only grown stronger since then."

"Grown stronger how?"

"No." He suddenly withdraws. "It's impossible to explain such a complicated and fragile idea at such a late hour, especially to a person who is tired and hasn't eaten all day and needs to worry about making his way home. Even if I find you a bed here, there's no way you'll fall asleep. So take my advice: get up and hit the road."

"You may be right. It is late, and we're both tired. And the drive back does worry me. So let's stop here and continue our conversation in Tel Aviv."

"No Tel Aviv, no conversation or meetings. Even this one was unnecessary from my standpoint, which is why it's the last one."

"And what about your epiphany?"

"It stays with me."

7

YOU STAND UP and take your car keys from the table, and you head for the big house, followed by the wiry-haired white dog from Kibbutz Re'im. You go through the main hall, where all the screens on the walls have gone blank, and through the hallways between the rooms, but this time you enter one of the bathrooms, remove your jacket and shirt in semidarkness, and douse your half-naked body with cold water to invigorate it. After changing batteries in your hearing aids to refresh them too and petting the dog who waited patiently beside you, you head back to the arbor. From the doorway you hear a reedy wail.

"What happened?"

"Uriel has you mixed up with his grandfather, my wife's father, who is no longer with us. He was upset to see you disappear."

"But I didn't disappear, Uriel, here I am." You lean over the young man and dare to wipe gently a tear from his pallid face.

"See." Trigano strokes his son. "It's not so easy to say goodbye to this grandpa. He keeps talking."

And you go on to describe Amsalem's investment offer for a new film, on the condition that Trigano write the script.

"That vegetable dealer? He's still hanging around?"

"He's no longer a vegetable dealer, now he's a successful building contractor."

"How old is he?"

"Over eighty. But fresh and youthful. After all, you were the one who introduced him to us."

"He's still willing to lose money on your movies?"

"He invests small but useful amounts. The film business gives him status among his friends, and he invites them to premieres and helps me fill the hall. You don't need to worry about him. Even when the movie fails, his contract ensures he won't lose money."

"I never worried about him. He's a wily bastard who knows how to take care of himself. So he's interested in some Turkish melodrama?"

"It could also be British. On television they showed a boy of fourteen from Liverpool who fathered a son. Amsalem decided that in this permissive generation, basic values are collapsing and the world is growing more absurd by the day, and he fondly remembers our early films, even though after every one he swore that we would never see another penny from him. Now suddenly he misses you. If Trigano is still up to it, he says, he should be the one to write the script. If he could plummet a train into a gorge so convincingly, he can make a schoolboy sire a baby, and concoct a tragic post-postmodern story out of it."

"Why tragic?"

"Because he suggests that the schoolboy, in the end, should plot against his own child in order to get back at the mother."

"So, in your old age, you finally found a fitting screenwriter."

"I listen to everyone. True, his ideas are lowbrow and primitive, but sometimes he comes up with something original, from the marketplace, from the tumult of life, like the idea for *Potatoes*, which was a very successful film."

"I didn't see it."

"So what do you say?"

"What can I say? I've already said everything. You can tell Amsalem that Trigano still exists, but not for films by Moses, because there is a deep abyss between him and the director."

"There you go again. You deepen it by the minute, make it ever darker. If there's an abyss between us, let's explore it. Enough with being proud and stubborn. Look at me. What do you see? An old teacher has come to you with goodwill. A penitent pilgrim."

"A penitent?" he says with disbelief. "Penance to whom?"

"To you."

Is it possible that the word *penitent*, uttered almost unconsciously, has softened his heart but might invite a daring demand of atonement? In any event it seems that your gentle hand on Uriel's cheek has quieted the boy. His deformed head has dropped, his eyes are shut, his breathing has grown heavier.

His father carefully wheels him back to the building. And now, alone at the table with no one nagging you, you take a look at what's before you, and poke around with knife and fork, and your appetite grows, and the hunger suppressed at the start of the evening erupts in force. The meat is cold by now. The unspecified internal organs are submerged in the sweetish sauce. But the fast you levied on yourself renders them delectable.

"You don't want me to heat up the meat for you?" You are startled by the farmer's wife standing behind you. "Why eat it cold?"

"No, I like it this way."

"A few minutes ago two rockets fell in Sderot, but they just sounded the all-clear, no need to worry."

You are now alone in the arbor, dogs crouching at your feet, mist rising from the earth. Trigano has not returned from putting his son to bed. Maybe he simply lay down and fell asleep beside him. Will a finale of dining alone top off a story about a director who tried his best to appease his screenwriter?

From behind the big house come sounds of screeching wheels and the clanging of cans. The big mule, wearing a sort of dunce cap, pulls the farmer in a little cart, bringing fresh milk for the residents. Raindrops penetrate the *sukkah*. Someone will need to show you the way home.

You are still as stone. A veteran artist waiting for a sign that will breathe life into a new creation.

8

SOME TIME PASSES before Trigano finally reappears, looking at you more charitably and apologizing. It was hard getting the boy to sleep. Meeting a stranger was enough to unsettle him. So he had to explain, to sing a song, tell a story. This time none of it calmed him; his father had to lie beside him and pretend he was falling asleep. "It's late, Moses, let's part amicably," he says and puts on his coat and his hat and takes a pipe from his coat pocket. "The way to Tel Aviv is simple, some seventy kilometers, but it's starting to rain, which doesn't bother Hamas. Let's say goodbye."

You don't budge.

The abyss . . .

Yes, the abyss. Trigano fills his pipe and lights it. No, he can't recall any other instance of a director and a screenwriter still troubled decades later by a scene that got canceled. And yet, an abyss. Even during the dubbing at the archive they all felt that the ending of the film was unclear and seemed pasted on. True enough, a weak and threadbare ending is no rarity in films, or plays, or books. Except that his original script had a proper, powerful ending, which was discarded out of cowardice. It wasn't to shock the audience that he wrote the closing scene. The thinking behind it was correct and human.

"The gifted former student, a dedicated army officer, who decided out of generosity and with full awareness to give birth to a child for a couple she loved, older people from a world utterly different from her own, Holocaust survivors, suddenly realized that with this noble act she had sentenced herself to be forever bound emotionally to a child whose life she will never really know. And yet, the tragedy of the adoptive parents, and the terror that dominates their memories, will inevitably become hers too and will cast their shadow on her entire future. So she decides to renege on her agreement to give the couple her baby. But out of pain and guilt over injuring those who have waited so eagerly, she wants to prove, mainly to herself, that she is not merely rebellious and independent, but also kind. When she leans over the beggar and pulls out her breast, she is saying, in effect: *Even as I go my way as a free woman, after giving up my baby to strangers, I do not turn my back on the world I have disappointed. I will care for you in your old age, I will comfort you, I will give you of myself.*

"And the actress and the director, who did not grasp the human content of the scene and saw only childish provocation, also could not understand the depth and the timelessness of its theme, which enriched the arts for generations."

"You didn't explain it that way when you fought for the scene . . . not a word about that."

"Because I myself didn't yet know what I was tapping into. Unaware of the historical reference, I still felt the power echoing from the depths compelling me not to give up the scene. I didn't know but I felt that the ending I invented, with all its ambiguity, was essentially a reconciliation, a potential point of departure for the next film."

And he stops, falls silent.

"Please, keep talking."

His look stabs you. He seems to be weighing whether you are worthy of further revelation. He looks at your plate then fills it with scraps from the table, and the dogs run to the trough near the arbor, where he tosses the remains of the meal.

"So?" And in your heart the possibility has already become certainty.

"You know or have maybe heard of the Latin concept of *Caritas Romana?*" he asks.

"Of course. Roman Charity."

"You knew? How did you —"

"Later," you interrupt in a teacher's commanding tone. "First tell me what about it moves you so much."

"In the cathedral museum, I stumbled upon a reproduction of a painting of Roman Charity by an unnamed artist. It seared my heart, and I realized that even as a young man without much education, I had tapped into an ancient story about a daughter who nurses an elderly father in prison. I understood then that the early scripts I wrote for you were not created in a vacuum but issued from something deeper and wider than my own little soul. I invented something that had been invented two thousand years before, in Europe. I, who came to Israel from a small town in Africa. Juan de Viola explained to me —"

"Juan de Viola!" you exclaim. "He hung that picture in our room, over the bed."

"Over your bed?"

"Yes, over our bed. The hotel borrows reproductions from the museum for their rooms."

"Wonderful, wise Juan . . ." gushes Trigano. "I told him about the other ending, the discarded one, and he went and hung it by your bed."

"He said nothing to me."

"Was this the first time you came upon the image of Roman Charity?"

"Yes. Despite my bourgeois upbringing, despite the home full of books, despite the history I studied at the university —"

"Studies that gave you no historical depth. Now you can understand the root of my anger. When you canceled that scene, you also trampled my self-confidence . . . my faith in my intuition, in the spiritual sources of my creativity . . . It's no accident that I then began to decline."

"Decline? Just a few hours ago I sat in that wonderful class of yours. Make no mistake, I now understand well the harm I caused you. Which is why I came to you tonight as a penitent."

"A penitent," he sneers, "a shallow word if not accompanied by an act of atonement."

"Atonement?" You smile. "What kind of atonement?"

"A simple atonement. I ask you, Moses, to reconstruct the lost scene."

"What? Shoot the film over again?"

"Not a film. The film is over and done. I want a scene of the myth that inspired me without my knowing, a scene of an old man, tied up, nursed by a young woman. I want you to reconstruct Roman Charity for me. A worthy classical theme."

"But how? One scene?"

"One shot. Just for me."

"What, get actors?"

"A young woman, whoever she may be. But a woman nursing."

"Nursing?"

"Yes, drops of milk must be seen on the old man's lips."

"You've gone too far . . ."

"No, I haven't."

"And the man?"

"The man? The man is the actual penitent."

"You mean —"

"That's the point. The old man on his knees is you."

"Me?"

"Why not? You are the man who suckles. You are the prisoner tied up. In body and character."

"Me!"

"Yes, who else? This is your atonement. The atonement of the director. You'll be in the scene, tied up and half naked, kneeling before a young woman who will nurse you. Look on the Internet for Roman Charity and you'll find dozens of pictures, and you can choose the one that suits you best."

"You're insane . . ."

"The insane one is you, who came down south on a winter night and asked to do penance. You junked a scene that was important and precious to me, and I will accept one still picture, on condition that you are the protagonist."

"Trigano, in the depths of your soul there is madness, and also cruelty."

"Perhaps. Do as you like. You came to me, not I to you."

A long silence. He sits stubbornly facing you, puffing smoke from his long pipe.

"You just want to disgrace me, humiliate me."

"There is no disgrace in art. The hour has come, Moses, at your age, for you to come to terms with that idea. Art makes the disgraceful beautiful and the repulsive meaningful. That's what I tried to explain to you then and you didn't understand. But you will understand when you perform the act yourself . . . with your own body. It will serve you well in the few years left you to make films."

Did he come up with the idea when he saw you in his studio, or did it crop up as he lay by his son, pretending to be asleep?

Again silence. Is he really waiting for an answer, or has he given up on you?

"And if I present you with such a picture," you say, challenging him like a partner in crime, "you'll agree to ask Ruth to repeat her blood tests?"

He tenses.

"Why is that so important to you? Do you intend to marry her?"

"Maybe. Why not? The hour has come."

He falls silent, shocked.

You put it more strongly. "If I present you with such a picture, you will convince her to repeat her blood tests."

He looks straight at you with the same hard eyes that were fixed on you long ago in the classroom.

"Yes," he says.

"Perhaps we'll renew our partnership —"

"Not so fast," he interrupts, then adds: "But no one will threaten any baby. Tell Amsalem he should confine his murderous fantasies to his own family."

nine

ROMAN CHARITY

1

"CAN AND WOULD you help me turn a verbal confession into a photographed atonement?" Moses asks the Dominican after finally getting through to his mobile. Manuel de Viola, who often makes the rounds of poor neighborhoods in the capital, is required to carry a cell phone to assist him in places where a monk's robe offers no protection. But Manuel, who has faith in human innocence, generally leaves the device turned off in the folds of his robe, using it only at night to check on his mother's welfare. So days went by before Moses could speak with him and explain what he needed and why. "I am willing," Moses tells him, "to dedicate my entire prize to this."

Manuel, who remembers the Israeli's confession, subscribes to the religious logic that such a confession demands continuity and perhaps absolution. And although he is appalled by the deviant nature of the screenwriter's request, he is neither willing nor able to refuse. "I must extinguish the fire I ignited in you," says the monk, his deliberate Hebrew reverberating in the tiny phone. He also expresses optimism that with the help of the prize money he will be able to cover the needs of a distressed neighborhood in Madrid.

Moses turns next to Toledano's son David, the photographer, and asks him to join his journey. "I need you to take only one picture in

Spain — specifically, an artistic picture of me beside a female character not yet chosen. The picture will be printed in my presence, in two copies. I will take custody of them, along with the film or memory chip of the camera, to make sure that the picture will never be duplicated and with the hope that over time it will be deleted from your memory. Yes, I could have found a Spanish photographer, but I would not trust him as I trust you, not because I know you, but because I knew your father, my friend and collaborator, and I'm certain that were he still alive, he would not hesitate for a minute to agree to my request.

"So, will you come with me?"

"If Abba wouldn't have hesitated, neither will I," answers the young man gallantly. He wants to know how many cameras to bring. "Two will be more than enough," Moses answers confidently, "we're talking about only one picture, but bring equipment that will work in dark places."

Moses has come to terms with the fact that he will part with his prize money; when all is said and done, the sum is puny, and spending it this way will not only please Trigano and open the door to a new partnership, but get Ruth to repeat her blood tests. Thus he treats himself to a business-class ticket, seating the young man in coach not so much out of stinginess or frugality but from concern that if the boy sits next to him on the plane, Moses will be forced to answer questions he would rather not yet address. But such worries are unfounded. At the airport it is amply clear that Toledano's son is a quiet and courteous young man and that the early loss of his father left him heir to the man's good qualities but not his troubled soul.

The white robe and black jacket, the cowl, the big copper cross dangling from his belt, distinguish Manuel de Viola amid the welcoming crowd. He and Moses bow slightly to each other, and Moses enthusiastically introduces the young cameraman.

"We too, like you Jews, seek to glide in the path of righteousness," says the Dominican as he takes hold of Moses' rolling suitcase, but it quickly becomes clear that the pursuit of virtue will not be simple. In an effort to help reduce the level of air pollution in Madrid, the man of God does not take taxis but rather travels by rail, which means they have to pick up the suitcase and carry it down rough and crooked stairs to a lower level, onto a platform from which they and grimy industrial workers, foreign laborers, African peddlers, and students in school uniforms pile into a commuter train that despite its dilapidated appearance takes off with a burst of energy.

Yair Moses is at peace. He is certain the monk knows his way, and that his religious presence shelters them from pickpockets. "Is the hotel in the center of the city?" he inquires hopefully, but it turns out that Manuel has chosen to put up the two Israelis at his mother's house. Moreover, he explains, Doña Elvira has purchased three small ceramic plates depicting the motif of Roman Charity, to provide the Israeli with added inspiration for his pose in the scene he will soon direct.

"What?" Moses is shocked. "You told your mother?"

"I did," says Manuel. He can conceal nothing from his mother. Luckily, his monastic vows have sentenced him to a life of bachelorhood, otherwise he would have been compelled to bare his wife's secrets too. But he reassures Moses: His mother may be trusted with secrets, his and those of others. Speaking frankly to her is like confessing to the Crucified One Who hears and understands everything but speaks not a word.

When they emerge from underground, dusk has fallen, but the streetlights are not yet on in the narrow alleys. The de Viola home is a large and attractive villa where during the civil war, family members remained amicable despite loyalties to opposing camps. But by the end of the century, they were forced to divide the big house into apartments for rental so that the aging actress could maintain her way of life and be dependent on the good graces of no one.

Although the monk often spends the night at his childhood home, mainly to lift his mother's spirits, he prefers not to use his key and risk frightening the elderly occupant, so he rings the bell, and they wait for the housekeeper to unlock the door. She leads them down a long and narrow corridor crowded with pictures and bookshelves to their room, at whose center stands only one bed, though a wide one, stocked with pillows and blankets.

Moses is startled. Must he again share his bed in Spain, and this time not with a character from his films but with an unfamiliar young man? But if this is the only guest room in the house, how can he embarrass the hostess by requesting another one? And it would not be right to send the young man to a hotel. In the distant past, when filming at an outdoor location, he and the cinematographer would sometimes share a little pup tent, and Toledano Senior had not pushed Moses around in his sleep, so why should the son be any different?

But the young cameraman can guess his misgivings and quickly announces that he will sleep on the rug, leaving the bed to Moses. And to minimize his presence he goes off to shower and change his clothes. Moses takes his toiletry kit and medicines from his suitcase and considers whether to hang his clothes in the closet, then decides to leave them folded in the valise. This is not a retrospective before a foreign audience or an appearance at a formal dinner but a secretive, revolutionary act that calls for wrinkled clothing. He feels the little bag containing the handcuffs and runs his hand over the red robe he borrowed from Ruth's studio, which he claimed he needed for his grandson's Purim costume. *How many times*, he chastises himself, *have I demanded that others, men and women, put on bizarre clothes and accessories and stand shamelessly before the camera? It's only right that for once I make the same demand of myself.* From his jacket pocket he removes an envelope, counts the prize money, deliberates whether to hide it and not risk carrying it in precarious streets, or take it with him and not leave it in a room with no lock on the door. Finally he decides to spread the risk. He hides a third of the money in a woolen sock; a third he shoves through a torn lining in the suitcase; and a third he replaces in his jacket pocket. The white robe and copper cross might be able to protect one thousand euros, but it's doubtful they could hold their own in the case of three.

The housekeeper appears in an embroidered apron and white cap straight from an old movie and invites them to supper at the bedside of their frail landlady. The two Israelis tiptoe into the bedroom, which is spacious and splendid enough for a banquet. The armchairs and couch are upholstered in a flowered fabric matching the window curtains, and small tables are arranged among them. In the corner stands a large round bed, and upon it sits a smiling Doña Elvira, the old actress, who seems to have shrunk since their meeting in Santiago. Moses approaches and does not stop at a handshake but lifts her hand to his lips, and holding it close he asks her how he has deserved such warm and devoted care from her and her two sons, for he is not even a descendant of the Spanish exiles and thus not properly entitled to compensation for injustices visited upon his ancestors.

Doña Elvira smiles feebly. In the evening, her English gets very shaky, and she requires the translation skills of her son, who has removed his robe and in his spotless white shirt looks like an elegant bearded bohemian.

Carafes of wine and cups are placed before the guests, and a small table is pulled from the side of the round bed. The housekeeper serves a platter of hot and cold tapas, and as they eat, Moses is shown three small ceramic plates embossed with colorful renderings of the Roman Charity scene, each with different characters and poses.

Moses feels the embossing with his fingertips and passes the plates to the young photographer, who is still unaware of the connection between them and his assignment. Moses explains to his hosts that since his first encounter with the reproduction by his bed at the Parador, he has studied the subject of Roman Charity, finding much material in books and on the Internet, and so when Trigano came to him with his astonishing demand, he knew that this evoked an ancient and venerable topic and did not rebuff his friend's fantasy with disgust. Indeed, the reproduction in his hotel room had been hung there at the initiative of Juan, who sowed the first seed, the point at which the involvement of the de Viola family in the act of atonement began. The reproduction he saw at the hotel will be the model for the scene he will direct and appear in himself, though in his case the nursing woman's gaze may be turned to the side — as he saw in some Renaissance paintings, as opposed to the Parador picture — so as not to embarrass her or the man. As to whether the woman should also hold a baby — that will depend on the circumstances. Moses would prefer to play the scene alone so Trigano could not claim afterward that the baby stole the atonement.

Yes, Trigano had admitted that when he thought of the ending to his script, he had not yet heard of Roman Charity, and after he discovered that his imagination was deeply rooted in classical art, his pain over the lost scene and anger over the insult by the director had flared up again. Clearly, then, at the outset of their renewed collaboration, it makes sense to reenact the scene in keeping with its classical roots. There is no point in masquerading as an old beggar to whom some unrelated woman exposes her breast. Only by getting to basics and re-creating the original source of the scene will it be possible to restore trust that was damaged — albeit in a discreet fashion, as one copy of the picture will be given to Trigano, and the other he will keep for himself, so he can privately enjoy his own daring, but the negative or memory chip will be destroyed so that the picture will never again be reproduced.

"That's what we agreed, am I right?" He turns to the young man drinking a glass of wine.

"Right."

He explains to Doña Elvira that David is the son of Toledano, the cinematographer of his early films. He too, like his boyhood friend Trigano, was upset at the time by the elimination of the scene, for which he had specially prepared soft, delicate lighting. But since Toledano the father knew Ruth from childhood, he understood her refusal, or at least accepted it, and unlike his friend, he did not break his tie with Moses but continued to collaborate with him until he lost his life in an unfortunate accident. Moses feels there is symbolic significance in his collaboration with the son who follows in his father's footsteps in the field of photography and who has carried everything necessary all the way from Israel on his back — except for the prize money, which Moses himself has carried.

"Do not grieve for the money," Manuel tells him in Hebrew, "it will be given to those who are truly in need."

"The money doesn't grieve me," replies Moses, "prizes come and go, but I fear humiliation, even before strangers I will never see again. I am not young nor am I an adventurer. I am a solid citizen in the last stages of his life."

Suddenly fearful, he whispers to the Spaniard: "Have you prepared the place? Found a suitable woman?"

"Don't worry," says the monk. "It may happen this very night."

2

THE PORTIONS OF tapas are small but varied, the meal pleasant and relaxed, so Moses is puzzled as to how and why the conversation comes around to the Marranos and the Inquisition, with Manuel trying to convince them that he is related to one of its top officials. He brings from the hallway two large paintings of family members, portraits of middle-aged men, severe-looking priests in white collars, then opens a Spanish encyclopedia of the history of the Inquisition and compares their pictures to that of a churchman from the sixteenth century, a cruel Inquisitor. In his opinion, anyone can see the similarity of the three, and some of their features have filtered down to him. We have a shared genetic destiny, says Manuel, who has switched into English laced with Spanish so his mother can participate in the conversation.

"Obsession . . ." scoffs his mother, sipping her herbal tea. In the vast round bed she looks like a dwarf. "An obsession to convince yourself you are a cousin of such a man," she says.

Manuel smiles sheepishly but carries on. If his ancestors persecuted New Christians and tortured those unable to prove the purity of their blood, then it is his responsibility to cleanse their sins by giving shelter to undocumented people of dubious origin — namely, illegal foreign workers.

"Obsession . . ." his mother says a third time, but now her tone suggests she has not merely come to terms with her younger son's obsession but rather enjoys it.

From the corridor comes the ringtone of the cell phone abandoned in the folds of the monk's robe. Manuel hurries to answer it, and his voice is heard in the distance, tense and excited. Moses smiles at the elderly hostess, nods his head in friendship, says nothing. David, steadily drinking wine, seems enchanted by the place he has implausibly landed, and he asks the director if he can take pictures of the room and the round bed with the old lady parked in its midst.

Moses refuses firmly. "No," he warns the young man, "do not photograph here, or anywhere else either. You have come to Spain for one picture only, which you will take in total secrecy. Limit your artistic passions to Israel, or come back to Spain on your own. As a cameraman you are here for me and subject to my orders."

The young man blanches. His eyes spring open, and he clenches his jaw. But he restrains himself and does not respond. Though the words were spoken in Hebrew, Doña Elvira senses the aggressive tone, and to calm the Israelis she dims the lights with a switch hidden by her bed. The darkness that minimizes her wrinkles enables the director's practiced eye to spot the signs of her former beauty that time has not erased.

"You, madam," says Moses in English, "are still very beautiful." Manuel returns from the corridor in time to repeat Moses' words in Spanish.

Doña Elvira does not smile or thank the guest; she throws him a sharp look. "Beauty is still important to you," she says and rings for the housekeeper, who arrives instantly, clears the dishes, and slides the lady's table back into the side of the round bed. Then, as they watch, she quickly and skillfully readies the bed for the night's rest. She tucks the old woman in a big blanket, spreads pillows around her in a circle, and crowns the remains of ancient beauty with a little white cap. The Israelis rise from their seats as the housekeeper is about to turn out the lights. But Moses is not done. He quietly approaches the actress's bed and says, "Yes, Doña Elvira, beauty is always important to a man, and especially at a hard time. And you know that a hard time awaits me."

Manuel guides the director and the photographer to their room and despite the early hour advises them to go to bed. Chances are the moment may be tonight.

"So soon?" Moses is confused. Manuel reports that a moral tug of war is taking place between financial temptation and the perversity of the quid pro quo. Although there is great hesitation, the people realize others will jump at the opportunity and they will lose out, and they say nighttime would be better for them than day. "After all," says Manuel, "the original Roman Charity took place in darkness; a prison cell is always dark."

Pondering the word *original*, Moses nods: "Who is the woman? Have you seen her?"

"I've never seen her. I only saw her husband."

"Husband," says Moses, "she has a husband?"

"Of course. If she is a nursing mother with a baby, there has to be a man, the baby's father. Pero, the nursing daughter in the Roman story, is not a holy virgin, and the father of her baby may have known that she went to the prison to save her father."

"Amazing," says Moses. "I have read and learned much about Roman Charity but have never come across any mention of the husband of the benevolent daughter."

"I exchanged a few words with the husband, and he will be there to supervise the photography and stand guard lest any harm befall his wife."

"But what harm could I do?" Moses protests. "My hands will be tied."

"Of course . . . of course. I also showed him pictures from art books. He is fearful, nonetheless, because it all seems odd to him. Understandable, no?"

"The fear is natural and appropriate, I feel it too, and perhaps you do as well. The crucial thing is for the photographer to remain calm."

They go into their room. The young Toledano sets up his bed on the rug in the corner, padding it with blankets and pillows, but the director decides to take a long shower. On returning, he finds that the photographer has turned the light off and burrowed beneath the blankets.

Moses appreciates the darkness. When he gets under the covers, he describes the details of the atonement to the young Toledano, its reasons and purposes. That way the photographer can be prepared mentally, not be surprised or confused. He is willing to undergo this debasement not only to renew his partnership with Shaul Trigano but to bring about Trigano's reconciliation with Ruth and persuade her to stop ignoring her illness.

From the sound of the young man's breathing, Moses senses the emotion of his listener. A long silence followed by a low voice: "All you've just said I've known all along, so nothing will shock or confuse me. I was surprised that a director of your caliber was willing to atone for what was lost long ago in the imaginary world of another artist. It seems, though, that despite all the films you've made without Trigano, collaboration with him is important to you. You are obviously prepared to tie your hands and suck from the breast of a complete stranger, who symbolizes another woman, a woman who made many people miserable."

"Many people?"

"Look, I don't need to tell you that my father's addiction to her ruined my mother's life. And when he died because of her, we were so angry with him that a long time passed before we could speak his name in the house. But if you're willing to humiliate yourself tonight for that woman, my collaboration can be a gesture toward my father, atonement for having hated him because of his love."

"In which case, it's a good thing I picked you for a partner." Moses plucks the hearing aids from his ears, tucks them in their little box, and covers his face with the blanket.

3

MOSES' FATIGUE CONQUERS his anxiety, so at three in the morning he needs to be shaken awake to restore his soul to reality. At first he has a hard time understanding that the reality is Spanish, and that he is being summoned to perform the deed that is his sole reason for being here. Manuel wears layman's clothes, no robe and no cross. Why? The Israeli is disappointed, not least out of concern for his own welfare in dark alleys. But the opposite is the case: they are going to a mixed neighborhood, also home to immigrants from North Africa, and Manuel deems it unwise to raise suspicions that a man of the Church is there to influence Muslims to convert. In that case, it might have been better to invite the man and his wife here and take the photograph in one of the rooms, says Moses. But Manuel cannot entangle his mother or the housekeeper in this story. There is always a chance that someone will be struck with remorse after the picture is taken and will come here and demand the film, or try to extort more money. Manuel believes it best that those involved in the matter not know of any specific place they could return to. Besides, he was careful not to reveal to them the national origin of the photographer and the man to be photographed. He merely spoke in general terms about artists from a faraway continent who wished to re-create a classical picture for a modern museum in their country.

"A modern museum . . . Nice touch."

In civilian clothes, at this hour of night, the monk looks tough and decisive. Before they leave he pours wine for everyone and prays for success, and once the handcuffs and robe join the camera equipment in the photographer's knapsack, they silently exit the house.

Wintry cold outside. And as they take their first steps Moses realizes that Manuel has every intention of taking them on foot to the appointed place, which he promises is not far. "No," says Moses, stopping at the street corner, "I can't go on foot tonight, let's take a taxi, even if it's close. I have plenty of money with me." But at such a late hour, approaching dawn, there are no taxis around. Manuel leads them on a shortcut through a deserted park, passing seesaws and slides, arriving finally at an apartment building where a few lights are burning.

Moses stops at the entrance. He demands that the middleman call a halt to secrecy and reveal the identity of the husband before whose wife he must kneel with cuffed hands.

Manuel is not prepared to supply the man's name, and the wife's name he doesn't know because he never saw her and didn't ask. He introduced himself to the man at the employment office he visits from time to time to help the unemployed with their requests. There he met a North African man of about sixty who seemed wary of approaching the clerk. Manuel spoke with him and was able to win his trust. The man is an illegal immigrant who slipped into Spain more than a year ago. He apparently fled his homeland following a run-in with the law and wandered for a few months in the south of Spain. There he met a young woman, also an illegal immigrant, who joined him and supported them both with odd jobs. But recently she bore him a child, and she is still worn out from the delivery, so given no alternative, he summoned his strength and went to the employment bureau. But when he found that they required papers, he was frightened.

"Does he speak Spanish?"

"Only a little. We managed the rest in Arabic, which I learned at the same time I learned Hebrew." At first the man was horrified, but the monk's robe combined with the Muslim's distress yielded the faith that proper boundaries would be observed.

"How much did you promise him?"

"A thousand euros."

"A thousand euros? You overdid it."

"But this family has no money for food, and you told me you were willing to sacrifice your entire prize, so I thought it would be best to be generous to the man and woman, even at the expense of others."

"Others? Meaning who?"

"I assumed," says the monk uneasily, "that the remainder of the money you got from my mother would be donated to charity."

Moses smiles. At this hour, at the entrance to this building, Manuel de Viola seems much more clever and practical than he did in the gloom of the confessional booth in the cathedral.

"You thought correctly," he says, laying a friendly hand on the monk's shoulder. "What is left we shall give to other needy people. Since the retrospective took place in Spain, it is right that the prize money also remain in Spain."

And they ascend a darkened stairway in a building that looks even shabbier on the inside than it did on the outside. They walk through narrow hallways filled with junk and rags and broken furniture and strollers. On an upper floor they are met by a tall, sturdy man, his dark hair sprinkled with gray. In a gesture of greeting he places his hand on his heart, then kisses his fingers as a sign of respect, and hurries them into his flat, locking the door behind them.

It is a rundown apartment, just one room and an improvised kitchen. On a clothesline in the kitchen hang cloth diapers. In one corner is a pile of empty bottles, apparently picked from trash cans to be exchanged for deposit money. Part of the room is set off behind a curtain stitched from old burlap bags. And as they enter Moses thinks he hears the feeble crying of a baby, or perhaps of a woman. The space is already arranged for the photography. A tattered sofa has been pushed to the side and a table laid on it upside down along with two chairs. But the space is not big enough for the required camera angle, and in the manner of cameramen confident of their craft, the photographer repositions a chest of drawers and other chairs. The North African stands silently to the side, transfixed by every movement of the foreigners. Manuel stands across from the Arab and gazes at him intently, as at a garden sculpture. "What do you think," whispers Moses to the photographer, "do you have enough light?" "No," answers Toledano, taking his flash from the knapsack and wondering how to set it up. "Come on, my friend," Moses says urgently, "let's try to get this over with." He suddenly feels dizzy and grabs hold of a chair. Is it the wine at three in the morning on an empty stomach, or is it the anxiety of humiliation surging in his mind? Frightened and amused by the situation, he closes his eyes. *It's been many years,* he thinks ruefully, *since there's been a woman by my side to make sure I don't fall.*

The photographer's energetic movements remind Moses of the young man's father. He sets one chair atop another and hangs the flash in the kitchen, among the diapers. A good thing he remembered to bring an extension cord from Israel, so he can unplug the refrigerator and use its socket to flood the room with light filtered through blue cellophane. This way the picture will acquire a slight aura of mystery. The North African disappears behind the thin burlap curtain, where the silhouette of the waiting woman is now visible. How nice, the light that all at once produces a woman, Moses rhapsodizes. He must produce a similar silhouette of a woman in his next film.

"If we've come this far," he says to David, "let's shoot the scene two ways, with two different cameras, then pick the right picture and destroy the others."

The North African paces around them like a caged tiger.

"Perhaps we should pay him in advance, calm him down," suggests Manuel in English.

"By all means," agrees Moses, and he hands him ten greenish bills, feeling he is sinking fast into a dream.

The photographer selects a lens and snaps it into the camera, takes out the red robe and handcuffs. Moses removes his topcoat and jacket and hesitates before dispensing with the shirt, then stands naked from the waist up. He wraps the robe around him like a skirt. He takes a chair and turns it sideways and sits on it as if on a footstool, spreading out the robe-skirt to conceal it, then puts his hands together behind his back and tells the photographer to place the handcuffs on him, and now that the ancient Cimon is ready to receive the nursing woman, the man goes to get her. From behind the curtain come whispers of an argument in Arabic in three distinct pitches, then silence. A few moments later, the curtain rises, as in a theater, revealing not one woman but two: an older, heavy one, holding the baby in her arms, and, walking behind her, a veiled woman with hands as black as night and a body so boyish she seems to be a daughter, not a spouse.

Seventy years ago, thinks Moses, trembling, *my mother fed me from a white breast, and now, as I approach death, the time has come for me to nurse from the black breast of a young girl. But I am still in control of the scene. This time I am the director and I am the screenwriter, and I am the actor whose lips will touch the warm nipple of the young black breast.* He is on the verge of losing consciousness from fear and joy. His head is slipping downward, but the photographer, standing on a chair and adjusting his lens, calls to him: "Wait a second, Moses, she has to take off the veil, otherwise when she leans toward you, your head will disappear under the cloth and the whole point of the picture will be lost." Moses freezes in place, his hands bound, unable to stand up, but he collects himself and conveys the request to Manuel in English, adding a literary rationale to the technical issue. "It makes no sense for the face of the daughter bestowing kindness to be veiled from her own father, so please ask the husband to remove the wife's veil for a few minutes. We paid him handsomely."

Manuel speaks to the man in Arabic that sounds formal and awkward, and the man turns to the two women and gives an order to the younger one, but she, agitated, shakes her head no. The man apparently tries to coax her, but she still refuses, and in the midst of their stormy exchange the word *yahud* is spoken, and again a second time; the Muslim has apparently identified them. And why not? After all, Hebrew can be heard anywhere in the world these days.

The young woman begins to wail. Is it the nationality of the old man about to press his hoary head to her breast that escalates her fear and resistance? For the wailing now segues into powerful crying, and when the older woman, who might be her mother or maybe another wife of the father of her baby, tries to pull the veil from her face, the young woman snatches the child with feral swiftness and vanishes behind the curtain in a storm of tears and shouting. The man and older woman are quick to follow.

Can it be, after forty years, that the scene has again eluded him? There's no doubt that the casting here is questionable. The money will alleviate genuine distress, but it cannot produce a credible, touching picture that enshrines a beautiful legend about a bold act of kindness. This is how it was with Ruth: a wise and experienced director knows that an actor cannot be forced to do something that contradicts his or her inner nature, even if the screenwriter believes he can bend the world to his will.

The shouting and weeping continue behind the curtain, and Moses, relieved, asks the photographer to free him from the handcuffs, dismantle the camera, take down the flash from the clothesline – in brief, to repeat what his father had done forty years before. Moses quickly takes off the skirt and puts his clothes back on. And to the utter astonishment of Manuel, he announces, "I am unwilling to force the young woman to remove the veil and thereby give offense to her faith. There's no choice – you will have to find a more harmonious collaborator." With a twist of irony, he adds: "Perhaps your forefathers were right after all when they believed that assumed identities are not to be trusted."

Even as Manuel's expression protests Moses' decision, the man returns. The young woman has asked that her eyes be covered when she nurses the Jew. He pleads with Manuel, pointing to his own face to show the boundary between hidden and revealed. "No, it's impossible not to have the woman's eyes in the shot," says Moses emphatically, "but I don't want to coerce her to expose them, so go tell her that we're giving up and leaving."

Manuel interprets. The man is shocked and angry. He seizes

the Spaniard as if about to tear his clothes, then turns to Moses and shouts his disappointment in shrill Arabic. "But the money?" whispers Manuel to the director, in English. "Leave them something to alleviate the misery you see around you." And Moses, with a dismissive wave and without hesitation, says, "Money is not the issue; he can keep what we've given him, to make up for the anguish we caused the woman and to save her from the abuse of that unhappy man. Please find me another woman, a free-spirited woman capable of looking straight at me with compassion and love. The prize has not been used up."

4

THERE WAS NO hope of finding a taxi, but it was near dawn and the subway was running. They traveled one stop and emerged into the street to find that during the short ride, subtle signs of a new day had crept into the sky of the Spanish capital. Again Manuel refrains from unlocking the door of his mother's house and rings for the housekeeper, who arrives barefoot in her bathrobe. "Is it over? The picture's been taken?" she inquires, hoping the guests will leave this very day. "Not yet," says Manuel, "they are staying until we find someone else more suitable." Moses, of course, can only guess at their Spanish conversation, but he gathers that the housekeeper, like her employer, knows why he has returned to Spain.

He asks for a glass of warm milk, and she invites him into the kitchen, seats him at the table, and serves him a slice of bread with butter. Though his hands were manacled for only a few minutes and show no signs of bruising, he continues to rub them. The excitement over the scene that nearly came to pass in the tiny apartment, the poignant entrance of the young black woman, his quick decision to withdraw — all this has left him enormously fatigued. "I want you to know," he says to Manuel, who comes in and sits beside him, "I have no regrets about backing out, or about the money we gave them. If we had insisted they return it, they might have responded with violence, and I've got enough Muslim disillusion at home, I don't need to arouse it elsewhere. So until you find me, today or tomorrow, a woman in need of both money and artistic adventure, a woman who will expose her face to uplift her soul, I, a man no longer young, will regain my strength under the covers."

And he does so. Pleased to have been saved at the last minute from a humiliating picture with a veiled young woman — and gratified to have chosen the right photographer, who hadn't lost his cool and with great professionalism had averted a mistake — he enters the bedroom, sees young Toledano sleeping soundly on his improvised bed, makes sure the money is still where he hid it, takes off his clothes, and puts on his pajamas. *All this was not for naught,* he says to himself. *I learned something, I tested myself. I rehearsed, though expensively.* He claps his hands and rubs them. The handcuffs actually felt good. True, the whole affair was more than a little mad, but if madness means liberation, it empowers art. And art, even in old age, is the purpose of his existence.

With this comforting thought he gives himself over to a deep sleep. When he wakes he finds a house flooded with midday sunlight but silent and empty. Young Toledano has probably gone for a walk in the city, Manuel has surely gone to find a barefaced woman, and the housekeeper has vanished, so he taps lightly on the bedroom door of the lady of the house, and, there being no reply, he opens it cautiously and finds her gone. But he doesn't retreat, instead entering to inspect and admire the round bed in daylight. *In the next film, or the one after,* he thinks, *we should build a round bed for a woman character waiting to die; this circularity has a calming metaphysical effect. After the shoot, I'll take the bed home with me. I have enough space in my bedroom.*

The room is clean and neat, the blankets folded, everything back in place. The Roman Charity plates are nowhere to be seen. On a little table sits the Spanish encyclopedia of the history of the Inquisition. Since he doesn't understand the text, Moses turns pages and looks at pictures of major figures and instruments of torture. He is so absorbed, he doesn't notice Doña Elvira soundlessly entering the bedroom, still wearing her coat and holding a pilgrim staff from Santiago de Compostela.

"Ah, Mr. Moses, here you are."

"I didn't find anyone at home, so I came looking for you," he says, and quickly rises to apologize for invading her room.

Doña Elvira calms him. Her house is wide open to him, and though she is sorry over the way Manuel had failed him with the North Africans, she is glad that the director and photographer will be guests in her home for another day.

It turns out that Manuel has gone to speak with a friend who works in the Department of Welfare, and the photographer took a trip to Toledo to see the place that gave its name to his ancestors.

"Everyone these days is looking for remote ancestors to get inspired by or argue with." Doña Elvira sighs. "Only last night I saw the childish confusion of my younger son, who thought he could help a Muslim family through absurd methods that violate their religion. The evening could have ended in disaster. The obsession to atone for the deeds of the Inquisition is indeed noble, but is that a reason for me not to have grandchildren? I've heard that you people serve God differently, and your priests and monks are allowed to marry and even have children."

"Many children, too many . . ."

"There is no such thing as too many. How many children do you have, Mr. Moses?"

"A son and daughter, and four grandchildren. Two grandchildren live in Germany and speak a language I don't understand, but two are in Israel, living nearby and very attached to me. Especially the older one, the grandson."

"In that case, you can think of yourself as a happy man."

"Thinking is easy, feeling is harder."

She smiles. She likes his answer. She lays the pilgrim staff at her feet, takes off her coat, sits down on her round bed, and calls for the housekeeper to bring tea and biscuits for her and the guest. As they drink their tea, Moses interrogates her about her life long ago in silent films. In what ways was it different — the manner of acting, the movements of the body, the relationship between actor and director — and how did music relate to the silent scenes? Ever since he returned to Israel from the retrospective, he's been thinking of making a silent film in the old style, toward the end of his career. Perhaps not full-length, but silent.

Doña Elvira does not envision great prospects for his silent film. In her day, the inter-titles between the scenes were brief and to the point, so as not to impede the flow of the action. People then were more intelligent and could read between the lines, even when the words were few and the sentences short. Today there is an inflation of words. Unless you repeat the same thing dozens of times, there's no way to get attention.

In the afternoon Manuel returns with encouraging news. He consulted with his Welfare Department friend, who is in charge of aid to artists in distress, especially foreigners from Eastern Europe recently landed in Spain — musicians, singers, actors. His friend, after Manuel explained the nature of the wish — without, heaven forbid, disclosing the identity of the wisher — promised to locate by this evening an actress who also happens to be a young mother and would consent, perhaps without pay, or for a small sum, to play the role of the daughter in the scene, out of loyalty to the grand classical tradition in which it stands.

"She must be paid," Moses interjects, "and generously."

"Yes . . . you are right . . . one may not exploit the actress," agrees Manuel, suggesting that something be given perhaps to the municipal official, who was enthusiastic about the possibility of an artist's atonement for an artist's sin. After examining the painting that Manuel showed him, the official proposed a location: the municipal supervisory department cellar, which has a high ceiling and a barred window. Such an atmosphere could enhance the credibility of the reenactment, and should the photographer require technical assistance, say a ladder to hold up the lighting, the guard on duty would be happy to help.

"I see that little by little, all of Spain will hear about my Roman Charity," jokes Moses. "I came all the way here to stay anonymous. In Israel there are no secrets."

"Even if all of Spain does hear," Manuel says, rising to the challenge, "after you leave, this country will forget you, whereas your country is always remembering the forgotten."

At four in the afternoon Toledano returns from Toledo, exhilarated. He bought another camera there and took dozens of pictures so he could show his younger brother the city that gave its name to their ancestors, then expelled them. I hope, he says to the director, that it was all right for me, without your express permission, to photograph streets and alleys and castles and rivers, and people, with a camera not associated with you, and to keep the pictures for myself.

"I hope so too," grumbles Moses.

The high spirits the young man brought inspire the older man to get out and breathe fresh air of his own. If the meeting again takes place at night, why wait around for tiny dinner portions served by the housekeeper, and the monk's theological chatter? Since the tea and biscuits, he has not eaten a thing. To be on the safe side, he asks his host to write the address and phone number of the house on three slips of paper, and briefly considers asking the old lady to lend him her pilgrim staff but deems it too intimate and takes an umbrella, which can serve as a stick if necessary, even though the skies of Madrid are calm and friendly. *More people will join my adventure tonight,* he thinks dolefully. *If only I had settled for a Muslim veil and a hidden face, I could have been on my way back to Israel this evening instead of wandering the streets of a foreign city.* Did the photographer's perfectionism arise merely from loyalty to the original scene, or is he using it to punish both the director and his father? What would it matter to Trigano if he got a picture of the director handcuffed before a veiled black woman? In fact, such a picture, hint-ing at the North African desert, might have fulfilled the scriptwriter's wish even more nobly.

With the three slips of paper in three different pockets, he undertakes a brisk walk to the city center. On arrival he slows his pace, strolls from plaza to plaza, contemplating statues of kings and generals, dropping occasional coins into the caps of young people pretending to be statues. He has never visited Madrid before and doesn't know what's worth seeing and what's not; he is not necessarily keen on churches and palaces and would rather soak up daily life. He pauses by shop windows, surveys the Spanish women passing by, in an effort to discover what still arouses him.

Since he has again abandoned his hearing aids by his bed, the city of Madrid feels hushed and mysterious in the reddening winter dusk. *Yes*, he berates himself, *tonight I need to be done with this craziness, no turning back. If she's a foreign immigrant, a young mother, an actress pining for a job, in exchange for a proper fee, she can inhabit the role. No humiliation, just connection with mythology.* The window of a small jewelry shop catches his eye. He looks at distinctive rings, bracelets, and watches, all devoid of price tags. He goes inside to inquire about cost, specifically watches. After protracted haggling he chooses a simple but elegant watch for Ruth, its hands and numbers legible by day and luminescent at night. It's about time she replaced the little watch with the blurry face she has worn since childhood. Besides, she deserves a portion of the prize, which will soon be down to its last penny. *Certainly I am not the first*, he says to himself. *Directors far greater than I have become entangled in obsessive relationships with actresses they eventually married.*

He tucks the gift box in his jacket pocket, pats one of the slips of paper, and decides to satisfy his hunger, selecting a restaurant not far from a big plaza. Though it is earlier than the usual Spanish dinnertime, and the waiters have not yet laid the tablecloths, he is greeted hospitably. His request is modest: a big plate of fried potatoes and a glass of red wine.

He sits at a table overlooking the plaza, where the streetlamps are not yet lighted, and eats with great gusto the potatoes browned gold in olive oil, and when the waiter, gratified by his pleasure, offers another portion, Moses happily accepts. Meanwhile the plaza is filling up with a large crowd. In the half-light, near a flight of steps, he can see the statue of a horse whose rider waves one hand in the air and holds a long spear in the other. "What's the name of this plaza?" he asks the waiter as he arrives with the bill. Plaza de España is the reply. Moses smiles. "In which case, I've come to the heart of Spain – I've landed well." The waiter goes on in English, but between the waiter's accent and the absence of the hearing aids, Moses doesn't understand a word. Once again he fears that Doña Elvira's housekeeper will think they are used earplugs and throw them in the wastebasket. *I still refuse to grant them the mandatory status of eyeglasses. The truth is that what I don't hear is usually not important, but what I don't see always is.* He leaves the waiter a generous tip and decides it's time to go home, since one can't call a private home a hotel, can one? He hands the taxi driver not one slip of paper but two, and the driver reads them both and finds a contradiction. As the taxi circles the plaza all the lights go on, and Moses manages a glimpse, alongside the horse and rider, of a mule whose rider's helmet is skewed backward. *Maybe these are Don Quixote and Sancho Panza,* he says to himself, *and why not? This is the right place.*

"I thought you'd decided to forget your atonement and disappear in the country that expelled my forefathers," the young photographer says half jestingly, half impertinently. The house is quiet and dark. Doña Elvira has eaten her dinner and is closeted in her bedroom; Manuel and the photographer have also had their meal and now sit in the kitchen, where the housekeeper is washing the dishes. Manuel reads aloud from the book of Psalms while the young photographer corrects his pronunciation and explains obscure Hebrew words to the best of his ability.

Moses heads for the bathroom. In a spontaneous decision, he shaves off his bohemian goatee. *Even a tiny symbolic beard,* he says to himself, *might repel a nursing woman and be a barrier between me and the breast.* And in the emotion of parting with such an unmistakable symbol of his character, he cuts himself, but succeeds in stemming the blood.

5

ON THE SECOND night the Dominican doesn't escort the Israelis on foot but rather takes them by tram to a large building surrounded by a high wall, where three figures await them at the iron gate. *I'm becoming famous in Spain.* Moses chuckles. Manuel introduces Moses to his friend, a former monk turned social worker in the city district, and to the night watchman of the municipal supervisory department, but not to the third person, who stands removed from the other two. Bundled in a winter coat, she now draws near and is revealed as Pero, the young daughter, the woman, the actress. Strands of blond hair poke from under her beret. The cigarette between her lips faintly illuminates her delicate, pale features, but she is wary of looking straight at Moses, who cordially shakes her damp, limp hand. Toledano introduces himself and says something to her that Moses doesn't catch, though he notices the embarrassed smile on her gaunt face.

The building was once a prison, and after Franco's death it became municipal offices. The watchman opens the gate and leads the five down stone steps to the prison cellar, now serving as an archive. *A mythological picture,* Moses says to himself, *with parking tickets and citations for building violations and other peccadilloes of the citizens of the capital of Spain.*

The light in the basement is feeble, and the cameraman and director understand that it will have to be significantly enhanced if they want to include the barred window, which is near the shadowy high ceiling. "Are these bars essential?" wonders Moses. "Essential?" The photographer shrugs. "Nothing is essential, but the bars in your picture will make it stronger and more credible. In many renditions of Roman Charity, the bars of the cell are visible. I think Trigano will be pleased to see bars in your picture," he adds. Hearing the name Trigano uttered by the photographer arouses vague anxiety in Moses, as if the two had conspired behind his back.

"Give it a try . . . what have we got to lose?"

The cameraman asks the guard for a ladder, takes out the extension cord he brought from Israel, and looks for a suitable socket. *Without the Israeli cord we'd be lost*, thinks Moses while the cameraman sets up the ladder opposite the barred window and mounts the flash on it, then looks through the lens to find the right spot for Cimon, the old father dying of hunger.

After the spot is designated the director takes off his coat and spreads it like a rug on the stone floor. Then, with expertise attained the night before, he repeats the ritual of undressing and dressing, then stacks up three thick folders of parking tickets to serve as the stool concealed by the robe, sits down, puts his hands behind his back, and waits for the young man to come down from the ladder and bind them.

The woman is frozen in place, keeping her distance. She does not remove her coat or even her French beret, merely studies the old Israeli with a blue-eyed gaze that blends anxiety and contempt. But when the light is focused on her, and with Moses sitting and waiting in his outlandish skirt, she takes off the beret and shakes out her hair, baring her tormented beauty.

"Maybe, like we did yesterday," the monk whispers to the director in English, "we should pay the woman in advance to calm her?"

"You're the one who needs calming, not she, but if it will ease your anxiety, take the wallet from the inside pocket of my jacket and give everyone what you promised. I hope you didn't promise the actress a thousand euros."

"No, no, only five hundred, she is after all an actress. Though she is also in deep distress, she is a real actress who has come to work here and not get charity."

He counts and recounts five greenish bank notes and then hands them to the young woman, whose face reddens; she is insulted by the advance payment. She looks at the bills with anger, like someone who doesn't know what to do with them. Then she sticks them in her coat pocket, quickly removes the coat, and unties her scarf, revealing a very white neck. But before taking off her sweater and blouse, she holds before her, like lines at a play rehearsal, the picture of Roman Charity handed her by the social worker and studies it.

Once Toledano has bound Moses' hands, she quietly and coolly takes off her sweater and her shirt, and, since she has prepared for the role, she is not wearing a bra. Her bare breasts are shapely and symmetrical, yet arouse compassion in their absolute whiteness, as if no blood flows in them, just pure milk. Only the nipples are red, sunken, as if burned. And when she raises her arms to brush her hair from her face, Moses spots blue track marks.

He looks at the photographer to see if he has noticed the marks, gestures to ask if they will be visible on camera. Toledano gives a little nod, meaning yes, they will, but signaling encouragement. "So," says Moses, "they brought me a junkie, no doubt about it. Her silence is deceiving." If he puts his lips on her nipple, he will suck not mother's milk but a drug. His face turns pale. A primal, childlike fear grips him. *How good*, he comforts himself, *that we've paid her; we can make a clean break right away with no contact, but respecting her professionalism.* However, the young woman, perhaps from the poison in her blood, does not sense the revulsion of the old man but sticks to the role assigned her and approaches him, no longer herself but Pero, the beneficent daughter who, according to the tale by Valerius Maximus, will now cradle the head of her manacled father dying of hunger and thirst, and nurse him with mercy.

Pleading desperately with his eyes, Moses signals to Toledano to click the camera, so the actress will realize she need do nothing more and her bare-breasted presence will suffice to achieve the desired picture. The flash floods the municipal cellar with blinding light again and again. The startled woman does not budge; Moses hunches over with eyes closed tight and struggles to stand, but his bound hands hobble him and he topples to his side at her feet.

Manuel cannot believe the scene is again unraveling, but the municipal social worker rushes to the Israeli rolling on the floor, quickly undoes his handcuffs, and pulls him to his feet, and, without asking him or the cameraman but with the insight of a former monk, he motions for the woman to put on her shirt. Yet she holds back, lingers before them with bare breasts and blue arms, pleading as if for her life in Slavic-inflected Spanish. The social worker takes her hand, calming her in her native tongue.

6

NOW THEY WON'T *just hear about me in Spain, they'll remember me.* Moses wants to tease Manuel de Viola for failing him yet again in his Christian innocence but decides not to tease or blame and just sits sulkily beside the taxi driver, gazing at the empty streets of Madrid, feeling the weight of the silence of the two men seated behind him. *No matter,* he promises himself, *tomorrow we leave for Israel. If Spain scares me, and Israel unnerves me, then it's best I give up on a new partnership with that old dreamer and look for a realistic screenplay, something psychological, family-based. That's what I'm still equipped to do.* Moses went to him to seek reconciliation not just for himself, but for Trigano, and especially for Ruth, so they could console her with a new role. But if Trigano insists on indulging the vengeful and childish temperament he brought with him from the Atlas Mountains, he'll end up in prideful isolation, and he will keep on teaching, as he did in the days he was an usher in that Jerusalem movie theater, what's right and what's wrong in the films of others but won't create anything of his own.

In their room he says nothing to the cameraman, who has undressed and curled up on his rug. They exchange looks. Can this young man empathize with his revulsion, or does he think the old man is fooling himself?

"How many pictures did you take?" Moses asks finally. "Two for sure," answers Toledano, "but I may have grabbed a third one." "Did you use your father's old camera, or the new digital one?" "The old camera." "Please take out the film now, so I can destroy it immediately," says Moses sharply. "Why destroy it?" says the photographer. "A pity to waste high-grade film we've barely used. When I develop it in Israel, I promise to destroy the pictures immediately."

"No," insists the director, "don't develop any picture. Take the film out now, please, and give it to me."

"You don't trust me? You don't believe me?"

"I believe you and trust you, but we are all human and can forget or be tempted. I'm not a totally anonymous person, and I have to protect my good name."

The young man jumps from his bed in his underwear, takes the camera, rips out the film, and gives it to Moses, who holds it up to the light to wipe out anything captured on it.

Then he undresses, goes to bed, gets under the blanket, turns out the light, and says to the young man, "Thank you for your restraint and your patience. Tomorrow we'll try to catch the first flight to Israel." "But why?" wonders the voice in the dark corner. "Why give up? If you made an agreement with Shaul Trigano, don't quit after two tries — you have money enough for a third. Listen, this may sound strange, but tonight, in the cellar, I had a thought that my father of blessed memory would be pleased if he knew you were trying to re-create the scene."

"It's not the same scene," says Moses.

"But it's still the true source, even if none of you knew it."

Moses says nothing. Turns his head to the wall and closes his eyes. The delicate breasts of the drugged woman hover before his eyes. Does the money he advanced her atone for the insult, or does he owe her an apology too?

Only after he swallows the sleeping pill designated for emergencies does he manage to banish his worries and fears to the outskirts of a soul striving for unconsciousness. And since the pill is joined to extreme fatigue produced by the night's adventures, not even the noonday sun pouring through the uncurtained window can wake him, nor is he affected by the clatter of the kitchen or the slamming of the front door. Only the gentle hand of the worried Doña Elvira lures the castaway consciousness to climb back to its owner and open his eyes.

Doña Elvira makes no apologies for the liberty she has taken, nor does she retreat from his bed, but instead brings a chair and sits beside him. A woman of ninety-four, an actress in both silent and talking films, wearing dark glasses to protect her eyes, begins to speak intimately to the foreigner aged seventy, as if he were her son.

"I know what happened to you last night. Not only did Manuel tell me; you will be surprised to hear that the young man you brought with you also tried to explain to me what happened. I think, Mr. Moses, that if you were frightened, it wasn't because of that poor girl. Manuel, who made sure you paid her in advance, foretold the future with his intuition and wanted her to feel she had done her job. For you know there is nothing more infuriating for an actor than when he or she is stopped in the middle and told, Get out of character and get back into yourself."

"Very true," says the director.

"But you were afraid not of the woman," continues Doña Elvira, "for how much could she hurt you, at your age? You, sir, permit me to interpret you, are frightened each time by the subject, by Roman Charity. The fear is understandable, because on second look this strange story — even though so many important artists drew inspiration from it and honored it for hundreds of years — this story remains perverse. Your screenwriter has no right to demand it of you. And yet, despite everything, it pains me that you will go back to your country empty-handed, that all of us here will give up on the picture."

"All of us?" he asks, startled, his white head resting on the pillow. "You care?"

"Of course I care. And it pains me that Manuel, whose achievements as an itinerant monk are so meager, will feel that he failed you too. Also the young man, who has gone to buy film to replace the roll you exposed yesterday, will feel disappointed, though he is just a technical person."

"A cinematographer is not just a technical person. In my profession I came to realize, time and time again, that everything depends on the cameraman."

"Perhaps not everything," Doña Elvira corrects him, "but a great deal."

Silence falls. Not since his childhood has a woman more than twenty years his senior sat by his side as he lay in bed with his head on the pillow. *What does this old lady want from me? Maybe, at my age, instead of a young girl nursing her father, an elderly mother should offer me her withered breast?*

Moses smiles at her contentedly. "Yes, Doña Elvira, I hear you."

"I think we must continue, not despair. Manuel wants to succeed, the cameraman wants to take pictures, your screenwriter wants to make peace. And it is also not good that the nice lady, your companion, should stay ill and without a role."

"I see you're on top of things. And if everybody wants this so badly, what choice do I have?"

"The scene, the picture, must be revived and immortalized, and I know exactly where this can be done without frightening you. My son Manuel, because of his obsession, is always looking for people in distress — foreigners, the sick, the unemployed — but a woman in distress, expecting kindness from you, cannot give you any Roman Charity. I prefer simple, happy people who combine the authentic with the classical, naturally and without fear."

"You are persuasive, but I don't really understand."

"Give me a little time to explain it to you in actions, not words. Don't hurry to leave Spain. Let me surprise you with something worthy of your talent, but as a very old woman, I can't surprise you with what will be, only with what was."

He tries to rise from the pillow, but his head feels like a block of lead.

"Good." He surrenders. "I am in your hands, but only till tomorrow."

7

THOUGH HUNGER AND thirst wake him as a rule, he is neither hungry nor thirsty now, and he sleeps soundly. At five in the afternoon Manuel shakes him firmly: "Come, Mr. Moses, we're going, and this time the journey is longer."

He responds to the call, rises, washes his face, puts on his clothes, and still feels no hunger. "Let's eat and drink on the road, no point in wasting time," he says.

Doña Elvira has called for her favorite cab – a boxy black one, London-style, easy for humans whose limbs have gone brittle to climb in and out of, and the seating is capacious, so passengers sitting face to face are compelled to be convivial, to exchange witticisms.

Manuel wears his monk's robe with all its accessories, and Doña Elvira is wrapped in a robe of green velvet she may have worn in one of her past roles as a femme fatale. The taxi sails away with the four of them, navigating the streets of Madrid and escaping the city by side roads – shortcuts that are sometimes unpaved – bringing them at nightfall to a rural area where buildings are few and far between, planted on large plots of land that in the past were probably flourishing estates and that today look desolate and abandoned. The buildings are big and dark, with occasional glimmers of light that might be electric or oil – the electrical poles are now fewer in number – and the narrowing and winding roads don't cross any railroad track or highway with a gas station or cafeteria to stop at. Now and then, it's possible on this clear winter's night to spot, on a distant hilltop, the vanes of a windmill, moving slowly, like the wings of a giant, languid bird.

"Will the driver have enough gas to get back?" Moses asks Manuel, who this time is taking his chances with air pollution.

"He is a veteran and reliable driver; Mother can always depend on him. He is from the area, and if he gets lost there'll always be a roadside inn where he can get directions."

"I haven't seen any roadside inn so far."

"That's because they're dark. Country people go to bed early, but don't worry, if you rouse them they get up right away."

Before long they indeed arrive at a darkened inn, and only after exiting the cab does Moses see the dim light within. By the side of the building stands a large carriage, its shafts resting on the ground, the unharnessed horses grazing nearby in a patch of soft grass. They enter a small dining hall with pots and pans hanging on the walls. In the middle is a large table, lit by oil lamps, surrounded by about ten men and women, laughing, enjoying food and drink; their colorful clothes seem like costumes. "Who are these people?" marvels Moses. "They are traveling actors," says Doña Elvira, greeting them.

The actors recognize her and make room for her and her companions. The innkeeper, a big-bellied Spaniard, greets the cabdriver warmly and pours the visitors wine in yellow ceramic cups. But Moses refuses any drink and ignores the platters of food that arrive at the table. Ever since the failed municipality cellar scene, he has, in effect, taken a vow of fasting. His eyes again take in the driver, now outside the cab, a short, chubby man, happy and content, loved and accepted by all, eating and drinking and laughing. Suddenly Moses thinks that he knows this character, that he ran into him in the distant past, but where and when? Can it be that the driver was once an actor in some film, or did he envision him when he read some old novel?

He doesn't ask Doña Elvira, who is engaged in cheerful conversation with the actors. Manuel urges him to eat. "We have far to go," he says, "you will die of hunger." But Moses resists. "No, thank you," he says, "even if I lose some weight there will still be more than enough of me left, maybe too much."

When they return to the cab they find the night has grown

brighter. The moon risen in the east floods the skies with magical milky light. "How can it be that not far from the capital city we are in such an empty, deserted landscape?" asks Moses. "So it only seems," answers Doña Elvira. "Many people live here, but the darkness conceals them from your sight."

It is near midnight when the black box arrives at an old farmhouse. A large dog greets them enthusiastically and jumps on the driver, whom he apparently knows or who might be his master. A country woman holding an oil lamp emerges out from the ground floor and bows to them deeply, and from behind her peek boys and girls of various ages. The driver hugs them all and picks them up. It would seem, says Moses to himself, not all the locals go to bed early. He looks at the cameraman carrying his gear from the cab, and thinks, *A fine young man. He is desperate to take pictures of the inn and the actors and the carriage and the grazing horses, but he respects my orders.*

The driver leads them to the rear of the farmhouse, and on the way they pass a stable where stand a horse and a mule, like old friends, snorting at a shared trough apparently stocked insufficiently, since the horse is gaunt, a skeleton of a horse.

In a rear building, near wooden stairs that appear singed by fire, are the scorched remnants of books in leather bindings. Moses trembles with all his being: *It seems I have reached a very important place.*

From the upper floor comes a man of about fifty, tall, as gaunt as the horse in the stable. His face is long, his eyes are sad, a tiny beard sprouts from his chin. *It's really him.* Tears fill the director's eyes. The knight is alive. His books were burned but he didn't die at the end of the story. Sancho Panza saved his master from deadly sanity and moved him to his house in the country, to his family and children, so he would no longer be alone in his delusions and frustrations.

The knight warmly welcomes the director and cameraman and their companions and takes them into a big room where on one wall hang an ancient helmet and spear, bent and dented over many years in battles, but gleaming with reality.

Toledano takes from his pack the old camera inherited from his father and measures the light with a meter.

Does this young man see what is going on here? Moses asks himself. Has he ever read the wonderful book? Today you can't rely on anyone's education.

His head is spinning, he feels his face is flushed, and Doña Elvira and Manuel are happy to see the eyes of the veteran director brimming with tears.

The two are chatting with the skinny man, and the Spanish they speak sounds different now, softer, less jarring, similar to the language he heard in his childhood in Jerusalem among the Sephardic Jews who lived there for many generations.

The chivalrous man, though he has probably not left this village for many years, is not taken by surprise at the request of the foreigner who has come from far away and scornfully refuses the payment offered by Manuel. He has no need of any payment. Even if they fill the trough to overflowing, the horse will never get fat.

He opens another door and escorts his guests into an inner room, and amid the shadows cast by the oil lamp appears a stout country woman sitting up in bed. It is hard to tell how old she is or if she is still nursing.

Toledano sets up his tripod and camera; this time he clearly needs to make do with the light of the oil lamp, for not only this house, but the whole area is without electricity, and the Israeli extension cord will be of no help.

"This is the place, this is the source," Moses says, and he takes off his overcoat, his jacket, and then his shirt and undershirt, and he allows the elderly Doña Elvira to place the robe on him but doesn't invite anyone to tie his hands.

"How is this?" he asks the cameraman. "Are you ready?"

"Do we have a choice?"

"Which camera do you want to start with?"

"My father's old camera. Only film can get the nuance, digital's not an option."

"Then let's begin."

"Yes," says Toledano, "but pay attention, Moses, I'm opening the aperture to the max and widening the lens, but you have to hold still, freeze in place, otherwise we won't get a picture out of this, only mush."

Moses approaches the country woman, who sits in her bed, and with his own hands he takes off her blouse and exposes her breasts. Though this is a country woman whose face is coarse and witless, she radiates a true and simple light. And Moses says to her in Hebrew, "I know who you are, you are Dulcinea, you are the fantasy, in person, the knight captured in the end." And facing a massive breast bisected by a bluish vein, he thrusts his hands behind him and declares that only the Knight of the Sorrowful Face may bind them.

A fragrant breeze blows through the window. *Am I hungry? Am I thirsty?* Moses asks himself. *If Dulcinea can feed me, it means she has borne the knight a child and the fantasy of his love is not merely the fruit of imagination.* The director brings his lips to the big brown nipple, and though this is a country breast, a magnificent breast, he is unsure whether he will find it soft or hard. The woman smiles and squeezes her breast, and between his lips Moses feels a first drop of milk.

The milk is warm – strong sweetish mother's milk with a mysterious taste, a hint perhaps of a country dish consumed by the woman. *Well, then, this is the fantasy. The inspiration I craved has returned,* he muses with joy, *I am drinking it straight into the chambers of my heart, against the reality that strangles us. My heart is intact, my daughter checked it not long ago. If so, this is my true retrospective, a retrospective meant from the start only for me.*

HAIFA, 2008–2010

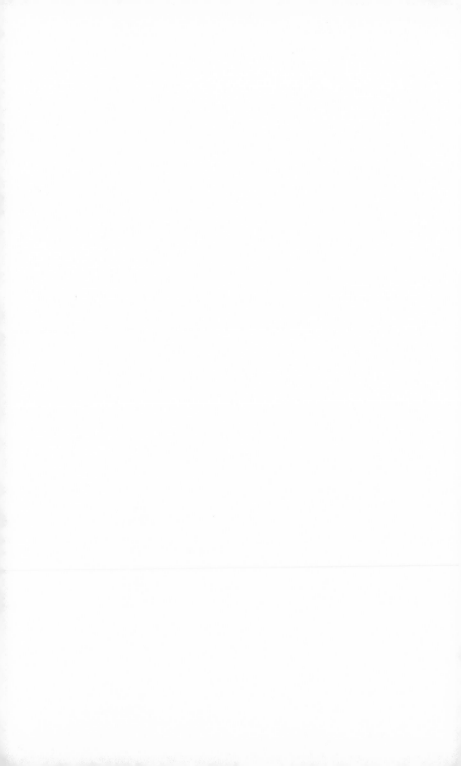